More praise for **WRACK and RUIN**

"Entertaining . . . a darn good story."   —*San Francisco Chronicle*

"The author of *Yellow* (2001) and *Country of Origin* (2004) delivers another warmly humorous take on identity. . . . a highly appealing novel that swerves ever so gracefully from rollicking humor to poignant moments of reflection."
—Joanne Wilkinson, *Booklist*

"This novel thrives on unlikely unions, unseemly humor and happy endings while maintaining a constant examination of family and identity, in keeping with the themes of the author's previous book."   —*Publishers Weekly*

"A modern day, multicultural, environmental, and existential farce . . . wildly colorful and articulate."   —Erin Connor, *Orion*

"An over-the-top black comedy of errors and absurdity . . . quirky characters, fleshed-out backstories, and a sharp attention to detail . . . engagingly comedic."   —William Hong, *Asia Pacific Arts*

WRACK and RUIN

Don Lee

W. W. NORTON & COMPANY | NEW YORK LONDON

A NOVEL

Portions of this novel originally appeared in
American Short Fiction and *Narrative*.

For information about permission to reproduce
selections from this book, write to Permissions,
W. W. Norton & Company, Inc.,
500 Fifth Avenue, New York, NY 10110

For information about special discounts for bulk purchases,
please contact W. W. Norton Special Sales
at specialsales@wwnorton.com or 800-233-4830

Manufacturing by RR Donnelley, Bloomsburg
Book design by Barbara M. Bachman
Production manager: Andrew Marasia

LIBRARY OF CONGRESS
CATALOGING-IN-PUBLICATION DATA

Lee, Don, 1959–
Wrack and ruin : a novel / Don Lee. — 1st ed.
p. cm.
ISBN 978-0-393-06232-8
1. Brothers—Fiction. 2. Sculptors—Fiction.
3. Farmers—Fiction. 4. Motion picture producers
and directors—Fiction. 5. California—Fiction. I. Title.
PS3562.E339W73 2008
813'.54—dc22

2007040464

ISBN 978-0-393-33475-3 pbk.

W. W. Norton & Company, Inc.
500 Fifth Avenue, New York, N.Y. 10110
www.wwnorton.com

W. W. Norton & Company Ltd.
Castle House, 75/76 Wells Street, London W1T 3QT

1 2 3 4 5 6 7 8 9 0

for

TERRY AND RICK

WRACK
and
RUIN

ALL THROUGH THE END OF AUGUST, THINGS KEPT BREAKING DOWN on Lyndon. First the PTO on one of his tractors gave out—an expensive and untimely repair. Then his computer crashed and burned, his dishwasher died, he cracked a molar on a popcorn kernel, and he got flats on consecutive days, both times from shiny new truss nails, the barbed shanks sunk deep into the same front right tire, very mysterious, since he had not been anywhere near a construction site.

Lyndon considered the string of breakages a sign, a harbinger of misfortune. His brother, Woody, after all, was coming to visit over Labor Day weekend—Woody, ever greedy and malevolent, sure to wreak some sort of havoc on Lyndon's life. Despite all evidence to the contrary, their mother used to say that Woody, whatever his faults and transgressions, meant well. Maybe he couldn't be trusted with the silverware, maybe he'd embezzle and lose his parents' entire portfolio (which, Lyndon had to keep reminding his mother, was exactly what Woody had done), but at least he *meant* well, she always insisted. He didn't mean well, Lyndon knew. Woody was a huckster, a misfit. He was a charlatan and a cheat. He was a liar. He was a thief. Until last summer, Lyndon had not talked to him for sixteen years.

But Lyndon wasn't focusing just yet on Woody, who wouldn't be arriving until the end of the week. He was too tired, too beleaguered by the everyday preoccupations of running his Brussels sprouts farm and welding business. He ordered a new transmission for his tractor. He had the flats on his tire patched and drove all the way over the hill to San Vicente, hoping to rescue his hard drive. He got a temporary crown on his tooth. He decided he could live without a dishwasher for a while, but then—what in the world was going on here?—he developed a migraine, accompanied overnight by a searing, debilitating neck spasm.

He could barely move, he was so paralyzed with pain. Multiple doses of ibuprofen provided no relief. Neither did a hot bath, stretching, ointment, or mentholated pads. What he really needed was a massage, which in Rosarita Bay presented a problem.

When Lyndon had first moved to the town, it had been a sleepy little backwater with a population of ten thousand. Less than an hour south of San Francisco on the coast, Rosarita Bay had been isolated and quiet, with no industry to speak of, surrounded by rolling foothills and farmland. It had been the perfect place for Lyndon, who, at the time, with his money and fame, could have chosen to live anywhere in the world, and several factors had assured him that the area would remain remote and bucolic. The first was geography. There were only two roads into town, Highway 1 along the coast and Highway 71 over the peninsula mountains, both of them just two lanes and prone to landslides, the traffic murderous going to and from San Francisco and San Vicente. The second was the weather. Gray and dismal almost year-round. It rained unceasingly during the winter, spring was cold and windy, and fog shrouded the town during the entire summer, leaving just two barely tolerable months, September and October. The overriding factor, however, had been the town's reputation as a developer's graveyard. Nothing ever got built in Rosarita Bay. Backed by some of the most stringent zoning regulations in the country, it was the prototypical land of NIMBY (Not in My Backyard), BANANA (Build Absolutely Nothing Anywhere Near Anything), CAVE (Citizens Against Virtually Everything), NOPE (Not on Planet Earth), and NOTE (Not Over There Either). Of course, with no tax base, no commerce, no easy way to commute to jobs, businesses kept failing, people kept moving out, and Rosarita Bay fell into disrepair. This was an acceptable trade-off to a lot of residents, who weren't so much environmentalists or conservationists but isolationists—independent spirits, loners, libertarians, iconoclasts, garden-variety curmudgeons, people such as Lyndon, who, on principle, did not like other people, regardless of whether they meant well or not. It was a wonderfully sad, forlorn, gone-to-seed town with gone-to-seed inhabitants, a good majority of whom, for one reason or another, preferred to be forgotten.

But in the past few years, a group of new, younger residents had somehow managed to get themselves elected to the town's governing council and planning, sewage, and water commissions, and things began to change. Subtly at first, then dramatically. A gated community of fancy homes sprang up one day. Hip coffeehouses and art galleries and restaurants started dotting Main Street. Near the Safeway a mile up Highway 1—heretofore the lone chain store permitted within town limits—a strip mall with, of all things, a McDonald's emerged. Revitalization was now the call of the day, and developers and builders and realtors were appearing in droves. Most startlingly, a proposal that had been shot down time and time again for thirty years—a massive hotel and conference center and golf course along prime ocean-front—all of a sudden got the go-ahead. The only thing stalling the project, in fact, was Lyndon, whose twenty-acre Brussels sprouts farm sat smack between the parcels for the hotel and golf course, meaning he was being pestered incessantly by attorneys and various developer minions, offering him ever more ridiculous sums of money to vacate.

All this growth and gentrification meant that Lyndon had a mystifying choice of remedies for his neck spasm. He could get reflexology, myofascial bodywork, or custom aromatherapy; he could get his body contoured and enlightened, detoxified and moisturized; he could get his polarity unblocked, his meridians balanced, his lymphatic fluids flowing; his life force could be integrated and viscerally manipulated; he could be empowered and stimulated and released with hot stones, seaweed wraps, salt scrubs, and parafango cellulite treatments; but he could *not*, apparently, get a simple old-fashioned massage wherein his muscles would be pounded and kneaded into submission.

California. After all of these years living in California, Lyndon still harbored certain prejudices from his former life as a New York artist, with an attendant East Coast disdain for anything New Age or holistic. The closest thing to a real massage he could find in Rosarita Bay was shiatsu, a Japanese variant of acupressure, and even that didn't look very promising, seeing the list of available "practitioners." Not an Asian name among them. Lyndon Song was half Korean American and half Chinese American, and although he didn't subscribe to any Old Country notions, he still would have been more comfortable with a shiate—if there was such a word—who had at least a dollop of Oriental blood.

The Coastside Institute of Shiatsu was a block off Main Street near the library, in a two-story house that had been divided into "medical" suites. Lyndon had called in advance for an appointment, but when he opened the door to the shiatsu institute, there was no one in the foyer. Though it was a bright day outside, the office was dim, the windows blocked off, lit by a few incandescent lamps. Music was playing—airy-fairy flutes and synthesizers and water effects. Beige linen curtains served as partitioning walls for the single large room, which was decorated here and there with the requisite shoji screens, bonsai trees, Japanese scrolls, and woodblock prints.

Lyndon took a seat in a chair and flipped through a magazine, *Massage & Bodywork*, forced to hold the pages directly in front of his face since he couldn't tilt his head. After five minutes, someone stepped from behind a curtain, and painfully he turned his body to look the person over. The woman wasn't the tie-dye-and-braids, earth-mother flake he had expected. She was petite, late thirties, Latina, dressed in a well-tailored blouse and slacks and nylon stockings. He opened his mouth to introduce himself, but she abruptly swung her finger to her lips and shushed him.

"Lyndon Song?" she whispered. She handed him a clipboard. "Could you fill this out? As completely as you can. I'll be right with you."

It was a four-page personal and medical history questionnaire, which seemed a bit excessive for a massage. In short order, the woman returned, escorting a blond teenage girl out the door, and then she sat down in front of Lyndon, who was laboring to finish the questionnaire.

"I'm Laura Díaz-McClatchey," she said. "It's your neck?"

"I woke up with it. I think I slept on it funny."

"You don't have to whisper anymore. Here, let me help you with that," she said, taking the clipboard from him. "Has this happened before?"

"Once last summer."

"You're, let's see, forty-three? And you're a welder on a farm."

"They're two separate jobs, farming and welding. I also fill in once in a while at the Oar House. As a bartender. I didn't put that down."

"Is your life stressful?"

"Occasionally."

"Any old injuries? Were you an athlete?"

"No."

"You look fit."

"I kayak. I run with my dog." The latter wasn't actually true anymore. He no longer ran the redwood trails every day, down to a two-mile jog on the beach every couple of weeks, and his dog no longer accompanied him. He didn't know why he was lying. Perhaps because his vanity was being engaged, and he wasn't above attending to his vanity. Despite her clipped, businesslike manner, Laura Díaz-McClatchey was undeniably attractive.

"What kind of dog?" she asked.

"Black Lab."

"I love Labs," she said. "Injuries?"

He was, in fact, falling apart in middle age: severely worn cartilage in both knees, the patellas floating on nothing, bursitis in his rotator cuff, a perpetually stiff lower back, a hip that clicked and hitched as if geared on an oblong.

She noted what he was willing to reveal—the knees and rotator cuff—on the questionnaire. "How have you been sleeping?" she asked.

"Okay. Once in a while I wake up in the middle of the night and can't go back to sleep."

"Why is that? Are you thinking about things?"

"I guess."

"What kinds of things?"

This was like going to a shrink, Lyndon thought. What kinds of things? His life, money, weeds and aphids, sparks and puddles and slag, sex, his aloneness, cormorants and least terns, reality TV, blue elderberries and flannel bush and cellulose and lamina and the transparency of shed snakeskin, the fetch of wind swells, pecorino cheese, the *cholo* in the low-rider who had nodded and let him go through the intersection first, X-ray machines, global destruction. A few other things. Laura Díaz-McClatchey waited for an answer. Brown eyes, skin that didn't need makeup. "I'm not sure," Lyndon told her. "Just random thoughts."

"What about your digestion?"

"What about it?"

"How are your bowel movements?"

He found the question highly invasive; this whole line of inquiry was far too hinky for his taste. "My bowel movements are fine."

She made another notation, raised her hand to scratch her nose, and said, "Song. Lyndon Song. I don't know why, but your name's very familiar to me. What about sexual activity?"

"Excuse me?"

"Are you sexually active?"

"Yes," he said automatically, although it had been a while.

"Married?"

"Divorced."

"Girlfriend? Or boyfriend?"

He looked at her. "None at the moment," he said, then realized this contradicted his answer about sexual activity.

"Girl?" She paused. "Or boy?"

She stared at him without a hint of mischief or irony. "I prefer women," he said, unable to read her. Was she flirting with him? This had always been one of his acute failings: even when women were throwing themselves at him, he often wondered if they were interested in him at all.

She nodded. "All righty. Shall we?"

She had him take off his shoes and led him into one of the curtained areas with a tatami floor. She asked him to remove his belt and anything from his pockets and lie on his back on the thin white futon on the floor, and she left him to settle in. Usually he would have been mortified by the idea of a stranger touching him. He was in too much pain to care, however, and from his research on the Internet at the library, he knew that the massage would be with his clothes on, a deep-tissue treatment with Laura Díaz-McClatchey applying pressure with her thumbs and palms on his muscles and joints.

"How are you feeling?" she asked, again whispering, when she rejoined him in the room. "Beginning to relax? Let me put this eye pillow on you."

It was a tiny pillow, maybe filled with flaxseeds, smelling of lavender. It weighed next to nothing, but it sank pleasingly into his eye sockets, blocking out all light, and instantly soothed him.

He sensed her kneeling down beside him. "I'm just going to take an assessment," she said, and she laid her hands on his stomach, probing and almost shifting aside his liver, stomach, and intestines, a weird, disquieting sensation that startled him and made him feel vulnerable.

"It's just my neck that's the problem," he said.

"It's all connected," she said. "Everyone assumes that things are isolated, but they're not. Every part speaks to another. Did you eat recently?"

"No."

"Hm," she said, sounding concerned.

"Something wrong?"

"Shhh. Can you turn onto your side?" The little pillow slipped off his face. "Close your eyes," she whispered. He lay on his side, and she positioned a large pillow under his knee as she gently angled his upper leg and straightened his arm. She placed her hands on his ribs and hip and pressed down with her body weight. She drew back momentarily, then pressed again.

"You can go harder than that," Lyndon said.

"Are you sure?"

"Don't hold back. The harder, the better. I want the full treatment."

"I don't know if you're ready for the full treatment. It might scare you."

A strange thing to say, Lyndon thought. "I'll be okay."

"Are you prepared for what might happen? People always think they're prepared, but they seldom are. They just become overwhelmed."

A tad melodramatic? "I'll be fine," he told her. "Really."

"Breathe in, breathe out," she said, and she pressed harder. He could hear her own breathing, inhaling and exhaling deeply through her nostrils as she weighted and unweighted, and he found himself mimicking her, breath for breath. As she turned him onto his other side, he caught a faint scent, not lavender, but something else, feminine, sensuous, her shampoo, perhaps. Wait, was that . . . chocolate? No, it was ice cream. Chocolate ice cream. Did ice cream have a smell?

"Breathe in, breathe out," she said.

She was strong, and she worked fluidly, moving to different parts of his body in a rhythmic, regimented sequence, his arms, his legs, flipping him to his stomach, then to his back again, pushing, pulling, stretching. It hurt at times, but he could feel his muscles loosening bit by bit. "Let it go. Relax," she said. He gave in to her touch. Her hands were emanating a discernible heat. It had been a while since he had been touched like this, and for a second he felt himself getting an erection and worried he would embarrass them both—this was why he had worn briefs instead of boxers, afraid of exactly this sort of involuntary response—yet he managed to contain it, and he let his mind sag into an agreeable nothingness. Eventually she moved up to his shoulders, neck, and head. He rode the current of her warm hands, allowing his body to ebb and flow with her propulsions, losing time until she roughly grasped his ankles and lifted his legs high into the air in a wide circle. She set his legs down and tugged on the cuffs of his pants and said, "Don't rush. Lie here till you're ready."

When he collected his wallet and keys and watch, he was surprised to see that an hour had passed. He walked out to the foyer, where she was sitting at the desk.

"How do you feel?" she asked.

"A little disoriented."

"You might feel achy later, but it'll go away."

He wrote her a check, including a small tip.

"Thank you," she said. "Come back if you need to."

"I will," he said fuzzily, and walked out blinking into the afternoon light.

He was groggy all evening, and the next day he didn't think the massage had helped that much, his neck still locked and rigid, his body indeed achy. He had difficulty driving, unable to see the periphery, which contributed to something bizarre happening. He was heading home in his truck when an object flew through the window directly past his eyes, almost hitting his face. He swerved and fishtailed and nearly collided head-on with a telephone pole. He was able to steer away at the last moment, but still ended up sideswiping the back panel of his truck, scraping it up good and busting out a taillight, as he saw when he stopped to examine the damage. He got back in the truck and looked at what had sailed through the window. It was a paper airplane, made with lined school paper, and there was a message written on it in a girl's looping script: "The First Noble Truth is that life is suffering. That must be why I met you." The curious thing was that he was on a broad swath of Highway 1 with nothing around except artichoke fields. Who had thrown the airplane? Had the message been meant for him? What were the chances it could hover and float across two lanes of highway and then dive through his open window as he was going sixty miles an hour? And what, pray tell, was the Second Noble Truth?

The paper airplane stuffed into his pocket, Lyndon returned to his farm. He grabbed the mail from his roadside box and unlocked his new driveway gate, which was plastered with signs: PRIVATE PROPERTY, NO TRESPASSING, KEEP OUT, DO NOT ENTER, THIS MEANS YOU, ASSHOLE, the last a handwritten amendment, owing to recent events. As he entered his kitchen, the telephone was ringing. He dumped his mail without looking at it into the trash can and opened his refrigerator door. The telephone was still ringing. He lifted the handset two inches from the cradle and dropped it down and resumed staring at the contents of his fridge. He had a hankering for ice cream. He had been craving ice cream since getting the massage the day before from Laura Díaz-McClatchey. Alas, there was none in the freezer, the closest substitute strawberry yogurt. He took the yogurt out to the porch, where long ago he had set up two Adirondack chairs to enjoy the view. The house—a large California Craftsman built in 1912 with wide eaves, gabled dormers, and shingle siding—sat on a rise of coastal bluffs. It was shaded on one side by a stand of red alders and blue gum eucalyptus and flanked on two other sides by his trucks, converted barn, two greenhouses built with plastic sheeting and aluminum frames, and a shed for his old Kubota and Massey Ferguson utility tractors. Around the shed were all the usual farm implements—row planter, cultivator, disc plow, spools of drip tape, compost spreader, everything looking rather rusty and worn. Down the dirt-and-gravel driveway was a muddy irrigation pond, bordered by stacks of aluminum pipes.

But from the porch, Lyndon couldn't see any of this. There was the Pacific Ocean on his right, his fields before him, and the inland hills. Sometimes, in the spring, he could see gray whales migrating north, seals and sea lions bobbing in the swells, brown pelicans skimming the surface. He could see his cover crops undulating in the breeze, the lush green of bell beans and barley broken by explosions of color from patches of wildflowers— the blue of Douglas irises, the orange of California poppies, the pink of hollyhocks, the gold of buttercups. He could see jackrabbits hopping behind the sagebrush and coyote bush at the edge of the bluff. He could see birds as they flew to the marsh preserve to the south, riding currents of air, the great blue herons and snowy egrets and red-winged blackbirds, the wrens and northern harriers, kites and gulls, and, all around the house— singing—white-crowned sparrows. He could see the terrace of foothills, the gentle slopes of pastureland leading to the canyon preserve of coastal redwoods, grass spotted with yellow mustard and red thistle.

Even today, absent of spring's colors, the view was magnificent, a screaming-red sunset with cirrus clouds on fire, and Lyndon, spooning yogurt into his mouth, wondered why he had ever stopped sitting on his porch. When had he begun to take all of this for granted? He felt good suddenly, calm and exhilarated and, inexplicably, very, very horny. He finished his yogurt, and instead of starting dinner, as he'd planned, he walked upstairs to his bedroom to masturbate—an uncharacteristic activity for him in his advanced age, at least before bedtime. Maybe once, twice a week, he would masturbate in bed before dropping off to sleep, more out of habit than anything else, but now he felt as randy as a pubescent boy, and he stroked away on his bed with urgent concentration, a vague picture of Laura Díaz-McClatchey— with her pantyhose and chocolate smell—in mind.

He heard a series of soft thumps. It was Bob, standing in the doorway, staring at him openmouthed, a new tennis ball on the floor between his feet.

"Get out of here, Bob!" Lyndon yelled, fumbling to cover himself with a sheet. He was appalled and chagrined, as if caught by his mother. "Git!"

Bob stood his ground until Lyndon threw a book—*The Stories of John Cheever*—at him, then he trudged down the hallway.

Lyndon thought of continuing with the matter at hand, but the mood had been lost. He went downstairs to the kitchen, fed Bob, and began preparing his own dinner, chopping zucchini and chicken to stir-fry and popping on the rice cooker.

Bob was ten years old. When he was younger, he used to follow Lyndon wherever he went, but now they were like roommates who'd grown disinterested in each other, occupying opposite ends of the house. No more trail-running together, no more sleeping at the foot of Lyndon's bed. Bob had his own dog door through the mudroom, and he came and went as he pleased. Sometimes Lyndon did not see him for days. In point of fact, Bob seemed depressed—listless. Lyndon couldn't remember the last time he'd even heard him bark. "You might think of it for yourself, you know," Lyndon said to Bob. "It might do you some good."

In the morning, Lyndon awoke feeling remarkably refreshed. His neck was loose, completely unencumbered, as if he'd never had a problem at all. He recalled the way Laura Díaz-McClatchey had tugged on his head and stroked the nape of his neck and cradled it in her hands, and he thought now—despite his resistance to such hokiness—that he had sensed a transference of some sort, that she had been channeling something—dare he say it?—a regenerative *energy* from her body to his.

Whatever the case, he was happy to be ambulatory again, for he was late in installing a job, a decorative iron doorframe for an art gallery. September was his busiest month, with everyone trying to gussy up their stores before the annual pumpkin festival in mid-October. (Rosarita Bay, along with a hundred other towns across the country, proclaimed itself the pumpkin capital of the world.) This year, though, August had been equally busy. There was going to be a chili and chowder cook-off on Labor Day weekend—another of the new mayor's ideas to drum up tourists.

Lyndon specialized in ornamental welding, although he was certified to weld anything from sheet metal to structural steel with gas or arc. Truth be told, he preferred down-and-dirty industrial jobs—tire rims, boat anchors, mufflers, and chassis—where he could simply lay down a bead and be in and out. Yet the money was in the fancier decorative work. He wasn't set up to cast or forge, but if he could order the components and fabricate them in his shop, if he could work cold with mild steels, bending wire or bars into scrolls, similar to the process he'd used for the delicate, ornate sculptures for which he had once been famous, he would take the job. Welding now brought him almost as much income as farming Brussels sprouts.

That afternoon on Main Street, after drilling into the masonry and caulking cracks with sealant, he bolted the iron archway and frame to the art gallery's entrance. The frame fit precisely, for which he took a moment of pride, and he thought, perhaps, that his streak of bad luck was over. He was finishing with some touch-ups of paint when Laura Díaz-McClatchey appeared, asking, "How's your neck doing?"

She was standing on the sidewalk behind him, wearing an outfit similar to when he'd last seen her—fitted polyester, pumps, another object lesson in rectitude—with a folded copy of *The New York Times* tucked underneath her arm.

"Better," he told her. "It's amazing, how much better it feels, actually." He swiveled his head from side to side to demonstrate.

"Good. I'm glad."

"Can I ask you something?" Lyndon said. "What exactly did you do to me? What was the full treatment?"

She was wearing sunglasses with small round lenses, and she slid them off her face and perched them on top of her head. "Why?" she said, scrutinizing him. "Do you feel different?"

"Yes."

"How so?" For the first time, he detected a glint of playfulness in her manner, a crack in the all-business façade she'd maintained throughout his visit to the institute. "How has it manifested itself," she persisted, "this feeling?"

"Never mind."

She smirked at him, as if she knew exactly what was up.

"How long have you been doing shiatsu?" Lyndon asked.

"Oh, I've practiced since I was a teenager," she said. She tossed the *Times* into a trash bin near the door. "My mother was a therapist in Berkeley. She trained me early. It goes back generations to Japan."

"You're part Japanese?"

"Middle name Kobayashi. But I've only done it professionally for a couple of months. It's not my life work, you know. I have a gift for it, but it's not what I was planning to do as a vocation. It's a punishment of sorts. I guess you could say I'm serving penance."

"For what?"

"I had a fall from grace. I'm in exile. I did a bad thing."

"What did you do?"

"I'm not ready to tell you yet."

Lyndon nodded. "Okay."

"I'll tell you about it when I get to know you better."

The implication intrigued him—that she intended to get to know him better. Laura Díaz-McClatchey dressed like an insurance agent (what was with the stockings? He remembered the sound of nylon sticking to tatami. Very impractical. They had to run all the time), but she was sexy in her own way, and she was becoming more mysterious, more appealing, with each exchange.

"Do you know anything about art?" she asked, turning toward the gallery.

"No."

She regarded him skeptically. "Really? Nothing?"

"I'm just a farmer."

"And welder-cum-bartender," she said. "Look at this shit. Who buys this crap? Who would want this on their walls?"

This gallery was like all the others on Main Street, filled with kitschy oil paintings of flowers, beaches, landscapes. "This town," Laura said. "There's no movie theater. There's no record store or bike shop. Yet they have a dozen so-called galleries wherein you may procure endless iterations of moonlit waves crashing onto rocks. I worry sometimes about the foundations of our democracy, the future of our cultural heritage, the sanctity of artistic integrity. Of course, then again, I'm an elitist snob and could give a rat's ass about the hoi polloi." She smiled—she was being facetious. Wasn't she? "Do you want to get some ice cream?" she asked.

Ice cream, Lyndon thought. Of course.

He stowed his tools and tarps and moved his truck around the corner to a side street, and they strolled down to Udderly Licious, an ice-cream shop with a faux-rustic décor near the creek bridge. They opened the door and walked in on two teenagers behind the counter in a passionate liplock, making out with hands grabbing and squeezing and clawing—oblivious.

Laura cleared her throat. The teenagers disengaged their mouths with—Lyndon swore—an audible pop. They stared at the adults in a confused haze, faces flushed and wet with saliva. "Hello, Jen," Laura said.

"Hi," the girl said slowly. "Hi." She let go of the boy, and they wiped their mouths and sorted their aprons. "This is André." The boy winked at them and carried two empty tubs into the back room.

"Isn't he beautiful?" the girl whispered to Laura.

The boy *was* beautiful, way out of the girl's league, really, tall and lanky, with stiff dyed-black hair.

"I don't know what happened. Last month, he didn't know I was *alive*. Can you believe it?"

Lyndon now recognized the girl—blond, a touch overweight, plain—as the client Laura had treated before him at the shiatsu institute.

"I'm happy for you," Laura said.

"I'm happy for *me*." The girl laughed. She pulled on a pair of disposable vinyl gloves. "The usual?"

"Well, what do you recommend today?" Laura asked.

"You're going to get something different?" the girl said.

"I don't know. I'm feeling adventurous."

They all looked at the signboard of flavors, of which there seemed to be as many varieties as there were massages in Rosarita Bay. Chunky Cantaloupe. Adzuki Beano. Almond Tofu Fruity. Chewy Louie. Ginger Molasses. Caramel Prune. Tullamore Dew.

"Go first," Laura said to Lyndon.

"A scoop of chocolate."

"Chocolate?" the girl said.

"Please."

"Double Dark? Rum? Amaretto? Mint? Cheesecake, Fudge, Peanut Butter? Tiramisu? Loco Mocha?"

"Plain chocolate."

"On a cone or cup?"

"Cone."

"Vanilla Cinnamon? Honey Wheat, White—"

"Plain sugar."

"Any sprinkles?"

He was afraid to ask.

"Walnuts, raisins, cookie dough, granola, gummy bears, pecan pralines—" the girl began.

"Nothing," Lyndon said.

"Okay, that's cool," Jen said. "You're a retro minimalist. Or maybe just a copycat."

Naturally, plain chocolate on a plain sugar cone, hold the sprinkles, was Laura Díaz-McClatchey's customary order.

"Who is that girl?" Lyndon asked as they walked out of the shop with their identical cones.

"Jen de Leuw."

"What's her story?"

"What do you mean?"

"Who is she?"

"I just told you."

"But what's she about?"

"I don't understand what you're asking. She's in high school. She was born and raised here. She works in an ice-cream store. She's in love with a boy. She came to me because she tweaked her back in field hockey. I don't really know anything more about her."

"Are you a Buddhist?" Lyndon asked.

The Second Noble Truth was that the origin of suffering was attachment. There were four Noble Truths in all, four tenets of Buddhism, which had been easy enough to track down on the Internet with the new computer he had been forced to buy, his old one beyond repair. All along, he had assumed that Laura Díaz-McClatchey had been the root of his erotic insurgency, all the mishaps and bad breaks and odd occurrences, his cosmos seemingly atilt. (The evening before, after his nightly bowl of 420 for dessert, he had masturbated in his bedroom, with the door locked, and once again this morning.) Now he reconsidered. Was Jen de Leuw, this dull, pudgy high school girl, responsible for everything? Had she written the message on the paper airplane? Had she, not Laura, been the source of the ice-cream smell, the font of weird energy that had been channeled into him, or was he imagining things, overanalyzing what was mere coincidence?

"Are you all right?" Laura asked.

"Fine," he told her.

She gave him a napkin, and they crossed the street.

"How long have you lived here?" she asked.

"Almost seventeen years."

"Extraordinary. Where were you before this?"

"New York," he said, licking his cone. "What about you?"

"San Francisco, by way of Chicago and Manhattan and Berlin and London and L.A. and Berkeley. I've circled the globe, and I ended up here, a rather sorry circumnavigation, wouldn't you say? What were you doing in New York?"

"Nothing very interesting."

"No? Just another anonymous soul in the Big Apple?"

"I suppose so."

"Really? Just another faceless cog?"

He was irritated by her tone. She seemed to be mocking him, and his sense of privacy felt infringed, much as it had been when she'd asked about his bowel movements. His response, then, surprised him. It came out before he'd even had time to construct it with any intent or meditation. "Do you want to go out to dinner sometime?" he asked.

"Dinner?"

"There're actually a couple of decent restaurants in town now. You might—"

They rounded the corner, and they happened upon a woman in a squat, hammering a nail—no doubt a shiny new truss nail—into the front right tire of his truck. After a final punctuating whack, the woman rose and turned. It was Sheila Lemke, the benefactor of Lyndon's most recent sexual activity and also, incidentally, the new mayor of Rosarita Bay. The three of them stood facing one another, Lyndon and Laura with their ice-cream cones, Sheila with her hammer, her expression caught between rage and horror and mad elation.

"Let me give you a piece of advice, sister," she said to Laura tremulously. "You're new here. You don't know this man's history. You don't want to get involved with him. You'll regret it. It'll be the biggest mistake of your life. He won't leave you alone. He'll haunt you. You won't be able to get rid of him. He seems nice enough on the outside, but he has bad intentions. He's not honest. He's a miserable excuse for a human being." She began to cry. "Oh, fuck me," she said in frustration, and swung the hammer against Lyndon's truck, leaving a nice little circular indentation on his door.

They watched Sheila as she broke into a full sprint down the street.

"I should explain," Lyndon said.

Laura's ice cream was dripping onto her hand. "I need to go," she said.

For the third time that month, Lyndon took out his jack and tire iron. He tightened the lug nuts on his spare, then drove to the service station on the corner of Highways 1 and 71, where he had the flat patched. The mechanic tried to convince him to let him, while he was there, fix his broken taillight, but Lyndon refused, which he immediately had occasion to regret, since he was stopped by a sheriff's patrol car just after he left the station. Lyndon rolled down his window and saw who was approaching in the side mirror: a tall, handsome man with prematurely white hair, splendidly combed in a short pompadour. Lieutenant Steven Lemke. Sheila's ex-husband.

"License and registration," he said.

"Steven, I'm not in the mood. I've had a bad stretch."

"And that's relevant how?"

"You're not really going to do this, are you?" Lyndon asked.

Steven rested his palm on the butt of his holstered gun. "Do you want me to add Section 148, obstruction?" he said.

He gave Lyndon a ticket not only for the taillight, but also for not wearing his seatbelt.

It was seven when Lyndon got home. A northwest breeze was stiffening, and it was noticeably colder. Fall would arrive in earnest soon. In a matter of weeks, it would be time to start harvesting his Brussels sprouts.

He entered the house through the mudroom. As usual, Bob was nowhere to be found, but Lyndon heard something odd inside—water running. Someone was taking a shower. Hesitantly he climbed the stairs, and as he reached the second floor, the valve to the shower squeaked shut. He stayed on the landing, unsure what to do next. The door to the bathroom was open, the light on, and he could hear the bather drawing back the shower curtain, toweling off, and running a brush through long hair, wet tips licking the air when the brush traveled past the ends.

The person—a woman—came out of the bathroom and pivoted down the hallway toward the bedrooms, away from Lyndon. She was naked, Asian, lean and muscled, skin slick and water-beaded. Lyndon took a step forward, and the floorboard beneath his foot creaked. They both stopped moving, a *tableau vivant,* frozen in identical positions, one foot in front of the other. Then Lyndon watched the woman's haunches and legs contract, and she whirled around, spinning twice in a spectacular fashion that was at once balletic and terrifying, and threw a roundhouse kick into his face. As he crashed against the wall and was going down to the floor, about to black out, he was cognizant of swallowing the temporary crown that had dislodged from his cracked molar—or what was now left of it.

CHAPTER 2

LING LING HAD NOT BEEN PART OF THE PLAN. WOODY WAS GOING TO drive from L.A. to San Francisco on Wednesday, take the actress to Sausalito on Thursday to see the director Dalton Lee, then go alone to Rosarita Bay, spending Friday night through Monday morning at Lyndon's farm. Yet the moment he arrived at the Fairmont Hotel on Wednesday evening, things began to unravel. An assistant manager took Woody aside and told him there had been an "incident." He bowed his head mournfully and said, "Actually, several incidents."

Ling Ling had assaulted two members of the hotel staff. Apparently her flight the day before from Hong Kong, despite the first-class passage, had been taxing on her, and she had lit upon the car driver and the bellhop and the desk clerk and the concierge at every turn with profane harangues. Yesterday evening, unhappy with the dinner wheeled into her suite, she had thrown a pot of coffee at the room service attendant. This morning, upset about being awakened prematurely, she had chased the hotel maid into the hallway and pushed over her cleaning cart and threatened to garrote her. This afternoon, there had been a fire. She had left a cigarette burning while taking a shower, and the cigarette had dropped off the ashtray, which she had placed on her *bed*, and set her sheets ablaze. Luckily the smoke detector had engaged and they'd been able to put out the fire before major damage had been done, but the fire alarms had been automatically tripped and the entire hotel had had to be evacuated.

"We have her in another suite now," the assistant manager said, "but we feel it'd be best for everyone concerned if the two of you would find different accommodations, somewhere other than the Fairmont."

Woody, tired from the long drive from L.A., still had his bags in his hands. "You want us to leave?" he asked.

"We feel it'd be best."

"Right now?"

"If you could."

Woody set down his satchels. One of those boxy things with rollers would have been more practical for travel, but these bags, made of the richest Italian leather, were so much more *stylish*. "I'm sorry for all the trouble," he said in a calm, reasoned voice. The assistant manager was in his thirties, short, and rather dainty—maybe gay, a Napoleon complex, no doubt, someone quick to feel slighted. As Nietzsche had once said, to predict the behavior of ordinary people, you only had to assume that they would try to escape a disagreeable situation with the smallest expenditure of intelligence. "I'll make sure there are no further incidents," Woody told him. "I'll take full responsibility for Ms. Yi from here on out. She's quite famous, you know."

"I've never heard of her," the assistant manager said.

"No? Yi Ling Ling? She's the queen of Hong Kong cinema." This was a stretch, Woody had to admit, but the truth was unimportant in these moments of negotiation. The words themselves, what was being said, didn't really matter. What counted was tone, modulation, the give and take in the power dynamic, the willingness to abdicate, when necessary, to a runty little homunculus like this assistant manager whose monthly salary, Woody was certain, didn't come close to the cost of his Italian leather bags. "But like so many people of privilege," Woody said, "she can be—well, let's just come right out and say it—woefully inconsiderate. I hope the room service attendant wasn't burned."

"Fortunately not."

"And the maid, she must have been pretty traumatized, I bet." Woody flashed his teeth, a dazzling set of porcelain veneers (two thousand dollars a pop), in a practiced, clubby smile, a smile, he knew, that soothed and reassured, that in its affability and munificent wattage asked, Is this, is anything, so serious as to be insurmountable? Can't we work this out? Aren't we all in this together?

"She'll be all right," the assistant manager said rather churlishly, not yet swayed.

"I'd be happy to cover the damages to the suite. Don't hesitate to put whatever amount you deem fit on my production company's credit card. As for your staff . . ." Here Woody opened his suit jacket and pulled out his money clip from his pants pocket. The sight of the clip—twenty-four-karat solid gold, with the red Harvard seal that Woody partially concealed with his thumb, enough to suggest a modicum of modesty, as if he meant to cover it, not wanting to brag, but not enough for the shield and its motto, VE-RI-TAS, to be unrecognizable to anyone who looked—always impressed people. Whenever he took it out and began unplucking the clip from his thick fold of one-hundred-dollar bills, he could see people's eyes grease in anticipation of a *transaction*, hallowed be thy name, *mirabile visu*. This simple exchange of legal tender for goods and services—was there anything more elemental, yet more beautiful? Money. No matter what anyone said, it was the answer to everything. When it came down to it, there was no human interaction that wasn't, at its core, a transaction. "I'd like to give the attendant and maid a small token of appreciation for their patience," Woody said, and flicked off two bills.

"That's not necessary," the assistant manager said.

"No, not necessary, but absolutely appropriate. And for you—" Flick, flick, flick. This was excessive, Woody knew. He couldn't really afford such extravagance, but he couldn't help himself, lost in the need to flaunt.

The assistant manager discreetly raised his hand. Stop, he was gesturing. Stop? Woody couldn't believe it. The little piss-ant was going to *refuse* him? But refuse him he did. "Could you leave the hotel within the hour?" he had the gall to say.

Ling Ling, of course, threw a horrendous fit about the situation, screaming at Woody incoherently—not the greatest way to be introduced to each other, having only talked on the phone until then. She wasn't exactly a pretty sight, either, nothing like the young, beautiful dynamo pictured in the dozens of Hong Kong action films she had made. But that had all been more than a decade ago. She was in her early forties now. Her face was bloated and wan, and she seemed weak, almost enfeebled, wheezing from the exertion of lifting her suitcases onto her bed. To top things off, she was drunk, completely soused. Instead of the svelte, glamorous, exquisitely fit kung fu goddess Woody had hoped to cast, he had before him a has-been, a pathetic chain-smoking barfly whose time had come and long gone. Yi Ling Ling hadn't had a decent part in years. No wonder she was here alone, without so much as a manager or a personal assis-tant, never mind an entourage, to keep her in check.

Due to the inanities of the movie business, however, Woody was stuck with her. Feasibility reports, income-to-cost ratios, audience demographics, liquidation breakdowns, global rights analyses, distribution window schedules, premium tie-in lists, ancillary licenses, completion bonds, gap financing, pre-sale agreements, foreign sales matrices, deal point arrays—he had carefully produced a slew of spreadsheet models and business plans for every imaginable contingency, every scenario considered and provided for, in order to make this film as profitable and successful as possible for all parties concerned, and the lead actress he'd almost signed, Vivienne Cheung, had been perfect for this hip, edgy action movie set in the Bay Area, an adaptation of a Hong Kong film that had been a hit for Yi Ling Ling fifteen years ago. The problem was, everyone along the way had had an idea, a suggestion, a "note," a teeny-weeny proposal for a teeny-weeny change in the script or talent or locale or period or genre. One teeny-weeny compromise had been tacked onto another, the biggest coming when Vivienne Cheung asked for too much money and a Chinese equity investor had an inspiration: Why not get Yi Ling Ling herself and make this a comeback vehicle for her? She'd once been a huge star overseas, and even after the extended slump in the Hong Kong film industry, her name still carried significant weight with foreign distributors and investors. It was a terrible idea, but to Woody's befuddlement and frustration it caught hold, and pretty soon his original sure-bet, win-win project had gotten watered down to a dead-on-arrival dog that no one really wanted to do anymore, but to which everyone was committed, money on the table.

Up to now, Woody had been making his money—a fair bit of money, if he did say so himself—as an intermediary between Hollywood and Asia. He negotiated the rights for American studios to remake films from Japan, Korea, Hong Kong, Thailand, Vietnam, and China. This movie, however, would be Woody's first as an independent producer. He was tired of letting everyone else take the credit for his discoveries, while he got a mere finder's fee. He wanted some input in how a movie was made. He wanted to go to festivals and premieres and stand with the stars and director. He wanted to take pride in something he'd created. He wanted to do his own remake. There was a lot riding on this project, a lot to fret about, a web of details and negotiations and transactions that required Woody's constant management and vigilance, lest it fall apart.

The fact was, this thing was still technically in development. He hadn't gotten the true green light yet. The complicated international financing for the movie now hinged on Ling Ling and the director Dalton Lee, whose first indie feature, a small, quirky thriller about members of a Chinese-American gang in San Francisco, had made a splash at Sundance last year. The film, *There Once Was a City*, had been done on the cheap on digital video, but the action scenes had possessed an uncommon immediacy. Dalton Lee had shot right beside the actors with handheld cameras, the frame always moving, herky-jerky. With grainy flashbacks and rapid-fire jump cuts and bleached, harsh hues, everything felt frenetic and spontaneous, as if a live event were unfolding before the audience's eyes, and the effect ratcheted up the film's intensity, making it unpredictable and vivid. Dalton had emerged from the festival as the season's new It Boy.

In a coup, Woody had locked him into a development deal, a pay-or-play guarantee that was one percent of the production performance fee, meaning Woody was obliged to give him $100,000 to sit on his ass while everything was being finalized. But word was that Dalton wasn't happy with the casting change, and Woody was supposed to take Ling Ling to meet him tomorrow. He needed Ling Ling to impress Dalton Lee. He needed her to be beautiful and charming and, above all else, sober.

Woody called his assistant in L.A., who found them two rooms at the Palace Hotel. Ling Ling passed out as soon as they were ensconced upstairs, and she didn't surface again until one-thirty the next afternoon. Their meeting with Dalton Lee in Sausalito was at five. She looked pale, hungover, but at least somewhat in control. She asked Woody to take her out to lunch, and he escorted her to a restaurant he knew in Union Square, three blocks away from the hotel (she insisted on taking a cab).

At the restaurant, Ling Ling, wearing huge, imperviously dark sunglasses, immediately ordered a brandy and ginger ale in a collins glass, not too much ice, please.

"I don't think you should," Woody told her.

"You don't think I should?" she said. She expelled a little chortle. "Oh, I most definitely think I should."

"It's important we're sharp for this meeting."

"Don't concern yourself," Ling Ling said. "Dalton Lee will love me. How could he not?"

She asked for a second brandy and ginger ale before they even ordered their meal, with which she wanted a nice little Bordeaux. After they finished eating, she lit a cigarette, and the waiter hurried over to the table and explained that there was no smoking permitted in the restaurant.

"Oh, I didn't know," Ling Ling said pleasantly in her melodious British accent—she had gone to boarding school in England—and, smiling at the waiter, continued to smoke.

The waiter, holding an ashtray, kept waiting for her to extinguish her cigarette, and Ling Ling kept ignoring him, flicking ashes into her water glass, until finally she had had enough, she said, of his snotty attitude.

"Do you know who I am?" Ling Ling asked the waiter.

"No."

"I'm Yi Ling Ling," she said.

"Is that supposed to mean something to me?" the waiter said.

Ling Ling dropped her cigarette into her water glass, picked it up, and pitched the contents into the waiter's face.

They were asked to leave the restaurant.

In the cab back to the hotel, Woody's cell phone rang. "I got bad news," his assistant, Roland, told him. "Dalton Lee's canceled."

"What do you mean he's canceled?"

"He said he has a family emergency and needs to go out of town."

"That's it? That's all he said?"

"That's all his people said. He wants to postpone until ten a.m. Monday."

"The little chickenshit. He couldn't even tell me directly. He has all my numbers. He better not be trying to wriggle out of this deal." Woody took out his PDA. "Give me the rest of my messages," he told Roland.

"You don't have any other messages."

"No messages?" Woody asked, feeling a pang of panic. There were always messages—messages from his accountant, his broker, his attorney, his unit production manager, messages from agents, producers, directors, managers, scriptwriters.

"Everyone's already left town for the weekend," Roland said.

"Oh, of course," Woody said, breathing relief. "Labor Day."

"Did you know that Labor Day was originally meant to honor the workers 'who from rude nature have delved and carved all the grandeur we behold'?" Roland said. "Isn't that a beautiful, poetic line?"

"I really don't give you enough to do, do I?" Woody said.

"Are you still going to your brother's?"

"Yeah, I guess."

"What are you going to do with Ling Ling, then?" Roland asked.

·   ·

IN THE END, WOODY had to bring her with him to Rosarita Bay. He was afraid to leave her in the city. God knew what kind of trouble she would get into on her own over the weekend, and he tried to convince himself that perhaps the delay was fortuitous. He might be able to dry her out a little, rein her in—a monumental delusion, he realized, when he returned to Lyndon's house and saw his brother unconscious on the floor, his hands and ankles hog-tied.

"What have you done?" he asked Ling Ling. "What is the *matter* with you?"

She was sitting cross-legged in the second-floor hallway, a drink and a cigarette in hand. He had left her for less than an hour, going into town to get some dinner for them.

"He snuck up behind me," she told him.

"He's my *brother*," Woody said. "This is his *house*."

"Oh," Ling Ling said. "I didn't know."

"Are you insane? Are you completely off your rocker?"

"Someone might be after me."

"What the hell are you talking about? Who?"

"I think someone might have followed me from Hong Kong."

"Why in the world would anyone do that?"

She began to speak, then stopped, as if she had lost her thought. "I don't know."

"Wonderful," Woody said. "Just dandy."

She had tied Lyndon with two electrical extension cords, and

Woody began unwrapping them. "I'm taking you to the airport tomorrow," he told her. "You can go back to Hong Kong. You're a disaster. I've seen prima donnas before, but this is beyond the pale. No wonder you haven't done anything in so long. Who would work with you? Don't you get it? You exist on reputation alone, and it's fading fast."

Wordlessly Ling Ling walked into one of the bedrooms and slammed the door.

Woody sat Lyndon up and lightly slapped his face. "Hey, hey."

Lyndon came to and slowly focused on his brother. "What the fuck, Woody. What the fuck."

They went to the kitchen, where Lyndon grabbed a bag of frozen peas from the freezer, banged on it with the base of his palm, and pressed it against his jaw.

"You have any whiskey?" Woody asked.

Lyndon nodded toward a cupboard, and Woody pulled out a bottle of Jack Daniel's and two glasses that were relatively clean. There was half a bottle of X.O. on the counter, which Ling Ling must have already pilfered. Woody made a note to himself to hide it. He poured two drinks and handed one to Lyndon, and they sat down at the kitchen table.

"You weren't supposed to be here until tomorrow," Lyndon said. He took a sip of the whiskey and grimaced.

As Woody spun off an explanation for his early arrival, his brother scowled and frowned. He appeared lean and tan. Woody supposed farming did that for him. Lyndon had gotten the looks in the family, a long, strong face with wavy hair that he had kept on the longish side. Woody's features were round, the classic big Korean head and pancake face. His hair was maddeningly straight, and his body naturally tended toward lumpy, which he had to curb with several torturous hours a week with a personal trainer. But at least he knew how to dress. Lyndon was wearing jeans, work boots, and a T-shirt that might have once been green but was now blue. Woody was, as usual, sharply garbed in a Hugo Boss suit, Paul Smith shirt, and Prada shoes.

"You could have called and given me some warning," Lyndon said.

"I tried. You never pick up the phone. You don't have voice mail or a machine."

"I disconnected it last week."

"Why?" Woody asked, knowing why but pretending not to.

Lyndon didn't answer, saying instead, "How'd you drive in, anyway? The gate was locked."

"I went around, through that little creek ditch. I have a Range Rover—six-speed, four-corner air suspension, and electronic traction control. It can roll through anything. You have a funny idea about security. All those KEEP OUT signs, the gate, you don't want any calls, but the doors to your house are wide open. You don't lock anything. What's going on? Who are you trying to avoid?"

"Woody, I told you this isn't a good time to visit," Lyndon said. "It's one thing for you to be here, but bringing along Mrs. Bruce Lee . . ."

"She's quite famous, you know. This movie's going to be an international blockbuster, like nothing you've ever seen. Arthouse noir meets Hong Kong cinema. It'll be groundbreaking. It's going to crossover a ton of markets. You've heard of the director Dalton Lee, haven't you? *There Once Was a City*? He got the Audience Award at Sundance last year."

Lyndon shook his head. "I don't see a lot of movies," he said.

What a miser, Woody thought. How miserly and mean and hateful of Lyndon not to give him an inch of encouragement, a charitable little pat-pat way-to-go, just the slightest recognition, the tiniest acknowledgment, that Woody was doing well finally, that he'd rebuilt his life, that he'd rebounded from the lowest of the low—God, he'd been down so low—and he was thriving now, doing something important, something creative. "Don't you think it's ironic," he said to Lyndon, "that we both ended up in the arts?"

Lyndon gave him a long irritated look. "You're staying the entire weekend? With her?"

"Would it put you out that much? You've got four bedrooms," Woody said. "Come on, we're supposed to be nice to each other."

They'd barely seen each other since that afternoon in the Boston courtroom when he'd been given a miraculous reprieve—unsupervised probation and fines instead of prison for the multiple charges of fraud and embezzlement he'd faced. The deal with the prosecutor had been contingent on full restitution, with interest, to his clients, and his parents had emptied out their life savings and taken out a second mortgage so he could pay back the money he owed. Thereafter, Lyndon, who'd advised their parents against bailing Woody out, had refused to have anything to do with him. Their sole encounter—silent, at that—had been at their father's funeral nine years ago. But then, last summer, their mother was ailing in the hospital, and she had gotten Woody and Lyndon to gather at her bedside, and she had implored them to reconcile. Once she had secured that promise, she had promptly recovered, bouncing back to a life that was far more active than ever before. She was, in fact, at that very moment, on a seniors' bicycle tour of Tuscany.

Woody looked at Lyndon. He had his fingers in his mouth, checking his teeth. Woody was almost two years older than his brother, but for so long, he'd been relegated the younger sibling, suffering Lyndon's condescension and disdain. How everything had changed. All through their childhood in Watsonville, seventy-five miles southeast of Rosarita Bay, Woody had been the overachiever, excelling academically, scoring a perfect 1600 on his SATs and getting into Harvard, while Lyndon, ever the dreamer, slacker, pothead, freak, barely squeaked into a no-name arts college in Maine that was practically a vocational school. Woody had been studious and disciplined and ambitious. He had worked at Credit Suisse First Boston, gotten his Series 7, and set off on his own as a financial planner. Lyndon, meanwhile, after a year on a commune farm where, predictably, he had grown marijuana, moved to New York City and became famous. Lyndon, who as a kid used to sit for hours over the same sheet of paper, a piece of charcoal in his fist, running it over and over in rectangles until the entire paper was blackened. Lyndon, who they used to worry was *autistic*. He became the toast of the art world, Lyndon did, his sculptures—these beastly, incomprehensible junk piles he'd weld together from scraps he found in dumpsters and vacant lots—selling for tens of thousands of dollars. He dated supermodels and appeared in a Gap ad. He was voted one of *People*'s Top 50 Most Beautiful People.

The inequities of the world had outraged Woody. Perhaps, he conceded, it was partly jealousy that had led him to overextend himself. He made a few strategic mistakes, a few disastrously bad plays in the market from which he could not recover, and he had been forced to fudge a few earnings reports. Soon, he found himself in something akin to a Ponzi scheme, making impossible guarantees to new clients in order to appease the demands and inquiries of old clients, who had included his parents. He didn't do anything blatantly illegal (or so he believed), just dumb and unethical. He lost everything—his securities licenses, his house, his fiancée, his good, hard-earned life.

At least he hadn't squandered his opportunities like Lyndon had, walking away from the art world at the height of his career. For what? To become a Brussels sprouts farmer, like some back-to-the-land tree hugger? To live in this musty house in this little howdy-doody town?

The house was neat and reasonably clean, but there was a clammy feel to it, the smell of mildew and mold, the vague whiff of decay. All the furnishings were a combination of Arts and Crafts and country casual, with lots of dark woods in the wainscoting, floors, and built-ins, mixed with knobby light oak chairs and pine tables and floral-patterned upholstery that was incipiently threadbare. Most unexpected were the antique plates, bottles, and bric-a-brac lining the shelves and mantel, and the framed watercolors of birds hanging on the walls. None of it seemed like Lyndon's style—not that he had ever really bothered to define a style of his own. It was decidedly retro décor, but not, Woody inferred, by choice. More by default. The whole house held the sad pall of dormancy.

"Have you bought anything new for this place in, say, the last seventeen years?" Woody asked Lyndon in the kitchen.

"Funny."

"No, seriously. The furniture came with the farm, didn't it? Everything in here you got lock, stock, and barrel, and you've been too lazy to change a thing."

"It's functional."

"It's rather pathetic, is what it is."

Clearly Lyndon had lived here alone all these years. No woman worth her salt would have stood for such decorative apathy. So depressing. Positively funereal. Hadn't he had a girlfriend in all this time? Woody didn't know. He had asked their mother once, but supposedly she did not know herself, or, as was more likely, she chose to respect Lyndon's privacy. The only sign of a female presence Woody had spotted in the house was a box of tampons. This wouldn't have been unusual in and of itself, but this was no ordinary box of tampons. Woody had found it in the closet upstairs while searching for extra sheets. It was a huge, industrial-bulk-sized box of generic-brand tampons, five hundred of them. Either Lyndon had a frugal girlfriend who was a heavy bleeder, or he was keeping them for some kinky purpose, trying to lure neighborhood girls, maybe, as the pied piper of sanitary protection.

Lyndon gestured toward the Styrofoam containers on the counter. "Is that food?"

"You hungry?"

They cracked open the containers of enchiladas verdes, and Lyndon handed him a plate and a fork and knife. Woody vigorously washed his hands in the sink and, while he was at it, scrubbed the fork and knife as well. He was a bit of a germaphobe—nothing really big, not a major deal, though his hygienic habits occasionally attracted attention, coming across, Woody conceded, as a little metrosexual and faggy. He wasn't a nut about it, just used common sense. He only really drew the line with public restrooms, anathema ever since he'd learned that toilets produced an aerosol effect when flushed, a mist that threw microscopic particles airborne as far as six feet away. At home, he always closed the toilet lid before flushing and, for good measure, kept his toothbrush in the medicine cabinet.

"I don't have time to entertain you two while you're here," Lyndon told him. "I'm getting ready for harvest."

"Don't worry about that."

"And tell her she can't smoke in the house. I hate the smell of cigarette smoke."

"All right, no problem," Woody said. He spooned out refried beans from a tub onto his plate and passed it on to Lyndon, who did the same with the tub of rice. They began to eat.

"What's there to do around here, anyway?" Woody asked. "Anything to see?"

"You got this at Diego's?"

"How'd you know?" The Styrofoam containers didn't have any identifying labels.

"Only Mexican restaurant in town. So you've seen Main Street. That's about it."

"That's hard to believe," Woody said, stuffing his mouth. The food was predictably mediocre, and Mexican was a flagrant deviation from his diet regimen, but he was hungrier than he'd thought.

"There's going to be a chili and chowder fest this weekend," Lyndon said. "There'll be some music, an arts and crafts fair."

"That's something, I guess. Is there a gym here?"

"YMCA."

"That'll have to do."

They ate their enchiladas. "Brussels sprouts," Woody said to Lyndon. "Leave it to you to grow the one vegetable everyone despises."

What a sorry life Lyndon led, Woody thought, alone and anonymous in this wretched little town and wretched little house that he was too cheap and indifferent to decorate. Everything about him bespoke isolation, failure, obsolescence. His brother was an idiot. Always had been, always would be. He deserved every last bit of the misfortunate that was certain—if Woody had anything to do with it—to befall him.

CHAPTER 3

IN THE EARLY MORNING FOG, LYNDON WENT OUT TO WALK HIS FIELDS. He took along a hula hoe, and he swept the loop of sharp steel attached to the end back and forth underneath the soil, cutting weeds. His bad weeds were amaranth—pigweed. They started out as tiny little things, no more than a quarter inch high, and if he didn't kill every last one of them, if he left a single one, it'd grow into a small Christmas tree.

He was worried about his plants. The week before, he had spent two days topping them, but then his irrigation pump had gone on the blink—yet another thing that had mysteriously broken down. He couldn't figure it out at first. The pump itself was fine, the motor in perfect working order, so he decided it had to be the electrical wire. Probably a gopher had eaten through a conduit and water had invaded, causing his four-hundred-foot wire to corrode in some interior connection. But he didn't know where. He had faced the prospect of having to dig up the whole thing. He had gotten lucky. He'd picked a side, the side starting at the irrigation pond, and he'd guessed right. He found the break within the first seventy feet. He'd lost a day, however—a day he'd needed to irrigate—and now his plants were looking a little stressed, a little blue instead of green.

Brussels sprouts were fussy, eccentric vegetables. They liked inhospitable climates like Rosarita Bay's, cool and dreary, next to the ocean, where the wind blew and blew and the fog lay over the marine terraces all day long. For a couple of hours in the early afternoon, the fog would recede and the sun would emerge and heavenly blue sky would yawn open, but then it'd all get swallowed up by the fog again. The Brussels sprouts loved it. They loved the cold evenings of fall, not even minding a mild frost, which actually improved the taste of the sprouts, making them sweeter and more tender. There wasn't much else that could be grown in this area that was as salt- and weather-tolerant. Artichokes, pumpkins, and Brussels sprouts were pretty much it.

Before Lyndon had taken over the farm, it had been run as a full-fledged commercial operation for three generations. When the patriarch died at the age of ninety-seven, though, his grandchildren weren't interested in carrying on with his legacy. They'd long ago moved to cities far and wide, and they were happy to let go of the property. Along with it came the house and all of its contents, as well as a farm manager and a crew of seven who had kept the Brussels sprouts doused with chemicals from start to finish: organophosphates like Lorsban and chlorinated hydrocarbons like DDT and then lindane. Lyndon hated it, the idea of it, the residue of all those pesticides and herbicides on the sprouts, the trace elements of toxins seeping into the earth and contaminating it for decades. But, contrary to assumptions, Lyndon wasn't a reformer. He wasn't some sort of idealistic, hippie-dippy enviro-activist, not even a vegetarian. He just wanted to farm in a way that was simple and pure, and keep his life uncomplicated. He laid off the manager and the crew, and stripped everything down so he could work the farm by himself. As it happened, going organic was the most lucrative option, a pragmatic decision more than a moral one. He planted only a total of one acre on his twenty-acre farm now, and he didn't spray at all, even with approved products on the OMRI list.

Some inspectors found it hard to believe that Lyndon could go no-spray organic monocrop and produce the Brussels sprouts that he did—dense, dark-green beauties, with tightly wrapped, unblemished leaves, firm but delicate, with a succulent, nutty flavor. These were Brussels sprouts the way they were meant to be, not the boiled, sulfurous, bitter mushballs with which most people were familiar. Lyndon's secret was to spread the plants out in small blocks of no more than six rows—two hundred plants per row. The minute you had too many rows together, you had problems. And in between blocks, he'd grow summer rye, barley, buckwheat, bell beans, and oats.

The cover crops were the key to everything. In the spring, Lyndon would mow them into tiny bits and disc them in. Everything would get incorporated into the soil, and all the microbes would begin to eat the chopped-up pieces of green-ery, and a tremendous amount of nitrogen would be seques-tered, equivalent to ten thousand pounds of fertilizer per acre. Meanwhile, he'd seed the Brussels sprouts in nursery flats in his greenhouse, then transplant the seedlings to the field, and, bar-ring trouble, they'd grow from six inches to over three feet. Big leaf petioles would spiral out from a thick central stalk, and at the base of each stem, buds would form into sprouts, elegant miniature cabbages shaded by an umbrella of leaves. At the end of September, Lyndon would crawl around the field with a jackknife and bucket, harvesting the early varieties, pick-ing from the bottom first, working his way up, and in October he'd hire a few people to help him break off the leaves and cut the stalks with machetes and haul them into the packing shed and desprout them en masse. Each stalk would yield eighty to a hundred sprouts, about two to three pounds, and at the end of the harvest, Lyndon might gross anywhere between fifty and seventy-five thousand dollars, about three times as much as he would have made growing Napa Valley Cabernet Sauvignon on the same acreage.

It was a tight, cost-efficient little operation if everything went well, but there were so many things, with the Brussels sprouts sitting out in the field for four months, that could go wrong. They were susceptible to all manner of disease and infestation. Clubroot, nematodes, black rot, powdery mildew, aphids, cabbage loopers, diamondback moths. To keep them at bay, Lyndon constantly rotated his crops, never planting in the same place for years, trading sprouts for cover crops, and he was always watching the soil, wondering whether it was too hot or too cold, whether it needed water or not. The soil had to be moist, the nutrients flowing, in order for his plants to be strong and healthy and growing. If they got too dry, they became stressed. As soon as they got stressed, aphids appeared. If the plants were too wet, however, he might get cabbage flies, maggots that chewed the roots and turned the plants purple. One part of the farm was always too wet or too dry. One corner had too much clay and poor drainage; another corner was too sandy or low on phosphorus or potassium. He was always looking at the colors, reds and purples on the leaves, or the tint of blue he saw now after his pump had failed and he'd missed irrigating by one day.

He was worried. He didn't need anything more to worry about. Woody being here. Getting assaulted by an aging kung fu actress on a bender.

She was standing outside the house when he came back from

the fields. Wearing a form-fitting baby-blue tracksuit, white kerchief, and large sunglasses, she was doing a tai chi routine, slowly shifting her weight, moving from one pose to the next, her hands soft, her arms flowing in graceful circles. It stilled Lyndon, witnessing the beauty of her movements, and for a second he thought he might have been too quick to dismiss her. But then she began coughing, a deep, hacking, lung-rattling cough that had her convulsing and doubling over and pounding her fist against her thigh. It seemed to last forever, the cough, and Lyndon began to wonder if he might have to call an ambulance. Finally it stopped, but she stayed bent over, hands on her hips, laboring to catch her breath. When she did, she hawked out a prodigious glob of phlegm, a righteous grade-A loogie, then reached into her pocket, pulled out a pack of cigarettes, and lit a butt, blowing out a plume of smoke as she walked away toward the bluff.

Out of the corner of his eye, Lyndon detected a tennis ball flying through the air and bouncing on the ground, Bob tearing after it. Oh, Bob. Where did he keep finding these tennis balls? It was Woody, of course, who was playing fetch with him. But as Lyndon rounded the corner of the house, he saw that Woody wasn't alone. A red SUV, decorated with flower-power splotches of pastel paint, was parked on the gravel driveway— the standard-issue vehicle for The Centurion Group, the developers of the hotel and golf course flanking his farm. Woody was talking to Ed Kitchell, the latest in a long string of polo-shirt-and-khaki-clad wonks who were trying to convince Lyndon to sell his property. Mud was on the SUV's tires, surely from following Woody's tracks through the creek ditch.

Lyndon went to his shed, dropped the hula hoe, and retrieved his Viper M1 semiautomatic rifle, a smaller version of an M16. He made sure it was locked and loaded and strode toward Kitchell. The gun had an extended barrel and a telescoping buttstock, which Lyndon braced against his shoulder. He took aim and fired at Kitchell. The shot missed, whizzing over Kitchell's head.

"Lyndon!" Kitchell screamed, ducking.

"You're not supposed to be here, Ed!" Lyndon screamed back.

"What are we going to do?" Kitchell said, his hands raised, backing up toward his car as Lyndon approached. "You won't answer your phone. We need to talk. We're running out of time."

These unannounced visits had been coming at a fever pitch of late. Apparently the design of the golf course was reaching a crucial juncture, a point of no return. After being harassed on and off the farm, Lyndon had applied for a temporary restraining order, and, to everyone's surprise, he had gotten exactly what he'd wanted. They couldn't come near him without first arranging a meeting via telephone, correspondence, or e-mail.

"I'm going to have you thrown in jail, Ed," Lyndon said. Even at this distance, he could smell Kitchell's awful cologne— Brut or Hai Karate.

"What about what you're doing to us?" Kitchell said. "To me *personally*. What about all that? You think that's legal? You think that's just fun and games? All the pranks? You're supposed to be cooperating with us, Lyndon, actively engaging in a dialogue. That's what the judge told you."

Lyndon fired off another round, which hissed past Kitchell's blow-dried blond hair and splattered against his SUV.

"Jesus!" Kitchell said.

"Watch it! Watch it!" Woody said to Lyndon. His shiny midnight-blue Range Rover was parked in front of Kitchell's SUV, which now had a new banana-yellow splotch to accompany the other blots of happy hues.

Lyndon had custom-ordered these Zap Talon paintball

shells. They were filled with permanent oil-based paint, not the usual water-soluble type, and they were guaranteed to be fast-drying. They were also advertised to be scented, alternately, with cat urine and doe in heat, although that claim had yet to be verified. He shot another paintball, this one lime-green, which tagged the back of Kitchell's SUV with goo as he sped away.

"You're a madman, you know that?" Woody said. He followed Lyndon into the house through the mudroom, where Lyndon peeled off his boots, then into the kitchen, where Lyndon began washing up at the sink.

"Are you insane?" Woody said. "Ten million dollars? They're offering you ten million dollars for your farm, and you've said no?"

"This is none of your business, Woody," Lyndon said, scrubbing his hands with Borax soap.

"Why are you even hesitating?" Woody asked. "Your place is only worth a fraction of that. You could ask for anything you want. You could probably push them to twelve million, maybe even fifteen."

"I'm not interested." He glanced at the kitchen table, where Woody had laid out his cell phone, headset, pager, PDA, BlackBerry, iPod, and laptop, which was open to a complex spreadsheet, all of them hooked up to a tangle of chargers.

"Fifteen million, Lyndon!"

Lyndon had been afraid of precisely this, that Woody would learn about The Centurion Group's offer while he was here for the weekend. Now he would never let go of it. "I'm not talking to you about this, Woody." He shut off the water, flicked his hands dry, and put on another pair of shoes.

"Where are you going?" Woody asked.

"I have things to do."

"What about lunch?"

"I told you, Woody, I don't have time to socialize with you."

"You have to eat, don't you?"

"I'll call you."

"Do you have a cell?"

"There are still pay phones around, you know," Lyndon said. "I'm not a complete yokel. I keep up with things. I have the Internet."

"You have dial-up, Lyndon. Dial-up. It's 2005. It's thirty-year-old technology. And you have a TV that gets reception for shit, no satellite or cable, never mind upgrading to digital, thank you very much, not even a DVD. What the hell do you do for entertainment? Read books? Have you become that much of a hick?"

"You might think of it for yourself. It might do you some good."

"Wait, hang on." Woody trailed after him as Lyndon walked to the door. "Here's my card with all my numbers. I might head into town. Your coffee, I'm sorry to say, stinks. And keep the gate unlocked, will you? It's a nuisance, but hardly a deterrent."

Lyndon put the card in his back pocket. "Do me a favor, Woody. Don't play fetch with Bob. He'll keep bringing you tennis balls, but ignore him. He's got bad hips. He shouldn't be running at all."

He took his panel truck with his welding equipment. He had a small wrought-iron sign frame that he needed to deliver later that morning. First he had to get fitted for another temporary crown. It took them over an hour to squeeze him in between appointments, at which point the dentist joked, "What'd you do, get into a fight?"

Lyndon installed the sign frame at the boutique on Main Street, and then drove up Highway 71 to Skyview Ridge Road, following the contours of the hillside to Sheila Lemke's house, a cedar-and-glass monstrosity with wraparound decks that she had bought from a former colleague.

Sheila had once been a high-powered attorney for a venture capital firm in Silicon Valley, but she had vested out her options long before the dot-com bust, escaping with a bundle of cash. Husband and child in tow, she had moved to Rosarita Bay eleven years ago when she was thirty. She had retired and divorced when she was thirty-one, and remarried when she was thirty-four. She'd stayed with Steven Lemke for three years, until she had left him for Lyndon.

Sheila answered the door with a cordless telephone pressed against her chest. "Just the person I wanted to see," she said balefully.

Lyndon waited. God, that face. What was it about her face that made him weak with devotion, willing to withstand her steady, withering scorn? She had blue eyes and straight auburn hair cut into a bob. She was slender, with long limbs, but really she was all mouth and sculpted cheekbones, her skin unnaturally pale, porcelaneous.

"Oh, all right," she said. "Come in. Let me finish this."

She took the phone with her down the hallway to her study, and Lyndon wandered into the living room. On a clear day, the house had a beautiful panoramic view of Rosarita Bay—the harbor to the north, the marsh to the south, the town in the middle, the Pacific everywhere beyond. Only it wasn't a clear day, the fog still a blanket. Lyndon's gaze settled instead on a line of chocolates on the dining room table. *Chocolates.* A dozen pieces of dark chocolate were on the table, each centered meticulously on individual white saucers, surrounded by stacks of photocopied articles and books: *Gourmet Chocolate, Purely Chocolate, The Bittersweet History of Chocolate.*

Sheila replaced the telephone in its charger and told Lyndon, "You wouldn't believe how many health and fire regulations are involved in running a chili cookoff. That's before we even begin to talk about the insurance issues."

"Wasn't the festival your idea?" Lyndon asked.

"That means I can't complain about it? Sit down. You're here, you might as well make yourself useful. What happened to your eye?"

Lyndon pulled out a chair. "Long story. It's fine." A small black bruise had arisen underneath his left eye. He had been kicked in the jaw, but somehow the damage had migrated up his face.

"Taste," Sheila said, pointing to a chocolate.

She seemed composed, none of the histrionics that were on display yesterday lying in wait, and apparently she didn't care to discuss what had happened, which was perfectly acceptable to Lyndon. If she wanted to pretend for the moment that all was normal, that no hammers had been wielded, no judgments of abject evil cast, so be it. He picked up the square of solid chocolate and opened wide to pop it into his mouth.

"No, no," Sheila gasped. "Not like that, you Neanderthal. This isn't a Hershey bar. These are gourmet chocolates. You taste them like you taste wine. Look at it first."

Lyndon looked, and saw a piece of plain chocolate.

Sheila sat down in the adjacent chair and leaned over. "Look at its surface, its texture. Turn it around in the light. See how smooth and unblemished it is? It has this silky sheen, no blooms from heat or moisture. See what I mean?"

"Okay, sure," he said, although he didn't.

"You feel it melting in your fingers? Chocolate stays solid up to 91.4 degrees and melts at 93.2. The quicker it melts, the better the chocolate. Now smell."

"When did you start learning about this?"

"A couple of days ago. It just came to me, this overwhelming craving for chocolate. It was the weirdest feeling."

Lyndon lifted the chocolate, and they bent down together and inhaled.

"Isn't that heavenly?" Sheila asked. "There are some incredibly subtle characteristics in here, floral and earthy and fruity all at once. These are all handmade, and they've got a high percentage of origin beans, cacao beans from the same country. Brazilian beans are smoky, Guyaquil are sweet, Madagascan more pungent. This one's the highest grade, a criollo from Venezuela."

It wasn't unusual for Sheila to take an impulsive interest in something and acquire an encyclopedic knowledge of the subject overnight. She was frighteningly intelligent and passionate, and Lyndon found her sexiest when she was engaged like this, embarking on a new pursuit.

"Breathe in again," she told Lyndon, "let the aroma settle."

Breathe in, breathe out, Lyndon thought. They smelled the chocolate together once more.

"Now snap off a piece and listen," Sheila said. "You hear that? A crisp, clean snap?"

Lyndon didn't hear much of anything. "Can I eat it now?"

Sheila frowned at him. "You are so male. You need instant gratification. All right, if you must, but don't chew it yet, just put it in your mouth."

Despite the lingering effects of Novocain, the hit of flavor immediately engulfed Lyndon, as if someone were peeling off his scalp. He'd never tasted chocolate anywhere near this sumptuous.

"Let it sit on your tongue," she told him. "It should feel firm but melt like butter, nice and smooth, without a residue. It shouldn't stick to the roof of your mouth or cling to your tongue. Connoisseurs call it a clean melt. Do you feel that?"

Lyndon tried to speak, but was momentarily incapacitated.

"Those are just the primary flavors," Sheila said. "Now chew on it, *slowly*, to release the secondary flavors. Roll it around with your tongue. Let it touch all four taste zones and get the full range of the flavors."

Lyndon, chewing, looked at her quizzically. Four taste zones?

"The tip of your tongue for sweet and salty," Sheila told him, "the sides for sour, the back for bitter. Do you notice how the taste changes as it goes to different parts of your mouth? Feel how long it lasts, how it rises and lingers, how varied yet balanced it is."

Lyndon could take it no more. He swallowed the chocolate. He was breathless, light-headed, zapped, delirious.

"Wasn't that sublime?" Sheila asked.

"Again," he said.

"Cleanse your palate first." She sliced a lime in the kitchen, squeezed a wedge in a glass of water, and gave it to Lyndon. "Rinse."

"You're going to make your own chocolates?"

"No, I'm going to sell them. I'm going to open a chocolate *boîte*, a boutique chocolate shop. I'm going to handpick my line from the best artisanal suppliers in San Francisco and have them delivered to me every day. You've heard of the health benefits of chocolate, haven't you? The flavonoids and antioxidants? And there's very little sugar in these chocolates, so less calories."

He could hear the sales pitch already, the formulation of a new business plan. Sheila liked starting businesses. In her relatively short time in Rosarita Bay, she had had three: a bakery, a flower shop, and a bookstore, all launched with the same zeal, all ending because of certain niggling, insurmountable obstacles. To wit, she had hated waking up early and didn't really enjoy baking, she was allergic to most flowers, no one read books anymore.

"All right, let's do another one," Sheila said. "I'll taste it with you. This one's a porcelana, the holy grail of criollos."

They looked at it, felt it, smelled it, listened to it, put it in their mouths, and swooned. Everything in Lyndon's mouth swelled and lifted, his vision blackened, he almost passed out. That buzz, that weird energy he'd felt after Laura Díaz-McClatchey's massage, returned, and he could see Sheila felt it, too, the two of them moaning, swaying, opening and closing their eyes, enraptured. They looked at each other, and they began kissing, an udderly licious liplock, tongues and chocolate commingling, rolling into all four taste zones. They fell to the floor, pawing each other, grabbing body parts, pulling on clothes, and Lyndon sank into the smell of her—her skin, hair—the feel of her, everything coming back to him, so familiar, he hadn't realized how much he'd missed her. But then Sheila pushed him away—an audible pop, Lyndon swore—and, long limbs punching and flailing at him, she perhaps inadvertently, perhaps intentionally, kicked him in the nuts.

Lyndon's brain exploded, his body combusted into flames. While he writhed in pain on the floor, Sheila stood and straightened her clothes. "I'm not falling for that again," she said to him. "You're crazy if you think I'll make that particular mistake again."

A year ago, she had ended it with Lyndon—another mandated shutdown in a relationship that had seemed more off than on. She was tired of his grumpiness, his solitary routines, she had said, she was tired of waiting for him to open himself up. She didn't understand him at all. When narcissism had become the national pastime, how was it that Lyndon could be so self-effacing, that he had so little interest in self-reflection? Clearly he wanted to be alone.

She got back together with Steven Lemke, only to walk into Lyndon's bedroom in the middle of the night two months ago and make love to him, descending upon him like a succubus, only immediately afterward to deem him a louse, a miserable excuse for a human being, why couldn't she accept that she couldn't change people, why did she keep falling for these blue-collar lunkheads, and demanded Lyndon stay away from her, stop stalking her, she never wanted to see him again, only to once again ask Steven to move out, admitting after much badgering and weeping (by Steven) that she had slept with Lyndon, making it twice that Lyndon had broken the covenant of Steven's marriage, which was why he was now giving Lyndon traffic tickets at every opportunity.

"I want you to get out," Sheila said. "I'm not another one of your floozies."

So now it was coming out, Lyndon thought, now they were going to get into it. "I just went to her for a massage."

"I see. A massage."

"Not that kind of massage," Lyndon said, gingerly standing up. "Shiatsu."

"You just move right along, don't you? You don't skip a beat."

"Sheila, you know I'm not like that. I've had five girlfriends in seventeen years."

"Not that you've been counting."

"What do you want me to do?" Lyndon asked. "You keep breaking up with me. You keep telling me you don't want to be with me."

"As any smart woman would do, someone as secretive as—"

"What's going on?" Lyndon asked. "Why are you putting nails in my tires? What was with the meltdown yesterday?"

"Go. Just go." She pointed to the front door.

On the threshold, Lyndon faced her and said, "You still love me, don't you, Sheila?"

"I don't."

"You do," he told her. "Just admit it. I'll admit it if you admit it."

It was true that they were completely unsuitable for each other. It was true that Sheila's election as mayor and her plans for Rosarita Bay had lodged a fundamental wedge between them. It was true that Lyndon had never asked Sheila to live with him or marry him, that he'd never fully let her into his life. Yet he'd loved her, he'd been happy with her, he'd given her as much as he was capable. He'd been brokenhearted when she'd left him and returned to Steven, and that one night together two months ago, madly fucking during a freak heat wave, unearthing all those emotions he'd had to work so hard to bury, only to have Sheila discard him once again, had been nearly as devastating for him. If anyone had the problem with constancy, with commitment, Lyndon thought, it was Sheila, not him—witness her inability to stick with any of her businesses.

"You should just go after your hot little tamale masseuse," Sheila said. "I'm serious. We are never going to get involved again, understand? There is zip chance. *Nada. Rien. Zenzen betsuni.*" She knew smatterings of five foreign languages but was fluent in none. "And I don't want Hana helping you with the harvest this year. I know she said she'd come home and give you a hand, but that's not going to happen."

"Why not?"

"You're not a very good influence."

"Come on."

"It's not in anyone's interests—and I mean practically the entire town, Lyndon—for you to have a good crop this year."

"You want me to go bankrupt?"

"I want you to sell your farm."

"Why? Why should it matter to you? You'll still get your windfall. You'll still get your tourists."

They'd had this debate so many times. Three hundred new jobs, tens of thousands of additional visitors, two million dollars a year in hotel occupancy and other taxes, The Centurion Group providing the funds for a new elementary school, weighed against higher property taxes and rents, more traffic, myriad environmental consequences, changing the nature of the town forever, paving away its rustic charm and leaving, in its wake, soulless sprawl.

"You know why, Lyndon," Sheila said. "Don't be disingenuous."

"Let them drive around!" he said.

The issue was, if Lyndon sold his land, the eighteenth hole of the golf course would be a long par-five that would hug the ocean and gently rise to the stunning vista of the six-story hotel on the bluff—a spectacular finishing hole that could rival the one at Pebble Beach, that one day might befit the hosting of a regular PGA tournament, or maybe even a U.S. Open. If Lyndon didn't sell, the eighteenth hole would be a short, lackluster par-three, after which golfers would have to climb into carts and drive around Lyndon's farm. The Centurion Group would have to reconfigure some other holes and change the layout of the course, truncating the total yardage far below championship level.

"It's their own damn fault," Lyndon said. "They were stupid to assume I'd sell out."

It was ludicrous, actually, for them to have gone ahead with the design and construction of the resort without securing an agreement from him. He was certain that heads—especially Kitchell's—would roll, which was why he didn't put it past them to try anything at this point, including, perhaps, pressing Sheila to influence Lyndon.

"Just take the money," Sheila said. "It's an obscene amount

of money. And you could use it, couldn't you? It mystifies me, what you've been doing. Don't you realize what's happening, how serious this is? All these pranks you've been playing—grow up, Lyndon. They haven't been helping. This latest one—"

"I had nothing to do with that." Up to now the vandalism and tomfoolery at the golf course had been minor—misdemeanor shenanigans and high jinks—but a few days ago, someone had tried to torch Kitchell's office trailer with a Molotov cocktail, melting the aluminum siding before·the fire was snuffed out.

"It's bordering on terrorism. People are telling Ed he should call the FBI or ATF."

"Next you'll blame the whale on me. I swear to you, it wasn't me."

"Just sell," Sheila said. "If you keep being difficult, the town might file for eminent domain."

This was a new threat, an ominous one. "You couldn't do that."

"I couldn't? The law's on our side."

"It'd get tied up in court for years."

"Don't be so sure. I'm still an attorney, remember."

"Why would you want to do something like that to me, Sheila? Something so mean, so malicious? What's gotten into you lately?"

Sheila's eyes narrowed, and he could tell she was tempted to say something glib and insulting to him, but the impulse gave way to another sentiment—a mixture of incomprehension and despair. "You've become like that whale to me, Lyndon. To tell you the truth, it would greatly simplify my life if you would just disappear from this town."

A few weeks ago, a dead humpback whale had washed ashore between the harbor and the site of the new hotel—a thirty-foot, thirty-five-ton calf that began to decompose while the town and various agencies argued over who was responsible for its disposal, the police and fire departments insisting it wasn't their problem, the National Marine Fisheries Service saying it was only charged with collecting data on the whale, not getting rid of it, the National Oceanic and Atmospheric Administration and the Gulf of the Farallones National Marine Sanctuary wanting to study it where it lay, the town and the harbormaster and the California State Park and Recreation Commission all claiming it was outside their jurisdiction. Meanwhile, the carcass sat on the beach for four days, stinking to high heaven, the stench wafting downwind to The Centurion Group's hotel, Ed Kitchell apoplectic because nothing was being done. At last, the harbor patrol and parks officials agreed to tow the whale several miles offshore, whereupon they would hand it off to a research foundation, which would haul it another twenty miles, where they hoped to observe a shark feeding frenzy. But they couldn't even manage to slide the whale past the surf, and while more arguments ensued over who was at fault, overnight, as mysteriously as it had arrived, the whale disappeared. Search teams unsuccessfully combed the shore for it, concluding it had floated back to sea with a rip current, and everyone forgot about the humpback until last week, when the whale showed up again, this time a couple of miles to the south, in a hard-to-access cove off the new golf course, in very sorry condition now. This time, none of the governmental agencies would get involved. The research foundation, after carting away some blubber, said they had all the material they needed, their crews busy with other projects, so several more days passed before, finally, Ed Kitchell had been forced to hire two private towboats to drag the rotting, putrid carcass—his own personal Moby-Dick—out to sea.

As Lyndon walked away from the house, he heard a series

of soft thumps. Hana Frost, Sheila's seventeen-year-old daughter from her first marriage, was shooting baskets at the end of
the driveway. Lyndon himself had replaced the old hoop over
the garage with this freestanding backboard when Hana had
expressed an interest in trying out for the junior varsity basketball team. The interest—an encouraging sign of group socialization, Sheila had said—had been short-lived. She didn't go to the
tryout, and she returned to holing up in her room with her guitar all day long, writing weepy little love-is-lost, tears-in-the-
rain songs.

"Game of Horse?" Hana asked him, dribbling the ball.

"Let's play Pig," Lyndon said. "I don't have that much time."

"What'd you do to your eye?"

"Never mind. Gimme." Hana tossed him the ball, and
Lyndon dribbled twice, pivoted, and threw up a sweet fade-
away jumper from twenty feet that arced high and rotated true
and hit nothing. Not the net, not the rim, not the backboard.
Nothing. *Nada. Rien.*

"Nice shot," Hana said with a laugh.

"That doesn't count. That was a warm-up."

"No way, José." She picked up the ball and dribbled to the
free throw line and smoothly fired a line drive, clanging the ball
off the front rim. A brick. This game would take a while. They
were both terrible at basketball.

Lyndon tried a little hook. Missed. Hana tried a baseline
turnaround. Missed. And so they went, trading misses, until
at last Hana awkwardly banked in a layup. Such a simple shot.
Lyndon flipped the ball up, a foregone conclusion, except it spun
around the rim and lipped out.

"Ha!" Hana said. "*P.*"

"Remind me why we do this again?" Lyndon said. "Is this
supposed to be fun?"

"It's fun for me."

They matched two more misses.

"Are you and Mom getting back together?" Hana asked.

She had always been like this with Lyndon, unusually frank, although she could be equally naïve. She was an odd bird, a contrarian, a loner, as intellectually gifted as her mother. She was due to start her freshman year at Stanford as a premed major in a few weeks.

"It doesn't look likely at this point," Lyndon said to her.

"Do you want to?"

"That's sort of between me and your mom, don't you think?"

"It does involve me, you know."

"I suppose it does," Lyndon said. "The answer is yes, I'd like to get back together with her, but she won't have me. She told me she doesn't want you at the farm this year." For the last three Octobers, Hana had helped him harvest his sprouts on weekends.

"We're fighting," Hana said.

"What about?"

"Isn't that between me and her?"

Lyndon lofted up a haymaker, grunting, his knees aching, his rotator cuff pinching, and, miracle of miracles, the ball ricocheted off the backboard and the rim and bounced into the air and swished through.

"That shouldn't count, it was so pitiful," Hana said.

"Chalk it up, sister."

Hana stepped to the same spot and threw up a prayer. She wasn't close.

"*P*," Lyndon said.

"You want to make this interesting?"

"My truck could use washing."

"Not a car wash."

"What, then?"

"Let's say a favor to be named later."

On her next turn, Hana jogged to the top of the key and shot a rainbow that dropped straight through the net. "Have you been practicing?" Lyndon asked. "You hustling me?" He took aim, let it fly, and shot another air ball.

"*P-I*," Hana said.

"Why do we do this?" Lyndon said. But he was enjoying the game. His relationship with Hana during the three years he'd dated Sheila had been a pleasant surprise. As moody and churlish as she could be, he had liked spending time with her, and he'd missed her company almost as much as Sheila's.

"Do you feel different lately?" she asked him.

"What do you mean?"

"Restless, antsy. I don't know. Everything's pulling at me," Hana said. "Is it the weather?"

"The weather's no different," Lyndon said.

"Maybe it's an influx of positive ions, or Mercury's in retrograde or something. Maybe just hormones. I've been jumping out of my skin. Do you think sex would help?"

It'd been a while since they'd talked, but the few times he'd run into Hana the last year, Lyndon had perceived a disturbing change in her. Before, she'd been all skinny arms and legs, wan, with lank hair and dark circles perpetually under her eyes, giving her the appearance of a junkie without the benefit of pharmaceutical agency. Partly this was due to her inimitable fashion sense, illustrated by the outfit she wore today: a thrift-shop brown cardigan, puke-green T-shirt, mango-orange skirt, black pantyhose, and square-toed clodhoppers. Now, though, not even her ugly clothes could conceal the startling fact that she had become, seemingly overnight, ripe with life. Her body had filled in with breasts and curves, her skin was plump and healthy, her lips larger, more protrusive. There was a new nubile, illicit quality to her. All of a sudden, she looked extremely fuckable. She was turning the heads of boys and men who'd heretofore not given her a moment's notice.

"I'm a little uncomfortable with this conversation," Lyndon told her.

"I'm still a virgin, you know," she said.

"I'm definitely uncomfortable." Lyndon—two men removed from Hana's father, the CFO of a software company whom she seldom saw anymore—had never been responsible for providing her with counsel or discipline, which, naturally, had accounted for their ease with one another. He liked that dynamic, and he didn't want to complicate it by knowing anything about her personal life. She was seventeen. He preferred she didn't have a personal life.

"I don't know squat about the world," she told him. "I don't know anything about *life*. I could end up like you."

"Meaning?"

"A recluse, a misanthrope. I've got to pop my cherry before I leave for school."

"Stop. I don't want to know," Lyndon said. He tried a little bank shot from five feet away and butchered it.

"I thought you were interested in my life."

"Some parts more than others," Lyndon said. "Anyway, I think you're sublimating. I think you're nervous about Sunday." The chili and chowder festival was going to be featuring some folk music, and Hana had won an open-mike competition at the Java Hut, the local coffeehouse, to perform a few songs on the main stage. Evidently she had learned a thing or two over the summer at a five-week program in Boston at the Berklee College of Music. Previously she had applied for regular admission as a full-time student there, but hadn't gotten in, much to the relief of her mother, who had been opposed to the idea from the start.

"Maybe I am a little," Hana said. "Give me some advice."

"When it comes down to it, life is suffering."

"What?"

"If you fall on your face, it won't be the end of the world." He didn't quite know what to make of Hana's musical aspirations. Everyone, even Steven Lemke, wanted to be an artist or performer these days, invariably for the wrong reasons.

"You're not helping." She made another layup.

"Do you know a girl named Jen de Leuw?" Lyndon asked.

"What?"

"She works at the ice-cream shop."

"I know exactly who she is. Why are you asking me about her?"

"No reason, really."

"No reason? No reason? You just happened to mention her? What a funny coincidence. What a monumental laugh! It just so happens I was going to let André Meeker relieve me of my virginity, until that fat bimbo came along."

"Forget I said anything." Wanting a quick escape, he muffed the layup on purpose—not that he would have necessarily made the shot if he'd really tried. "Okay, that's Pig. I gotta go."

What was wrong with everyone? he wondered as he drove back down the hill.

It was one o'clock. He hadn't called Woody about lunch, and he had half a mind to turn east on Highway 71 and weasel out of town for the afternoon. Sometime or another he had to drive to Salinas to get the waxed cardboard boxes and perforated plastic bags with which he packed his Brussels sprouts—why not go now? That would kill at least five or six hours. He needed to be in his pickup, though, not his crowded panel truck, and he wanted to do some work in his barn this afternoon. He supposed he couldn't evade Woody the entire weekend.

It was awkward for Lyndon, trying to go along with this new mode of fraternal détente. He couldn't get used to it, couldn't quite slip into the pretense that everything was fine, they could pal around, eat meals and hang out together.

As children, they had fought continually, more than once coming to blows. Woody had been a geeky kid, chubby and ungainly, always trying too hard to be liked. He'd been obsessed with getting into Harvard and, toward that goal, had enrolled in all sorts of extracurricular activities and sports, none of which he'd executed with the least bit of passion, everything just a means to an end, a tally of participation. Lyndon didn't know where Woody had picked up this single-minded pursuit for achievement. Their parents hadn't been particularly demanding in that regard, never meting out any bourgeois, upwardly mobile, model-minority pressure for their sons to go Ivy League (in contrast, say, to what Sheila expected of Hana). No, Wooddough had somehow come up with this compulsion all by his lonesome, and when Lyndon hadn't been busy ignoring or mocking or despising his brother, he had felt a little sorry for him.

In adulthood, whatever sympathy he'd had for Woody vitrified into pure hostility. It'd only been in the past few years that he had thawed at all, that he'd begun to feel it might be time to make peace with him. He hadn't been willing to initiate anything, of course. Someone or something else had to do it for him. Frankly, he had been waiting for Woody to beg. Their mother's deathbed charade had been transparent, but serviceable. She had looked awful in the hospital, weak and jaundiced. She hadn't been able to eat or drink or go to the bathroom for days. It turned out she'd had a simple intestinal blockage that merely required a twenty-minute endoscopic procedure, but she had milked the situation for all it was worth. Lyndon knew she was faking it, and so did Woody, and the fact that no one called her on it was their gift to her.

Still, Woody—with those ridiculous blond highlights in his hair, his cartoonishly white teeth and plucked eyebrows, his garish clothes and SUV—remained inimical to everything Lyndon believed in, and despite his best intentions, Lyndon could barely stand to be in the same room with him. Thanksgiving and Christmas last year had been excruciating, but even worse had been Lyndon's visit to L.A. in February. Woody lived in the Hollywood Hills in a one-story house with a partial view of the city, a cool, modernist affair with a flat roof and white stucco walls and sliding glass doors, minimally furnished with sleek chrome and leather showpieces, everything in black or gray or white. He'd hired an interior designer, Woody had said with pride. The house was beautiful, all right, but cheerless, without any character, and that was what Lyndon felt as Woody dragged him to studios and restaurants and clubs, continually pointing out famous people Lyndon had never heard of. It all looked good, but it was so vacuous. He couldn't get out of the city fast enough.

This was the thing about family: you were forced into an intimacy with people with whom, given a choice, you would never care to associate. It was so much easier to cast people off than to have to deal with them. People were difficult, annoying, intrusive. If only he didn't have to bother with people, if only he could be left alone—that was all he really asked. Why was that so much to ask?

Yet, to his bewilderment, he always seemed to be doing things that jeopardized his seclusion, inviting complications. Sheila, for one. The nails in his tire, the shrieking, the antagonism—they were something new, however. They weren't at all like her.

Sheila could be prickly and capricious and a little crazy at times (although not this crazy), but she was generally kind, reflective, occasionally wistful. Really, the most reckless thing she had ever done was fall in love with Lyndon.

Four years ago, November 2001, she had hired him to build a spiral steel staircase in her new bookstore on Main Street. It was supposed to have been a relatively simple and quick job—two weeks on the outside, from ordering the materials to applying the protective coat. She was in a rush. Her store was scheduled to open soon, and everything else was essentially done: the cherry bookshelves, the maple floors, the interior stonework. Yet there'd been some sort of snafu with the original designer and contractor, who'd installed a beautiful mahogany ladder to a small storage loft near the back of the store. Neither had accounted for a county building code that stipulated strict modes of access, even for a passageway that would only be used by staff. The ladder had to come down and be replaced with a staircase.

"You don't seem too upset," Lyndon had told her.

"These things happen," she said. "This isn't my first store."

Having weathered his share of mercurial clients, Lyndon appreciated her composure and levelheadedness. With the many tradespeople and vendors and inspectors she had to deal with throughout the day, she never yelled, never got flustered, was decisive and polite and resolute. This was a woman who knew what she was doing. She knew how to listen, negotiate, compromise. She wasn't affected by internal quirks or idiosyncrasies. She didn't let anything perturb her personally. It was all just business. All the more which made her behavior with Lyndon perplexing.

She initially told him she didn't care what the spiral staircase would look like. She didn't want any decorative or ornamental touches, interested solely in its functionality and completion. That was what she told him. So he got some twelve-gauge steel plates with a nonskid diamond pattern, cut them into treads, and started tacking them to a center pole. He added mild-steel rods for balusters and a stainless-steel handrail, welded out all the joints, and ground out the points.

Yet, when he had completed the staircase's raw construction, she balked. She walked around it, studying it. "It looks so . . . industrial," she said.

"You told me you didn't care how it looks."

"I know, but I didn't realize it'd be . . . I don't know," she said, faltering unexpectedly. The stitch weld marks underneath the treads, where they met the support brackets at a right angle, especially bothered her. "They're unseemly. Isn't there a way you could make them . . . seamless? Cover them up and make them smooth?"

At that point, it would have been cheaper and less time-consuming to tear apart the whole thing and build a new one. What they eventually agreed upon was to have Lyndon apply Bondo—auto body filler—on the underside of each tread. He'd put down a thick caulk-like bead to cover up the weld marks, mold a concave curve on each side of each T-joint, and sand it down so everything would be flush and seamless. However, there was no way to do any of this except *by hand*.

It was tedious, backbreaking work, sitting on the steps and contorting his body to reach up to the next tread. Lemke Books had its grand opening before he was able to finish, and he had to come in during off-hours, mornings or nights, when it'd be just him and Sheila inside the store.

Then, after he finished smoothing down the Bondo, there was the issue of painting the stairs. He had to hang a well of plastic sheeting around the staircase, attach a portable ventilation system, and spray on two coats of primer, three coats of oil-based enamel, and a final coat of polyurethane sealant, all of which he thought was overkill for an interior staircase that would get little traffic. And since it was "unsightly" to have the plastic sheeting hanging there during business hours, Sheila asked him to take it down and put it back up each night. Then she changed her mind—twice—about the color of the paint, deciding she wanted a slightly different shade of blue-black after he'd applied the final sealant on the previous one, which meant he had to sand it all down again to the primer, requiring a week's more work.

"Am I being difficult?" she asked. "Do you mind?"

Normally he would have minded; he would have minded a great deal. But he was almost sanguine, because she was now paying him by the hour, and because she was always apologetic and a little shy with Lyndon, and because each amendment, each additional task, gave him the opportunity to spend more time with Sheila, this pretty, competent redhead, with her clear blue eyes and sharply carved face. There was something irrefutable between them, a flirtation, an attraction. He'd sensed it early on, and he knew she did, too, from their second day in the store together, when she got off the phone after arguing with her daughter about homework, the parent promoting the virtues of ambition and discipline to the child. Offhandedly, Sheila had said to Lyndon, "You agree with me, don't you?" and he'd said, "If you must know, I've always taken a principled stand against ambition and discipline."

She'd stepped back then, regarding him, her curiosity piqued. What have we here? he could read in her eyes. "That's not very reassuring to hear," she said, "considering I've just hired you."

"You're going to have to keep a close eye on me, then."

They chatted over the many weeks he worked on the staircase. About their present lives, their childhoods, how and why they had arrived in Rosarita Bay. She had grown up in Chicago, gone to Northwestern, and then Stanford Law. She'd met her first husband, Chris Frost, in Palo Alto while he was getting a combined JD/MBA degree, and they had lived almost exclusively in San Francisco, most recently in Noe Valley, before moving to the coast. She had wanted to get out of the city, out of the congestion and traffic and stress of urban life.

"The world seemed so much coarser to me all of a sudden," she told Lyndon, and talked about an amorphous yet acute feeling of malaise that had weighed down on her. "I was looking for quiet. I was looking for escape."

Lyndon was customarily evasive with her about his former career as a sculptor. As far as anyone in town knew, he'd only had middling success as an artist in New York, and this was the assumption Sheila herself drew, based on his reticence.

"It didn't work out very well for you, did it?" she said one night, arranging books in the travel section while he stirred paint.

"No," he told her, which wasn't, strictly speaking, a lie, although he'd had solo exhibitions all over the world, his work appearing in the Museum of Modern Art, the Whitney, the Centre Pompidou, and the Tate Collection, and he'd been featured in *Vogue* and *Life* and *People* and had regularly been fodder for the gossip tabloids.

"I'm surrounded by failed artists," Sheila said.

"Oh?"

"My daughter, she sings and plays guitar. She's pretty bad right now—no big surprise, she's thirteen—but there's something there. Even I can tell she has some natural talent. But know what? I'm never going to tell her that. I'm never going to encourage her one iota in that direction."

"Why not?"

"I've seen what hope can do to people, to dreamers."

"You wanted to be an artist?" Lyndon asked.

"No. Not me. My husband. My second husband, Steven Lemke. He's a sergeant with the sheriff's office. Do you know him?"

Lyndon had an image of a tall man with remarkably lustrous dark brown hair. He nodded. "I think he's given me a parking ticket or two."

She stared at the rack of travel guides. "Does it make more sense to order this by country or region?"

"Region," he told her.

"I keep signing up for language classes," she said, "but keep dropping out of them. I've always wanted to travel."

"Why haven't you?"

"Difficult with a child."

"And a new business," he said.

She shuffled a row of books—Japan next to China. "Sometimes," she said, "it doesn't feel like it was a matter of making a good choice or a bad choice, of missing an opportunity or not. I just wasn't paying attention. I looked up one day and found myself where I am, and now I have fewer and fewer chances to do anything about it."

He didn't exactly understand the antecedents of this statement, but she was suddenly naked to him—lonely.

"Do you read much?" she asked.

"I like a good mystery now and then," he said. "No, not much, I'm afraid."

"I'll let you in on a little secret," she said. "I don't think this bookstore has a chance of surviving."

"No?"

"No. I can say that almost definitively."

"You haven't been open a month yet."

"I'd give it a year at most," she said. "Independent bookstores are relics, dinosaurs. There's no market for books anymore."

"Then why are you doing this?"

"I had a misguided notion it'd cheer up Steven," she told him. "I thought—and this is how desperate I've become—it might help save our marriage."

"Are you succeeding?"

"No."

Steven was an aspiring fiction writer—or, before summarily quitting earlier that spring, he had been for twenty years. In that time, he had produced three novels and reams of short stories. He had attended dozens of workshops, panels, and conferences, pored over a multitude of how-to-get-published books and magazines, entered contest after contest, applied for every conceivable fellowship, submitted his manuscripts to hundreds of literary magazines, editors, and agents, all to no avail, unable to publish anything, save for a handful of vignettes in a few inconsequential, obscure journals. All the while, he had been convinced he was a genius, that his experimental narratives were not being appreciated because they were too advanced, too sophisticated, for mainstream publishers. He had been absolutely secure about his gifts as a writer.

"That's an admirable quality to have as an artist, and maybe a necessary one," Lyndon said. "The only problem with it is, one can be wrong. What did you think? Was his stuff any good?"

"I don't know. I can't really say," Sheila told him. "I don't have a lot of expertise in the matter. I can't really judge."

"What did you major in in college?"

"Literature."

"What?"

"His prose style was always a little idiosyncratic, his characters generally unsympathetic, unlikable, and his vision was, well, let's say it was sort of harsh, apocalyptic."

"I'm beginning to understand."

Sheila had offered to pay to have Steven's stories and novels self-published, but he'd said no, insisting that the traditional arbiters of the literary world should recognize his work.

"It was so sad to see all these self-addressed, stamped envelopes coming back from magazines," she said, "after Steven had waited months, sometimes over a year, for an answer. He'd just want a little encouragement, a note, a handwritten 'Thanks' or 'Sorry' or just someone's *initials* scribbled on it, some acknowledgment that his stories merited the briefest human response, but they always just contained blank form rejection slips. They were like little deaths, one after another, those slips, for him and for me. It's terrible to see someone's dreams die before you."

Steven started sending vituperative letters to the magazine editors, sometimes phoning them, demanding to know if his stories had even been read, or merely funneled into the slush pile for an intern to process. Sheila told him this strategy would not help his cause, since he often ended up soliciting the identical editors with more of his stories, but Steven would not listen.

The final indignity came during the latest round of trying to get his novel into print—the same one he'd written in his early thirties, which he annually revised and retitled and resubmitted. (He had not, in truth, written anything new in years, devoting himself instead to learning the ins and outs—the trick, there had to be a trick—of the business.) He sent the novel to every major and then every minor publisher, and then every first-book competition, each one for which he duly mailed in his twenty-five-dollar entry fee with a photocopy of his 744-page manuscript, double-spaced, paginated, no contact or identifying information anywhere except on a cover page to ensure anonymity and avoid conflicts of interest. He received form rejection letters from every contest apart from one, which had a handwritten note on it. The note—unsigned—read: "The world might be a better place if Steven Lemke would just get a clue." Soon afterward, the results of the contest were announced, and Steven learned that the winner had been the judge's former student—perhaps, it was rumored, even the judge's former lover.

Ever since, Steven had been on a campaign, dedicating every waking spare hour to exposing the corruption inherent in the publishing industry. It was all a sham, a charade, completely unethical and elitist. The entire enterprise was rigged. All the awards, grants, fellowships, and contracts went to favorites and sycophants and the select few who managed to inveigle themselves—with youth and good looks and connections—into the inner circle. The literary establishment was a cowardly, complacent old New Yorkers' club that excluded outsiders and shut its eyes to anything that was different, innovative, anything with real guts, anything that dared to challenge the status quo. Steven now was a leading contributor to muckraking writers' forums and blogs. He badgered the IRS, trying to get them to revoke the tax exemptions of certain nonprofit small presses. He pestered attorney generals, asking them to charge contest organizers with fraud. He bombarded editors with chastising e-mails, deriding their highfalutin magazines and publishing houses as torpid and moribund. He posted nasty online reviews of books by new writers, particularly contest winners, assailing their careerism and mediocrity. It didn't trouble him that he never read the books. He never read anything anymore. He hated everything he cracked open.

"It's making him go gray," Sheila said. "Literally. His latest pet peeve is with minority writers. He claims most of their books would never have seen the light of day if they'd been white, that they're getting the benefit of literary affirmative action. He's coming off as vaguely racist."

"I don't know if there's much that's vague about that."

"Steven is not a racist," she said. "Really, he's not. I would never tolerate that. Underneath, he's a good, honorable man. That's why it's so tragic, what all of this has done to him."

"Did it ever occur to him that if he'd spent as much energy writing as he did trying to get published, he might have gotten further?" Lyndon asked.

"Owing to residual loyalty, I cannot comment," she said.

The irony was, it had been a love of books that had brought Sheila and Steven together. They had met in a book club, sharing a passion for reading, a fervent conviction that fiction mattered, that novels and stories could change and shape lives, even whole societies.

She reached behind her and pulled out a volume of Chekhov. "There's nothing with more elegance and power in such a simple package," she said. "When you read a good book, it stays with you forever. It teaches you about family, about love, about the dialectic of being an individual and finding community. It teaches you about the search for connection. What could be more meaningful than that?"

He guessed she had used this argument many times before. To bank managers and investors, to the zoning board and the planning commission. Nonetheless, as she spoke, she was ardent, earnest, and he saw a light in her, an incandescence—perhaps she was a dreamer after all, a romantic.

"That's what we used to believe, Steven and me," she said. "Enough to have always fantasized about owning a bookstore together. But he's no longer a believer, and I don't know if I am, either."

"Because of what happened to him?" Lyndon said.

"Partly," Sheila said, tucking the Chekhov back into its slot.

"But it's more . . . I just don't know if novels are relevant anymore. I don't know if they can tell us anything about the world today."

"Do they really need to?" Lyndon asked. "Is that the role of art?"

"You think it should just be entertainment?"

"Hardly. But that's not why people make art."

"Why do they?"

He shrugged.

"If you had to say."

"If I had to say," Lyndon told her, "I'd say that it's enough to provoke the imagination, which in its own way instills compassion. But from the point of view of an artist, I'd say that art, at its core, is a quest for transcendence, for purity." This was from an old speech of his own, a sound bite he'd manufactured long ago for interviews.

"You know," Sheila said after a pause, "there's more to you than meets the eye."

"That's called a backhanded compliment, I think."

"The weld marks never really bothered me," she said to him. "The paint was fine the first time. You must've thought I was a complete bitch."

"Not at all."

"I put you through hell for nothing."

"You don't have to explain."

"It was just an excuse."

"Didn't you just tell me I'm not as dumb as I look? It's all right," he said. "I know. I know."

       ■   ■   ■

WHEN LYNDON GOT HOME, he found Yi Ling Ling standing at his kitchen sink, barefoot in her blue tracksuit, dumping out the contents of his entire liquor cabinet. Presently she was holding a bottle of Jack Daniel's upside down over the drain.

"This is so liberating," she said, eyes agleam. "I've had my last drink, you see. You're witnessing a new YLL. I'm going to cleanse myself of all impurities. This air, this wonderful air here, I just breathe it in and feel this *clarity*. There's something about this place, this farm—it's transformative. I hear the ocean, the wind, all these birds. It moves me. I feel all this *energy*. Did I do that to your eye?"

"Yes."

"I'm sorry," she said. "I only have the vaguest recollection of it, to tell you the truth. I think I was having an adverse reaction to some medication I was taking for jet lag." She had finished with the Jack Daniel's and was now pouring out a bottle of Tanqueray. "Things are so alive here. I feel everything *growing*. I never imagined the countryside could be so invigorating."

"You know, other people might want a drink now and then," Lyndon told her.

She looked at the gin splashing out, then flipped the bottle upright. "Oh, of course, I don't know what I was thinking," she said, giggling.

She returned the remaining bottles to the cupboard, and he put the empty ones into the trash. "Where's Woody?" he asked.

"I don't know, really. He sort of abandoned me. He said he'd be right back, but that was hours ago."

"Do you want some lunch?" Lyndon asked.

"Thank you. I'm famished. Just give me a minute to change, and I'll be ready to go."

"I was thinking of just making some sandwiches for us."

"Really? Here?" Ling Ling asked. "You're going to cook?"

She sat down at the table and watched him prepare the sandwiches, apparently fascinated with his culinary ability. The attention made him nervous, which led him to be a little care-less as he moved a cutting board from one counter to another, allowing a paring knife to slide off and drop.

The knife hung suspended in the air, the tip an inch above his bare foot. With impossibly fast reflexes, Ling Ling had stretched out to catch the handle of the knife in midflight. Balanced on her chair, she was laid out horizontal to the floor, arm and legs fully extended, toes curled around the knob of a cupboard door for a fulcrum. She rose and handed Lyndon the knife.

"Thank you," he choked out.

"Don't mention it," she said. She absently rubbed her shoul-der. "Do you know somewhere I could get a massage?"

Lyndon cut the sandwiches in half. "There's nowhere to get a massage in this town," he told her. "None." He plated the sandwiches with some potato chips and sweet gherkins, popped open cans of diet soda for them, and joined Ling Ling at the kitchen table.

She picked up her sandwich, took a bite, and grunted appre-ciatively. "This is marvelous. You're really very talented."

"I think it's something even you might be able to manage."

She laughed uproariously—a heehawing horse laugh. Relaxed like this, without her sunglasses for once, she was pretty, Lyndon had to confess. "Woody tells me you were once famous," Ling Ling said.

This was all Lyndon needed—for Woody to reveal the details of his past to everyone in town.

"How famous were you?" she asked.

"Not really famous. I could walk down the street unmo-lested, if that's what you mean."

"I was famous once."

"I gathered."

"I could never, not ever, walk down the street unmolested. So

I never walked anywhere. I always had a car and driver. I never had to do my own cooking, or cleaning, or laundry. I never had to go to the market or the chemist. I never had to stand in a line and wait for anything, ever."

"Some of that sounds very appealing."

"Oh, it's sensational, until you lose it. Then it's humbling. Then it's humiliating. It's degrading, for example, to go to the bank and be utterly *lost* when it comes to using the automated teller machine and having people treat you as if you were a useless *git*." With the expulsion of the last word, she angrily bared her teeth, but then eased into an ironic smile. "You may have noticed, I have a slight problem with being told what to do. I like being the one who tells people what to do. What kind of sandwich is this again?"

"Grilled cheese with tomato."

"Grilled cheese with tomato," she said. "It's heavenly. Could you make this for me every day I'm here?"

"I'll see what I can do."

She picked up a gherkin, turned it in the light and examined its texture, sniffed it, and put it back down on her plate. "Tell me about Brussels sprouts. Do you actually like Brussels sprouts?"

"Sure," Lyndon said, although frequently he was disgusted by them, the taste of them, the smell of them, God, sometimes he didn't think he could look at another fucking Brussels sprout if his life depended on it. He was used to defending Brussels sprouts, however, and he knew dozens of ways to make them palatable. He knew how to sauté them, bake them, steam, fry, boil, braise, roast, stew, and blanch them. He knew how to serve them lyonnaised, au gratin, and à la barigoule. He knew how to make them with peanut butter, chestnuts, gorgonzola, Hollandaise sauce, grapes, pomegranate molasses, Beaujolais, curry powder, fresh dill, clarified brown butter, pimientos, soy sauce, balsamic vinegar, and marjoram. His head overflowed with recipes for Brussels sprouts, although he seldom ate them anymore. Teaching himself how to prepare Brussels sprouts, he had learned to be a pretty good cook, but he rarely cooked anything more complicated than a stir-fry. It seemed he was full of talents that were of no particular use to anyone.

"Do you miss New York City?" Ling Ling asked.

"No."

"Don't you miss your celebrity?"

"No."

"This is enough for you, being a farmer?"

"Yes."

"I miss it—all of it," Ling Ling told him. "I miss being recognized. Mobbed. Adored. I miss the tabloids and the paparazzi, the autograph hounds, the stalkers. I miss my *youth*, I guess is what I'm saying. It's so unfair that we have to age. It's a rotten trick, really."

"I like being my age. All those things I used to worry about when I was younger, I don't worry about them anymore. It's a relief."

"What sorts of things did you worry about?"

"Everything," Lyndon said. He took her plate and cleared the table.

Bob made one of his infrequent appearances, stretching through the dog door and plodding into the kitchen, nails clicking on the floor. Ling Ling watched him sniff at his food bowl, then lick, and lick, and lick at his water, a prolonged drink that seemed without end. "What a fascinating animal," Ling Ling said. "Is he always so thirsty?"

"He'll drink from anywhere," Lyndon said.

Bob traipsed back outside, and Ling Ling said, "Go on. What did you worry about?"

"I worried constantly what people were thinking about me." Lyndon dumped the remnants of food into the trash, put the pan in the sink, dripped a little detergent in it, and turned on the water. "I worried I was making a fool of myself but didn't realize it. I worried I was becoming an asshole, and then I worried I was no longer worried about being an asshole."

Lyndon remembered one Christmas when he and Woody were home from college. Their mother was arguing with Woody—Lyndon couldn't recall about what anymore—and Woody unleashed a familiar plaint: that she loved Lyndon more, that Lyndon was her favorite. Later that evening, as she and Lyndon were washing the dishes, she admitted that what Woody had said was true. She did love Lyndon more, he had always been her favorite. She said she'd started becoming frightened of Woody—frightened of her own son—when he was in high school. Frightened of his ambition and materialism and preoccupation with status, of his aggression and the way he treated women, girls. She'd realized she was raising a boy who was becoming exactly the type of man she'd always despised. She was raising an asshole. His mother had then burst into tears in the kitchen and made Lyndon promise never to reveal to Woody what she had just said.

"I don't see it," Ling Ling told him. "I don't see an asshole in you, and I've seen a lot of them in my time."

"A few people would disagree," Lyndon said.

Ling Ling stepped outside to smoke a cigarette. As she came back into the house, a high-pitched alarm began ratcheting up from the mudroom. "What on earth is that noise?" she asked. "I heard it a while ago."

"It's the driveway sensor."

"Is it supposed to keep going like that?"

It wasn't. Instead of a short chirp, the sensor was emitting a continuous whine. Lyndon pushed the kill switch on the console in the mudroom, but the piercing whine continued. He banged on the console, to no effect. The noise was getting louder, more shrill, intolerable. He lifted the console off its mount and tugged on the wires in the wall and ripped them off the back of the console. The noise stopped.

He expected to see Woody driving to the house, but it was JuJu LeMay. Lyndon could hear his rattling, spluttering, rusted-out Toyota—with the soundtrack of his head-banging music—approaching long before he could see the car.

JuJu skidded to a stop, flung open the door, and extricated himself from the seat. "Hey," he said tiredly. He was unshaven, his skin an unhealthy bluish tint, dark patches beneath his eyes.

"Hey," Lyndon said.

"Beelzebub called. Wants to know if you can fill in for Pauly tonight."

JuJu worked as a bartender at the Oar House, where Lyndon occasionally picked up shifts, and Lyndon had been hiring him along with Hana to harvest his sprouts in October. Dreadlocked and tattooed, JuJu was a former surfer, originally from Santa Cruz, who had been in the seventh year of a Ph.D. program in Mesoamerican studies at UCSC before, at long last, he'd dropped out to surf full-time. He had been peerless at Rummy Creek, the big-wave break just north of Rosarita Bay that fired up thunderous monster barrels during the winter. A photograph of him—dropping down the sixty-foot vertical face of a hella-cious peak—landed JuJu on the cover of *Surfer* magazine, and he went pro, started getting sponsors. But then two years ago, on a relatively placid, windless day at Rummy Creek, the water green and glassy, he'd lost his left foot to a roving great white shark. He had been straddling his board, waiting for a set, and he'd felt a tug on his leg, then unbelievable pain. He never even saw the shark. He was fitted with various prosthetics, the latest a carbon-fiber-titanium marvel that was so well designed, strangers sometimes didn't realize he was a gimp.

"I don't know if I can work tonight," Lyndon told him. "I have visitors."

JuJu gaped open his mouth, mocking disbelief. "*You?* Have *visitors?*"

"You know what?" Lyndon said. "Tell him I'll do it. I'm sure I'll need a break later."

"Who are your visitors?"

"My brother."

"I didn't even know you *had* a brother," JuJu said. "You are full of secrets and surprises, my friend. I want to meet him. Where is he?"

"Out."

"How long is he staying?"

"Too long."

"Oh, I see," JuJu said, "some fraternal antipathy. Well, then, let's see how our little girls are doing, shall we? How are they looking? Want to take a drive out and visit? What's up with the black eye?"

They climbed into Lyndon's pickup and drove down the tractor path, spinning on the dirt at the turns. JuJu huddled on the passenger seat in his fleece jacket, sniffling snot—a perpetual cold he couldn't seem to shake. He wasn't looking good. He looked, in fact, strung out.

"You've been monkeywrenching on your own, haven't you?" Lyndon asked.

"Hey, that wasn't me."

"The stuff we've been doing, they've been kind of funny and juvenile and innocuous, but a Molotov cocktail—"

"Dude, I'm telling you, it wasn't me."

It had begun with a childish little prank. After the heavy equipment to clear-cut the adjoining land had first rolled in, Lyndon and JuJu had gone out one night and poured popcorn kernels into the exhaust pipes of some of the bulldozers and excavators, so when the engines were started the next morning, the kernels heated and popped and streamed out of the pipes. Then—they weren't too inventive yet, still strictly high school—Lyndon and JuJu ordered fifty anchovy pizzas for delivery to The Centurion Group's project managers in their office trailer. Then they signed them up for free trial subscriptions to a passel of rather hard-core homosexual porn magazines. Then they slipped sugar into the gas tanks of a few backhoes and front loaders. Then sand. Then dozens and dozens of tampons. After that, things got a bit out of hand.

It was Ed Kitchell's fault, really. In January, Kitchell and his project managers woke up the entire town with a parade. They drove their red SUVs in a caravan down every street in Rosarita Bay, shouting and singing and blaring music. It became apparent that the principals of The Centurion Group were all alumni of the University of Southern California, and that many of the project managers were former Yell Leaders for the Trojans football team. This was why the company SUVs were painted cardinal-red with gold trim, and why the hotel and clubhouse and McMansions along the fairways were taking on, as they were being built, a distinctly Romanesque cast, with porticos and Corinthian columns.

The project managers were celebrating USC's victory the night before in the national championship game, hanging out of the SUV windows with megaphones in their white V-necked USC sweaters, singing the school's alma mater and fight song, the accompaniment for which they blasted out of an elaborate PA system. Once in a while they jumped out of their cars and did back handsprings and formed standing pyramids and dropped to the ground for linked push-ups in the shape of a T.

Worst of all was Ed Kitchell. Muscle-bound Ed Kitchell was galloping half naked up and down the streets astride a huge white horse—a rented Andalusian, Lyndon later learned, just like USC's mascot—dudded up in a skimpy Tommy Trojan outfit: leather tunic and skirt, knee boots, a silver helmet with a plume of feathers. Very authentic-looking, and with good reason. Ed Kitchell *had been* Tommy Trojan in college. This was the costume he had worn at games.

Lyndon and JuJu had been sitting in Lyndon's pickup, stuck at an intersection, appalled by the spectacle before them. Ed Kitchell rode his horse past the truck, yanked on the reins, spun the horse around, and made it whinny and rear up on its hind legs, affording them a nice view of its genitalia. Dropping the horse back down, Kitchell brandished his sword at Lyndon and JuJu, the muscles in his arm bulging, neck veins popping, and said, in a low voice thick with contempt, "Hail to the conquering heroes, you worthless shits." It was too much to bear. It was, for all intents and purposes, a declaration of war.

But it had been more than a month since Lyndon and JuJu had ventured out for any of their little stunts. JuJu had to be sneaking out solo.

"Okay," JuJu said in the pickup, "I'll admit I've been doing a few tiny little jokey pranks on my own—"

"JuJu . . ."

"Harmless, man. They've been absolutely harmless—small-time, trick-or-treat, negligible nonsense. You know me. I'm a pacifist. I'd never do anything like firebomb a trailer."

Lyndon wasn't so sure. JuJu had succumbed to a rash of self-destructive behavior of late. He'd been let go from his two other jobs—clerking in a surfboard shop and washing boats down at the harbor—and was forever close to being fired from the Oar House. General attitude problems, absenteeism, maybe skimming off the till. Recently he'd gotten into a bar fight, beaten soundly. He wrote a couple of bad checks and had been fined and almost jailed. He'd developed a form of road rage, following drivers who'd offended him until they parked, whereupon he'd slit the paint on their cars with a razor-sharp box cutter, the lacerations unnoticeable until they rusted.

"If it wasn't you, who, then?" Lyndon asked.

"Beats fuck out of me. Maybe the real PLF's come in."

The PLF was the Planet Liberation Front, an extremist organization that advocated ecotage—sabotage, property destruction, mischief, and vandalism in the name of environmental activism. They busted windows, put spikes in trees, and mailed letters containing razor blades. They booby-trapped construction sites, sliced power lines, and set buildings on fire. As an organization, they were highly decentralized, divided into cells that operated independently. Theoretically, anyone who adopted the organization's ideology could claim to be a member, and people were welcome to monkeywrench to their heart's content in the organization's name, tagging their handiwork with the initials PLF.

"You should have never sprayed that on the dump truck," Lyndon told JuJu. "That was just inviting trouble."

"It seemed kind of funny at the time. You thought so yourself, if I recall."

"I can't be responsible for my actions when I'm under the influence," Lyndon said.

"Exactly my point, bro. Now slow down, slow down." Ahead of them was a thicket of bushes and trees. JuJu leaned his torso out the window and inhaled deeply. "Holy mother of Chong, you smell that? That's unbelievable."

Lyndon drove the rest of the way to the edge of the thicket and killed the engine. They began walking into the bushes and were overwhelmed by the aroma of the marijuana plants. There were five of them here, a second cluster of five more plants hidden in another part of the farm. The plants were Durban Poison, a cross between a South African sativa strain and a potent early Dutch skunk. They had grown to over six feet tall, springing up in the shape of Christmas trees with the alacrity of amaranth, and Lyndon and JuJu could almost see the THC crystallizing and dripping off the plants. They had huge leaves and long, compact, extremely resinous buds. Once harvested and dried, they would have a sweet, earthy flavor with a hint of anise and, according to reports, a clean, uplifting, trippy high.

"Don't you think they're ready?" JuJu asked.

"They're not ready."

"They look ready."

"They're not," Lyndon told him.

"We can't just pick some off the top?" JuJu asked. "They look so ripe. We pick some off the top, that might help the buds on the bottom, don't you think?"

"Take my word for it, JuJu, it's too early to harvest them."

They got back in the pickup and drove to the other cluster of plants.

Lyndon didn't think of himself as a stoner or an addict. He was a recreational user. He only smoked at night when he was home, alone, and knew he wouldn't be going out or driving. True, he smoked a bowl of 420 almost every night, and if he missed a night he got jittery and restive, but, by and large, it didn't have much effect on him. It didn't alter his behavior, really, nor his perceptions. He was inured to it. To him, it was a pleasant indulgence, like a glass of wine with dinner, that hurt no one.

The plants in the second thicket of bushes were equally healthy and robust. "You have got a mongo green thumb, man," JuJu said, standing before the plants. "I can't believe all of them came through. Every single one of them. You said we'd lose more than half to disease and mold."

"We got lucky."

"We should have done this eons ago," JuJu said. "Simply fucking outstanding."

This was the first time Lyndon had tried to grow marijuana on his farm, and he hadn't expected to be so successful. To be on the safe side, he had planted quadruple the amount he and JuJu would need for a year's personal supply. In retrospect, the pot had been easier to grow than Brussels sprouts. They had the same growing cycle, and all Lyndon had needed to do was bury pipe extensions from his sprouts to irrigate them simultaneously with drip tape.

"So, what should we do with the surplus?" JuJu asked. "There's no way we can smoke all of this ourselves, you know."

"Don't even think about it," Lyndon told him.

"Come on, nothing serious, just to some friends."

"No." Lyndon waded through the bushes toward open air.

"Just for some pocket change," JuJu said.

"No, JuJu, we are not going to start dealing. We *agreed*. This is strictly for personal consumption." Lyndon had been apprehensive about exactly this. Up to now a socialist, JuJu had become an opportunist. He had all sorts of entrepreneurial ideas lately, from the way the Oar House should be run to how Lyndon should operate his farm. He thought Lyndon should diversify his crops and "profit streams"—growing pumpkins, lettuce, and Christmas trees, establishing farm tours, U-pick programs, school field trips, pony and hay rides. He talked about direct-market sales like CSAs, farmstands, restaurants, country stores. He admired what other local farmers were doing to pull in tourists during the pumpkin festival and suggested Lyndon follow suit. Attractions for kids like a haunted house, face-painting, inflatable jumps, slides, electric trains, even the two Asian elephants, Esther and Louise, that one family farm had brought in to sell rides—JuJu thought these made good business sense. It was downright scary, what JuJu was turning into. A capitalist. A mercenary. A hustler. Lyndon wouldn't have been surprised to find out that it had been JuJu's plan all along to sell the pot.

"Lyndey, we could both use the money," JuJu said.

Lyndon had a sudden alarming thought. "You haven't told anybody about this, have you? Have you?"

"No."

"I'm not kidding, JuJu. This would be cultivation with intent to sell, a felony, serious prison time. You better not have told anyone. You didn't, did you?"

JuJu stalled, his mouth contorting. "I may have mentioned it, in passing, as an inconsequential sidebar, to one or two very close compadres, who'd never, in a million years—"

"Oh, God," Lyndon said. "Who? Who'd you tell?"

"They'd never utter a peep to anyone. Tank and Skunk." Tank and Skunk B. were two of his old surfing buddies, not the most reputable people in the world.

"Great. Just great," Lyndon said. He went to his pickup, opened the storage bin in the truck bed, and pulled out a machete.

"What are you doing?" JuJu asked.

Lyndon walked toward the plants. "These are gone. They were never here. They never existed. I'm taking them down and burning them."

"Don't, don't!" JuJu said. "Come on, Lyndey, they'll keep their mouths shut. I promise. Fuck, you can't destroy these beauties. It'd be a monumental waste. It'd be sacrilegious."

"You know how happy Steven Lemke would be to put me in jail? Not to mention Ed Kitchell?"

"Tank and Skunk, they're cool, man. I can count on them with my *life*. You know that." Tank and Skunk B. had been in the lineup with JuJu when the great white had attacked him, and they had used a wetsuit zipper strap as a tourniquet to stanch the bleeding and paddled him to shore. "Hey, come on," JuJu said. "Everything's cool. I—" He tripped on an irrigation pipe and stumbled to the ground.

"Hey, you all right?" Lyndon asked.

JuJu turned himself over and slowly sat up. "Everything's hurtling toward oblivion," he said. "It's meaningless, man. It's fucking meaningless. Look at me. I didn't firebomb that trailer, but yeah, I would've liked to. I want to take things down. I want to fucking destroy everything. This is the only thing I have to look forward to, Lyndon, our little project. It's all I've got. Don't take it away from me. I'm asking you, let me have my fun. Let me have this small amusement."

Lyndon looked down at JuJu, concerned for him. "You need to talk to them," he said after a moment. "Make sure they understand."

"Okay, okay."

"I'm not kidding, JuJu. The first sign word's leaked, I take it all down. Shit like this, it has a way of getting out, and it does, Sunny Padaca will come after us with more than a machete." Sunny Padaca was the town's resident pot supplier, not a man to piss off.

"I gotcha, I gotcha. Don't worry," JuJu said, getting up.

Lyndon put away the machete. "Okay, then."

"Okay," JuJu said. "Fuck, you damn near gave me a heart attack. I'm too delicate for this much excitement so early in the day."

Returning to the house, Lyndon took the path next to the

bluffs, and JuJu, toking on a fatty to calm himself, gazed out at the ocean. "Wanna take the boats out? It's flat, not much wind."

Lyndon knew JuJu didn't really want to take the boats out; it was just bravado. "I need to do some work," he said.

"You work too much," JuJu said. "You need to recreate more." He pinched the cherry off his joint and stuck the remainder in his shirt pocket. "You know Ed Kitchell's moved into one of the model homes on the golf course? They got guards all over the place now, but there's an easy way to circumvent that particular nuisance. What say, Kemo Sabe? Kitchell and his boys are going to be gone tomorrow night. He's flying to L.A. for USC's home opener."

"Jesus, JuJu, you are incorrigible." How had he let so much potential calamity enter the confines of his deeply ordered life? He didn't understand himself sometimes.

As they came up to the house, Lyndon spotted Ling Ling outside again, doing another kung fu routine on the grass, not tai chi this time, but something faster, flashing punches and kicks, blocks and traps.

"What do we have here?" JuJu said. "Holy mother of Jackie Chan, you know who that is?"

"She's an actress."

"Not just an *actress*," JuJu admonished. "That's like saying Elvis was just a singer. That's Yi Ling Ling! She's a legend in the kung fu world. What's she doing here?"

"She's with my brother."

"She's your brother's *girlfriend*?"

"No. She's going to be in a movie he's producing."

"Your brother's a *movie producer*? You've been holding out on me, Grasshopper."

JuJu had been obsessed for a while with the old TV series

Kung Fu, a stoner show if there ever was one, able to quote Caine with uncanny fluency and frequency: *"Before we wake, we cannot know that what we dreamed does not exist."*

They got out of the pickup, and JuJu bounded toward Ling Ling. *"Nehih ho ma*, Yi Ling Ling," he said, bowing with his left palm covering his right fist. *"M sai hak hei."*

Ling Ling looked pleased. She bowed back, hands in the same position. "Thank you," she said.

"I'm sorry, don't let us interrupt your training. But I would be honored if we could observe."

She smiled demurely. "By all means."

She stepped to the middle of the yard, rolled her head to get her neck loose, hopped up and down a few times, did several knee bends, and flapped her arms, then put her feet together and took a deep breath. She lunged forward, arms whirling, fingers freeze-framing into claws, and continued—leaping, kicking, striking, slowing, stopping, bursting onward, all of it accompanied by explosive shouts and yips. At one point, she unfurled her arms like a whip and let them quiver in front of her, her body jerking as if electrified—a human vibrato. Then she twirled in a circle, dipped down, twisted, and threw her body upward so she was horizontal as both legs scissor-kicked the air.

"Ooh, butterfly kicks," JuJu whispered.

She touched down and dipped and twisted and kicked again, but something happened this time, and she fell, landing flat on her face, dirt clouding out from the impact.

JuJu ran to Ling Ling, who was momentarily immobile on the ground. "Are you all right, Ms. Yi?" he asked, helping her up.

"I'm afraid I'm a little out of shape," Ling Ling said, chagrined, brushing dirt from her tracksuit.

"Out of shape? No, I don't believe so," JuJu told her. "Perhaps distracted and unnecessarily burdened by trivialities. It looks to me you simply need someone to help you, someone to take care of things for you, so you can concentrate on your training."

"Yes?"

"Like a personal assistant," JuJu said. "Or a manager."

Ling Ling took stock of JuJu, examining him from head to toe. "I think you may be right."

"And I happen to know someone who would be perfect for the job," JuJu said.

"Oh, you do, do you?" Ling Ling said. They both laughed, and she hooked her arm around JuJu's and led him to the house. "Are you a BK transtibial?" she asked, watching him walk on the dirt.

"How did you know that?"

"Oh, I have some experience in this area."

CHAPTER 4

NSIDE CUCHI'S COUNTRY STORE ON MAIN STREET, WOODY STARED DOWN
at his loafers, his poor Berluti loafers, which were spotted with mud. He had been careful this morning, going from
Lyndon's house to his car, hopping on tiptoe from one dry spot
to another on the dirt driveway, but still his shoes had gotten spoiled. He couldn't believe how much dirt was getting on
him—on his clothes, his Range Rover, his *person*—embedding
itself into every crevice and fold. He didn't know how it was
possible, when he hadn't touched anything, hadn't even gone
into the fields.

He had not been able to sleep much the night before. After
eating dinner with Lyndon, Woody had cleaned his guest
room—just a cursory wipe-down with a bath towel, nothing too
obsessive. He was trying hard to be more relaxed, to let things
go more. *Let it go, let it go*, his therapist, Dan, kept telling him on
the phone. (Woody didn't have time for office visits and spoke
to Dan only on his cell phone, usually while driving.) As Woody
lay in bed last night, however, on sheets as faded and threadbare
as the upholstery downstairs, he was kept awake by the sound
of the wind outside, buffeting against the windows, the house

ıg. The smell of the room started bothering him—musty, ...ewy. His breathing began to fracture. His lungs constricted, ıd he wheezed a little. How old was this mattress? he wondered. Had this been the previous owner's room, the grandfather's? Had he died on this bed? Woody began picturing the old man decomposing in his grave, maggots eating away his corpse, all those bugs and worms in the ground outside, and Woody's skin began to itch. He felt things crawling on him. Bedbugs. Dust mites. He was swaddled in their feces and body parts, they were feeding on his skin.

He went downstairs, found cleaning supplies, and scrubbed down the entire room, dusting, polishing, mopping, vacuuming the mattress and drapes. He was tempted to do the rest of the house; he'd taken care of the bathroom already. Once he got going, it was difficult to stop. This was why he kept firing his house cleaners. He would see they'd missed a spot, moved something. He would get out a sponge, reposition an item, and pretty soon he'd reclean the whole house. He was a bit of a neatnik— nothing really big, not a major deal, not too obsessive. When he went to other people's homes, he had the compulsion to tidy things up a little, clean, rearrange. From experience, he knew people were offended by this, and he was trying to reform.

In the store, he looked for some shoe wipes and polish, but there wasn't much of a selection, just a couple of cans of old Kiwi black. How did people live in this town? There were a half dozen coffeehouses on Main Street, a wealth of choice that had surprised him, but they were bereft in almost every other basic service. He hadn't been able to locate a shoe store or a dry cleaner, driving round and round. More astonishingly, there did not appear to be a cineplex anywhere in or near Rosarita Bay. How could they not have a single movie theater? They didn't have a car wash, either. His tires, the beautiful twenty-inch chrome alloy wheels on his Range Rover, were caked in mud, the Buckingham Blue Metallic paint streaked with crud. His Range Rover wasn't meant to go through creek ditches. It was meant for the quadrangle of L.A. freeways, the 405, 101, 134, and 10. It was meant for pulling up to Morton's, Spago, the Ivy, and Mr Chow, to the Skybar, the Viper Room, the Whisky Bar. It was meant to impress. It wasn't meant to get dirty.

He walked down the aisles, searching for the diaper section. He'd learned that, in a pinch, baby wipes—the ones for sensitive skin—were versatile cleaning cloths. Alcohol- and perfume-free, hypoallergenic.

It was an odd store. There were groceries, mostly gourmet and organic, and a butcher and deli counter. There was a bakery, a variety of cheeses, wines, homemade jams, relishes, and salad dressings, and a mishmash of housewares, personal hygiene products, and curios. In one corner, they had jeans, hip waders, fishing lures, and, honest to God, cowboy boots. All of it was stocked haphazardly on towering shelves divided by very narrow aisles, one of which he entered to discover two overweight young women stuffing a bottle of shampoo and a six-pack of soap bars, respectively, in the waistbands of their pants.

Maybe they weren't so young. It was hard to tell. One was short, Asian, the other tall, blond. They were layered in ratty fleece jackets, peasant blouses, T-shirts, and cargo pants, a couple of pairs each, and they wore floppy legionnaire hats with neck drapes and heavy hiking boots. Their hair was matted, faces grimy with soot, glowering at him. They looked like they'd been marooned somewhere and pushed to extremes. They looked dangerous, as if they had had to eat one of their own, and might tear into Woody at any moment. He backed out of the aisle.

He located his baby wipes and paid for them at the checkout stand, then went outside to clean his shoes. As he was crouched down, working on some mud that was wedged into the crack above one sole, he saw two muddy pairs of hiking boots step into view on the sidewalk. They stopped directly in front of him. "They make an Argosy laden with gold out of a floating butterfly," one of them said, "and these stupid grown-ups try to translate these things into uninteresting facts."

Woody rose and faced the two women. He didn't know which had spoken, but, vaguely, he knew that quote, knew that voice.

"How much wood would a woodchuck chuck, if a woodchuck could chuck wood?" the Asian girl said.

That voice—low and smoky. It tugged at him, plucked at the recesses of his past. "Do I know you?" Woody asked.

The women were expressionless, dour. "As much wood as a woodchuck would," the blond girl said, "if a woodchuck could chuck wood."

"What's this about?" he asked. "What do you want?"

"Got any wood, Mr. Woody Wood*pecker*?" the Asian girl said.

"Who are you?"

She broke into a wide grin. "Woodrow Wilson Song, don't you recognize me? It's Trudy, Trudy Nguyen! Or Thorneberry! Trudy Thorneberry! Kyle's sister!"

Kyle Thorneberry had been Woody's best friend at Harvard. Trudy had been Kyle's younger sister, adopted from Vietnam, a shy, scrawny little girl who hardly ever spoke, six, eight years old when Woody knew her, barely registering a presence during his visits to the Thorneberrys' house during the holidays, significant to him then only because she was Asian, making him wonder about Kyle, their friendship, if the real reason they were buddies was because Kyle was following some sort of familial streak of charity involving Orientals.

Trudy threw herself at Woody and hugged him, something underneath her jacket making her body feel like jagged edges. She was filthy and smelled terrible. It was difficult for him not to recoil.

"My God," she said. "How have you been?"

"I've been good, good," Woody told her. Hadn't she heard how he'd really been? But it seemed she had suffered her own fall from grace. The Thorneberrys had been very wealthy. Clearly Trudy had become estranged from the family and was now destitute, homeless, perhaps. "What about you?" he asked. "What have you been doing with yourself all these years? What's brought you here?" Drugs, Woody imagined.

"We've been recovering the plovers in Bidwell Marsh Preserve," Trudy told him.

"What?"

"The marsh south of here. This is Margot, by the way."

"Schrempp," she barked.

"Excuse me?"

"Margot Schrempp." She was a big-boned woman, toothy, with black horn-rimmed glasses.

They shook hands—his fingers squeezed inside Margot's strong grip—after which Woody, without thinking, cleaned his hands with the baby wipe he was still holding. "What'd you say you're recovering?" he asked Trudy.

"The western snowy plover."

"That's a bird?"

The girls laughed.

"Yes, a bird," Trudy said. "A shorebird. We're relocating them to a new breeding habitat. They were displaced by the golf course they're building, so we've been trying to get them to establish new colonies in the marsh preserve."

"How long have you been doing this?"

"All summer," Margot said. "This is our third seabird restoration project. We did the common murre at Devil's Slide last year, and two years ago the roseate tern in Maine."

"You've been camping?"

"Can you tell?" Trudy said.

"We're a little rank, aren't we?" Margot said. "It's funny how all I really want right now is a hot bath. I'd pretty much do anything for a hot bath. Anything."

"Have you ever been to the preserve?" Trudy asked.

"No. I only got in town yesterday."

"You're here on vacation?"

"I'm visiting my brother. He has a Brussels sprouts farm here."

"That's wonderful. I love Brussels sprouts," Trudy said. "What about you? What are you doing these days? Are you still in investment banking?"

Woody couldn't tell if she was being sincere. "No, I'm a movie producer in L.A."

"Really? What kind of movies?"

"Anything we might have seen?" Margot asked.

He mentioned a few of his most famous remakes, slick reiterations of Asian horror and action films that, despite being bland Westernizations of the original hits, had been extremely profitable: *The Well*, *Lethal Enforcer*, *Warrior of Wonder*, *Lying in Wait*.

The girls shrugged apologetically, not recognizing any of the titles. "We don't catch many films, actually," Trudy said.

"You should really see the preserve," Margot said. "It's only twelve miles down the coast."

"I'll try to stop by sometime."

"Are you busy right now?" Trudy asked.

"Now?" Woody said. "Not really, I guess."

"Because you should really see it, and, um, we could really use a ride."

"A ride?"

"Our car died last month. We sold it for scrap," Trudy said. "We've been hitching, or trying to, but for some reason people won't stop for us."

"It's perplexing," Margot said, "two comely ladies like us, don't you think? I'm telling you, T., we need to show more skin."

"We'd really appreciate it," Trudy said. "We walked all the way into town today. We're exhausted."

The thought of these two foul castaways in his pristine car was not at all appealing, but reluctantly he consented. He wanted to find out more about Trudy, or, more to the point, about Kyle. He led them to his Range Rover, Margot limping so noticeably, Woody wondered if she had a knee brace or an artificial leg under her fat cargo pants.

"This is your car?" Trudy asked.

"Yes."

"It's an SUV," she said. "We can't ride in an SUV."

"You can't?"

"No. We're diametrically opposed to SUVs."

"Oh, come on," Margot said to Trudy. "We can make an exception just this once, can't we?" She pouted at Trudy pleadingly. "We need to get back to our little fledglings."

Trudy climbed onto the front passenger seat, Margot in back. Once the doors were shut, their smell was overpowering. Woody turned on the air-conditioning and rolled down his window, then put the Range Rover in reverse.

"Look! The car has a camera!" Margot said. She pointed at the touchscreen on his dashboard. There was a camera mounted on the tail of his SUV, transmitting a wide-angle rearview color image whenever he backed up. "That is so cool!"

"There's a GPS navigation system, too," Woody said. "Give me the address for the preserve. I'll plug it in."

"It doesn't have an address," Trudy told him.

"What about something nearby?"

"Just head south on Highway 1. I'll tell you where to turn."

Once away from the store, the girls began pulling things out from underneath their clothes, not just the shampoo and bars of soap, but also toothpaste, floss, blocks of cheese, zucchinis, tomatoes, bananas, packages of pasta, carrots, a sack of potatoes, a bottle of Italian dressing, a jar of Dijon mustard, bags of trail mix, they kept coming, how had they been able to get away with shoplifting all of these things? As they voided item after item, tossing them into a rucksack, the girls got smaller and smaller, their clothes seeming to deflate, and Woody realized they weren't the slightest bit overweight, were, in fact, rather malnourished, which they proved with their next flurry of actions, Margot swinging her leg on top of the back seat and extracting, hand over hand, an impossibly long baguette from the cuff of her pants leg. Trudy tore the cellophane off some cheese with her teeth, and Margot whipped out an enormous bowie knife as Trudy dug her thumbs into the baguette, creating a channel, and Margot cut into the cheese and handed rough hunks off to Trudy, who crammed them into the bread and ripped the loaf in half and gave one to Margot, and immediately they began ravishing the sandwiches.

"Sorry," Trudy said, her mouth full. "We haven't eaten since yesterday morning. Want some?"

"No, thanks," Woody said, aghast by the crumbs and bits of cheese dropping onto his seats and carpeting.

Within seconds, the girls had wolfed down the sandwiches and then swallowed several bananas and shoveled away the bags of trail mix, washing it down with a gargantuan bottle of water they split between them. Finally sated, Trudy, breathing heavily, told Woody, "We've sort of run out of funds, if we're being too subtle for you. We were supposed to get some money wired to us, but there was a snag. I feel terrible about stealing from a mom-and-pop, but it's too difficult to shoplift at the Safeway with their security."

"Who's been paying you to restore the birds?" he asked. "The park service? The Audubon Society?"

"Oh, we don't get paid," she said.

"Hey, what are these things?" Margot asked, pointing at the video screens embedded into the backs of the front headrests.

"It's a DVD player."

"No kidding?" She saw the remote control in front of her and punched a button, which instantly resumed playing the movie that was still docked midscene.

"You don't get paid?" Woody said.

Margot turned up the sound on the 360-degree Harman Kardon Logic digital surround-sound system.

"He took the fucking bags," a character said.

"That fucking snitch," another character said. *"He thinks he can fuck with us? No one fucks with us."*

"We're volunteers," Trudy told Woody, raising her voice over the dialogue.

"I don't understand. You're not real researchers?"

"We're trained field biologists. Margot and I have degrees in environmental science from UVM."

Vermont, Woody thought. It figured. "Are you writing a book or something?"

"Why do you ask?"

"What are you trying to get out of the project?"

"Get out of it? We're trying to save the birds. There used to be tens of thousands of snowy plovers along the West Coast, but now there're only about fifteen hundred. It's a travesty, what the government's done, allowing all these developments up and down the coast. The plover's on the federal Endangered Species list, but somehow this conglomerate got approval for this stupid golf course and completely disrupted their nesting grounds."

"We are going to fuck him up good, know what I mean?"

"Fucking right we are. Better fucking believe it. The Messiah is coming to visit you with righteous indignation, brother Judas."

"Margot," Trudy said, swiveling around to face her friend, who was mindlessly engrossed in the movie. "Margot!" Trudy screamed.

"What?" Margot screamed back.

"Can you turn that down?"

"What?"

"I cannot *believe* you. You have been behaving *heinously* today." Margot flipped her the bird.

"Pop open that panel," Woody told her. Margot did, and pulled out a pair of wireless headphones. Woody used the touchscreen to redirect the soundtrack.

"Thank you," Trudy said. "What *is* that DVD?"

"Lying in Wait."

"That's one of your movies?"

"Yeah," Woody said, feeling strangely embarrassed. "But my next project, it'll be—"

"That's the type of movies you make?"

"My next one, I've got Dalton Lee directing." She didn't know who Dalton Lee was. "It's going to be an art-house film." He began telling her the plot, but as he did so, he couldn't even convince himself that it wouldn't be another genre movie.

"It sounds . . . ," Trudy said. "I don't know . . ." She was disappointed in him, it was plain to see. "You really look wonderful, Woody. You're dressed so beautifully. I'm glad you're on your feet again. I guess you had it pretty rough for a while, didn't you?" she said.

So she knew. "Kyle told you?"

She nodded.

"Can I ask you something? Did you have a falling out with your family?"

"Why do you think that?" she said sarcastically. "I'm not in contact with them at all anymore."

"But you still talk to Kyle, don't you? How's he doing?"

She turned to him. "Woody, don't you know?"

He had lost touch with Kyle, with everyone else from Harvard, after he had been indicted. The last he'd heard, Kyle was leading the convertible arbitrage investment team for Goldman Sachs in Manhattan and living in Westchester County, married, with three kids, inhabiting the very sort of life Woody had hoped he would have. He purposely tried to avoid news of his former friends, but no matter what he did, somehow the Harvard alumni office always tracked him down, forwarding donation pleas and newsletters and magazines wherever he moved. He always dumped them straight into the trash, unopened. "Do I know what?" he asked.

"He died," Trudy said.

Woody thought he had misunderstood her at first. "What happened? When?"

"He committed suicide. Four years ago."

"What?"

"He shot himself on Christmas Day, 2001. He drove to the train station in White Plains and sat in his car and shot himself in the parking lot."

"My God," Woody said.

They didn't speak the rest of the way to Bidwell Marsh Preserve, listening uncomfortably to Margot's punctuated laughs, gasps, and snorts as she watched the movie. They drove past farms, cow pastures, and rolling hills, and when the highway dipped into a wooded area, Trudy had him turn onto an unmarked dirt road. They bumped down the ruts, the road narrowing dramatically and becoming rougher, making the Range Rover rock and pitch, the engine grinding a bit. After a mile or so, the road ended at a clearing of sorts, although it wasn't very wide at all, and Woody worried he wouldn't be able to turn around.

Trudy opened her door and hoisted the rucksack. "Hey, let's go, Margot," she said.

"Let me just finish this scene," Margot shouted, still wearing the headphones. "This thing is a hoot!"

"Trudy," Woody said. "Was something happening with Kyle? With his career? Was he in trouble?"

"No, he wasn't in trouble," she said, climbing out of the car. "Not in that way."

"Why, then? Why'd he do it?"

Trudy shifted the straps of the rucksack on her shoulders. "I don't know. He was unhappy. Obviously he was unhappy. That was a stupid thing to say."

"Did he leave a note?"

"I guess you could call it a note," she told him. "He scribbled a line on the back of an envelope, a utility bill. It said, 'I have everything.'"

"That's it? That's all he wrote?"

"Yes." She banged her hand on the back window. "Margot! Get out of this car right this instant. I am so disgusted with you." She walked around to the driver's side and said to Woody, "Come see the plovers."

"I can't right now. I have an appointment."

"Come tomorrow, then. Just walk down the path to the ocean." She pointed to a trail he hadn't noticed.

"Okay, I'll try."

"Promise?"

"I promise." He took out his money clip and flicked off several bills. "Trudy, here, take this."

"No, I couldn't."

"Take it," he said.

She accepted the money and awkwardly leaned through the window and hugged him. "It's so good to see you, Woody," she said. "When I was little, I was deeply in love with you."

HE DIDN'T KNOW WHAT to do with the news. Kyle Thorneberry—he'd committed suicide? It was impossible. It didn't make sense. There had to have been a reason, something must have happened—with his job, with his marriage, with money. Woody didn't care what Trudy had said. People didn't kill themselves for no reason, they didn't blow their brains out because *they had everything.* Something must have been in the offing, a scandal of some sort: Kyle had made a colossal mistake that would soon be exposed, an error in judgment that would cost Goldman Sachs billions, for that was the rarefied, almost unimaginable arena in which Kyle had worked, responsible for billions of dollars. Or maybe the SEC or the attorney general, with so much attention being paid to hedge fund managers then, was investigating his division and was about to come down on him. He was going to be fired, humiliated, disgraced, possibly jailed. Or it could have been drugs, gambling, a sexual indiscretion or, more likely, perversion, an incurable disease—*something.* There had to have been something going on. Maybe he'd even been murdered, his death set up to look like a suicide.

As soon as he emerged from the dirt road and was back onto the highway, Woody carefully enunciated, "Call Roland," activating the hands-free phone in his car, which automatically extended the antenna mounted on the roof and made the call to his assistant.

"Yallow," Roland said.

"Where the hell are you?" Woody asked. It had taken Roland nearly four rings to answer, and there was a lot of background noise, people talking, laughing. Had the little pipsqueak skipped out of the office early? Was he forwarding calls to his cell phone? He'd caught him doing exactly that once before.

"I'm in a restaurant," Roland said. "I'm eating lunch."

It was almost one o'clock. Lyndon—what a surprise—had not called Woody about lunch.

"Which restaurant?" Woody asked.

"Chow Bella, the new fusion place on La Cienega."

"How is it?"

"Not bad."

"What'd you order?"

"Pizza. Peking duck pizza."

Woody didn't believe him. Roland was a stickler about his cholesterol intake, and he rarely went out for lunch, preferring a regular office delivery of specialty macrobiotic meals. Woody knew a way to ferret him out. "This is a bad connection," he said. "Let me call you back. I'll call you on the restaurant landline."

"But I hear you clear as a bell."

"You're breaking up on my end."

"Call me direct on my cell," Roland said. "I've got five bars. It's the forwarding that's probably the problem."

"Let's just use the landline. Go over to the hostess."

"Woody, wait," Roland said. "I'm, uh, actually not at the restaurant. I'm in, well, a bar."

"You are this close to being fired, Roland."

"Oh, come on, chill out, Woody."

"Chill out? Chill out? Are you out of your mind? Are you drunk?"

"It's Friday afternoon, Labor Day weekend! I went in this morning and took care of that contract and then sat on my ass with nothing to do. I told you, everyone's already shut down for the weekend. So I decided to call it a day. Is that so unreasonable? You're on vacation yourself."

"This is not a vacation, and you are not me. You do not get to do what I do. This is not a socialist enterprise. This is an unwavering state of fascist rule. Do you understand me?"

What Woody got in response was not the appropriate contriteness, not an apology, not simpering pleas to be returned to Woody's good graces, but a sigh, a loud insolent sigh, full of attitude, full of like-I-could-really-give-a-shit presumption, that might as well have been a Bronx cheer.

"If you say so," Roland told Woody.

"Wrong answer, you little pissant. You have an hour to clear out of the office," Woody said, and hung up. He had had enough of Roland. He was efficient and knowledgeable, but young, twenty-six, and overly ambitious. He thought he was capable of taking over Woody's job. He was a good assistant, really the best he'd ever had, but Woody would find another assistant. He could not let this type of insubordination stand. Once you allowed someone to undermine your authority, once you tolerated the slightest breach in hierarchy, the game was lost. People had to know their place. No one ever wanted to *stay* in his place, of course. That was just human nature. People were solipsistic, and ultimately no one ever did anything that wouldn't redound to them, that wouldn't be in their self-interests. It was an evolutionary fact, a principle of behavior that was predictable and immutable and therefore comforting. In this Darwinian world of winners and losers, altruism was an illusion, loyalty a sham.

Respect was not something you earned. You established it by force and manipulation. You coerced it into being because you had something of value that the other person did not. That was the definition of power, and if it wasn't ingrained over and over by brute example, you were open to mutiny, betrayal, to disasters and defeats, to endless snubs and slights.

This had been the problem with the assistant manager at the Fairmont Hotel, the arrogant little runtface who'd had the temerity to rebuff him. Woody had misread the situation, he saw now. He had been turning it over in his mind, examining it, "particalizing it," as he liked to say, not able to let it go. (*Let it go, let it go. Breathe in, then breathe out, and feel it releasing, dissipating into the air into nothing,* his therapist, Dan, told him uselessly.) Erroneously he had believed the assistant manager would be impressed by money, tendered with a soft, egalitarian touch, but people like that needed to be quickly cowed, reminded of their puniness and impotence and immediately put in their *place.* Woody had played it all wrong.

He knew how to play Roland, however. He didn't really want to fire him. For the most part, he did an excellent job, and they had a good rapport. And, sad as it was to admit, Roland was as close to a friend as Woody had in L.A. He was indulging in a little bluff, just as he had been bluffing with Ling Ling, never intending to send her back to Hong Kong this morning, when she had, as he'd known she would, meekly asked for his forgiveness.

He decided to let Roland sweat it out for a while. He had to eat something. He was famished. He drove back to town and parked. He'd intended to find a deli in which he could get, as prescribed by his personal nutritionist, a good, healthy, low-fat, low-carb sandwich—turkey with lettuce and tomato on whole grain, maybe a skosh of mustard—but Roland's mention of Chow Bella whetted his appetite for Italian, and he found a trattoria called

La Bettola on Main Street. The place wasn't Drago or Valentino in L.A., but it wasn't bad, not bad at all. This morning, he'd even discovered a funky gourmet coffeehouse, Java Hut, that had an outstanding Jamaican Blue Mountain. This town was growing on him. It had a few things to say for itself.

In the trattoria, he ordered a linguini carbonara with poached egg, smoked bacon, and parmesan—he couldn't help himself— followed by a tiramisu—he couldn't resist—with a *tiny* scoop of amaretto gelato on the side and a *tiny* biscotto, washed down with an espresso.

He had a few problems with impulse control. With eating, of course, maintaining his weight an issue all his life, but also with everything else, a general impetuosity, unable to contain himself, his mind and body always revving, never able to sit still. An image consultant had once told him that to perfect the art of cool, he had to stop gesturing and moving around so much, not be so twitchy. Yet it was precisely this adrenalized intensity that was his sine qua non. He was a rainmaker, a go-getter. He needed that jack, that juice. While he was utterly terrified of failure, he was, paradoxically, at his best on the brink, on the precipice. It was the only way he knew how to live.

Walking out of the trattoria, he felt good, fairly relaxed, indeed almost as if he were on a vacation. On the sidewalk, he tucked his headset over his ear and phoned the office.

"You're not really going to fire me, are you?" Roland asked.

"I called for a temp. She should be there any minute. Give her the keys and the alarm code and all your passwords."

"Woody, let's not do this."

"And the key card for the garage."

"Let's make up."

"I wouldn't put me down as a reference, if I were you."

"Okay, I'm sorry."

Woody, restraining a laugh—he was the master of the universe, the king of cunning—waited a full five seconds before speaking. "Are you?" he asked.

"Yes, I'm sorry. You were right, I was wrong."

Woody waited another five seconds, then said, "I need you to do something for me."

"Whatever you want."

He told Roland to hire a private investigator in Manhattan to find out everything possible about Kyle Thorneberry of White Plains, New York.

"You know it's after five in New York."

"Do PIs only work nine-to-five?"

"It might be hard to find one, that's all I'm saying, especially on—"

"Yeah, yeah, Labor Day weekend." He could hear computer keys clicking on the other end—Roland most likely checking his e-mail. "When you find one—a good one, Roland, not some drunk hack—call me."

"Who is this guy Thorneberry?"

"He was my best friend. He killed himself."

The typing stopped. "Oh, Woody, I'm sorry. Why didn't you just say so?"

Sympathy. What an odd sensation it was, to be on the receiving end of it. Woody couldn't remember the last time anyone had felt sorry for him—genuinely sorry, without an accompanying tinge of shame. After the indictment, he had been shunned by everyone he knew—his friends, his colleagues—a pariah. Only his mother would talk to him. His father, at least he still deigned to see him. But Lyndon, so cold and self-righteous, had abandoned him completely. His own brother, his only sibling.

Woody moved from Boston to L.A., city of Annulment and Angulation. Everyone had some sort of a scheme there, an angle, a gimmick or hustle, a can't-miss racket to hit the big time. One's past did not matter. You could erase history, reinvent it. Second acts were not only possible in L.A., but celebrated. The deeper you hit bottom, in fact, the better. Self-destruction, addiction, sorrow, pain, misery, practically any malfeasance short of pederasty was okay, it could be forgiven, if you were willing to work hard and persevere and single-mindedly apply yourself to The Dream. Everyone loved a good comeback story. With some luck and plenty of guile, you could get those vectors of fortune to realign themselves and intersect in a wondrous new confabulation of status and achievement.

Not that it had been easy for Woody, not that he hadn't wanted, many a time, to drive somewhere, a parking lot beside the ocean, say, at the end of the continent, and shoot himself in the head, or take the sweeping elevated ramp that connected the Santa Monica Freeway to 405 North and turn the wheel just a hair to punch through the guardrail, the lights of the city before him, and fly into the relief of nothingness. He'd had plenty of those moments, all right, feelings of hopelessness and utter despair, while he lived in an SRO in Korea Town with a filthy, disgusting bathroom down the hall and worked in a liquor store; while he peddled stereos at the Crenshaw Wal-Mart and used cars in Gardena; while he sold pirated DVDs and VCDs from Hong Kong in Santee Alley. He didn't know how he would ever be able to repair his life, be anything but destitute, banished to this pathetic, anonymous life working *retail*. He was a Harvard graduate, for God's sake!—although he never put that down anymore on his many job application forms, since it would only guarantee that he would not get the job, the manager thinking Woody was lying, embellishing, there was something seriously smelly here, really Woody would have had a better chance saying he was a graduate of Lompoc Correctional.

It was ludicrous, this consignment into ruin. Here he was—after making two hundred large a year and owning a house in Lexington and being engaged to a gorgeous PR flack who would have made an ideal trophy wife—now living among bums, wetbacks, winos, junkies and whores, Jesus freaks, wiggers, pimps, boojies, and bhindus—the scum, the dregs, the bottom of the barrel. And then there were the nitwits who came to Hollywood believing they could be stars, and the dipshits with their fast-buck infomercial fantasies, and the numbnuts with their conspiracy theories, and the chuckleheads with their sunny, feel-good, self-help prescriptions for alternative health and twelve-step programs. Pathetic losers, all of them, and Woody was, unbelievably, *one* of them, *a retail clerk*, destined to rot in this dismal menial existence, so very small-time. He could not abide such mediocrity.

He bought a gun, a Saturday night special called a Bryco Model 38, for seventy-five dollars off a tong gangbanger. He took it out every night and stared at it. It was comforting to see it there, to know that if things became truly unbearable, he had an out. He learned how to do it properly. Sticking the barrel in his mouth and angling it too high might mean blasting away his sinus cavities and eyes and frontal lobe but leaving him alive—blind, without a face, lobotomized. Temple shots had the same potential for error. Pointing the gun too low in his mouth might miss the brain stem and hit his spinal cord, rendering him a quadriplegic. The best bet was just behind or directly in one ear, aimed at the other. The bullet would obliterate all the vital parts of his brain and he wouldn't hear or feel a thing.

He wondered what Kyle had done. What kind of gun, ammo, had he used? Hollow points? Hollow points would have been prudent.

Woody's therapist, Dan, was a smart guy, but every now and

then he said some incredibly moronic things. One time, when Woody had been anxious about a particular project, Dan, trying to reassure him, had asked, "Well, what's the worst that could happen if this doesn't work out?" *What was the worst that could happen?* He could lose everything—again. Everyone could desert him—again. He could be out on the streets—again. It'd happened once before, there was nothing to say it couldn't all happen again. He couldn't afford to start over a second time. Maybe once he could manage it, maybe while he was still in his early thirties, he could recover as he had, talking his way from hawking bootleg DVDs to importing them, from distributing Hong Kong theatrical releases to brokering remake options. Maybe once, but not twice. Not at this point in his life, not at this stage. If the worst happened, he'd have no choice but to do what Kyle Thorneberry had done, load the brand-new Glock 17 that was nestled in the drawer of Woody's nightstand in L.A. and level the muzzle in his ear and pull the trigger.

That was why he was willing to do whatever it took to keep this film he was producing afloat. Sure, he knew now that it probably wouldn't be the artistic gem he'd hoped for, but with Dalton Lee directing, it wouldn't be a complete turkey, either, and it would still make a profit, which Woody had ensured with his presales of foreign distribution and ancillary rights. Yet his own compensation package wouldn't begin kicking in until principal photography, and he wouldn't see any real money until well after the film was out. As a first-time producer, he wasn't going to get first-dollar gross receipts, he was going to have to wait for net-profit participation, and this meant, for the moment, that he was dangerously leveraged, both personally and with his company, especially now that the remake business was drying up.

All of which justified in his mind what he was doing now, driving past a tract of model homes, past dirt contours of a golf course, past a fountain with a statue of a Trojan soldier that was, strangely, being watched by an armed security guard, past a row of parked cardinal-red SUVs with gold trim, almost all of them garnished with splotches of pastel paint, up the sweeping curve of a driveway to a massive hotel under construction, perched grandly on a cliff overlooking the ocean.

Woody got out of his car and walked toward the hulking structure, which was bustling with construction workers moving I-beams and bolting prefab panels into the façade. The hotel was fronted by three long tiers of arches and columns, an architectural flourish that was aggressively out of place in the seaside landscape. Woody was trying to decide what it reminded him of, and just as he heard someone say, "Heads up," he'd determined that the exterior was modeled after the Colosseum in Rome.

He turned around and saw a football silhouetted against the gray sky, spiraling through the air and gaining speed as it arced down toward his face. Reflexively he raised his arms, and the ball bounced hard off his hands. He had never been much of an athlete, despite his resolves, many times during his youth, to become one, someone with easy grace and effortless coordination, someone like Ed Kitchell, who jogged over to Woody, swept up the football from the ground with one hand, and, still running, flipped it behind his back and caught it in front of him, seemingly without looking.

He shook Woody's hand, crushing his fingers. Despite the cool weather, he wasn't wearing a jacket or sweater, and his big muscular physique was apparent in his tight red polo shirt. He was around Woody's age, and had a youthful, handsome countenance—jutting square jaw, blond hair, a classic Californian. "So what do you think of the place?" he asked. "Pretty fucking spectacular, isn't it?"

"Incredible."

"You should see the layout of the course. You play golf?"

"No," Woody told him. "I've gone out a few times, but I was pretty awful."

"Well, it doesn't happen overnight, you know. It takes patience. Did you take lessons?"

"A couple."

"You see, that's the problem. You can't have some half-assed club pro giving you a few perfunctory tips and then letting you loose on the course. It's like anything else. You need to build on the fundamentals and get a good foundation down. Those fundamentals will extrapolate into everything you do thereafter. Like when I tossed you the ball. Your hands weren't right. To catch a ball above the waist, your index fingers and thumbs should be in a triangle, like this, right in front of your face. Try it out."

Just from this small speech, Woody gleaned a lot about Kitchell. He was presumptuous, peremptory, a man who always thought he knew better, who liked to tell people what to do, and even though Woody resented his condescension—he wasn't a complete geek, he knew how to catch a damn football, he'd been caught by surprise, that was all—he was willing to indulge him, putting his index fingers and thumbs together.

"Keep your elbows slightly bent, fingers spread out," Kitchell said. "You see, you've formed a target with your triangle. Catch the nose of the ball in the target. Just watch the tip of the ball all the way in, and when you catch it, absorb the force by bringing your hands and arms into your body, and tuck it in tight." He backed up. "Ready?"

Woody nodded, thinking, Just throw the fucking thing already. He wasn't here to play games.

Kitchell chucked the football, and Woody caught it snugly in his triangled hands. "That was a perfect catch, chief," Kitchell told him, and Woody, despite himself, felt pleased. He threw the ball back to Kitchell, who said, "Hey, got some zip there. You work out?"

"When I can," Woody said.

They tossed the football back and forth a few more times.

"This is what they're supposed to teach kids in Pee Wee," Kitchell said, "but some of these coaches these days, I don't know where they find them, they don't know shit, and as a consequence we get these punks on the team now, they're gifted, athletically they're in the absolute nth-teenth percentile, the stratosphere, but they think they can shake and bake and juke and high-step like it's hip-hop on the field. They're more worried about style points than just catching the fucking ball and tucking it in. Drives me fucking insane."

They kept passing the football, finding a nice rhythm. Woody hated to admit it, but he was enjoying himself. It reminded him of college, whiling away late afternoons along the Charles River with Kyle, tossing a Frisbee.

"Now you got it," Kitchell said. "Now you're cooking."

Woody smiled. He knew precisely what was going on here, what Kitchell's use of profanity, his rants about the sorry state of sports instruction, were all about. There were so many subtleties in the dynamics of male socialization, but Woody, if anything, had an astute understanding of human behavior, which was the key to his Machiavellian success in the art of negotiation. Subconsciously or not, Kitchell, in pointing out Woody's athletic deficiencies, had established his position at the top of the dominance hierarchy as the alpha dog, and now, after chipping away at his ego, in effect emasculating him, he was giving Woody positive reinforcement to bond them in a mentor-protégé relationship, make Woody feel grateful for the attention and guidance, solidifying Kitchell's standing as a leader to follow and trust.

If that was what Kitchell needed, he would give it to him. He didn't mind pretending to accede, because, really, when it came down to it, Kitchell was a simplistic oaf, just another pushy dunderheaded jock, and as long as he was under the illusion that he was in control, he would be easy to manipulate. "You must have played college ball," Woody said. He could tell by the expression on Kitchell's face—pride mixed with regret—that this had been precisely the right thing to posit.

"I was supposed to," Kitchell said. "I had a scholarship to USC all lined up, and then I blew out my ACL. I was a pretty fucking good wideout, if I do say so myself. I was an absolute *specimen* then."

"Looks like you could still take the field today," Woody said, pupil honoring master.

Kitchell said, "Well, I don't know about that," but clearly he agreed. "So I did what I could to support the team. I became a Yell Leader. My last two years, I was Tommy Trojan."

"Jesus, you got to hang out with those cheerleaders?"

"We called them Song Girls back then. Now—another inane victim of political correctness—they're called Song Leaders. But yeah, we got to travel with the girls, if you know what I mean."

"God, those sweaters and little skirts, they get me every time. Year in and year out, they're the hottest squad out there."

"You have no idea how hot," Kitchell said, and winked.

This was another pattern in the ritual of male bonding: after admiring each other's physical attributes, you had to engage in some gratuitous braggadocio about *pussy*, lest anyone get confused by the homosexual overtones of the conversation.

They repaired to the main office trailer, the siding of which was melted and blackened, as if from a small fire.

"Accident?" Woody asked.

"Not an accident," Kitchell said. "Just the latest handiwork of a nutjob terrorist who's been having a lot of yucks at our expense. Very probably your brother."

Inside, besides the expected desks, laptops, whiteboards, hard hats, walkie-talkies, and blueprints, the trailer was festooned with USC regalia: pennants, posters, framed photos of Kitchell as Tommy Trojan with his band of Yell Leaders, umbrellas wrapped in cellophane, stacks of baseball caps, mugs, a row of miniature helmets.

"Looks like a campus store," Woody said.

"We don't like visitors to leave empty-handed. Where'd you go to school?"

"Cambridge," Woody said.

"Cambridge. As in Cambridge, England? Oxbridge?"

"Cambridge, Massachusetts."

"Oh, *Harvard*," Kitchell said. "It's interesting how people from Harvard will never come straight out and say they went to Harvard, but somehow, within the first five minutes of meeting them, it's worked into the conversation."

"It's part of our noblesse oblige."

"Well, that's very impressive," Kitchell said. "No Division 1-A football, mind you, but an impressive school. And there's the Harvard-Yale game."

"Always an occasion."

"Maybe I can convert you into a Trojan fan now that you're on the West Coast. I'm going to the home opener tomorrow. You should make a point of catching it on TV. Here, take one of these." He picked a USC baseball cap off a stack and gave it to Woody. "Just don't let your brother see you with it. Had a chance to talk to him yet?"

"He wasn't very receptive to the subject."

"Oh, really? I'm surprised."

They sat down on opposite sides of a desk, and Woody filled

Kitchell in on Lyndon's financial situation, which he had ascertained this morning, snooping through his brother's papers.

Kitchell, after listening to Woody's report, frowned. "Well, we know all of this already. They said you were close to him. You think you'll be able to change his mind?"

"I don't know," Woody said.

SBK, the gigantic multinational conglomerate that owned The Centurion Group, also had a division that ran a subsidiary with a controlling share in a corporation that had a major stake in one of the foreign distributors that was partially bankrolling Woody's movie. It was pure chance that the link between the Song brothers had been discovered. SBK owned thousands of businesses, and usually its divisions, with so many diversified interests in so many different industries, were run independently of one another, but somehow, someone, while investigating Lyndon, had put it together, and a few weeks ago, the head of the German distribution company had met with Woody and asked him to do them a small favor, go up to Rosarita Bay and talk to his brother, see what his weaknesses were, how he might be influenced. The request hadn't been presented as a direct quid pro quo, nothing as crass as that—the distribution deal, after all, had already been signed—but deals could be broken, of course. So Woody had agreed, and he had made some assurances he shouldn't have made: that he and Lyndon were quite close, that Lyndon would listen to him.

"You know, I take pride in my ability to read people," Kitchell said. "I don't know anything about the movie business, for instance, but I can look in your eyes, and I see passion and purpose there, and I know you care about what you do, you care about this movie you're making. I can communicate with you."

"We both understand the nature of transactional exigencies."

"Exactly," Kitchell said, then added, "I think. Anyway, I can tell you're someone I can sit down with at the bargaining table. Not that this is the case, because it's far from it, but it wouldn't even matter if we didn't like each other. There's something you want, something we want, that's an equation with an attainable solution. On the off chance we couldn't come to terms, I'd understand why on a primary level. But it's more likely than not we'd work something out, even if one party had to accept a less than equitable distribution, because we both realize there's no stopping the momentum of commerce. Try, and you'll get steamrolled. Doing nothing is indefensible. It's a ruthless world, and inertia will crush you. So, like it or not, you negotiate, you compromise, you fight and squawk, eventually you sign on the dotted line and move on. This is what reasonable people do."

"We'd reach a *modus vivendi*," Woody said.

"Right," Kitchell told him. "If you say so. Your brother, though—I just don't understand him at all. Nothing he does makes sense to me. Why won't he accept the deal? It's a very generous deal."

"You won't get an argument from me about that," Woody said.

Kitchell opened his laptop and called up several screens that displayed radar images and sophisticated weather graphics. "Feel like taking a ride? You're not afraid to fly, are you?"

Kitchell led Woody outside to the far side of the hotel, where a helicopter was parked on the grass. Seeing Woody hesitate, Kitchell said, "Don't worry. I'm CFII-rated with over a thousand hours."

After Kitchell performed a walk-around inspection of the helicopter, which was painted in the same cardinal-red with gold trim as The Centurion Group's SUVs, they climbed into the cockpit and strapped themselves into the surprisingly plush leather seats. "This is a Bell 206 LongRanger," Kitchell told him.

"It's about as good as they come." He went through a preflight checklist and fired up the turbine engine, the rotors whump-whumping to life, and then Kitchell lifted a lever on his left, and they wobbled up five feet off the ground and hovered rather precariously, Woody, his heart racing, looking down between his legs through the bubbled bottom window, no longer quite subscribing to the concept of man in flight. Kitchell shifted his feet on the pedals, and the helicopter rotated slightly to the right, and then he eased forward the yoke or joystick or whatever it was called, and they began *moving*, nose pitched down into the wind, accelerating up and away quickly toward the ocean, directly toward several seagulls that were gliding over the shore. Instead of getting out of the way, the birds started flapping right into their path, and Kitchell climbed and banked steeper to avoid them.

"Fucking gulls," he said. "Nothing but a nuisance."

Woody could hear him perfectly with the noise-canceling headphones. "You ever hit a bird?" he asked.

"Me, personally?" They were flying past Lyndon's property, and they both looked down at the house and farm before Kitchell continued. "No, but it's been known to happen. It's actually more common than you'd think."

If a teeny little tweety bird hit the rotors, he told Woody, it wasn't a problem, it'd simply be vaporized, you'd see this little pink poof, and it'd be gone. But it was things like geese, flocks of geese, you had to worry about. They could break your rotor tip cap or go through your windshield and incapacitate you or worse.

"Birds in general are so stupid," Kitchell said. "A couple of years back, an eagle hit the main rotors of an AH-1 Cobra and got cut in half and hit the tail, busted the drive shaft, so the thing autorotated and the crew had to egress, ten million dollars down the drain, all because an eagle couldn't distinguish a military attack helicopter from a Chihuahua. But what can you do? Most windshields are only rated impact-resistant for a one-kilogram bird. They analyze these things with bird-strike tests, using gas cannons. In England, Rolls-Royce has a contract with a farmer to raise turkeys the same weight and size, and when they have a new engine, the turkeys are trucked to the plant and shot right into the fan blades. Only reason the remains aren't used for in-flight meals," Kitchell said, "is the feathers are too hard to pluck." He laughed.

They flew down the coast, surveying the golf course, much of it still dirt, only the vague outlines of fairways discernible. Excavators and backhoes rooted into the ground. Two bulldozers with a chain between them mowed down a row of trees, knocking them over one after another like pickets.

"Isn't it beautiful?" Kitchell asked.

Woody hardly thought so, but then the fog lifted before them, and he saw the Pacific crashing onto the craggy shore, the precipitous sandstone bluffs, and, farther down, a line of beaches and the marshes where he had dropped off Trudy and Margot earlier. Below them now, some of the golf course had been sculpted and laid down with grass—poa annua on the greens and ryegrass on the fairways, Kitchell told him—and indeed it was beautiful, breathtaking, the wild, windswept contrast of colors, the majestic collision of land and water.

It was exhilarating being in the helicopter. The minute he got back to L.A., he was going to sign up for flying lessons. How cool would it be, casually saying to people, "Feel like taking a ride? You're not afraid to fly, are you?"

"Are you married? Have any kids?" Kitchell asked.

"No."

"My wife died thirteen years ago. Breast cancer. We never had children. Ever since she died, I've gone from project to project, resort to resort, all over the country, all over the world. I'll tell you the truth, a lot of the time, I didn't give a shit about what I was building. It was just a job to me. I'd wrap it up and go on to the next one. But this feels different. I'm prouder of this than anything I've ever done. I feel like I'm building something significant here, something of permanence, know what I mean? I've come to love this area. After I finish this resort, I'm thinking of quitting and settling down here. I don't know what I'll do, maybe run a charter service, do whatever I need to do to make ends meet—fire-fight, cropdusting. I want to help revitalize this town. I'd like to coach the high school football team. Does that sound crazy?"

Yes, Woody thought. It sounded crazy. This town might be growing on him, but he could never live here, and he didn't see why anyone who had a choice would ever consider it.

Kitchell banked the helicopter around, and they headed back to the hotel, following the jagged coastline. "This is what I don't get about your brother. He doesn't seem to *care*, doesn't seem *committed* to anything. Not to this town, not to this community, not even to farming. His finances are in tatters, he doesn't have any political or environmental objections to what we're doing. Why doesn't he sell?"

"He's a very stubborn person."

"People are stubborn because they want to prove a point. It might contradict their best interests, it might be downright silly, but they'll do it out of spite. What's his point?"

"I don't really know," Woody said. "I'm working on it." The problem was, despite his dedication to therapy and all manner of self-improvement and personal growth, Woody wasn't quite sure it was possible to convert people. One of his greatest fears was the possibility of eternal recurrence, that everything he'd been through would keep repeating itself, that nothing would change. He knew that, as Nietzsche had said, he needed to embrace *amor fati*, his love of fate. He needed to trust that all the suffering and loss he'd endured was ultimately good, that everything that'd happened had a predestined purpose. Only then could he stimulate a transformation of consciousness. But he didn't know. Could people really change? Could they be redeemed? Or would Woody always be the same person, just as Lyndon, in all likelihood, would always be intractable, and Kitchell a major dick?

"Well, we need you to work a little faster," Kitchell told him. "To be honest, we're already in the eleventh hour. We really can't wait much longer before things become desperate."

"And then what?" Woody asked.

"Then we'll have to do something more persuasive."

Right then an object flew past them, close enough to startle them both and make Kitchell jostle the joystick and cause the helicopter to hiccup and veer.

"What was that? A bird?" Woody asked. The object had been small and light brown, but he hadn't perceived wings or a beak or tail. It'd been shaped, he thought, like an ovoid.

Kitchell was bewildered himself. "I think it was . . ."

"A potato?" Woody asked.

.   .   .

THERE WAS A FAT PERSON inside Woody, a person who was tired of being oppressed and denied, a person who wanted Woody to stop working so hard and accept the inevitable, that he wasn't meant to be skinny or cut or buffed, he was meant to be pudgy, a little roly-poly. He was meant to have love handles and man breasts. He was meant to have a neck hump and static-abrading thighs, loose flab quavering beneath his flesh, gelatinous blubber and tissue and lard shifting and heaving in pendulous slabs.

He was meant to be a deep-fried butterball, cured salt pork, vegetable shortening oozing out of sausage casings, a saturated swillbelly, a Mr. Blimpy, Shamu, a Doughboy Two-Ton Krispy Kreme Blobbo Chunkmeister Potato Head.

It was exhausting not to be those things. It took so much effort. Every day for the rest of his life, he would have to diet and exercise to keep that slow but inexorable accretion of fat at bay, submit to the cardio, the machines, the free weights and stability balls and resistance bands. Sometimes he wondered if he shouldn't just surrender, throw out his injection-molded sneakers and special moisture-wicking performance wear and stuff down churros and pizzas and steak-and-cheese subs slathered with mayonnaise. Was it so wrong to be fat? Was it such a disgrace?

Well, yes, in Hollywood, even for people behind the camera, it was. These things mattered a great deal in a town that sustained itself on superficial illusions. Your looks, your body, every aspect of your appearance—they all bespoke who you were. They were a reflection of your character and prosperity. They defined you. As much as he hated it, Woody would have to keep working out, keep starving himself, keep getting facials and manicures and eyebrow plucks.

He drove to the Rosarita Bay YMCA, stopping on a side street first to change clothes in his car. In his house in the Hollywood Hills, he had a fancy multistation gym, a complete set of chrome barbells and dumbbells, a treadmill, stair climber, and spinning bike. Jorgy Hecker, his sadistic Danish personal trainer, came over to the house four mornings a week to put him through his cruel paces. "More more more!" Jorgy would heckle. "*Ja*, Woody. *Smuk, smuk!*" It took Woody months to realize Jorgy wasn't calling him a schmuck, but saying beautiful in Danish. There was never any call for Woody to go to a health club except when he was traveling. Hotel fitness centers, although less than ideal, were tolerable since he could change and shower in his room, but gyms were a problem for Woody. It wasn't just the locker rooms—horrific breeding grounds for athlete's foot, jock itch, plantar warts, fecal coliforms; he avoided locker rooms at all costs—but all those sweating bodies in contact with the machines and equipment. All sorts of bacteria, fungi, and pathogens thrived in health clubs: cold and influenza viruses, *E. coli*, staphylococcus, salmonella, streptococcus, mycotoxins, even hepatitis A.

He brought his own towels and spray bottle to the YMCA. As far as Y's went, it was a pretty decent facility, less than ten years old. They had a pool, a sizable basketball gymnasium, racquetball and handball courts, and a boxing room. The main fitness area was partitioned into separate sections: free weights, cardio, and strength apparatus, mainly Universal machines and a line of new Nautilus equipment.

Jorgy had customized a gym workout on a chart for Woody, and he dutifully started with a warm-up on a recumbent bike after disinfecting it. He squirted the display panel, seat, and handgrips with his spray bottle, which was filled with a special antibacterial solution, wiped everything dry with his red towel, laid out his green towel on the seat, and patted the sweat on his face with his blue towel. He followed the same routine on the Nautilus leg extension machine. Jorgy's chart was very specific. He harped all the time about mixing free weights with machines, not isolating muscle groups, but Woody, best intentions aside, didn't feel up to it today. He was tired, tired of lunges and squats and deadlifts. He wanted a nice, easy workout. He would just stick to the machines, and fuck the two sets, he'd do just one. Next were leg curls, then hip adductions and adductors.

As he moved to the pec fly machine, spraying and wiping, a woman walked up to him and said, "Is there something about me you find particularly objectionable?"

"Pardon?"

The woman was fortyish, past her prime but still attractive, Woody supposed, if you went for the relo, subdivision, possibly-moist-under-the-hood type. She was willowy and thin, but incipiently poochy—a burgeoning convexity to her stomach that no amount of exercise, he could have told her, would ever be able to rescind. She apparently had a workout chart similar to Woody's, for he had been following her down the line of machines, hopping on each one she vacated.

"I'm not even sweating," she said, "but I'm still using my towel on everything after I'm done, per the rules and regulations and per common courtesy. Yet you persist in doing a Haz-Mat scrub-down on every surface I touch. So I ask you, is there something so offensive about me that's compelling you to execute such a thorough decontamination?"

"It's nothing personal."

"I see, nothing personal. Well, excuse me, but I do take it personally. Very personally."

"I'm just sort of . . . I have a thing about germs," Woody told her.

She regarded his face, and then gave him the once-over. "Is that an antibacterial spray?" she asked, looking at his bottle.

"Yes."

"You know it doesn't protect against viruses. It's a myth."

"It's been proven to be effective on—"

"I've read the studies," she said. "You've fallen for clever marketing, that's all. The active ingredient is triclosan. It's registered with the EPA as a pesticide. What it'll do in the long run is weaken your immune system because you're not being exposed to beneficial bacteria. Furthermore, now that everyone's using it, it'll eventually create superbugs resistant to antibiotics."

This woman was scary, Woody thought. Quarrelsome, formidable, relentless. "Thank you for that information," he said. "You've been very enlightening."

"Oh, I see," she said. "Now I get dismissive attitude. You think I'm some sort of idiot suburban biddy who doesn't know her head from her ass. Well, you know where you can stick that attitude." She grabbed her towel, huffed off to the mats on the other side of the room, and began pumping through a series of crunches.

Woody resumed his workout, going a little quicker down the line—pec flies, overhead presses, lat pulldowns. He was doing compound rows when his cell phone rang. He reached down inside his gear bag, pulled out his Bluetooth headset, and looped it over his ear.

Roland said he had found a private investigator named Christopher Cross with the Allegiance International Security Service.

"You lazy weasel," Woody told Roland. "You just went to the Yellow Pages and started with the A's."

"No, no. He comes highly recommended."

"By whom?"

"He's an advisor to *Law & Order*. An ex-cop, NYPD, Criminal Investigations Unit."

Law & Order? Actually a pretty smart move. Maybe he should give Roland a break. "What's his number? Hang on."

The scary woman was standing in front of him again, saying, "Excuse me."

"Tell him to call me," Woody said to Roland, and pushed the disconnect button. "Yes?" he asked the woman.

She pointed to a sign on the wall. "There's a policy against using cell phones on the premises."

Lady, he thought, you really need to get laid. "Oh. I'm sorry. I didn't know."

After a pointed stare, the woman went back to the mats.

Woody changed his phone ringer to vibrate and grabbed the handles of the compound-row machine to finish his set. Not that he himself had been laid recently, he thought. How long had it been? Almost a year now. The last had been Annabelle, a twenty-four-year-old D-girl with Miramax who'd sucked two pairs of Manolo Blahniks and a Versace dress and a substantial portion of her car lease out of Woody before dumping him. She had been, however, gorgeous. A woman his age had once asked Woody why he dated younger women, and he had wanted to tell her, Why? Because I *can*. Why in the world would I go out with someone like you when I can wedge inside the sweet loins of a taut-skinned, perky-breasted knockout half my age?

His phone was illuminating and vibrating in his gear bag. He glanced down at the caller ID screen: 212 area code, New York. He palmed his headset and crept into the hallway.

It was Christopher Cross. Why did that name sound so familiar? "What have you found out?" Woody whispered.

"I can't hear you very well. Is this a bad connection?"

Cross hadn't discovered much about Kyle Thorneberry: Sudbury, Massachusetts; Buckingham Browne & Nichols; Harvard; Wharton; Morgan Stanley; Goldman Sachs; house in White Plains; wife, three kids; no criminal record; cause of death conclusive as suicide; firearm registered to his name.

"You're reading me the obituary," Woody said. "I could have gone to the library and looked all this up on LexisNexis."

"I've been on the case all of five minutes," Cross said.

Someone tapped Woody on the shoulder.

"You never learn, do you?" the Gestapo woman said.

Woody cupped his hand over the boom mike and said to her, "Look, I'm in the *hallway*, okay?"

"No cell phones on the *premises*. You understand what *premises* means?"

"I'll get off in a second."

"No, right now. You will get off right now."

"What is your *problem*, lady? What is it that you find so objectionable about me? Because quite frankly your attitude sucks, and I think you know where you can stick it."

She took a deep breath, held it, and let it out, then inhaled again. Woody knew what she was doing, a self-control trick taught to him by Dan: when you feel like exploding, breathe in, breathe out. "Who are you?" she asked. "What are you doing in Rosarita Bay?"

"I'm Woody Song. I'm here visiting my brother. Not that it's any of your business."

The anger seemed to sap out of her then, replaced by genuine bewilderment. "You're Lyndon's brother?"

"You know Lyndon?"

"Hello?" Cross said on the headset. "Hello?"

"Do I know Lyndon?" the woman said. "Do I know Lyndon Baines Song? I thought I did, I'd hoped I did, but I guess I don't. I don't think, really, I know who he is at all." And with that, she walked away.

What an odd woman, Woody thought. He took his hand off the headset. "You still there?" he asked.

"Yes," Cross said.

"I want you to look into Thorneberry's family as well. They're loaded. He had an adopted sister named Trudy. She's going by Trudy Nguyen now. See what you can find out about her relationship with the parents. Have they cut her off, does she have a trust fund or something? Look into her father. When I think back on it, Mr. Thorneberry was kind of a dodgy character. Maybe, I don't know, he touched his kids inappropriately." Woody heard the two-tone chirp of the call being disconnected. "Hello?" He moved to the doorway and saw the Nazi matron holding up his cell phone. She gave it to a burly young man in a white YMCA shirt, who carried Woody's gear bag and his colored towels and spray bottle to him.

"Sorry, bud," the young man said, "you're going to have to leave."

"You're kicking me out?" Woody said. "For taking one lousy call?"

"She said it was several. We have a policy—"

"Okay, okay, I'll keep it shut off. Let me finish my workout. I'm almost done."

The young man shook his head. "No can do. She was pretty clear."

"Who *is* that woman?"

"She's on the board of directors here. She's the mayor."

He went out to his Range Rover, which he'd parked on the street beside the front door, and there was a ticket on his windshield. Wonderful. Everything magnanimous he'd been thinking about this town, he took back. It was a shithole of a town, an uptight, small-minded, never-would-be hicksville of a town.

The thing on his windshield was not, upon further inspection, a parking ticket. It was a paper airplane, made with a sheet torn from a spiral notebook, and it had a handwritten message on it: "The Second Noble Truth is that the origin of suffering is attachment. Small wonder you're so miserable." Woody crushed the airplane into a ball and tossed it into the gutter.

He dumped his workout gear into his car and drove out of town, back onto Highway 1. It'd started out as a decent day and had become an annoying day, he was thinking, just as it turned worse. He almost hit a dog. He was distracted for a second, fiddling with his satellite radio, and the dog darted across the highway in front of him. He should have just run the goddamn thing over, but in a moment of weakness, he let some deep-seated, regrettable instinct for kindness get the better of him, and he swerved to avoid it, fishtailing and almost rolling over, skidding off the road and down an embankment and into a tree.

"Fuck!" he screamed.

He didn't hit the tree hard enough to deploy the air bag, but his bumper was squashed, his diamond-mesh chrome grill was dented, his left Xenon-gas headlight was shattered. As he crouched down to check the damage a little closer, he heard a noise behind him, and he could make out the outline of the dog in the bushes. He realized then that he had flashed on an image of Lyndon's dog, Bob, running across the road, and that was why he had swerved. But it hadn't been Bob on the road. This was not Bob in the bushes. It was a coyote.

Still in a crouch, Woody slowly backed away, then jumped into his car and shut the door. Thankfully the Rover started without a problem, the wheels gripping securely as he sped up the embankment in reverse, watching his dashboard screen as it displayed the sky and then the highway and then an eighteen-wheeler barreling down on him.

"Fuck!" he screamed. He slammed on his brakes and reflex-ively covered his head with his arms as the truck's horn howled. He could feel the vibration of its weight and speed and proximity as it came on top of him, but it missed the Rover, a whump of air violently rocking the car as it passed, horn bending in its wake.

Woody watched the truck disappear down the highway. "Asshole," he said pointlessly.

He went back to Lyndon's farm, where a rusty old Toyota was parked in the driveway. Woody heard a commotion, a series of pounding noises, in one of the greenhouses, and opened the door to see Ling Ling working on a wing chun dummy—a training device that looked like a denuded tree. It had a big freestanding trunk with a dozen thick logs branching out of it at odd angles, and Ling Ling was smacking them silly, both arms moving at once in rapid-fire contrapuntal synchronicity, as if parrying an attack.

"Outstanding, outstanding!" a dreadlocked kid standing beside her said. He gave her a towel and a water bottle, and when he noticed Woody at the door, he bounded over to him with a weird lurching gait and enthusiastically introduced himself as JuJu LeMay, Lyndon's friend and coworker. "So you're Lyndon's brother!"

"What are you doing? Where'd you get all this stuff?" Besides the wing chun dummy, there were swords, staffs, boxing gloves, and pads spread out on the floor.

"We're training!" the kid said. On second thought, he wasn't a kid, more likely in his thirties. "I borrowed the gear from the kung fu studio in town," he said. "I tell you, they were mighty excited and accommodating once they heard Yi Ling Ling was here, training for her new film."

Finally someone knew who she was.

"Ms. Yi is a marvel, isn't she? A whirling dervish," JuJu said, although she wasn't whirling at the moment. She was sweating and breathing heavily, gulping down water from the bottle, her face red from exertion. Maybe this much activity was not totally advisable, given her poor condition. But she was also doing something Woody had not witnessed once during the two days he'd been with her—she was smiling. She was *happy*.

"Don't push her too hard," Woody told him. "I don't think she's lifted anything heavier than a bottle in years."

"I'm going to take good care of her," JuJu said. "This movie of yours sounds fantastic. Dalton Lee and Yi Ling Ling! What a bravura pairing! An absolute stroke of genius! It's a thrill for me to be involved in this project, even in this humble role."

"Well, I appreciate it."

"Let me know if you need anything, anything at all. To be frank, I'm a little underemployed these days, so I've got a lot of free time. Maybe, I don't know, I can be of service to you in a more formal capacity. Something more substantive? Just a thought."

Even in Rosarita Bay, everyone had an angle. "I'll keep that in mind. You know where Lyndon is?"

He was in the barn. Barn was a bit of a misnomer. There was a huge barnlike structure behind Lyndon's house, but, as far as Woody could tell, it wasn't a barn used for farming. He didn't know what Lyndon was using it for. The barn doors were blocked by a permanent addition, essentially a large windowless shed in which Lyndon had set up a welding workshop, and in which he was now assembling some baker's shelves.

The shed was well lit and neat, concrete floor swept clean, and Woody walked around, examining the tools of the trade: welding tanks and machines, a generator, grinders, sanders, drills, all sorts of clamps and jigs and vises, racks of rods, steel plates, square tubes, and angle irons, a couple of overhead pulley blocks with chains. What interested him most, though, were the sliding barn doors that took up an entire side of the shed. The doors were shut and secured with a heavy-duty chrome padlock.

"What have you got behind there?" Woody asked. "What are you hiding?"

"It's just storage," Lyndon said.

Unlikely, Woody thought. Too impractical. He couldn't get anything in and out. "I was up last night and saw sparks from inside."

Lyndon tilted up his protective shield. "Were you vacuuming? I thought I heard someone vacuuming."

"I had insomnia," Woody said. Actually, after he had scoured his bedroom, he had gone outside and sat in the back seat of the Rover and watched part of the DVD for *Lying in Wait*. It was difficult for him to sleep without watching some TV each night. "What happened to our lunch?" he asked.

"I got hung up with an installation."

"Maybe you should do this full-time. It seems more profitable than farming."

Lyndon clamped an S-scroll to a support frame. "That's your professional opinion?"

"It's like any business. Your investment is in material, labor, and overhead, and your success depends on getting a superior return on your investment, with a product that has a different form of value from your competitor's. The problem with farming is you have variables you can't control, like weather. Is that what happened to you the last few years?"

"What have you been doing? Looking through my books?"

"I was poking around your house a little this morning and came across some of your ledgers," Woody said.

"Jesus, Woody. You don't understand boundaries, do you?"

"You're on the verge of bankruptcy. You've got a bridge loan due at the end of the year."

"I've had a little run of bad luck," Lyndon admitted. "Moth infestation one year, heavy rains the next. I'll be all right."

"You're one bad harvest away from going belly-up. Your finances are a complete mess. You have credit-card debt! How could you let it get this bad? What happened to all your money, Lyndon? What'd you do with it all?"

"Besides help out Mom and Dad all those years?"

"The guilt trip's getting old. I've been helping her out, too, you know."

"There was never as much money as people believed," Lyndon said.

"You should have invested it," Woody said.

"You mean with you?"

An unnecessary low blow, Woody thought. "You're going to have to take this deal, you know."

Lyndon put on his gloves, turned on his welding machine, and flipped down his shield, then touched the electrode down where the S-scroll met the frame, crackling the air and suffusing it with the smell of burnt metal.

"You could do anything you want," Woody said. "You could go anywhere. You don't need this."

Lyndon threw off his gloves and shut off the machine. "Where would I go?"

"You have to face up to it. Small farms are obsolete. This way of life doesn't exist anymore. Don't you see? You're a walking anachronism. But you love farming so much, you buy another farm. With ten million, you'd have another twenty years to run that one into the ground."

His brother tilted the frame, tapped on it with a hammer, and blew off excess chips. "Now that you've explained it to me," he said, "it's so simple."

"What are you going to do?"

"Probably nothing," Lyndon said.

"What's the matter with you? You act like you have options, like something will miraculously drop out of the sky and save you. Why aren't you panicking? You could be *homeless.*" Kitchell was right: his brother was an enigma, nothing he did made sense, he didn't seem to care, as apathetic about losing his farm as he had been about losing his art career. "Let me talk to Kitchell for you," he said. "I'm sure I could squeeze twelve from him without a problem."

"You're not going to do anything for me, Woody. You're going to stay out of this."

"I can help you," Woody said. "You won't let me help you?"

"No."

"You're the king of no," Woody said. All of a sudden he remembered who Christopher Cross was—a one-hit wonder on the radio in the early eighties. How'd the song go? *Sailing*, na-da-da, *sailing* . . . Woody had loved the song, as mushy and sentimental as it was, when it'd first come out, but, as always, they'd killed it, overplaying the song until it became parodic. Could this possibly be the same Christopher Cross? Had the singer finally gotten sick of the endless nostalgia tours, the yesteryear retrospectives, the sad hide-the-belly-with-long-jackets, huffing-geezer podunk club dates, and become a private investigator with the Allegiance International Security Service? Doubtful. It had to be just a coincidence.

"You know the problem with us?" Woody said to Lyndon. "We're fucking typical Asian men. We don't talk. We're emotionally inaccessible."

"What have you been doing, going to therapy?"

"You might try it yourself. It might do you some good," Woody said. "Don't you think it's odd we both ended up alone, without a family?"

"I like my life," Lyndon said.

Woody looked at his brother, standing there in his dirty leather bib apron in the cheerless shed. "I don't know what to do with you," he said.

Sailing, na-da-da, *sailing* . . . Now that the song was in his head, he'd never get rid of it. He was tired. He wanted to get out of his workout clothes and take a shower. He wanted something to drink—a bubble tea, perhaps, or a smoothie. He had an urge for something with lingering texture and coolness, something refreshing and nautically brisk.

"You have any ice cream?" he asked his brother.

CHAPTER 5

THE OAR HOUSE HAD ONCE BEEN A COWBOY BAR CALLED THE LONE Night Cantina, but about ten years ago it had been bought by Milton Everhart, Rosarita Bay's harbormaster, who, instead of getting rid of the existing décor, had simply begun nailing nautical castoffs around, over, and eventually above the cowpoke memorabilia. First came a single wooden oar from an old dinghy, then another. Then brass clocks, compasses, portholes, binoculars, sextants, ship's wheels. When the walls were completely covered over, Milty started hanging things from the ceiling: anchors, diver's helmets, lanterns, fishing nets, glass floats, buoys, bells, and fenders, plastic parrots, the old dinghies themselves. It looked like a cramped, run-down harbor museum—or a very disorganized curios shop—and it always felt a tad dangerous in there, the ornaments hovering haphazardly overhead from wires that seemed too thin and scant for the load.

With the funky atmosphere, the Jimmy Buffett tunes on the jukebox, and Milty's reputation as a raconteur, the Oar House became one of the most popular bars in Rosarita Bay, a friendly neighborhood place for boaters and fishermen to come in for a few beers, a game of pool, and the occasional dominoes tournament. It had been a great place to work, very casual and relaxed, and Lyndon had liked being a bartender there. He'd had plenty of bartending gigs during his starving-artist days in New York, way back when, and though it had been a little demoralizing, the necessity, at this point in his life, to look for part-time work, the Oar House hadn't been that bad, kind of fun, actually, to get off the farm one night a week, mingle with townsfolk, develop friendships with the patrons and other servers, one or two with whom Lyndon, over the years, had had brief affairs.

But everything changed this summer when Milty sold the bar and retired to Key West. The new owner, Mark Beezle, a.k.a. Beelzebub, the Prince of Evil Spirits, the Patron God of the Philistines, was a former manager of a T.G.I. Friday's, and he was the biggest pinhead any of them had ever seen. A bean counter extraordinaire, he brought along all of his corporate accounting practices and procedures, raising the prices, instituting strict cost control measures, and casting a dreary pall over the staff.

Today, as Lyndon and JuJu came in, Beelzebub greeted them with his latest mandate: uniforms. Milty had let them wear whatever they'd wanted, although the mufti had naturally gravitated toward Hawaiian shirts and sandals. Beelzebub handed them dark red polo shirts with a new emblem—the blond blade of an oar underlining the logotype—and told them to wear the shirts with khaki pants from here on out.

"You have got to be kidding," Lyndon said. They'd look just like the wonks at The Centurion Group.

"They're nice shirts," Beelzebub said. "I didn't go cheap on them." He was wearing one himself, form-fitting and tucked in, unfortunate choices that outlined the pear of his narrow shoulders and prodigious butt.

This was the problem with working in the service industry.

It wasn't the customers, although they could be a pain in the ass, since Lyndon usually saw them in the worst state known to man—drinking on an empty stomach—and people often wanted to talk to him, confide in him, be entertained, be his friend. No, the real problem was the managers, the bosses, the petty dickheads who needed, at every opportunity, to assert their authority and prop their puny egos by demeaning their employees and chipping away at their dignity.

"Hey, you look cute in that shirt, bro," JuJu said.

"Shut up," Lyndon told him.

"I suppose we shouldn't begrudge Beelzebub," JuJu said. "He's really just a sad little man. He hates his life. That's why he's like he is with us. But it's so hard not to despise him, you know? Not to wish him monumental harm. Not to wish this rattrap wouldn't just cave in on the weasel's head. Jesus, I don't even own a pair of khakis."

Lyndon didn't, either. He had Carhartt bibs and coveralls. He had dirty blue jeans and clean blue jeans, and one pair of nice black jeans for evenings out. He possessed only one suit, black, which he'd purchased for his father's funeral. It was a little tacky-looking, and the sleeves were too short. This had been a major point of contention in his relationship with Sheila: what the hell was she doing with a man who owned just one off-the-rack suit, she couldn't take him anywhere, she couldn't get him to go to parties or benefits with her, to the ballet or concerts, to galleries or fancy restaurants, to the city or practically anywhere.

His brother had suggested a therapist. On Sheila's recommendation, Lyndon had been to several. A Jungian therapist had certified him a classic introvert, feeling drained in a crowd, whereas an extrovert would have been energized. A psychodynamic therapist laid the blame on his parents—uncommunicative father, meddlesome, perfectionist mother. A cognitive-behavior therapist surmised he had social anxiety disorder, a fear of being judged. Lyndon thought they were all hacks and quacks, and when the last one kept saying Lyndon seemed "diffident" when he meant to declare him "indifferent," Lyndon quit for good, indifferent to anyone who could not distinguish the difference.

He and JuJu set up their stations for the night, cutting up fruit for the garnishes, mixing the mixers, restocking the coolers, changing the kegs, lugging in tubs of ice, washing glasses. They needed extra birdbaths—martini glasses. It was Martini Night.

Beelzebub hadn't gotten around to fiddling with the décor yet, but he was experimenting with various concepts to draw more business, hiring a DJ for Oldies Night, a dance instructor for Salsa Night, making Nestor, the cook, assay beyond his usual repertoire of burgers and nachos into a vast new menu of happy-hour appetizers, ranging from tapas and dim sum to bruschetta and goat cheese fondue.

The martinis for Martini Night were an abomination. Lyndon was old school when it came to martinis. Fill a shaker with ice, splash in a tiny bit of Cinzano vermouth and immediately strain it out, pour in Bombay Sapphire gin, swirl the shaker seven times, strain it into a chilled birdbath, garnish with two olives. Vodka was outré, any other accoutrements were sacrilegious, and flavoring in the booze was simply heinous. Yet on the Oar House list of martinis was now an Appletini, a Mochatini, and a truly revolting concoction called an Orangetini. It made Lyndon's skin crawl whenever he had to make one.

Which, thankfully, was not too often, for despite Beelzebub's efforts, the theme nights and special drinks and appetizers had not lured in a bustling new yuppie clientele. Instead, they had to settle for holdovers from Milty's old gang and a few walk-ins

like Tank and Skunk B., JuJu's pals, who'd made a habit of trying to stump the bartenders with calls for exotic drinks, names
they liked saying: Ginger Not Mary Ann, Dirty Nipple.

They came in just after sundown, and when JuJu asked what
they wanted, Tank and Skunk B. shouted in unison, "Adiós
Motherfucker!"

JuJu squinted at them. "*¿Qué?*"

"Adiós Motherfucker!" the boys shouted again, and began
cackling.

The drink was not in Beelzebub's drink recipe book, which
meant it was not in the new POS computer, which meant JuJu
would have to enter the ingredients for the drink manually into
the register—that is, if he could figure out what they were.

"You know it?" he asked Lyndon.

It happened that he did. It was a frat-boy drink, a cruise-
ship, spring-break, amateur's drink, a rancid-tasting nail in the
head that smelled like rocket fuel, designed purely for projectile inebriation: half an ounce each of vodka, rum, tequila, gin,
and Blue Curaçao, two ounces respectively of sour mix and 7UP.
While Lyndon made the drinks, JuJu punched them up on the
touchscreen computer, and Tank and Skunk B. kept laughing, having a high time, oohing and aahing about the drinks'
aquamarine glow, clinking their glasses and cheering, "Adiós
Motherfucker!," faux-choking and pounding their chests.

JuJu gave them the tab. "Nineteen ninety-five," he announced.

The boys stared dumbly at the check.

"Each, motherfuckers."

Thereafter, they stuck to beer.

There was a bit of a predinner rush, if it could be called that, a
few more customers, a few Mochatinis, and then the place emptied
out again, deadsville, which gave Skunk and Tank B. occasion to
hold forth on their favorite subject—sex—not that either, at least

in recent memory, had had much more than anecdotal experience with it. Eventually Skunk got around to a story he'd heard from a nurse about a Russian guy who'd come to the hospital because he'd once been in the army in Siberia, and the soldiers there—little-known fact—had nothing better to do than get wasted on vodka and inject silicon into their penises to make them bigger, and this guy's silicon had migrated up to his stomach, requiring surgery, and the nurse had taken a peek as he was being prepped.

"What'd it look like?" Tank asked Skunk.

"She said it looked just like a gigantic Campbell's soup can," Skunk said.

"No."

"Yes."

"Dude, fuck if I'll ever be able to eat tomato soup again."

As they continued to yap, JuJu pondered the empty bar and said to Lyndon, "You know what we need in here? Flat-screen TVs. *Images*, man. It's become a spectator culture, that's the phenomenology of the postmillennial age. People need images flashing around to signify experiential reality."

"The last thing I need is Ed Kitchell coming in here with his Yell Leaders to watch football games. Because he'd do that, you know, just to yank my chain."

"Tomorrow night, Lyndey. They'll be out of town. A little monkeywrenching to soothe the soul?"

Lyndon was tempted, but said, "Can't risk getting caught." He went into the back cooler to change the canisters of beverage syrup and CO_2 for the soda guns, and when he came out, he found Laura Díaz-McClatchey standing near the entrance, scanning the bar. She looked, as always, as if she'd just left the insurance office, buttoned-down in a taupe pantsuit.

"There you are," she said. "I was wondering if you'd be working tonight." She pulled out a stool and sat at the bar, all eyes on her.

Lyndon put down a coaster. "What can I get you? Martini?"

She looked at the list of martinis and grimaced. "How about a sidecar?"

A sidecar was a good, old-fashioned American drink, very elegant: cognac, Cointreau, and lemon juice. "Sugar on the rim?" Lyndon asked.

"Let's skip."

"Preference on the cognac?"

"Martell VSOP?"

Another good choice. Not the most expensive, but smooth and mellow, and it stood up well to ice and mixing.

"With a twist," she said.

She was impressing him more and more, forgoing the usual froufrou garnish of a cherry and orange slice. He poured, and she sipped.

"Perfect," she pronounced, and they smiled at each other.

Mandy, one of the waitresses, laid her tray on the counter and, smacking gum, said, "Vodka cranberry Stoli orange juice."

Mandy had syrup for brains. Lyndon loathed the way she called out her drinks, always having to decode the order. Did she mean a Cape Cod and a Stoli screwdriver? A madras? Two vodka neats with juice backs? There were myriad possibilities.

He noticed Mandy had twisted the bottom hem of her new polo shirt into a knot to expose her lardy midriff. When had showing off how flabby you were become a commendable fashion trend? Who had convinced the diet-challenged functional illiterates of the world that this might be construed as sexy?

"Your eloquence is exceeded only by your charm," Lyndon said to her.

"Thanks," she chirped, taking it as a compliment.

Lyndon was going to clarify, but let it go. After she left with the drinks (she had meant a Stoli Cape Cod and an OJ), Laura told him, "You have a way with women."

"You noticed?" He wiped down the counter, then leaned toward her. "Listen, I'm sorry about the . . . incident yesterday."

"I have to say, it spooked me a little," Laura told him. She cocked her head and peered at his face. "Is that a black eye?"

"It's nothing."

"Did that woman do that to you? She hit you?"

"No, it wasn't her. It was . . . someone else. An accident."

Laura straightened up on her stool. "What are you, the town roué?"

"Hardly."

"Are you sure? Not that it would necessarily be a bad thing. Sometimes a little experience can be, shall we say, useful."

This Laura Díaz-McClatchey, she had a way of being provocative.

"Who was that woman with the hammer, anyway?" she asked. "Your ex-wife?"

"No, she's my—" He didn't know how to describe Sheila.

"An ex, though?" Laura said. "As in former, erewhile, ancient history, now extinct?"

"Yes," Lyndon said.

"You're no longer involved with her?"

Lyndon thought about what Sheila had told him this morning: *Nada. Rien. Zenzen betsuni.* "No."

"So she's just a stalker, a wigged-out ex-lover who's so enraged and embittered with you, she's inflicting bodily harm on your truck and besmirching your reputation in front of every woman you associate with. Is that the gist of it?"

"That about sums it up."

Laura nodded. "All righty. I can live with that." She extracted a scrap of paper and a pen from her purse. "I can't stay, but the other day, you were saying something about dinner." She wrote down her phone number and slid the paper across the counter. It was an ATM receipt. She had $83.57 in her checking account.

"Tomorrow night?" Laura asked.

Why not? he thought. Hadn't Sheila told him to go ahead, to move on, to forget about her? "Tomorrow night," he said.

She stood and took out her wallet. "What's the damage?"

"It's on me."

"Call me," she said at the door.

As he entered the comp on the register, JuJu knocked into him with his shoulder. "Lyndey, you old *dog*, you!"

"Shut up, JuJu."

"You've been holding out on me, Kemo Sabe. Who's the *chica*? Where'd you meet her?"

"I got a massage from her," Lyndon told him.

"Oh, I *see*," JuJu said.

"Not that kind of massage."

Yet Lyndon felt good. The day had taken an unexpected turn, an intriguing dip and declension. Sheila notwithstanding, he hadn't had a real date in years.

The night progressed quickly, busy all of a sudden, actually two-deep at the bar at one point. This was a different type of crowd than they were used to seeing, more affluent, sophisticated, definitely out-of-towners. A lot of gin and tonics, Cosmo's, and margaritas. They were savvy enough to decline the specialty martinis and order them dry or dirty. Most of them were visiting Rosarita Bay, it happened, wonder of wonders, kudos to the mayor, who knew what she was doing after all, for the chili and chowder festival.

But as this wave of customers was beginning to thin out, Sunny Padaca, the big-kahuna pot dealer, decided to make an unpropitious visit. Sunny was a Filipino-Samoan moke from the wrong side of Oahu, and he came in with two of his *vato* buzz-cut crew, mowing through people to the bar, a barrel felling trees. "Howzit, brah," he said, grinning at Lyndon. He wanted three Kamikazes and three Anchor Steams.

"A little off the beaten path for you, isn't it?" Lyndon said as he prepared the shooters. Sunny never dropped by the Oar House, preferring to ensconce himself in the Memory Den, a dive near the harbor.

"I like to diversify once in a while," Sunny said. "Check up on the little people. What have you been up to? You and the pogo stick keeping out of trouble?" He gazed over at JuJu, and then at Tank and Skunk B. "Or looking for it?"

Oh, fuck, Lyndon thought. He knows. Sunny had heard about the plants, and he assumed Lyndon and JuJu were planning to sell the pot, horning in on his action.

"I never look for trouble," Lyndon said.

"Yeah? You sure about that?" Sunny said. "Because I've been hearing things to the contrary. Little birdies are tweet-tweeting little rumors, rumors that you're engaging in some extracurricular activities."

Here it comes, Lyndon thought. *Adiós*, motherfucker.

"You know what the tweet-tweet is?" Sunny asked.

"No."

Sunny beamed. "I hear you firebombed that developer's trailer. Damn, that is fucking righteous, Linda."

"That wasn't me," Lyndon said, his knees sagging with relief.

"Yeah, right." Sunny laughed. He held out his fist for a conspiratorial bump, and Lyndon, not wanting to be ungracious, knocked his knuckles against Sunny's. "You have some serious *cojones,* bruddah," Sunny said. "I didn't figure you to be such a badass."

"You're giving me more credit than I deserve."

"No, really, you're a man after my own heart." He looked over again to JuJu, Tank, and Skunk B.—Larry, Curly, and Moe—and suddenly he wasn't smiling anymore. "You don't take shit from anyone, yeah? Someone pisses on you, you piss right back. You let them know you're not fucking around, this is serious business, it's not for amateurs, people can get hurt."

Oh, fuck, Lyndon thought. He lined up the shots and beers on the bar. "On me," he said.

"Hey, that's da kine, brah."

Lyndon grabbed JuJu from his station. "We're going out tonight and cutting down the plants," he whispered.

"Take it easy. He doesn't know anything."

"Tank and Skunk talked."

"They didn't. I made them swear on their mothers. You're being paranoid, Lyndon. Sunny practically French-kissed you just now. He's never that friendly with anyone."

"He's playing me."

"Come on," JuJu said. "Everything's cool."

Everything was not cool. Woody and Ling Ling appeared at that very moment, creating a small stir, ridiculously overdressed for the place, his brother in another one of his slick suits, Ling Ling in sparkling red sequin.

"What the hell are they doing here?" Lyndon said. He'd told them he was busy tonight, they would have to fend for themselves, and had given them several good dinner suggestions, all of them out of town.

"I told Ling Ling to drop by," JuJu said. "A problem?"

Yes, a problem. He hadn't wanted Woody to know that he was moonlighting as a bartender, particularly after their discussion earlier today about his money woes. He still couldn't believe Woody had gone through his accounts.

"Cute shirt," his brother said.

Ling Ling leaned over the bar and animatedly kissed JuJu on the cheeks, and Tank and Skunk B. gawked.

"She's in a good mood," Lyndon said. "Got a head start at dinner?"

"She's actually on the wagon tonight," Woody said. "Your little helper's become my little helper. He's had a positive influence on her. She can't shut up about how alive she feels. Get a Maker's on the rocks? And a ginger ale for her."

Lyndon poured the bourbon for his brother, who took out a money clip of crisp folded bills with a flourish.

"It's on me," Lyndon said. ·

"Oh?" Woody said. "Well, thank you kindly." He flicked off a fifty, dropped it into the tip jar. He raised his glass and drank, glancing up at the jumble of ornaments suspended from the ceiling, then eyed the pool table in the back of the room. "Ling Ling, you were in *Black Widow Undercover*, weren't you?" he said. "Did you really learn to play pool for that, or was it all special effects?"

Woody had been a fair pool player in high school, hustling orders of french fries and burgers in the rec room of the Watsonville YMCA.

"I think I hear a challenge in that inquiry," Ling Ling said. "Prepare to be humiliated." She placed her hand on his forearm, as if being escorted into a ballroom, and they cut a regal swath through the bar.

"Where'd all these *women* come from all of a sudden?" Tank asked JuJu.

"Yeah, what's going on at that farm?" Skunk B. added.

"You know who she is?" JuJu said excitedly.

"Orangetini gin Sierra Tanqueray tonic," Mandy called to him.

Oh, fuck me, Lyndon thought. But things began winding

down; they'd be closing soon. Bars had to shut down at midnight in Rosarita Bay, an antiquated, provincial regulation for which Lyndon was thankful. There'd be an hour of cleanup, and if he was lucky, he'd be home in bed by one-thirty.

"You're pulling the tap wrong," Beelzebub told him as he was drawing a beer.

"How so?" He was pulling the tap handle as he'd always pulled it, the way he'd been taught on his first job in New York, grabbing it at the base and tugging it with a quick smooth motion.

"Pull it from the top."

"That'll put air in it. It'll draw foamy."

"Exactly," Beelzebub said. "We want more foam. The difference between no foam and an inch of foam is forty-three glasses per half barrel."

There was a commotion near the pool table, Woody and Ling Ling high-fiving each other. Apparently they were playing as a team against someone, and then Lyndon made out who their opponents were: Sunny Padaca and one of his posse. Sunny did not look happy.

"Friends of yours?" Beelzebub asked.

"In a manner of speaking."

"You haven't been entering all your comps." Beelzebub had a handwritten list on an index card, and he was checking it against the POS computer. "You're missing two Kamikazes."

"What have you been doing, spying on us?" Lyndon asked. He wouldn't have put it past him to have installed a hidden camera.

"I hired a bar spotter," Beelzebub said.

"You what?" Lyndon asked. He'd paid a narc to watch them? Lyndon recalled a woman who'd sat at the bar most of the night, scribbling in a journal and nursing coffee. He'd taken her for a wannabe poet.

"I did an audit," Beelzebub said. "We've been losing 28.7 percent to shrinkage, which means you guys have been either overpouring, giving out too many comps, stealing outright, or all three."

Woody cracked in a shot, and Ling Ling whooped. Lyndon hoped there was no money on the game. Sunny did not like to lose—at anything.

JuJu said to Beelzebub, "The Kamikazes are on my ticket."

Beelzebub looked at the computer again. "So they are. But that still leaves you in the negative by five, Lyndon. Seven comps. You shouldn't be so generous with your friends."

A roar emanated from the back of the room, a bone-rattling primal yowl. Head tipped back, lips prized open to bare a massive dark maw, Sunny was screaming, enraged. He snapped the pool cue in two against his knee and, raising one of the splintered sticks into the air, started moving toward Woody.

By the time Lyndon and JuJu got to the pool table, Ling Ling had already intervened. She'd kicked the pool cue from Sunny's hand, and, with a variety of yips and shrieks, she was running through a long series of maneuvers in front of Sunny, punching and kicking the air, faster and even more impressive than her demonstration that afternoon at the farm. Sunny was stunned and mesmerized at first, and now he was, of all things, giggling, seemingly delighted by the exhibition as Ling Ling skipped and whirled into her butterfly kicks, scissoring her legs, going higher and higher until she accidentally clipped one of the lanterns hanging from the ceiling with the back of her heel, shattering the glass in the antique lamp. The lantern bobbled, there was the ping of wire snapping, and it crashed to the floor.

They all stood motionless, holding their breath, staring not down at the lantern, but up, up at the vast, ponderous scrapheap hovering above them as they divined what might happen next: junkyard Armageddon.

Everything swayed and creaked, the buoys and diver's helmets and old dinghies rocking and yawing, moving in unison to an invisible swell. But it held, nothing else fell, they were safe. Everyone began laughing nervously.

A faint ping sounded, a guitar string breaking. Then another, and another, like the detonation of sequential charges to implode a building. Wire after wire popped, and everything started crashing down, bells, anchors, oars.

"Move, move, move!" Sunny said, shoving people aside.

"Oh, fuck," Beelzebub said.

They ran toward the exits, toward the storeroom and office and kitchen, everyone except Mandy, who stood glaciated, still holding her tray aloft, midriff protruding, as the detritus fell and exploded toward her.

She was directly underneath a dinghy, a rotted, weather-beaten ten-foot bucket that easily weighed two hundred pounds. Lyndon didn't really want to, but he did. He pushed Mandy out of the way, and in her stead accepted her fate, deserved as it was—to be smote from the earth, obliterated by the boat, crushed by hull and keel.

ALTRUISM WAS NEVER REWARDED. Lyndon thought he'd have learned this by now. The bar was a wreck. It'd be closed for months. Beelzebub fired Lyndon and JuJu on the spot. Mandy, who'd escaped with nary a scratch, her job secure if and when the Oar House ever reopened, nonetheless threatened to sue, sue for emotional distress, post-traumatic whatsit, there had to be something she could get out of this. Didn't Lyndon grab her tit as he was shoving her, wasn't that sexual harassment? Couldn't she sue Lyndon or that Chinese woman or Lyndon's brother for the wages and tips she'd miss during the renovations?

It was a wonder Beelzebub didn't threaten to sue them as well, but, not knowing any better, he insisted Sunny Padaca be held accountable. He called in the police, railing about malicious destruction of property, assault and battery, reckless endangerment, inciting a riot.

"How'd I know you'd be in the middle of this?" Steven Lemke said to Lyndon.

As it happened, he arrested Sunny—not for destroying the Oar House, but for an outstanding warrant: he'd skipped bail on trafficking charges in Hawaii, and Sunny was taken to the sheriff's substation to await transport to the San Vicente County jail, from which he would be extradited to Honolulu.

No one was hurt other than Lyndon. He'd blacked out for a few minutes, and JuJu drove him to St. Catherine Hospital in Moss Beach, four towns to the north, for a gash on his forehead that would require five stitches, and also for his right knee, which would no longer bend correctly, yet which the doctor pronounced was just sprained, no ligament tears, necessitating a thick neoprene brace but no surgery. It took hours to get this diagnosis. It wasn't much of a hospital, more like a clinic, with only one doctor on call, and, concerned that Lyndon had been knocked unconscious twice in two days, he wanted to keep Lyndon overnight for observation and possibly transfer him to San Vicente Memorial for a CT scan.

All Lyndon could think about was the hospital bill. He already owed the dentist for two visits—thank God the temporary crown had held this time—with a third scheduled to cement a permanent crown over his molar. He couldn't afford an overnight stay at the hospital. He had medical insurance, but of the catastrophic variety, with an outrageously high deductible, almost useless.

Against the doctor's advice, he went home, head throbbing, body limping and beat. It must have been four o'clock by the time he fell asleep, and he didn't wake up until nearly nine, uncharacteristically late for him. Everything in a gray haze, he hobbled into the hallway to the bathroom, badly needing to piss. He heard rain, rain was splashing on his legs, it was odd, he didn't think it'd rain today. He glanced down, and realized he was pissing on the closed toilet lid. Christ, who had put down the toilet lid?

He cleaned the toilet and the floor and washed his legs and hands and examined himself in the mirror. He looked quite terrible, his face collapsing with fatigue, eyes rimmed red, a bruised knot welling underneath the bandage that covered his stitches. He staggered out into the hallway. Woody's room was empty, his bed neatly made. Ling Ling, however, was still in hers, and she was not alone. JuJu was asleep underneath the covers with her, Lyndon saw through the cracked-open doorway. He had a vague memory of being awoken by an earthquake in the middle of the night, a dream of tremors, the walls shuddering, a woman crying for help, a blue parrot flapping wildly toward him, waves cresting, a boat capsizing and flipping on top of him and trapping him in blackness. It hadn't been an earthquake that had plagued his sleep, it'd been fucking. People fucking in his house.

He needed to walk his fields. He strapped on his knee brace and got dressed, microwaved some instant coffee and put it in a covered plastic mug, and went outside. The weather had turned, the fog gone, just bright sunshine and blue skies, no wind at all. Good for the tourists, not so good for his plants. He was still worried about missing that one day of irrigation when his pump had gone out of commission.

Water. So much of farming was about water. There was a ranch above town, the fields now fallow. For generations, the Nielsen family had dammed a creek to form reservoirs for their irrigation water, but various agencies—California Fish and Game, NOAA Fisheries, U.S. Fish and Wildlife—had suddenly decreed their dams prevented steelhead and coho salmon, threatened species, from swimming upstream to spawn. Forced to dismantle the dams, the Nielsens had tried, without success, putting in wells, and then tried to obtain permits to install new irrigation ponds—"off-stream impoundments," the government called them—but learned it would take years and hundreds of thousands of dollars to get approval, due to the endangered red-legged frogs and San Francisco garter snakes that would make the ponds their habitat.

Lyndon felt fortunate not to have any such problems with his water supply. Arroyo Tunitas, the creek that bordered his property and fed his pond, ran down to the golf course as well, and The Centurion Group had once threatened to contest his water rights, but it became a moot point when the town—acquiescing to environmental groups—decided the hotel and golf course would have to recycle wastewater to qualify for zoning.

Lyndon grabbed his hula hoe and headed to the block nearest to his house. If there was trouble, it'd appear first in the field closest to the upwind bluff. Limping—good God, his knee hurt—he looked at the color of the plants. They were a healthy green. They didn't seem stressed. They were nearing maturity and very leafy, but were standing up nicely. He moved to the next block, his head beginning to clear as he walked along the ocean in the crisp, clean air, listening to the birds. He heard the call of a red-winged blackbird, *check*, *deeek*, and turned toward a stand of red alders. He stared at the lichen and moss mottling the bark, a swaying branch, the bobbing yellow catkins, and there, spreading its wings, was the bird, glossy black, with star-tlingly red patches on its shoulders.

Out here, Lyndon's senses always felt heightened, every-thing—light, shadows, contours, textures, colors—more vivid. These quiet mornings alone in the fields, next to the sea, they were what he loved most about farming. The purity of the natural world, the sweet fruit of gestation and growth, the blooming of his labors. It was ridiculous to say, but he always felt a little regret-ful when it came time to harvest the plants, stripping the stalks and then mowing everything down. He'd have to remind himself that this was the ineluctable cycle of nature. As they always did, he and JuJu would go down to Baja in January to camp and kayak, and then he would return to chores and repairs, getting supplies and making preparations during the dead time of the winter rains, and then it'd all begin again, another year, another season, another spring, deciding on seeds—Oliver, Diablo, Trafalgar, or Jade—and where to plant them, prepping the fields, mowing the cover crops, discing them in, getting it level.

He was not going to give this up. He had crawled over every inch of this land. He knew every contour of it, every tree and knoll. He knew its moods and vagaries, its contradic-tions and inclinations, its bounty and wrath. He knew it better than any lover he had ever had. Whatever happened here—good or bad—was his doing, and his alone. It didn't depend on the judgments of other people, on others' approval or favor or consent, on arbitrary designations or ordinations. He made all the choices and had to live with them, and sometimes he was rewarded, sometimes not. Sometimes he'd do everything right, and it still wouldn't matter—he'd fail anyway. Whether he was here or not, it would go on, this cycle, for thousands of years, like it had before him. Knowing this was humbling. It made him feel insignificant, and paradoxically that feeling was useful, freeing. He would do whatever it took to keep this farm, even if it meant turning down ten, twelve, fifteen million from The Centurion Group, even if it meant going against Sheila's wishes or half the town's. He couldn't fathom trying to start a new farm somewhere else, not with the regulatory mess that would surely clutter every step. It would be easier, as the Nielsen family did, to simply quit. They'd sold their ranch to a land trust for far less than what they could have gotten from a developer. "At least it'll never become a fucking subdivision," Jon Nielsen had said. Lyndon supposed he could do the same—turn to a land trust. He had been solicited by more than one. Quite aggressively, in fact. But he still believed he could get through this year in the black, as long as everything went right this season. He had to have this harvest. He didn't know how he'd continue next year, or the year after that, but those questions would be irrelevant if he didn't have a good harvest this year.

He waded through the inside rows of a block, squinting, the glare of the morning sun making it hard to see. He should have brought sunglasses. But eventually he did see something, a few bottom leaves that were a little wrinkled, slightly cupped. He got down on his hands and knees in the dirt, inspecting the undersides of the leaves, feeling the sap. Soon enough, he found them, exactly what he'd feared, near the bottom stems, in the crevices of the plants. Gray spots, like waxed cigarette ash. Nascent colonies of aphids.

He sprint-hopped back to the house, where JuJu was at the stove in the kitchen, Ling Ling sitting at the table. "This is a wonderful American tradition," she said to Lyndon, "the men cooking for the women."

"Want an omelet?" JuJu asked.

"I need your help," Lyndon said.

He could still save the block of plants if he got water on them and changed the microclimate. Aphids didn't like it too wet. He needed to do it with overheads, though. Drip tape wouldn't cut it. He had to haul the aluminum pipes to the field with his tractor and set them up parallel to the rows of plants, put a rise on one end so the pipes would be at an angle and shoot the water in an arc, and run them for at least half the day.

Ling Ling volunteered to go out with them, and they worked without a break for two hours. Lyndon didn't know if their efforts would have any real effect. Tomorrow he'd do a foliar application of rock dust, another thing aphids disliked, but he didn't really understand what was going on. The plants weren't strong enough to fight off the pests, and he didn't know why. At least the other blocks appeared safe. There was always a certain percentage loss with no-spray organic, and he could afford to sacrifice a few rows, but not more than that.

After they came back from the fields, they took turns showering, and Lyndon made grilled cheese and tomato sandwiches for them for lunch, during which Ling Ling apologized for precipitating the damage to the bar that had cost them their jobs.

It was sweet of her—a sober, sincere gesture. "It was only a matter of time before we would've been sacked," Lyndon told her.

She and JuJu began clearing the table and washing the dishes, and Lyndon went to his workshop to finish the baker's shelves he'd started yesterday. He was spraying primer on the supports when Hana Frost knocked on the door and rolled in her bicycle.

"Wow, you look like shit!" she told him.

"Thanks. Hello to you, too."

"I heard what happened at the Oar House."

"The little birdies in this town travel fast, don't they?"

She had a crack on the frame of her bicycle where the bottom tube met the headset, and she asked if he could fix it.

"Easy enough to do," he said, "but it's not going to look very pretty when I'm done."

He could have taken the bike apart to its bare frame and sandblasted the paint clean, but he had neither the time nor the desire. It was a cheap mountain bike. There should have been a thick even weld around the entire tube end, but the manufacturer had done a shoddy job, the bead thin and spotty. He took the bike outside and applied some paint and epoxy remover to the cracked joint.

"We need to let it set for a few minutes," he told Hana.

"Do you think I'm attractive?" she asked.

Not this again, he thought. "Don't you realize how pretty you've become? Even those clothes can't hide that."

"What's wrong with my clothes?" She had on a baggy red Stanford sweatshirt over a turquoise housedress, gray knee socks, and brown Birkenstocks.

"Am I missing something?" Lyndon asked. "Is that supposed to be hip? The anti-fashion fashion?"

"Like you know about fashion."

"As everyone keeps telling me."

"If I changed the way I dress, would boys find me sexier?"

"I don't know," Lyndon said. "Don't ask me these things. Ask your friends. Ask your mother."

"I'm asking you."

"God, I hate these conversations. I already told you I think you're attractive."

"Attractive's one thing, sexy's another," Hana said. "This is what I've heard about men: they see a woman, and they make an instant assessment—they think, *Yes I do*, or *No I don't*. Do you look at me and think, *Yes I do*?"

"Do I think you could be marriage material for someone?"

"Do you think about fucking me?"

"Hana!" Was this the favor she had intended to name later? That he deflower her? "Jesus Christ! There are boundaries here," he said. "I'm forty-three years old. You're seventeen. I used to date your mother. I was practically your stepfather. It's against the law and morally indefensible in five different ways to even think about this."

"I'm not asking you to fuck me," Hana said.

"Well, thank God for that."

"I want André Meeker to fuck me."

"Okay, good. Well, not good, but at least appropriate."

He wiped the stripping solvent off with a cloth and carried the bike inside, where he clamped it to his table and began attacking the old weld joint with a wire brush, a file, a piece of steel wool, an emery cloth, a sheet of sandpaper.

"Why wouldn't he fuck me?" Hana asked. "I threw myself at him. I said, Here, here I am, I'm yours, you can have me, and he decided to go out with that fat cow instead. Why? Why, Lyndon?"

"I don't know, Hana. If you want my honest and objective opinion, he's a complete wanker and dipshit moron to pick Jen de Leuw over you."

"I'm in love with him," Hana said. "I've been in love with him since sixth grade. I know what you're going to say—I'll get over it, I'm young, I'll fall in love a dozen more times—but it's not like that. I'm not thinking forever. He's actually pretty dumb. No genius, that boy, not much upstairs, and he's got some kooky ideas about the environment. Plus, he's got unbelievably bad taste in music. But he's so beautiful. It's almost criminal, how beautiful he is, don't you think? You know how long I've been planning this? You know how much work it's taken? It was destined, don't you see? It was meant to *be*. Then he starts working at Udderly Licious and hanging out with Jen de Leuw, and before I know it, it all falls apart. God, it's so unfair. Why did this have to happen, Lyndon?"

"I wish I could do something to help."

"There is something," Hana said.

"What?"

"André has a little habit. He's kind of like you."

"In what way?" Lyndon asked, cleaning the bike frame with acetone.

"He's kind of a pothead."

He wiped his hands and looked at Hana. "What are you talking about? I don't smoke pot."

"Oh, come on, Lyndon, you think I'm that naïve? All those times you were at our house, and you'd have to go out 'for a walk' after dinner?"

"I'm a closet cigarette smoker."

"No, you're not."

"Sometimes I just need my alone time."

"Stop."

"How long have you known about this?" he asked.

"Forever. It wasn't hard to figure out, seeing you and JuJu together."

"Does your mom know? About me?"

"She'd be an idiot if she doesn't."

"Do you smoke pot?" Lyndon asked.

"I've tried it a few times. With André. Sunny Padaca was his dealer."

"Do you do other drugs?"

"I'm not a junkie, Lyndon. Don't worry. But now that Sunny's been arrested, André's going to get desperate pretty soon. I'll be in a position of power, if you help me out."

Now Lyndon became truly alarmed. Did she know he was growing? Was he going to have every teenage stoner in town hitting him up for ganja?

"Could you give me a couple of joints?" Hana asked. "If I could just get André alone, if I could get him a little buzzed, I think nature would take its course. I'll pay you, if you want. You're probably worried about your supply as well, with Sunny in jail."

Lyndon breathed easier: she didn't know. "I'm not going to give you anything, Hana. I'm not going to contribute to the delinquency of a minor, especially knowing you want it to seduce someone. God, what would your mother do if she found out?"

"She'd never have to know."

"These things have a way of surfacing eventually."

"Are you still hoping to get back together with her?"

"I'm a slow learner," he said. In fact, Lyndon had decided this morning, after finishing with the irrigation pipes, that he wouldn't call Laura Díaz-McClatchey about dinner tonight. He didn't want to start something new. He wanted everything to stay the same. He wanted Sheila back.

"She's going on a date with that developer guy, Ed Kitchell," Hana told him.

"What?"

"I picked up the extension by mistake last night. They're going out to dinner on Monday."

It was impossible. It was just not possible. "They're getting together to talk business," he said. The Centurion Group was sponsoring the chili and chowder festival. They were probably planning a postmortem, strictly business. Or perhaps it was another insidious, conniving, cowardly attempt by Kitchell to pressure Sheila into swaying him. But not a date.

"No, I can tell the difference," Hana said.

"Are you sure? Ed Kitchell?"

"He's a jerk, but they're sort of a good match, you know. All she cares about is money. That's why you two could never make it work. She's a philistine. She always has been."

"That's a little harsh."

"Yeah? She's making me go to Stanford." She looked down at her sweatshirt. "Premed. Whoever said I wanted to be a doctor?"

"I believe you did," he told her. "That's all you talked about a couple of years ago. Don't you remember? Doctors Without Borders?"

"I got into Berklee College of Music."

"I thought they rejected you."

"I applied again for the spring, and they just accepted me. But she says I can't go. I want to be a songwriter."

"You can go to Stanford and still be a songwriter."

"That's what she says. Maybe you'd feel differently if you'd done better in New York."

"Now you're getting mean." Over the years, since he had never refuted Sheila's initial assumption that he had failed as a sculptor, a certain mythology had developed, the extent of his defeat leavening to an image of carnage.

"It doesn't help that Steven was such a miserable hack," Hana said.

"Okay," Lyndon said, his feelings for Steven notwithstanding, "I think that's uncalled-for."

"You haven't heard me lately," Hana said. "I'm *good* now. You'll see tomorrow when I play at the festival."

"I'm planning to be there. Stand back a little while I do this." He turned on his Heli-Arc machine, flipped down his helmet, and scratched the tip of the tungsten electrode against the bike frame to strike an arc, then dipped the filler rod down to form a sturdy molten puddle.

"I told Berklee I'd come in January," Hana said. "I haven't told Mom."

"You are full of surprises today." He closed the cylinder valve, purged the gas line, and switched off the machine. He lifted the bike off the table and set it down in front of Hana. "You're all set."

"You think I'm crazy."

"Is this what you really want to do? Write songs, sing?" he asked.

"Yes."

"Do you love it? I mean really love it?"

"Yes."

"Let me ask you, answer honestly, is it just because you want to be famous?"

"I don't care about that shit," Hana told him.

"Answer honestly, really think about this, you feel you can't *not* do it, that even if you wanted to, you couldn't let it go?"

"You know how I feel, don't you?"

Maybe what he said next was out of spite, to hurt Sheila. "Do it, then."

"Really? You mean it?"

"But go to Stanford first for a semester. At the end of the semester, if you're still sure you want to do it, transfer."

"What if Mom won't pay for it?" Hana asked. "They didn't offer me a scholarship."

"Isn't your father responsible for college?"

"That wasn't part of the settlement. She wanted full control."

"Apply for funding again," Lyndon said. "Get a job. Get a loan. If you want it, you'll find a way."

"Okay, thanks," Hana said. "Your opinion's important to me. Are you going to give me the joints now?"

"No."

"Why not?"

"Didn't I tell you already? Life is suffering."

Lyndon sent her home, went to the kitchen, and called Laura Díaz-McClatchey.

CHAPTER 6

H E COULDN'T FIND THE TURNOFF AT FIRST. HE WENT BACK AND forth on Highway 1, looking for the little dirt road down which Trudy had directed him, but it was nowhere to be seen. As he backtracked through the wooded area of Bidwell Marsh Preserve, his Rover began making a funny noise. The engine or radiator or something or another was misperforming, the car's usual fine-tuned purr interrupted on occasion with a disturbing stutter. Had he sustained more damage than he thought when he had crashed into the tree yesterday? Not merely cosmetic—cosmetic was bad enough—but mechanical or structural as well? The prospect was troubling. It was extremely doubtful there would be a qualified service center anywhere in the vicinity.

Woody had a headache. He hadn't gotten to sleep until late the night before, wired from his near-death experience at the Oar House. Then, just as he was dropping off, Ling Ling and JuJu had started giggling and tussling in the bedroom next door, and very distinctly they had started fucking, going at it with an unbelievable racket, banging the bed against the wall, Ling Ling yipping and screeching as if she were whipping through one of her kung fu routines. What the hell were they doing in there? It went on and on—it seemed impossible for two people to fuck that long with such no-tomorrow gymnastic vigor. Woody finally had to succumb to a sleeping pill.

Somehow, though, the clamor of birds outside pierced through his narcotic slumber in the early a.m., and he awoke with a start, an epiphany fully enunciated in his head, one that surprised him with its clarity but which vanished as abruptly as it had appeared. Afterward, he'd been unable to fall back asleep. Goddamn birds. They were perched in a tree right beside the house, singing happily. What were they so fucking happy about?

Now, despite two espressos at the Java Hut, he was still hungover and bleary from the sleeping pill. Maybe he needed to adjust his meds. He was on five different medications for his cholesterol, high blood pressure, anxiety, allergies, and male pattern baldness (he was receding just a touch in his temples), as well as an antidepressant and a mild stimulant for possible adult attention-deficit hyperactivity disorder, and antibiotics for some pimples on his back that wouldn't go away, not to mention the beta blockers he sometimes took before important pitch meetings, the sleeping pills from which he was trying to wean himself, the Viagra he didn't really need but used purely as a precautionary measure, and the inhalers for the asthma he was convinced he had. Some of these had been prescribed by his primary care physician, dermatologist, and allergist, most had not. Woody doctor-shopped, and whatever he couldn't get from a doctor, like for the asthma, which, perplexingly, no one would confirm as a diagnosis, he bought on the black market or the Internet. And, of course, there were also his protein and ephedra supplements to burn fat and build muscle, his Omega-3 and flaxseed and various vitamins, his glucosamine chondroitin for his creaky knees, and his acidophilus and enzyme tablets, without which, owing to lactose intolerance, he would not have been able to enjoy that delicious linguini carbonara the day before. Modern medicine was a wonderful thing.

At last he spotted the dirt road. Or so he thought. He turned into it, and immediately it seemed bumpier and narrower than he'd remembered. The Rover bounced haphazardly, the engine grinding; parts of the car seemed to be flying apart, clanging. Was this the right way? He didn't recognize a thing. Yet he didn't have room to turn around, and it was too difficult to try to exit in reverse, so he kept going—forever, it seemed. There was definitely something wrong with the Rover, and the last thing he wanted was to get stuck out here. The car was bucking crazily. Maybe it was the axle or the electronic suspension system—he knew nothing about cars. He hated going to garages, because there he was in an inferior position, never sure if he was being ripped off. That was one of the reasons he got a new car every two years, before the warranty expired.

He broke through to the clearing. He shut off the ignition, and the Rover spluttered to a rest. God knew if he would be able to start it again. He got out of the car, spread a towel on the ground, and changed into a pair of old jeans and a T-shirt he'd snatched from Lyndon's closet and some rubber boots he'd found in the mudroom. Everything was a bit tight, and certainly the outfit was the nadir of fashion, but it'd have to do. His own clothes were completely unfeasible for this walk into the marsh. He started down the trail that Trudy had pointed out to him.

He had been thinking about Trudy, what she had said, that, as a little girl, she had been deeply in love with him. The confession had puzzled him. Not many women—none, in fact— had ever professed such a sentiment to him. Had it merely been a schoolgirl's crush on a brother's friend, bolstered by the happenstance that Woody was one of the few Asians she knew, or had there been something about him—a trait or quality—that Trudy had found particularly admirable? He couldn't imagine what that might have been.

During those summer and Thanksgiving visits, he had been preoccupied with trying to impress Mr. and Mrs. Thorneberry, or "Buzz" and "Tinker," thinking they might serve as important connections in the future. His entire time at Harvard, he had been continually on edge, wondering how he was coming off, what people thought of him, if he was being patronized or ridiculed, where he fit in on the pecking order of the Future Leaders of the Ruling Privileged Wasp Elite. He studied hard, but nothing came to him naturally. He always found himself cramming, secretly relying on CliffsNotes, his grades never more than average. He knew he was out of his league intellectually, and he wasn't particularly witty or funny, and as he struggled to partake in his classmates' repartee, it became clear he didn't have an original thought in his head. So he memorized esoterica—polysyllabic buzzwords and Latin phrases and quotations from Nietzsche and Schopenhauer—to parcel out in moments of insecurity. Intimidated as he was, he determined early on that he couldn't waste his time with middle-class scholarship kids like himself on the lower rung. He had to prioritize and network. He had to befriend people according to their utility, their value in what they might be able to provide him after graduation—a strategy that proved wise. Kyle, although failing to help Woody with the top investment banks in Manhattan, had used a family entrée to get him the job at Credit Suisse First Boston, and other classmates had been essential assets when he'd hung out a shingle as a financial planner, though neither they nor Kyle had enough faith in Woody, he was wounded to discover, to entrust him with their own money.

The trail became less distinct all of a sudden, the path blending in with the grass and the roots of the trees. He soon had to brush aside branches and brambles, and he began to sweat. He was under the canopy of the trees, but the sun was hot and bright today, insects homing in on his flesh. He should have brought along bug spray. And sunscreen. A hat. And water. He'd imagined a leisurely little stroll along a wide marked trail to the beach, not an arduous trek through jungle forest that required a machete. He carefully sidled past some spiny bushes, worried about ticks, Lyme disease. The ground was slippery, wild mushrooms popping out of the rotting vegetation. These birds above him, they were making such a din, shrieking like monkeys. Why were they being so noisy? Was it because the sun was out, or was it because there was something they were afraid of nearby? Could there be bears in the marsh? Or maybe that coyote.

He was feeling the burblings of panic. It shouldn't have taken so long to reach the ocean, and he feared he might be lost. He flipped open his cell phone. No reception, of course. He wished he had one of those portable GPS units. He looked up to see where the sun was, and walked right into a spider web, which wrapped around his face. He spat and clawed, brushing off the threads. He stepped into a space between the trees and looked up again. The sun in the morning would be in the east. If he kept going in the opposite direction, he'd eventually find the ocean, wouldn't he? He'd never been a Boy Scout. All he knew about the outdoors, he'd learned from TV and the movies. He hated the outdoors. He didn't understand the appeal of hiking or camping at all.

He heard the sound of running water. He burst through a thicket and came upon a meadow with a creek. Thank God, open air. He'd follow the creek to the sea. Simple enough. He wasn't lost at all. He didn't know why he'd been concerned. He wasn't an idiot. He didn't need Boy Scout or wilderness training. He could figure these things out on his own. He was a Harvard graduate, after all.

The meadow turned into marsh, and the creek widened into an estuary. He could hear breaking waves, see dunes ahead, a sign on a post: WESTERN SNOWY PLOVER NESTING AREA. BEACH AND DUNE AREAS BEHIND THIS SIGN ARE OFF LIMITS. SNOWY PLOVERS ARE PROTECTED UNDER THE ENDANGERED SPECIES ACT.

The ground got muddier as he walked onto the flats behind the sign. It'd been a good idea, these rubber boots of Lyndon's, but nonetheless each step was becoming more of an ordeal, his feet sinking deeper and deeper into the alluvial muck. He was having to yank his legs up as if in a snowdrift, breaking the suction of the mud. As snug as the boots fit on his feet, he slipped out of one, lost his balance, and fell on his back.

"Fuck!"

He was lying in the sludge, up to his ass in it, and the mud stank horribly, putrid from the marsh. He pulled himself upright, tugged the boot loose, and put it back on. He was caked in mud, soaked to the bone. He had a choice before him now. The mudflats broadened out away from the marsh, and he could cut across them or stick to the firmer ground alongside the trees, parallel to the beach, and circle back on the sand. He stiffly proceeded straight ahead. It couldn't get any worse, he thought. He was already soiled through and through.

He stepped into some sort of soft spot in the mud, and he sank all the way down to his knees. He wiggled his feet, trying to pry himself free, but only sank farther, now to his crotch. This wasn't mud. This was a weird kind of liquefied sand. Quicksand. He jerked his legs and flailed his arms, and descended to his waist. He was trapped, he couldn't move.

"Help!" he screamed. *"Help!"*

It came back to him, that profound revelation with which he had awoken earlier this morning. It must have been a delayed reaction, his brain, choosing to defer processing events until he was asleep, in shock from the string of close encounters with death—the car accident, the coyote, the truck on the highway, Sunny Padaca threatening to flagellate him in the Oar House, the piles of junk from the ceiling about to compress him into cookie dough. He had woken up knowing something with anguished, crystalline certitude: he did not want to die alone. And coupled with this thought was a startling resolution: he wanted—right away, if possible—to get married and have children.

But he would not have the chance to do any of that now. He would suffer the most hideous of deaths, exposure and starvation, blistering in the hot sun, and he'd be out here alone, no one missing him for hours, no one even knowing he'd ventured out to the marsh, damn this place, damn this town, damn his brother for his intransigence and stupidity.

He closed his eyes and yelled, over and over, *"Help!"* Was there an afterlife? he wondered. Had there been any purpose, any meaning, to his tortured, cursed existence? Why hadn't his parents raised him with a religion?

"Years that whirl me I know not whither, substances mock and elude me."

The two of them, Trudy and Margot, were standing behind him, wearing shorts and tank tops, looking very tan and sinewy.

"Get me out!" Woody pleaded.

"You're really not in any danger, you know," Trudy told him.

"Unless you were to fall face-first," Margot said. "Then you might be in trouble."

"The more you struggle, the more you sink," Trudy said.

"The human body's less dense than the quicksand. If you relax and lie on your back, you'll actually float. Into the destructive elements immerse."

"Density's one thing," Margot said. "A lot of it has to do with lack of movement to reduce viscosity."

"You're saying that's an equal factor?" Trudy asked.

"I don't know about equal, but contributing."

"That's a crock."

"When you lie still, you're increasing surface area."

"The density of the human body's 62.4 pounds per cubic foot."

"Hey," Woody said weakly.

"Give or take," Margot said.

"What's that supposed to mean?"

"It's not an absolute. It's an average. Depends on a lot of variables. Body fat, temperature."

"Excuse me."

"The density of quicksand is 125," Trudy said. "Almost double the density of water. A couple of pounds here and there aren't going to make a difference."

"Depends," Margot said.

"On what?"

"Uh, ladies?"

"Sedimentary composition. Sand-water ratio. Salinity."

"Are you just going to contradict everything I say today?" Trudy said. "Is that your explicit objective? Did you wake up and tell yourself, I have an idea, I'll just be the biggest pain in the ass I can possibly be?"

"That's right, because it's always, always all about you, isn't it, T.?"

"Hey!" Woody yelled. "A little help here?"

They pulled him out of the quicksand and, refusing to speak

to each other, led him to their campsite at the edge of the woods, near the beach. Their little hideaway was neater and more organized than he would have guessed. They had a big tent, two collapsible chairs around a fire pit, a cooking area with pots and pans and stuff sacks hanging from a wire strung tight between trees, and even a hammock. Off to the side was a little garden with lettuce and green onions. There wasn't a piece of litter anywhere in sight.

"Okay, strip," Trudy told him.

"What?"

"You're filthy. Take off your clothes, and I'll wash them for you."

"What will I wear in the meantime?"

"Margot will lend you something. It should fit. She's got a gargantuan ass."

"Like you should talk," Margot said.

"Lard ass."

"Tub of shit."

These jabs held little weight. Trudy was tiny, and although Margot was a big girl, with the solidity of a former athlete—swimming, rowing, perhaps—she, like Trudy, looked gaunt and severely underfed.

"Camel toe," said Trudy.

"Hatchet wound," said Margot.

"Catcher's mitt."

"Stench trench."

Trudy glared at Margot and hissed out, "Motherfucking bitch cunt slut whorebag cocksucker. Cum-belching cancer-eating dildo-humping donkey punch. Scaly rimjob turd-licking white-trash lesbo dyke."

Margot gaped at Trudy, utterly abashed. She snatched up a fishing rod and vanished into the woods.

"I don't know if you've noticed," Trudy said to Woody, "but we've begun to get on each other's nerves."

He changed into a pair of Margot's shorts and a denim shirt, and Trudy took his clothes to the creek, where she rinsed the mud out of them while Woody washed up.

"Want to see the plovers now?" she asked after she had hung the clothes to dry. "You're in for a treat. The last chick has just hatched."

She packed a few things into her rucksack and showed him the way to the trail, which was well marked in this portion of the marsh. As they walked along, Trudy pointed out plants and wildflowers: buckwheat, beach primrose, yarrow, Nutall's milk vetch.

"This is an amazing marsh," she said. "It's got such a varied ecosystem—all the willows and cattails are perfect for nesting. One-fifth of all North American bird species have been spotted here. You hear the wrens?"

Woody looked up at the sky. "Those are vultures, aren't they?"

"What?" She laughed. "No, they're red-winged blackbirds. There's an egret, and you see over there? There're a bunch of great blue herons in the eucalyptus."

They traversed a tidal flat, the mud sucking on his boots again, sloshed through the shallow mouth of the estuary, and then climbed the back of some dunes. "Crouch down," Trudy said. At the top of the dune, he followed her into the entrance of a well-disguised blind, jury-rigged with white canvas, tent poles, and driftwood, that had just enough room for two people. A telescope on a tripod peeped through an observation slot at the beach below. Trudy put her eye to the scope and trained it across the sand. "Here, take a look," she said.

They switched places, and Woody squinted through the eyepiece. He saw sand and debris, but no birds. "Where are they?"

"Don't you see them?" Trudy got on her knees next to him and peered through a pair of binoculars. "Look beside that clump of kelp."

He saw one of the plovers finally, a little gray-brown puffball on legs, scurrying down to the water's edge, stopping and pecking into the wet sand. "It's so *tiny*," he said. It looked no bigger than a child's fist.

"That's Eyebo, and Whygo's right behind him."

"Eyebo and Whygo?"

"Acronyms for their bands. AY:BO and WY:GO, father and mother. You see the color bands on their legs? You read them from top to bottom, left to right. Aqua, yellow, blue, orange. White, yellow, green, orange."

He watched AY:BO skitter up the beach, moving like a high-speed windup toy, but suddenly he disappeared—a vapor. "Where'd he go?"

"He's just sitting down. That's how they camouflage themselves. All they need to do is hunker down to blend in with the sand."

Woody spotted him again, running up to a circular fence. He zipped through the wire mesh to two little chicks and straddled his legs over them. He squatted down, covering them with his belly.

"He's brooding the chicks, keeping them warm," Trudy said. "When they hatch, they can't thermoregulate themselves yet."

"The mother doesn't do that?"

"Not with snowies. The father raises them until they fledge. WY:GO, the mother, will probably take off in a few days and breed with another male. Plovers are—to use the catchword of the day—polyamorous. This is a really late-season nest. We actually got to see them copulate. It was quite shocking. I thought it'd be a quickie insemination—you know, wham-bam—but it lasted much longer than I would have thought. Boy oh boy, AY:BO has got some *stamina*!"

Plovers bred on wide open beaches, sand pits, and salt pans, Trudy told him, and made their nests by scraping a depression in the sand and spreading pieces of driftwood, shells, and seaweed alongside it. After a pair of plovers laid their eggs, both sexes took turns incubating them for about a month, the female during the day, the male at night. The clutch size was usually three eggs—minute brown-speckled eggs that were barely visible even to the trained eye, easy to step on by accident—but if too many of them were lost during the long incubation, by high tides or blowing sand or predators, or if their habitat was disturbed too frequently, the pair would abandon the nest. After hatching, the chicks would almost immediately begin foraging on their own, led by the adults away from the nest to areas where they could peck up brine flies, larvae, insects, and amphipods. They could roam up to half a mile a day in search of food. The chicks would not be able to fly for four weeks, and thus were particularly vulnerable until they fledged.

The odds were against them. They were fragile, defenseless birds, preyed upon by seagulls, crows, ravens, foxes, skunks, raccoons, falcons, owls, dogs, cats, pretty much every animal on the coast. But what really spooked plovers were people. Any sort of threatening human activity in the vicinity might make them abandon their eggs or chicks.

"What we're trying to do," Trudy said, "is increase the number of fledglings from one to one-point-five per breeding pair. That's the difference between a population on the decline and one on the rise."

"How many have fledged while you've been here?"

"Three."

"*Three?* You've camped here all summer for *three* fledglings?"

"There might be more if some of this clutch makes it. But it's more complicated than that. We're trying to establish this as a new breeding ground. If we're successful this season, they'll come back next year."

They were using methods based on the theory of social attraction, developed by a biologist named Stephen Kress, the head of the National Audubon Society's Seabird Restoration Program. The idea was to lure birds into building new colonies with everything from recordings and mirrors to fake eggs and mating perfumes. Plovers didn't really nest in colonies, but they could be enticed into aggregating in suitable habitats. The first thing Trudy and Margot had done was dig out the nonnative beachgrass, which had been imported for erosion control but had become invasive. Next, in the cleared sand, they had scattered oyster shells and decoys, widely spacing them apart, and put up signs and symbolic fencing—posts linked with string—restricting the entire dune area. Then they had waited. They watched the plovers build nests, marked their locations, erected enclosures around them, cleared sand from eggs after storms, surveyed the numbers and dates of eggs and chicks, banded the birds, monitored their feedings, and chased away predators.

"They put a garbage dump at the end of the golf course," Trudy said, "and that's attracted more gulls and coyotes. You know what kind of an environmental blight golf courses are? An eighteen-hole golf course uses eight hundred thousand gallons of water a day, and requires *four tons* of germicides, pesticides, and herbicides every year. Most of the chemicals are carcinogenic—organophosphates, methylmercury. They run off and leach into the ground and kill everything within miles for generations. All of this development—it's all big-boxification and Sprawl-Mart. Forty-six acres of farmland are paved over every hour in this country, and the agribusiness that's left, you just don't know what the hell you're eating anymore, all these GMOs, cows and chickens fed with corn and soybean pumped up with antibiotics that breed resistant stains of bacteria, these farmed fish with PCBs. It's Frankenfood. You just can't imagine the consequences. That's the problem: it's a lack of imagination. Your SUV, for example. You know it produces one pound of CO_2 for every mile you drive? You drive twenty thousand miles a year, that's ten tons of CO_2 expelled into the air annually. Multiply that by a billion cars, along with all the methane and chlorofluorocarbons released every day, and you wonder why the ozone layer is being depleted, why there's a hole over the Arctic Circle, why there's global warming?"

Woody was disquieted by her rant. Almost certainly she was the person who had been vandalizing The Centurion Group's property. "I've been thinking of trading in my Rover," he said apologetically. "It's been giving me trouble lately, anyway. Maybe I'll get a hybrid."

She laughed. "I get carried away sometimes. Margot keeps saying I have anger management issues."

"My brother's Brussels sprouts are completely organic. He doesn't spray at all."

"One of the few remaining heroes. You two close?"

"Very close," Woody said, looking through the telescope again. There was some brightly colored webbing lining the top of the nest enclosure. "What's that strip of orange for?"

"To prevent bird strikes," she said.

Stupid birds, he thought.

Suddenly alert, Trudy grabbed her rucksack and pulled out a slingshot. She loaded it with a pebble and flicked it out of the observation slot. Woody watched the pebble whiz toward a seagull on the beach, making it scamper and flush away. "Fucking gulls," she said.

"Let me ask you something," Woody said. "It seems, well, kind of dumb for the plovers to make their nests in the wide open like this, where they're so vulnerable to predators and people. Aren't you interfering with the course of natural selection by protecting them? If they're so weak, maybe they're meant to go extinct."

"It might seem dumb to you, but they were doing just fine until now. They've successfully reproduced in a very harsh environment for thousands of years. Death—even extinction—is part of the natural cycle of things, but what's happening to them now is unnatural. It's solely because of man encroaching on their habitat. So we can passively watch the demise of a species, or do something about it. I don't think there's a choice. We have an obligation, a stewardship role, to save them."

The argument sounded like it was straight out of a lobbyist's manual for the Audubon Society, and Woody didn't buy it. It was easy to spout these bleeding-feather bromides, to squawk as a radical environmentalist, when you had a trust fund. Last night he had again talked to Christopher Cross, who had told him that Buzz Thorneberry had contributed ten thousand dollars a year—the maximum allowed without incurring inheritance taxes—in Trudy's name to a trust since she was first adopted. According to Cross, Trudy had not spoken to the Thorneberrys in over three years, but Buzz was still putting money in the trust, so now she was worth half a million dollars. Yes, she had never withdrawn a cent of it, but still, the money was there. She always had it to fall back upon. She had, anytime she needed it, the sanctuary of wealth. "Isn't man part of evolution?" he asked. "Isn't progress supposed to be ruthless?"

Trudy tucked back her hair and sighed. "You don't appreciate how everything is related, how miraculous it is. You breathe in and you breathe out, and you don't think anything of it. But on an atomic, molecular level, we're recycling the universe with each breath. Don't roll your eyes at me. There's a dynamic balance between every organism. We expel carbon, and it's taken in by plants, which in turn release oxygen, which in turn is taken in by animals, and it circles around and around, so that eventually all the atoms in our bodies are exchanged with every living creature from the dawn of time. We have the atoms of our ancestors in each of us. You have Mahatma Gandhi, the Buddha, inside you right now! The whole planet, everyone dead and alive, is breathing together! Isn't that remarkable to think?"

"Are you a Buddhist?"

"I've studied Buddhism, and I have Buddhist aspirations, but it seems I have certain aggressive tendencies that are contradictory to the basic precepts," she said, smiling. "The Dalai Lama says his true religion is kindness. Isn't that beautiful? I'd like to be able to say that for myself, but it's such an effort when there's all this greed and evil around you. Do you think of yourself as a good person?"

The question, as simple as it was, unsettled Woody. Nietzsche had said that what was good was anything that heightened the feeling of power, the will to power, power itself; what was bad was anything born of weakness; what constituted happiness was the feeling of that power growing, of resistance being overcome. But, as usually defined, was Woody a good person? He wanted to say yes, but if he had to be honest, he would have to say, fundamentally, no.

"I met a woman in town the other day," Trudy said. "She's decided to give up everything and leave her family for a year to become a Tibetan nun. She's going to Nepal next week. She told me the Buddha used to say the human condition is like a man shot by an arrow. The man will flail and wail, but instead of seeking immediate help, he'll first demand to know who fired the arrow, why did this happen, what did this have to do with him, how can he avenge this act, be compensated, why is life so unfair, why is he so unlucky. He's not dealing with the problem at hand, the here and now. He's not awake. It's what Buddhists call our 'monkey mind.' We keep swinging from past regrets to future worries, we vacillate between longing and loathing, craving and jealousy. That's what poisons the arrow, not the arrow itself, because we're not aware of what's happening in the bloom of the present moment."

Woody had to confess to himself, this was exactly what he did all the time, fixate on the past and the future.

"Tell me," Trudy said, "which way is the wind coming from?"

"Hm?"

"The wind. It's coming from the northwest. The tide's coming back in. You see that dark patch of water there, where it looks a little windier, where there're more ripples? Notice anything unusual?"

"Not really."

"The patch is moving. It's going *toward* the wind. Keep an eye on it."

Nothing happened for a while. A couple of small birds hovered over the surface, following the drifting patch of water, then a few more. Without warning, a whole flock of them appeared, and they began diving frantically into the water, churning it into a boil.

"What's happening?" Woody asked. It frightened him a little, the ferocity with which the birds were plunging into the ocean.

"Terns. There's a school of mackerel or sardines chasing some baitfish—smelt or anchovies—up to the surface, and the terns are feeding on them. Look above."

A bigger bird—dark and bulky—was flying overhead, about fifty feet above the sea, and when it reached the terns, it folded its wings and plummeted head-first into the water with a huge splash.

"Whoa!" Woody said.

When the bird surfaced, there was a large pouch of skin bulging beneath its bill, water draining from it as it lifted into the air.

"That's a brown pelican, the only nonwhite pelican in the world," Trudy said. "It's on the endangered list as well, because of DDT. It can hold three gallons of water and fish in its pouch."

"That's amazing."

"What I'm saying is, it's too easy for people to live in climate-controlled isolation and not *see* what's around them. Even when people go into nature, they approach it all wrong. Have you ever read Edmund Burke? Yet another dead white male chauvinist, but never mind. He tried to come up with an explanation for our taste in art, especially landscape art, and he said things are either beautiful or sublime. The beautiful has a nurturing quality. It's sexy, because it stirs our instinct for self-propagation. The sublime is awe-inspiring and terrifying, like the Alps or the Grand Canyon. It's an encounter with otherness, and elicits an impulse for self-preservation. Later on, they added the picturesque, landscapes that are pleasant and domestic, reassuring. What's the problem with this? I think we could all use several doses of the beautiful and the sublime every day, jolt us out of our complacency, but these categories, they're just another example of anthropocentrism. Ultimately it's glorifying man's dominion over nature. Saying something is beautiful or ugly, sublime or picturesque, is beside the point. It's *arrogant*. To truly appreciate nature, be a part of it, you have to replace arrogance with humility. Then you'll begin to see. There's so much to see, even in the smallest things."

She picked up a pebble and handed it to Woody. "Climbers have this exercise," she said. "They're faced with a big wall and have to figure out a route on it, and they get overwhelmed by its complexity. So they start with something smaller, a boulder. They look at the holes and cracks, get tuned in to it, and then shift those doors of perceptions over to the wall. If you look at a pebble, really look at it, you can do the same thing. Look at the surface, at its texture and variations, the microscopic indentations and crevices. You see what I mean? There's grandeur in a pebble."

It was getting hot in the blind, and Woody wiped the sweat from his forehead. He held the pebble in his fingers and turned it around in the sunlight, staring hard at it. It was a pebble. He didn't see grandeur. He shook his head.

"You think I'm full of shit, don't you?" Trudy asked.

"The air is getting kind of thick in here."

"There have been days when I've stared at the sky and the ocean and the horizon from this spot, and I've felt the earth rolling underneath me."

"What do you mean?"

"If you sit still and really concentrate, you can feel the earth spinning on its axis," she said.

"Now you're making fun of me."

"No, no, really," she said. "It's being aware. There's a canyon of redwoods just above the marsh. I should take you to the hot springs up there. A couple of months ago, I found this waterfall, and I sat across from it for over an hour, and after a while I could follow individual particles of water flowing over the edge. Then I glanced over at the rock beside the waterfall, and I could see it flowing, too."

"The rock."

"Yes!"

"You did this without drugs."

"Yes! We think of rock as being solid and unchanging, but it's not. Nothing is. Everything in the universe is in flux. Molecules in motion, recycling. Everything's a shimmering dance of energy."

She nodded at him gleefully. He hadn't figured her to be such a crystal-gazing flake, tripping out on vision quests in the wild.

"Did one of your parents do something to Kyle?" he asked.

"Buzz and Tinker?"

"Did something happen to him? Or to you?"

"You're still looking for an answer as to why he killed him-self," she said. "You're not going to find it. There wasn't any abuse or childhood trauma. Buzz and Tinker are only guilty of being rich and white and narrow-minded. Otherwise they're well-meaning people."

"Why are you no longer talking to them, then?"

She picked at a scab on her knee. "I went to Vietnam three years ago, after Kyle died. I went to find my birth parents."

"Did you?"

"No. But a trip like that, of course I came back and noth-ing was the same. It made me realize I didn't belong there, in Vietnam, but where did I belong? It magnified all the issues I'd had with Buzz and Tinker, and they weren't very happy with the choices I was making, anyway, and without any sort of conscious decision, on my part or theirs, we cut each other off. It's kind of weird how easily something like that can happen. You wouldn't think it'd be so easy, but as time goes by, it gets too awkward to reconnect."

Woody knew all too well how easily these things could hap-pen. "How much did Kyle tell you about me?"

"Not much. You went bust. You lost pretty much everything."

"I almost went to federal prison."

"He didn't tell me it'd been that bad."

"Was Kyle, I don't know—was he ashamed of me?"

"Ashamed? That's an odd thing to ask. To tell you the truth, I don't think it was that momentous to him. He felt bad for you, but you guys weren't really that tight, were you?"

"We were best friends," Woody said.

"You were? I always thought you were, you know, roommates—not really friends. I didn't know you two kept up after school."

Was that the way Kyle had regarded him? As a mere roommate? Someone to be tolerated, a hanger-on, like a pathetic little brother? Trudy was right—they hadn't really kept up after graduation, living in separate cities, each involved with their own careers and lives—but it made Woody heartsick to think that that was all he had meant to Kyle.

"Are you proud of what you're doing now?" Trudy asked. "Producing movies?"

"Proud?" he asked. "Sure. Why do you ask?"

"They seem so violent, your movies," she said.

"Dalton Lee is going to be directing my new one," he said. She stared at him blankly. He'd forgotten she didn't know who Dalton Lee was.

"When I was little," Trudy said, "I liked you because you wanted so badly to fit in. Maybe it was just status-seeking Twinkie-ism, but it was endearing to me, how hard you tried, because I was feeling the exact same thing. It took me years not to care. You know, Woody, it's such a relief not to care." She scooted up to the observation slot. "We should go down soon," she said, looking through the telescope. "If you could do anything—let's say money wasn't a problem, let's say you didn't care what anyone thought—what would you do?"

"I like what I do."

"Something different, something else. What would you do?"

It was a silly hypothetical exercise, but he decided to indulge her. "I'd own an ice-cream store," he said, grabbing at the first thing that came to mind.

"An ice-cream store! That's great. Why an ice-cream store?"

"The transactions are always brief, no service complications, no returns, and people are always happy in ice-cream stores," Woody said. He was only thinking of it because last night, after taking a chance on a Japanese restaurant on Main Street for dinner, which turned out to be surprisingly decent (Lyndon had recommended a couple of restaurants miles away, but Woody hadn't felt like driving that far, especially with a busted head-light), he had wanted ice cream for dessert, and he and Ling Ling had gone to a little shop called Udderly Licious.

Trudy told him it was time to head down to the nest. After lengthy instructions, she led him to the beach, keeping between the water's edge and the wrack line of seaweed.

"Don't look at me, don't look at me!" Trudy said, carrying a rake over her shoulder. "Look where you're stepping!"

"Okay, okay!" he told her.

As they neared the fence enclosure, AY:BO did precisely what Trudy had predicted. He flew around them, twittering *whit curr, whit curr, terwheeit,* and then performed a broken-wing display, flaring out a wing and dragging it behind him while he limped in the sand, pretending to be injured, offering himself as bait to lure them away from the chicks. This was con-siderably better, Trudy had told Woody, than what they'd had to endure with the roseate terns, who dive-bombed intruders, pecking at their heads and shitting on them. They'd had to wear hats made of plywood.

"Watch where you're going for WY:GO," she said. "She's got to be crouched in a depression somewhere."

Trudy plopped a bright orange baseball cap into the middle of the enclosure and opened up the fence. "All right, you
can come up here now." She knelt down, unzipped her rucksack,
and extracted tools. "This is what we're going to put on the one
that's just hatched. USFWS Size 1B." It was a silver aluminum
band less than the size of a pinkie fingernail, etched with nine
numbers and the inscription CALL 1-800-327-BAND.

"You're not putting four bands on it?"

"Later. It's too weak for adult bracelets."

"How will you catch it?"

"Mist nets. With the bands, we'll be able to trace its movements throughout its entire life span. People will send reports
from all over the world to the Bird Banding Laboratory in
Laurel, Maryland. I'm sure in a few months there'll be a sight-
ing in Baja. That's where they'll starting migrating to when they
fledge. Ready?"

She lifted the baseball hat and revealed the two chicks. It
was breathtaking, how minuscule they were, mere cotton balls.
Trudy gently picked up the one they'd already banded and
placed it in the overturned baseball cap, then cupped the newly
hatched chick in her hand, measured it with a ruler, dropped it
into a pouch, and weighed it with a little spring scale.

"Doesn't this . . . traumatize them?" Woody asked.

"I don't think so, but we can't really know, I suppose."

She was being exceedingly careful handling the bird, and it
seemed to fall into a docile trance. "It's so calm," Woody said as
Trudy clipped the band loosely on the chick's leg.

"This is what's called a bander's grip. When you hold on to
its shoulders like this, they don't struggle, for some reason." She
took a piece of orange plastic and wrapped it over the aluminum band. "There. Hold both your hands out." She deposited
the chick onto his palms.

It weighed nothing. He could barely feel its wings and feet paddling against his skin. "My God," he said, "how do these things survive?" It was truly miraculous.

As they retreated from the nest, Trudy raked over their footprints all the way to the wrack line, and then they walked back to the blind on the wet sand.

"Thank you for letting me do that," Woody told her.

"You're welcome," she said. "You know, you should spend the day with me. You look so much more relaxed already. You need to learn how to relax, Woodrow."

But when they reached the blind, Trudy herself was anything but relaxed, abruptly throwing down the rake and peeling off the straps of her rucksack. "I don't believe it. What the fuck are they *doing* here?"

"Who?"

She tore up the dune and dived through the observation slot. Woody looked down the beach and saw a horse. A couple was riding on it together, bareback. As they got closer, Woody realized they were facing each other, entangled, kissing. The woman was straddling the man, who wore shorts but was shirtless. With each clop, she was bouncing up, and so was her skirt, flipping up to reveal lily-white ass cheeks. Improbably but unmistakably, the couple was fucking on the horse. Then Woody recognized them. They worked in the very ice-cream store, Udderly Licious, he had gone to last night. The black-haired skinny boy and blond pudgy girl behind the counter. They were locked into each other, bumping up and down with the horse, *into* it. Nothing could separate them, nothing could pull them apart. They could not be distracted or denied, they were the planet's only inhabitants. It was stunning to behold, these kids on the horse, riding along the ocean, making love. Incredibly romantic. The sun was high in the sky, waves were crashing onto the shore, the grass and the sage above the dunes were waving in the breeze. Woody breathed in the clean, bountiful air. He could hear the birdsong. So many birds! This place, this vast stretch of windswept dunes, so wild, such a stark, beautiful no-man's-land—it was magnificent. Youth! Life! Love! The propagation of the species!

"Motherfuckers!"

Trudy was running down the dune with a rifle—it looked like an old Winchester from the movies; was everyone an armed vigilante in this town?—and she was snapping forward the lever action to cock and load the gun. "Get the fuck out of here!" she yelled. She raised the rifle and braced the butt against her shoulder, taking dead aim, dispensing with any warning shots.

"Wait!" Woody said. "I know them! They're just kids!"

Trudy fired anyway, but the rifle didn't make the noise he'd expected—just a soft *thunk*. The shot wasn't close, apparently, but she now had the attention of the boy and girl, who turned to them quizzically. Trudy reloaded. "Go away! Go away!" she screamed. She fired another shot.

Frightened, the boy yanked on the reins of the horse and spun it around and hightailed it back down the beach in the direction they'd come, the girl clutching on to him.

"Unbelievable," Trudy muttered. "Can't they read? It's not like we don't have enough signs down there."

"They're just teenagers. They work at the ice-cream shop on Main Street," Woody said. Immediately he regretted telling her this: she could be fanatical enough to pursue further retribution.

"There's a stable south of here. Everyone's been warned time and time again. Last month that guy from the golf course development came through on a white Andalusian, wearing this outrageous getup, like a Trojan soldier. What a pervert. I scared the shit out of him, I'm happy to say."

"You're going to hurt someone with that gun one of these days."

"I doubt it," Trudy said. "This isn't a real rifle. It's a pellet gun."

"Yoo-hoo!"

Grinning, Margot was standing at the top of the dune, an Amazonian warrior goddess, feet planted wide apart, arms spread in triumph, brandishing her fishing pole in one hand and a huge fish in the other.

Trudy trudged up the sand, dropped her pellet gun, and wrapped her arms around Margot, sinking her head against her chest in a prolonged hug. All was forgiven.

.   .   .

THE GIRLS GUTTED AND scaled the trout in the creek, and then cooked it in a large bamboo steamer over a fire with scallions, potatoes, and carrots, serving it with a sauce of Italian dressing and Dijon mustard. The meal was astonishingly good. The outdoors made everything taste infinitely better.

After lunch, Woody changed back into his own clothes, which had dried by then, and they returned to the blind and watched AY:BO and WY:GO lead their two chicks to forage. Then they strolled behind the dunes, climbed the towering sandstone bluffs topped with wind-sculpted Monterey cypress, and navigated down the cliffs to the rocky shale reefs, exposed by the low tide. A sea otter was bobbing offshore in the golden-green kelp beds, and a couple of harbor seals were sunning themselves on the rocks. Yet the real view was in the tidal pools. Woody had never seen anything like it, the bold, iridescent colors, the variety of sea life in the small puddles of water: giant blue and green fluorescent anemones, hermit crabs, sculpins, starfish.

"What's that?" he kept asking.

Red and purple algae, bright green surf grass, pricklebacks, black turban snails. Simply out of this world.

Next they walked up the marsh trail, crossed Highway 1, and hiked through the canyon into the hills. The path was covered on all sides by big-leaf maples, willows, madrones, and alders, and the damp spongy topsoil was spotted with Calypso orchids and banana slugs, the ugliest, most peculiar creatures Woody had ever encountered—huge, neon-yellow, with black spots and a meaty hump on their backs, like mutated snails without shells.

"They're hermaphrodites," Trudy told him.

Farther along, there were newts, salamanders, and red-legged frogs along the creek, and when they reached a meadow of ridgetop chaparral, they had a view of the glittering Pacific.

"Look!" Trudy whispered.

For one glorious, heart-stuttering moment, Woody caught a glimpse of a black-tailed deer bounding into the manzanita.

They kept climbing, surrounded by groves of live oaks and old-growth redwoods towering three hundred feet above their heads. Gray squirrels and raccoons scampered among the brambles, and thrushes and warblers flitted overhead, joined occasionally by yellow-bellied sapsuckers, woodpeckers, and western tanagers.

At last they arrived at the hot springs—a boulder-lined pool ten feet in diameter, next to a cold brook. Trudy and Margot, as casual as could be, stripped off their clothes, tiptoed into the pool, and eased into it.

"Aren't you getting in?" Trudy asked.

Woody had not foreseen that they would be naked in the hot springs. He was self-conscious about exposing his body to begin with, and now that he'd hesitated, he would have to undress as the girls watched.

"Come on," Margot said. "Don't be shy. You know what they say: it's not the size of the boat, but the motion of the ocean."

He took off his clothes.

"Well, ahoy there, matey," Margot said, giggling.

"What's the temperature of that water?" he asked, covering his genitals with his hands.

"It's just right," Trudy said. "Around a hundred degrees."

Exactly as he feared. Bacteria grew best at body temperature: 98.6 degrees. Who knew how many people had been in these springs, what sorts of fungi were growing in there?

"We won't bite," Margot said. "Unless, of course, you want us to."

Into the destructive elements immerse, he remembered Trudy saying. He needed to inject some spontaneity into his life, take some risks, *let it go*. He stepped into the hot springs. The water was warm and had a slightly sulfurous smell. It felt quite pleasant, actually. He took a seat between the girls and leaned back against the rocks.

"How does it feel?" Trudy asked.

"Pretty nice," Woody admitted. It was very relaxing, sitting in the water next to the ferns and the trees and the stream.

Margot leaned forward for Trudy's rucksack, tugged out a joint and a book of matches, and fired it up, using only the tips of her fingers to keep it dry. She sucked in a toke and expelled a long, thick column of blue smoke. Trudy did the same and said to Woody, "Care for a taste?"

He hadn't smoked pot in many years, perhaps since Harvard—unlike Lyndon, who, he knew, was still a habitual pothead. Woody had found a stash of marijuana in his workshop when he'd been rooting through the farm. "Why not?" he said. He took the joint from Trudy. He inhaled deeply, held it for as long as he could, and breathed out.

They sat quietly in the hot springs pool, passing the joint back and forth, listening to the brook and the birds and the insects scraping in the trees. Closing his eyes, Woody breathed in through his nose and smelled dried pine needles and something minty, almost lemony—a very agreeable, lush forest smell. He let his arms and legs float in the water, could feel himself drift.

"Well, lookie here," Margot said. "A wooden dinghy."

"Hm?" he asked, dreamily opening his eyes.

"Your sloop has hoisted its sail." She was glancing down between his legs.

He saw that he had an enormous erection. It was odd. He hadn't been thinking about anything sexual. His mind had been completely blank, granted he had noted earlier the girls' perky, supple breasts.

"It's alive, it's alive!" Margot said.

"Oh, don't laugh," Trudy said. "It's a very natural thing."

Under normal circumstances, Woody would have been terribly embarrassed, but he wasn't at all bothered. "Got wood," he said, chuckling. "Woody Woodpecker Peckerwood. If a woodchuck could chuck wood."

"Well, aye-aye, Captain," Margot said.

"Do you guys know the song 'Sailing'?" he asked. They didn't seem to know it. When had the song come out? The early eighties? They were probably too young to remember. "By Christopher Cross?" He closed his eyes again and hummed out, *"Sailing, na-da-da, sailing."* He wished he could remember the lyrics to the song. He could hear the opening swell of the violins, the plinking repetition of the guitar intro—or had it been a piano? He could vaguely make out Christopher Cross's nasal voice, but not any of the words. *"Sailing,"* Woody sang, "na-da-da, *sailing."*

Something squeezed his penis. "Whatza?" he said, blinking. Trudy had her hand clasped around his penis, which to his surprise was still erect.

"Shhh," she said. "Close your eyes. Lay back. Feel the earth rolling underneath you. Flow with it. Remember the poisoned arrow?"

He did as she told him, shutting his eyes and breathing, staying in the present moment, letting her stroke his penis with one hand, and then two. No, that was Margot's hand, joining Trudy's, together moving with the lightest, gentlest touch. These girls were so nice to do this for him.

Somehow, he knew it wouldn't go any further than this—no pressure about what would happen next, whom he should kiss or touch first, how he would perform in a ménage à trois, although a ménage à trois intrigued him, he'd never been in a ménage à trois, maybe later they'd engage in a ménage à trois in earnest, which he wouldn't mind, he wouldn't mind that at all—but for now, he recognized that this would be an isolated episode, really it was the most natural thing in the world to occur, his penis just happened to be erect, and they decided to give him some relief, like standing behind a friend and giving her shoulders a casual massage, no come-on, as it were, just an amiable, spontaneous act of goodwill.

And that was what it ended up to be. He ejaculated, shuddering and spasming with an intensity he hadn't experienced in years, and they sat in the hot springs for a while longer, and then they dressed and leisurely hiked back down the canyon, enjoying the scenery, smiling at each other, not having to say a word.

What a day. What a lovely, lovely day.

　　　　·　　　　·　　　　·

AT DUSK, HE DROVE BACK to the farm, and found it empty. It seemed that everyone had gone out to dinner without him. He made three plain cheese sandwiches for himself, polished off two cups of yogurt, an entire bag of potato chips, and a full can of cashews, diet be damned, and gulped down two beers and several glasses of tap water. After he finished eating, he was sleepy, but at the same time restless. He had this great vibe, this groovy energy, coursing through him, and wanted it to continue.

He went into Lyndon's workshop and pulled out his brother's stash from a cabinet underneath the bench and packed the bowl in Lyndon's ceramic bong. The pipe wouldn't draw well at first, and Woody thought it might be broken, but then he figured out he needed to keep his thumb over a hole on the back of the bong while he inhaled, filling the chamber, at which point he could suck up its contents. This was strong stuff, much stronger than the joint the girls had had. As he smoked the bowl, he stared at the padlocked barn doors. What was behind there? He examined the big chrome lock, wondering if he could pick it. He straightened out a paper clip and jiggled it around the keyhole, but the tumblers wouldn't budge. He gave up and rolled a couple of joints for later, which, given his inexperience and inebriated state, was difficult to do. He kept ripping the paper or making the joint too loose, not spreading the pot evenly enough, before he was able to lick closed two little fatsos.

He replaced Lyndon's bong and plastic baggie of weed in the cabinet and stumbled outside. It was such a clear night. He looked up and, even with a partial moon out, saw billions of stars—stunning. He never saw stars like this in L.A. He craned his head from side to side, trying to take in the breadth of the firmament, and almost fell over. "Whoa, Nellie," he said aloud, dizzy, and laughed. When had he ever said *Whoa, Nellie?*

He heard a soft thump at his feet. Bob was standing in front of him, a tennis ball on the dirt. "Heya, Bob," Woody said. "What's up?"

Bob picked up the tennis ball with his teeth, dropped it, and looked at Woody expectantly.

"Don't you know you have bad hips? It's not good for you to be playing fetch."

Bob stood his ground, waiting.

"Oh, just once," Woody said. "Just once can't hurt, right?" Perhaps Lyndon was being overly protective—a dog hypochondriac. Who knew better than a dog what his body was capable of? Maybe his hips had healed, regenerated, and he was being deprived of play, of *joy*.

Woody grabbed the ball, reared back, and threw it as far as he could. Bob loped after it, running just fine, running so easily, in fact, that he was able to snatch up the bouncing ball without breaking stride. Yet, instead of returning to Woody, he kept going, jogging away from the house, into the fields.

"Bob, boy-o, where you going? That's not the object of the game, chief. You're supposed to bring it back to me, you stupid dog."

Woody followed Bob into the fields, but each time he thought he was catching up to him, he'd lose him again. Woody walked on the tractor path beside the bluffs, gazing at the ocean, which glinted with silvery reflections. At the end of the path, he spotted Bob again, looking back at him, tennis ball still in his mouth, as if he were intentionally leading him somewhere.

"Where you taking me, Bob?"

Bob trotted inland through a block of Brussels sprouts. Woody strolled after him, and on impulse stripped a sprout off a stalk and munched down on it. It was remarkably good, with an intricate sweetness, like honeysuckle.

He crossed a field of grass, which waved in the light wind— a west wind, he knew, if anyone were to ask. It was a heavenly feeling, wading through the waist-high grass, like fording a river. In the middle of the field, he lay down, letting the grass tickle his face, and stared up at the stars, watching some wispy clouds float across the sky. *"Sailing,"* he sang.

He lay quietly in the grass, and made promises to himself: He was going to become a Buddhist. In the morning, he'd find a bookstore in town and read up on Buddhism. He'd learn to meditate. Maybe he'd try to locate that Tibetan nun Trudy had met and solicit some advice from her. Maybe he'd go to a monastery himself for a while. Lying in the field, he could hear insects burrowing in the dirt. He could feel the grass and the Brussels sprouts growing. He could feel the goodness in him blossoming. He was a good person. Whatever faults he had, he was—deep down—good.

When he got up, he spied Bob cutting into a thicket of bushes and trees. Woody smelled something, like the aroma of mint he'd detected in the redwoods, but far more pungent. As he neared the thicket, the smell grew stronger, almost making his eyes water. What the hell *was* that? He pushed through the bushes and uncovered a handful of marijuana plants, taller than he was, staggering in their robustness.

Edging closer to the plants, he tripped on a root. On closer examination, it wasn't a root. It was an aluminum pipe, which was connected to black hoses laid out to irrigate the cannabis.

"Lyndon," he said. "You son of a bitch."

People never changed. His brother, the old commune hippie, was growing pot. That was what he had locked away in his barn. He was harvesting pot in there, probably cultivating more plants indoors, a hydroponic lab. That explained the sparks Woody had seen the previous night: Lyndon had been welding grow lights overhead, hanging them from the rafters. He was planning to save his farm *by dealing*. What a hypocrite. So much for his condescension, all those years of lording over Woody with his moral superiority. He and Lyndon weren't that different, after all—they were both willing to do whatever was necessary, even if it meant skirting the rules or the law, to get what they wanted. At a different point in his life—say, yesterday—Woody might have worked this discovery to his advantage, used it to hurt Lyndon, but interestingly he didn't feel, at the moment, vengeful. He was, more than anything, amused. Live and let live, he thought.

He lurched through the thicket into a clearing on the other side and lit a joint. It popped and sparked as he inhaled. He had neglected to remove the seeds and stems. Still, it was serviceable, his buzz intensifying with a hallucinogenic patina, allowing him to see more clearly in the dark, as if he had night-vision goggles, everything aglow in green.

He saw Bob, crouching beside some shrubs. He was growling at him.

"Bob, don't be scared. It's me, my friend," Woody said.

Bob snarled louder. He took a step closer and tensed his haunches and hind legs, as if he were about to pounce on him.

On closer examination, it was not Bob. It was the coyote.

CHAPTER 7

SHE PICKED THE SPOT: SUNAKU, A NEW RESTAURANT ON MAIN STREET fashioned after a Japanese *izakaya*, or pub, which served little dishes, tapas-style. A few years back, another Japanese restaurant called the Banzai Pipeline had opened in town, an ambitious project with trendy designs, flashily appointed with water cascading down copper walls. The owner, Duncan Roh, had, by coincidence, retired from the same venture capital firm where Sheila had worked and used to surf Rummy Creek with JuJu, Tank, and Skunk B. The restaurant had failed miserably, closing after just nine months. Duncan and his wife, Lily, had moved to Hawaii, where he was from, and Sheila had bought his house. Rosarita Bay hadn't been ready for upscale sushi then, but it might have fared better now.

Sunaku was packed. Lyndon was wearing his nicest pair of jeans—his black jeans—and a long-sleeved oxford shirt. He felt silly and fatigued and nervous, and he had half a mind to flee. What was he doing, going on a date? At least the other diners were mostly tourists, no locals of any real acquaintance here to witness this debacle. He sidled past the crowd in the foyer; he had had the foresight to make a reservation. The hostess led him to a table for two beside the front window, and Laura Díaz-McClatchey joined him shortly thereafter, wearing a dress for a change, rather than a pantsuit, her hair down and falling freely over her shoulders.

Awkwardly—what was the protocol? kiss on the cheek? a hug?—they shook hands and sat down.

"What happened to you?" Laura asked, looking at the Band-Aid on Lyndon's forehead.

"It's nothing," he told her.

Unfolding her napkin over her lap, she said, "You know, I didn't think you were going to call me. You waited long enough. I thought you were going to stand me up."

"That was rude of me."

"It was," she said. "But I'm willing to forgive you this one transgression. Just one, though."

They occupied themselves debating what to order, reading over the extensive menu, interrupted briefly by the waitress, who pointed out the specials marked on paper strips on the walls. The waitress took their drink orders—hot sake for her, a bottle of Sapporo for him—and then they deliberated over the dishes again, Laura unable to decide, and Lyndon realized that she was as flustered as he was, stalling, for after exhausting all the happy rituals and distractions of the pre-meal, picking out what they wanted to eat and getting their drinks and relating their order to the waitress and toasting and drinking, they stared at each other with sudden vacuous panic, neither having anything to say whatsoever.

Laura fumbled with her tiny sake cup, refilling it. "So you had some sort of accident?" she asked feebly, her usual self-assurance and verve nowhere in evidence, and Lyndon, who had hoped she would carry the conversation for them, hastily poured himself another glass of beer and told her about the destruction at the bar, the rolling, thunderous descent of nautical junk, which mercifully presented her with a conversational thread, thin as it was, and they grabbed at it like a lifeline: she talked about an earthquake when she'd been living in San Francisco, it was evening, and she was in the Sunset District, overlooking Ocean Beach, and swore she saw the sea light up, glowing green, and Lyndon excitedly said it must have been plankton, which becomes phosphorescent when disturbed, and he described kayaking at night in Baja, how the plankton would sparkle in the boat's wake and on the blades of his paddle, the experience of swimming in it, psychedelic fairy lights bursting off his fingers, dolphins zipping underwater, making the depths look like they were being fractured with lightning, and Laura asked what kind of fish he spotted down there, she was an occasional diver, she had gotten certified on a vacation in Bonaire, and he told her about the bluespotted cornetfish, the moray eels, the sergeant majors, the devil rays and king angelfish and porcupine puffers, and of course the gray whales, migrating five thousand miles from the Bering Sea to the Sea of Cortés, and she remarked how surprised she'd been, on a whale watch once, to learn that whales had terrible breath, smelling like bay mud from eating all that shrimp, but they were so majestic and huge, the way they arced to the surface and slipped beneath the water, coming up for three breaths and then, fluking their tails, diving deep for ten minutes, and Lyndon asked if she'd heard about the humpback whale that had washed ashore and the ensuing fiasco, and of course she had, who hadn't, which gave Lyndon and Laura, despite their guilt over laughing about the death and undignified disposition of an endangered species, a good, hearty chortle, except then, as their laughter faded, they realized, just as they had been lulled into thinking that things were going well, just as they were beginning to relax, that they had run out of things to say, the balls dropping, the roof deflating, the tanks wheezing into the most dreaded of all moments during a first date, dead air—good God, why did people go on dates? why would anyone willingly subject themselves to this type of torture?—when, in desperation, people were liable to resort to anything—where was their *food*, goddammit?—uttering something they didn't intend to, something ill-advised, the last thing they planned to say, simply to keep the conversation going, keep the evening alive—he was overboard, sharks afoot—which was what Lyndon did, blurting out to Laura, "I have something I need to confess to you."

"What?" she asked.

And now, even though he knew it was a mistake, he couldn't retreat, he couldn't think of anything else to confess. "I told you I'm divorced. The truth is, I've never been married."

"Why would you lie about that?"

Lyndon squirmed in his chair. Where was their food? If the restaurant was tapas-style, weren't the first dishes supposed to come out right away? "It's easier sometimes to just say I'm divorced," he told her, "instead of having to explain why I've never been married."

"Why is it you've never been married?"

"You really want an answer to that?"

"You're not ugly—you're rather handsome, in fact," Laura said. "I bet you were quite hot in your twenties and thirties. You're no dummy. Granted, you're a farmer-slash-welder-slash-ex-bartender, but you're no hick. The verdict's still out on your sense of humor, but you have your charms nonetheless. I'm sure you've had plenty of women falling for you. So why haven't you fallen for one of them? Is it because you're looking for perfection? Or is it that you're afraid it'll be expected of you?"

"That's too simplistic."

"Is it?"

Was it that simple? He didn't know, really. Almost all of human behavior, he believed, could be reduced to one thing: people were terrified of being alone. He didn't want to be alone, but it was getting harder for him, each year, to imagine being with someone, living with someone, revealing himself—all of his quirks and neuroses and secrets, his little pot habit, for example, and what he was hiding in his barn. The thing was, he was generally okay with being alone. He liked his privacy. He liked his routines, his freedom, his unaccountability, and he didn't really want to change. He had said to Sheila once that he thought the perfect marriage would be one in which husband and wife kept not just separate rooms, but separate houses. Why did they necessarily have to live together? Why did they have to decide which property to dissolve and which to share? (Before The Centurion Group had appeared, Sheila had said she would be willing to move to Lyndon's farm, but his house would need a complete teardown, no doubt to be replaced with a swanky pre-fab McMansion of her choosing.) The true comfort of a relationship, Lyndon had said, came from being able to rely on each other when needed—for emotional support, for companionship, for sex, for a bulwark against the howling existential abyss. It didn't come from being together so much you drove each other to lunacy and thoughts of grievous bodily harm. It didn't come from learning each other's every peccadillo, from bumping into all the opposing tendencies and noisy intrusions of everyday conjugal life. Ubiquity was not constancy. Make no mistake, he'd said, he was willing to "commit" to her, but he could be there for Sheila without always being *with* her.

Sheila didn't see the wisdom in such an arrangement. "You don't want a wife," she had said. "You want a fuck buddy."

It mystified Lyndon why she assumed marriage and/or cohab-

itation would improve matters. He and Sheila were so different. They fought all the time. Sometimes he wondered why she
wanted to be with him at all. Yet he had another theory about
relationships that explained their attraction, explained almost
every woebegone impulse vis-à-vis men and women, which
was that people were drawn to each other because of comple-
mentary pathologies. Everyone had a sickness—a discontent-
ment, an absence—and, subconsciously, couples nourished one
another's sicknesses. Without them, the relationships would fail.
Lyndon and Sheila's arguments, their frustrations and impasses
and maddening discords, were likely the entire basis for their
affinity. What would happen if they changed that dynamic?
Would they even be attracted to each other anymore?

"I have a confession to make of my own," Laura Díaz-
McClatchey said.

"You do?" Lyndon asked. He ran through several incarnations
with which this confession might present itself—all salacious.

But he had to wait. Their food finally came, two waitresses
bringing out all of their backed-up orders at once, the grilled
asparagus and eggplant, yakitori, the duck breast marinated in
sake, tempura, braised short ribs with daikon, fried softshell
crabs, soba salad, gyoza, marinated mackerel, steamed egg cus-
tard, ohitashi, and potato croquettes. There wasn't enough room
on the table for everything, the rims of plates stacked on top
of one another. Looking at the spread in totality, they realized
they'd ordered way too much food. Still, they dug in, welcom-
ing the respite.

They ate and ate, drank more beer and sake, and skipped
from one inconsequential subject to another in a free-flowing
manner, loose enough now that Lyndon had nearly forgotten
about her confession until she said, "So, the thing I wanted to
tell you . . ."

"Let me guess: you're an ex-con?" he joked. A bad joke. He was bad at jokes.

"What?"

"You said you did a bad thing before."

"Oh," she said. "No, no time in the big house, but another type of purgatory. This is related to what I want to tell you." She hesitated, playing with her chopsticks.

"Don't stop now," he said. "You have my undivided attention."

She laid the chopsticks down on the table, squeezed them together so they were parallel, and looked up at Lyndon. "I know who you are," she said.

"What do you mean?"

"I know you were Lyndon Song the sculptor."

Lyndon grimaced. Things had been going so nicely. He had actually begun to enjoy himself, and he'd been entertaining the possibility that something might happen with Laura Díaz-McClatchey, that he might indeed move on. "What did you do, Google me?" he asked testily. There really was too much information on the Internet. He had always expected Sheila or Hana to do a search on him and discover the truth about his artistic career, at which point he would have been willing to divulge all the sordid details, but they never had.

"As a matter of fact, I did," Laura said, "but only to refresh my memory. You see, I'm a curator. Or, rather, I *was* a curator, at MoCA in San Francisco." She leaned across the table and, faux-confidentially, whispered, "I got fired earlier this year."

"Why were you fired?"

"It's a long, convoluted story," she said, "uninteresting to anyone but me."

"The short version."

"All righty," Laura said. "I was having an affair with a dealer, which was really no big deal, everyone in the art world, as you know, sleeps with everyone else. But I acquired some of his artists' works at maybe a tad higher than market price, which, again, was more a failure of judgment than anything else, maybe a tiny conflict of interest, not a huge amount of money, though. But what I didn't know was that my boss at MoCA, the executive director, with whom I'd never seen eye to eye on the collections, had also had an affair with said dealer not too long ago, and he was still pissed about the way it'd ended, and he saw this as a great opportunity to exact his revenge on the dealer and get rid of me at the same time, so he talked the board into letting me go. You see, nothing very dramatic. But it's not so easy to get hired by another museum when you have the taint of impropriety on you."

"So that's why you're now giving massages in Rosarita Bay."

"Yes."

"Were you in love with him?" Lyndon asked.

"Said dealer? Oh, I don't know. I thought I was."

"What about him? Did he love you?"

"Or was he just using me? I keep asking myself the same thing, though I shouldn't be so naïve."

"You're no longer involved."

"It's funny how that's worked out, now that you mention it, how he hasn't called since I moved down here."

"I'm sorry."

She wagged her head as if to say no matter, but obviously it did. "What about you?" she asked. "Why did you leave New York? Why did you quit?"

He sighed. "Long, convoluted story, uninteresting to everyone, including me."

"You were a *star*," Laura said. "The first Asian American to be included in the Whitney Biennial. *Arts in America* called you the discovery of the decade. You weren't even thirty!"

"Ancient history," Lyndon said.

"That's what I mean. You walked away at the height of your fame. You just vanished, and now you're barely a footnote in art history texts. You were on your way to becoming a major figure in late-twentieth-century art. Why in the world did you give that up?"

He didn't want to talk about it. He hadn't, in fact, ever talked about it since coming to Rosarita Bay, and now he felt he'd lost the capacity to explain it, the reasons ill-defined and hazy to him. An unexamined life was a life easily forgotten. Everything in New York had happened within the space of four years, from his arrival to his departure, from bleak obscurity to head-of-the-line celebrity. Blink, and it was gone, another life, or someone else's life, a pothead's woozy recollections that could be, in fact, erroneous, an elaborate web of synaptic constructs that was largely fabricated.

He had gotten jobs as a bartender and as a welder in a machine shop and rented a loft on the border of Chinatown and the Lower East Side, no running hot water, a single space heater that was so anemic, he had to wear a coat and half-fingered gloves while he worked during the winter. The East Village was the hot spot then, Jeff Koons and Keith Haring and Jean-Michel Basquiat, everything about spontaneity, post-abstract abstraction in the form of performance art, video art, graffiti art, appropriation art, street art. Homespun, raw, wild, often silly, they showed their work in makeshift storefront galleries, not caring about buyers or portfolios or reviews, reveling in the pure joy of creation. Was it good art? Maybe, maybe not, but who gave a shit? They just went with it, the more outrageous and absurd the better.

It lasted about five minutes. If there was money to be made, the high-profile SoHo galleries were willing to ditch the Neo-

Expressionists of the day and poach on the East Village. And there was plenty of money to go around. Auctions were fetching record prices. Wall Street was booming, and all those profits from leveraged buyouts had to go somewhere.

At first, Lyndon was welding together pieces from scraps he'd found in junkyards or pilfered from construction sites: manhole covers, rebar, pipes, metal grates, industrial fans, stadium lights, exhaust vents. He'd amass the sculptures on the floor and walk around them, and while he thought the essential structure was almost there, the scale and perspective wouldn't feel right. He wanted to get beyond the junk aesthetic and animate his sculptures, disorient them. He puzzled over it for months, dissatisfied, and then got an idea. He remembered the Korean screens his parents had at home, folding panels made of rice paper and silk layered over wood latticework, depicting a continuous landscape of lotus blossoms, fish, and birds. He made frames of steel and iron, cut his sculptures apart, positioned them onto the frames, and hung them upright as wall reliefs, sectioned into polyptychs. Then he sandblasted and oxidized the surfaces with hydrochloric acid to get a rich texture of rust, with hues of reds, browns, orange, and black. Afterward, he applied a hot patina, heating the metal with a torch, spraying on a nitrate solution, brushing on a thick coat of wax while the metal was still warm, and putting on a clear protective coating to deepen the subtle shades of blues and greens.

This is it, this is it, he thought. He had found his medium, his process. He stayed in his loft for days at a time, not sleeping, forgetting to eat, his clothes dotted with burn holes, his head swimming from the fumes. All he wanted to do was work.

In due course, he was plucked up by Alvin Zukof, a SoHo gallery owner who was a kingmaker. First a group show, and then a solo show, and then Lyndon had exhibitions in Zurich, London, Tokyo, Venice, and São Paulo.

He was mortified by his quick ascension. He liked that his work was being recognized, and he sort of liked the money—it was ludicrous, how much money he was making—and for a while he liked the women, but he hadn't anticipated that he would have to *talk* to people so much, that he would have to attend openings and glad-hand buyers and schmooze critics, that he'd have to go to parties and clubs and act interested in other people's lives, that everything he said and did or didn't say or do would be noted and disseminated and almost always misinterpreted and politicized, for there was, right from the start, a perplexing tenor to the reception of his work.

He didn't title any of his sculptures, but Alvin Zukof insisted on having titles. "It's boring, as well as impractical, to title everything *Untitled*!" he said. Not much older than Lyndon, Alvin was an heir to a Pittsburgh steel magnate. He was a bit of a dandy—custom-tailored hipster suits with narrow lapels and trousers, always accented with a silk breast-pocket kerchief—and he liked to wear his hair long, swept back regally from his veiny temples. He had a fondness for cocaine and Dom Pérignon and young men, usually in combination. An intellectual jokester, with degrees in physics and literary theory from Yale, he convinced Lyndon to let him devise the titles of the sculptures for him—pseudo-postmodern, ironic nonsense titles: *Toward a Generic Theory of Small-World Estimation. Contemporary Uses in Finite Paramimetic Infirmity. Endoplasmic Necrophagia in Omniphallic Cacophony.* The exhibition catalogues adopted the same mock-serious tone, Alvin composing pretentious, incomprehensible treatises about spatial dissonance, dystopian visions, entropic associations, and Bataille's concept of the *informe*, about subverting symbols of technology in order to probe the nature of seeing and perception and deliver a scathing indictment of the military-industrial complex.

Yet, in their reviews, art critics latched on to an entirely different subtext, one that baffled Lyndon. With a wall relief he had crisscrossed with I-beams and barbed wire, they saw a reference to hedgehogs—tank obstacles—similar to those in the DMZ between North and South Korea, and talked about connotations of divided homelands and crossing borders. With a wall relief incorporating an aluminum boat he'd dissected into strips, thin as spaghetti, they saw a reference to Marco Polo's voyage to the Orient and his fallacious claim to have introduced noodles to the Chinese, and talked about issues of migration and cultural appropriation. With a wall relief he'd studded with thousands of intricate projections of rods and wires, like twisted tree branches, they saw a reference to elk antlers and the Korean custom of ingesting powdered antlers as an aphrodisiac, and talked about stereotypes that belittled the virility of Asian men.

And the interviews—they kept asking Lyndon about ethnicity and identity, about assimilation and diaspora, about racism and post-colonialism. Apparently he was not an artist. He was an Asian-American artist. Nearly every article had some sort of cutesy analogy to chopsticks or kimchi or the melting pot.

People—journalists, collectors, patrons—felt they had license to ask Lyndon any question about his personal life, and they were usually the most inane, ignorant questions.

"How'd you learn to speak English so well?" they would ask.

"Well, actually, you know, I was born and raised in California."

"You seem so Americanized."

"Well, actually, you know, that's probably because I'm an American."

As condescending and stupid and racist as these people were, Lyndon was assiduously polite and patient with them. He didn't reveal that he was annoyed or hurt or angry. He pretended to be grateful. Grateful for the attention. And, as a result, he felt like a whore.

A new series of sculptures proved to be even more problematic. These wall reliefs were of the same scale as the previous work, finished with the same process, but instead of jutting projections of steel or found objects, they presented mashed-together, warped prisms and polyhedrons made from wire mesh—a quasi-extension of Cubist constructivism. As geometrical as they were, the sculptures were unsettling for their asymmetry, the angles and planes somehow distorted and surreal, the vertices seeming to move as you surveyed them, the perception of depth eerily unfixed. The material with which they were made appeared dimensionally unstable, the permeability of the wire mesh contributing to a shimmering spatial fragility. Examined closer, the rusty, patinaed mesh ended up to be a pointillistic trick. The wire mesh wasn't wire mesh. It was, actually, a linkage of thousands of tiny ideograms that looked like Chinese characters, each one delicately bent by hand with scroll benders and homemade jigs and then welded together. The catch—and the root of the subsequent controversy—was that Lyndon did not know Chinese, so he had made the characters up. They looked authentic, but they were meaningless.

The critics saw references to origami and takeout boxes and Mao's Cultural Revolution, and talked about the inutility of culture, the mutability of language, the disarticulation of syntax, the metaphysical cages of silence and paradox, the unraveling and erasure of signifiers, the ossification of repressive symbology.

This time, though, there was an additional source of criticism, quite vociferous, and it came from other Asian Americans. They accused Lyndon of exploiting his ethnicity, of being a phony, of falsely exoticizing his work in order to cash in. At the same time, somewhat contradictorily, they condemned him for not challenging the media's narrow categorization of his sculptures and life as "Asian American," for willingly ghettoizing himself.

"How's it feel to be the Uncle Tong of the art world?" he was asked.

He started hearing things over the grapevine, things other artists—white artists—were saying, the consensus being that his accomplishments were directly and solely attributable to multiculturalism, the largesse of political correctness. He was, they were saying, merely the color of the month.

And then everyone really turned against him. For his next show, he abandoned the wall reliefs and hung his sculptures from the ceiling with filaments like kinetic mobiles, a phantasmagoria of birds and fish and crustaceans hovering in the air, appearing to be flying or swimming by, all the animals—constructed with fine interweaved strands of bent wire—bulbous and garish-looking, as if mutated. The animals were an abstract *écorché*, horrifying, really, his usual acid treatment making the animals look like they had been skinned and eviscerated, tendons and muscles exposed, yet they were, at least to some people, also unexpectedly beautiful. Lyndon had taken a vacation to Belize and gone kayaking for the first time, and he had been fascinated by the laughing gulls and red-footed boobies as he'd paddled into mangrove coves, by the fish bending and flicking with the current, the bright green and pink coral and sea grass and sponges and turtles he'd glimpsed through the clear blue water.

Alvin, undeterred in his penchant for pedantic wisecracking, named the new show "Certain Epistemological Issues of Bestial Perversion," and in the catalogue quoted Foucault's introduction to *The Order of Things*, in which Foucault described how all of his familiar landmarks of thought, "all the ordered surfaces and all the planes with which we are accustomed to tame the wild profusion of existing things" and distinguish "between

the Same and the Other," had been annihilated when reading about Borges's discovery of an ancient method of taxon-
omy in a Chinese encyclopedia called the *Celestial Emporium of
Benevolent Knowledge*, which delineated fourteen different types
of animals:

1. those belonging to the Emperor,
2. embalmed ones,
3. those that are trained,
4. suckling pigs,
5. mermaids,
6. fabulous ones,
7. stray dogs,
8. those included in the present classification,
9. those that tremble as if they are mad,
10. innumerable ones,
11. those drawn with a very fine camelhair brush,
12. et cetera,
13. those that have just broken a flower vase,
14. those that from a long way off look like flies.

The critics were not amused. They dismissed the sculptures as kitsch. They had the substance of tchotchkes, they said,
if that. They were unmitigated trash. They were equivalent
to taxidermy, belonging in the American Museum of Natural
History (which happened to be Lyndon's favorite museum in
New York).

He got shellacked by the Asian-American pundits as well,
this time for *not* including any discernible Asian references in the
mobiles, regardless of what the catalogue was trying to appropriate. They rebuked him for trying to deny his cultural heritage
and whitewashing himself. For being, in short, a Twinkie.

It was a disaster, the show, and Lyndon could sense the disappointment in the collectors who had heretofore been devoted to him, his peers, his friends. "I saw your show," they'd say when he ran into them on the street or in a store, and Lyndon would wait inquiringly. "It's good," they'd say tersely, eschewing further comment, and it'd be clear they thought nothing of the sort. They were *embarrassed* for him. They were thinking: the old stuff was better; he'd lost it; he was a has-been.

Alvin tried to be encouraging. "Listen," he said, "it's all a wink and a nod, and if they're too dense to get the joke, fuck 'em!"

But that was the troubling part. It *hadn't* been a joke, and Lyndon began to doubt himself. Sometimes he fumed about the stupidity of these critics, who were, let's face it, all failed artists themselves, bitter they couldn't cut it as painters or sculptors or whatever, and now they were consumed with schadenfreude, and they couldn't write worth a damn, anyway, their reviews hackneyed and facile. But more often than not, Lyndon wondered if maybe they were right. Maybe he was a fraud. Maybe he didn't have any talent.

Every casual remark became telling. If someone said she really loved his wall reliefs, he assumed she hated the mobiles. If someone asked why he had made a certain choice in his work, he assumed it was a veiled dig that it had been the wrong choice. If someone said Lyndon was a genius, he assumed he was being ridiculed.

Whenever another artist got a coveted exhibition or a good review or an award or grant, he was rent with jealousy. He wished his friends ill will. He thought everyone detested him, and why shouldn't they, he was prickling with so much self-loathing. Everything about the city began to irritate him: it was so crowded and *hostile*, no one had any manners, all the noise, the traffic, buses screeching, music blaring, the endless construction projects, the honking and sirens, always there were people yelling, the fucking homeless and crazies, every sound making him jolt. He never went out anymore. He had occasional thoughts of suicide.

He wanted to stop being judged. He wanted to stop being expected to come up with something new and brilliant every year. He wanted to stop having to measure up to his early success. He wanted to stop being so afraid—of failure, of not being respected or liked, of performing badly, of making a fool of himself. He wanted it all to stop. It'd be such a relief to stop, he thought, to disappear, go someplace where no one knew him, do something simple and unambitious for a living.

Alvin gave him an escape. He had a client who was building a house in Sagaponack, and he intended to install one of Lyndon's wall reliefs in his living room. Except the wall relief didn't quite fit the proportions of the house, a little too large for it. The client asked Alvin to ask Lyndon if he could purchase just three panels of the sculpture rather than all four.

"You think this is *decoration*?" Lyndon asked. He told Alvin he had always been skeptical about his qualifications as a dealer, and now he knew those reservations had been warranted. He told him he knew nothing about art, and called him a charlatan, a huckster. He told him he was no better than a furniture salesman, just looking to make a quick buck, but money didn't buy integrity, and said he no longer represented him.

Lyndon left New York, and on his way home to Watsonville from San Francisco, he pulled off Highway 1 into Rosarita Bay for coffee. He saw a real estate circular about the farm for sale at a bargain price—it was a time when family farms were routinely being foreclosed. On a whim, he took a look and bought it, attracted mostly by the enormous gambrel barn with its white pine siding, cedar shingles, and copper flashing.

For a couple of years, there were a few letters from dealers and curators, inquiring about representation and shows and exhibitions, all of which he never answered, tossing them into the trash, and then the letters abruptly stopped coming. It was both comforting and depressing to realize that he could drop out as he had and, in the end, not really be missed.

A footnote in art history, Laura Díaz-McClatchey had said. The waitresses cleared the plates from the table and gave them cups of hot green tea.

Why had he quit? Laura wanted to know. What could he tell her? That he had despised the person that he'd become? That he'd turned into a complete raving, megalomaniacal asshole?

"It wasn't anything dramatic," he said to her.

"You don't want to talk about it."

"No."

"You don't like me anymore," Laura said. "I'm being a snoop and a nudge. I've offended you, and now you won't want to get ice cream with me for dessert."

"That ice cream is pretty fabulous," he said. He turned up his palm—a gesture of concession. "I just got tired of the scene. It would have been nice if the work had been its own reward, and you could somehow remove ego from the equation. It would've been nice if you could just make things, follow the original impulse into infinite variations, and not have to finish them for the sake of a show. But that wasn't the case. I got fed up with it. I wanted a normal life. An average life."

On the way to the restaurant tonight, after parking his pickup far down Main Street, several blocks already closed off for the stages and booths for tomorrow's festival, Lyndon had walked down the sidewalk and found another paper airplane, stuck in a bush. Folded on the same lined school paper was the message: "The Third Noble Truth is that the cessation of suffering is attainable. With you around, I DON'T THINK SO." From his earlier research on the Internet, Lyndon knew that the Buddha had said suffering could be ended by acquiring dispassion—freeing yourself from attachment, getting beyond the self—and that was precisely what Lyndon had been unable to do as an artist. He'd been unable to let it—let anything—go.

"You don't regret it, leaving when you did?" Laura asked.

"No. I don't think about it all that much, if you want to know the truth."

"What about your obligations as an artist?"

"My obligations?"

"What you were doing was important to a lot of people."

"It wasn't any great loss to mankind when I stopped making art."

"You stopped sculpting entirely?" she asked.

"Yes."

"I find that hard to believe."

"Why?"

"Let me ask you, what went through your head as you started a sculpture? What did you see?"

"I didn't see anything." These sorts of discussions were invariably difficult for him. People expected him to reveal something profound, but the reality was always much more prosaic—or simply impossible to articulate. "I'd just be conscious of a . . . I don't know how to explain it." He thought of the sensation that had run through his body after Laura had given him the massage. "This energy," he told her, not believing the words were coming from his mouth. "I'd start a piece, and I'd just see it flowing in front of me, like it wasn't solid matter anymore, but viscous, with a life of its own."

She nodded. "Like *ki*, Japanese for *chi*," she said. "That ability, that gift, it doesn't just disappear. You can't just turn it off with a switch."

"Well, apparently I did."

He paid the check. It was a rather hefty check. He understood this protocol of dating, though, regardless of the date's outcome (not entirely pleasant, by his estimation, but perhaps salvageable)—that she would offer to split the bill, and he should say thank you, but refuse—and while the waitress took away his credit card, Laura excused herself to go to the bathroom, after which they planned to go to Udderly Licious for dessert.

At the table, Lyndon was staring out the window when he saw Sheila walking by. He sucked in his breath, trying to summon invisibility, as if a large predatory beast were slinking past him. She kept going, head down, preoccupied with jotting a note down on a clipboard—she must have been overseeing the preparations down the street for the festival. Lyndon breathed out, heart hammering, and gulped from his glass of water, only to have Sheila backtrack to the window and peer in at Lyndon.

"What are you doing here?" she asked after she came into the restaurant. She glanced at the empty chair across from Lyndon. "Are you on a date?"

He didn't know what to say. "It's not really a date."

"What is it, then?"

"It's just a dinner. A friendly dinner."

"With your masseuse?" she asked.

"Sheila, it was a spontaneous thing. I didn't really—"

"Did you tell Hana she could go to Berklee?"

"Absolutely not. I said she should go to Stanford first and then see how she feels."

"You have some nerve," Sheila said. "God knows why, but

she listens to you, and now she has it in her head she'll transfer out in the spring. You have no right, Lyndon. This songwriting thing will be her ruin. It'll break her heart. How could you do this to her? To me?"

"She's an adult, Sheila."

"She's seventeen."

"It's not a matter of growing out of it."

"You mean she has to get it out of her system, like you did? Like Steven? Fall flat on her face and be humiliated? Then she can hole away on a pathetic little farm with no prospects of solvency? You've never been a parent. You don't know what it is to want to protect your child from pain. Thanks for telling me, by the way, that your brother's visiting you. I thought you no longer spoke to him."

"It wasn't my idea for him to come," he said. "He sort of foisted it upon me."

"Were you going to introduce me to him?"

"You know, I'm confused, Sheila. Didn't you tell me you didn't want to see me anymore? I think, actually, you were very explicit about that. Am I still obliged to tell you everything?"

"Like you ever did," she said.

"Are you going on a date with Ed Kitchell?" Lyndon asked.

She looked at him, slack-jawed. "What did you say? Who told you that?"

"Are you?"

"That's none of your business."

"I think it is. I think it's very much my business. Don't do it. Don't go out with him."

"Why not?" she asked.

"He's a *dick*, Sheila," he told her. "He's only trying to get to me through you."

"That would be the only reason he would want to ask me out?"

"Are you really going to see him?"

"Maybe it's just a friendly dinner, a spontaneous little happenstance."

By happenstance, Laura returned to the table from the bathroom then, and Sheila turned to her, and then turned to Lyndon, the three of them held in an abeyance of shared terror for a moment, and then Sheila picked up Lyndon's glass of water, pitched its contents into his face, and left the restaurant.

Lyndon was no longer in the mood for ice cream. "Could we just call it a night?" he said to Laura.

But to his embarrassment, his credit card was declined, and he had to give the waitress another one, and he and Laura had to sit there for a while, water dripping off his head, before they could depart, watched by everyone in the restaurant.

"I guess that could have gone better," Laura said on the sidewalk.

They exchanged quick goodnights and went their separate ways.

Could this weekend, Lyndon thought, get any worse? As he approached his pickup, it looked a little funny to him, something off about it. He slowly grasped that it was parked lower to the ground than it should have been, and when he bent down for a closer look, he saw that his tires, all four of them, were completely flat. There was also something on his windshield— a parking ticket. He had misread the hours on the posted signs restricting access for the festival. The officer of record who had issued the ticket was Lieutenant Steven Lemke.

Laura, driving by, spotted Lyndon sitting on the curb and offered him a ride home. He didn't have much choice. All the service stations in town were closed, and when he'd called the auto club from the pay phone on the corner, they'd said it would take over an hour to get a tow truck over the hill.

"That woman is a menace," Laura said as she swung onto Highway 1. "You ought to get a restraining order."

"That might be difficult," he said.

"Why?"

"She's kind of connected, politically, in this town."

"I'd be careful if I were you," she said. "She might try to hurt you."

"She's not that crazy," Lyndon told her.

"Look what she did to your tires."

She had a point. Instead of a truss nail, Sheila had cut his tires this time with a knife, a hunting knife with a very sharp clipped blade, maybe a bowie, by the looks of it.

They didn't say much else on the drive to the farm, all pretenses of a romantic future between them now evaporated. As they bumped up the dirt road to the house, Laura gazed at his barn. "Is that your studio?" she asked.

"The shed's my welding workshop," Lyndon said. "The rest is for tractors."

A sound—like a shotgun blast—cracked the air, and Laura flinched. "What was that?" she asked.

Near the bluff, Ling Ling was laughing raucously. Standing with JuJu, she was holding what looked like a white bazooka over her shoulder.

"Spud gun," Lyndon said.

"What?" Laura asked.

He and JuJu had built the potato cannon a few months ago, using pipe cement, duct tape, and PVC for the five-foot barrel and combustion chamber, into which they'd embedded a barbeque spark igniter.

From Laura's car, they watched JuJu fold over a green glow stick to activate it, stuff it into a potato, and jam it down the barrel of the spud gun with a broomstick. He unscrewed the end cap from the combustion chamber, sprayed Right Guard deodorant (the best fuel vapor, they'd found) into it, screwed the cap back on, and gave the cannon back to Ling Ling, who lifted it onto her shoulder and aimed it toward the ocean.

"Fire in the hole, little fishies!" JuJu called out.

"Fire in the hole!" Ling Ling yelled. "Spuds away!" She pressed the igniter, and flames flashed out of the barrel, the recoil making her tip back. The potato hurled out into the night sky, arcing almost two hundred yards, the glow stick wobbling fluorescently like an errant tracer bullet before it disappeared into the water. Ling Ling and JuJu whooped and high-fived. The spud cannon had a range of a quarter of a mile. The day before, Lyndon had fired a potato at The Centurion Group's helicopter, which Ed Kitchell had had the nerve to steer down for a flyby, and Lyndon had nearly hit him.

"Friends of yours?" Laura asked.

"In a manner of speaking."

"Can I see your barn?"

"There's nothing to see."

"You're still making art in there, aren't you?"

"No," Lyndon said.

"What you told me before," Laura said, "that you just want to be average, that's bullshit. That's a luxury of choice only artists who've been successful can afford, and it's insulting to those of us who haven't."

"You're an artist?"

"I was. A painter. I was awful. A teacher convinced me early on I didn't have what it takes. It killed me to hear that from her, it really did, but now I'm grateful to her. It saved me a lot of unhappiness, years I would've wasted when I could have found something else to do to make a contribution, like being a curator. So quitting like you did, with all the talent you had, with everything you could've still accomplished, especially for artists of color? I don't care what the circumstances were. So what if it was hard? So what if you were miserable? So what if you got a few bad reviews and your dealer was an idiot? So what if you were saddled with identity politics? So what if the art world was pretentious and filled with mean-spirited, backstabbing jackasses? Quitting was a betrayal. It was selfish. It was an act of cowardice."

Lyndon opened the door and started to get out of the car, angry. Laura Díaz-McClatchey knew nothing about art. No wonder she had failed as a curator. She had never been a real player. Her drab clothes were the first clue. She would never be anything more than small-time.

But then he turned back to her and asked, "How do you know she was right?"

"Who?"

"Your teacher. How do you know she was right about you? Maybe she was wrong. Maybe you should have kept painting."

"My stuff was crap. I kept making this series with a little girl in a pinafore and patent leather shoes. I don't know why, but I was obsessed with her. I always had her flying, and I gave her two heads. They were ghastly."

"You might have gotten better," Lyndon said.

"I wasn't gifted."

"You could have still worked at it. Who knows what might have happened?"

She shook her head. "I wasn't ever going to be good."

"What makes you so sure?"

"I didn't want it enough."

"That's my point," Lyndon said. "You have to want it. It's pointless unless you want it."

.   .   .

AT ONE-THIRTY in the morning, he shook awake JuJu, who was curled up in bed with Ling Ling. "Time to monkey around," Lyndon whispered to him.

JuJu smiled and said, half-lidded, "*Semper fi*, dude."

In Lyndon's workshop, they prepared for the nighttime assault, applying camouflage on their faces and toking up. "We need to figure out a plan," Lyndon said.

JuJu pulled out a list from his pocket that itemized all the supplies needed for each room. "I've got everything packed up in the trunk of my car."

"How long have you been working on this?" Lyndon asked.

JuJu sucked up the smoke in the bong and eked out, holding his breath, "Days."

"Seen Woody tonight?" Lyndon asked.

"Nope."

"His car's in the driveway, but he's not in his room," Lyndon said.

All weekend, he had been so anxious about Woody meddling in his affairs, yet Lyndon had hardly seen his brother during his stay on his farm, and now, despite himself, he was getting a little worried about him. Woody had left the house in the morning while they were all still asleep, presumably had returned in his SUV this evening while they were out to dinner, and had ransacked Lyndon's kitchen, leaving a mess, empty cups of yogurt and cans of beer and potato chips and bread crumbs lying on the counters. But that had been hours ago. Where could he be?

"Someone might've picked him up, given him a ride," JuJu said. "Maybe he's on a date. Maybe he got lucky."

Lyndon repacked the bowl in the bong. "With who?"

"I don't know, maybe he met someone. Stranger things have been happening," JuJu said. "Lyndey, has everything felt weird to you lately? I have this overriding sense of coincidence, of synchronicity, all of a sudden—a vortical, Yoyodynean, *realismo mágico* imbrication of fates. Something's shifted in the cosmos, and everything just feels wondrous and right and kind of amazing. You grooving on that, too?"

"No." He didn't see convergence; he saw chaos, anarchy, his carefully constructed world flying apart.

"Struck out on your date, huh?"

"Shut up, JuJu."

"You came home pretty early. Things didn't click with her?"

"It was just a friendly dinner."

"Sorry, dude, that's cold. I hate when women just want to be friends. It goes against every evolutionary instinct known to man to be just friends with a woman. What's the point of being friends?"

They walked over to the shed and stowed their paddles, PFD vests, and Ziploc bags of monkeywrenching ordnances inside their kayaks, then—with JuJu at the bow and Lyndon at the stern—they took a grab loop in each hand and carried the two boats into the fields, toward a path down the bluff where they could put in on the beach. With JuJu's prosthetic foot and Lyndon's knee brace, they were both limping on the dirt, but they somehow managed to hobble in time.

It was a calm night. No wind, little swell, a few scattered clouds, a waning crescent moon, enough for them to see but not enough for them to be seen. They'd have a quiet, easy little paddle, no worries. They were both expert kayakers and weren't going far, but it was always a little dicey taking the boats out on the ocean at night, particularly when they were a tad high, and, understandably, JuJu still got spooked out there, imagining what was lurking underneath. Last year, he had thought something had bumped his kayak while they were paddling through a kelp bed. He'd become hysterical and, to Lyndon's bewilderment, had pulled out a *revolver* from beneath his PFD—some cheap Saturday night special he'd bought on the street in the Tenderloin, expressly for this contingency—and begun firing indiscriminately into the water. He'd let go of his paddle and, swiveling in his cockpit, lost his balance and capsized his kayak. Without his paddle, he couldn't Eskimo roll, so Lyndon kept waiting for JuJu to pop off his spray skirt and do a wet exit, not a big deal, nothing to panic over, but seconds passed, and he didn't appear. Lyndon dove down and saw JuJu sitting upside down, immobile. He thought he was unconscious at first, but he wasn't, seemingly drifting in a current of capitulation, waiting to drown. Lyndon had dragged him to the surface and, hanging on to their kayaks, swum him in. What had bumped JuJu's kayak? A sea otter. Lyndon had seen it floating on its back, balancing a rock on its belly and whacking a clam against it with its paws, glancing dumbfoundedly at the two men as they laboriously kicked to shore.

Surely that incident—as well as the humpback carcass that had come ashore and the discussion about a shark feeding frenzy—was on JuJu's mind as they headed toward the water now, making him more jittery than usual, which must have been why he dropped the kayaks and screamed spasmodically when Woody emerged from the bushes in front of them with Bob.

"Jesus Christ!" JuJu said. "You scared the *shit* out of me!"

"I was almost attacked by a coyote!" Woody said elatedly, his face alight with joy. "But Bob—*Bob!*—" He knelt down and hugged Bob, who listlessly held a tennis ball in his mouth.

"Bob saved me! He barked and growled, and he scared the coyote away!"

"Bob did that?" Lyndon asked.

"It was the most incredible thing!"

"Dude," JuJu said, "you're bleeding."

Woody touched the blood that was caked on the left side of his face. "Oh, an owl surprised me, and I fell and hit my head on a rock or something. I think I was knocked out for a while. What time is it?"

"It's almost two," Lyndon said.

"*Really?* I'm not tired at all. I am wide awake. I've had the most wonderful day. You guys are going out on your kayaks? It's a beautiful night for it."

He didn't seem puzzled by Lyndon and JuJu's appearance, the jungle fatigues underneath their spray skirts, the loam and light green camouflage paint streaked on their faces, the fake squirrel ears and reindeer antlers affixed to the tops of their heads.

Instead, with a beatific smile on his face, Woody rhapsodized about walking the fields, the smells and colors of the vegetation, the lovely contours of the land, the sanctity of the dirt, how he'd become one with the earth. "I even took a shit in the woods!" he said. "Can you believe it? Do you know what a breakthrough that is for me? I haven't taken any meds or supplements since this morning, and I feel great! I used leaves for toilet paper!"

"Are those my clothes?" Lyndon asked.

"Have you ever read Edmund Burke?" Woody asked. "The beautiful and the sublime? Beauty has nurtured me, and I know what terror is now, I've seen the sublime in it. I've encountered the other, and I've conquered it. I've never been so alive! This is a magical place, Lyndon. This farm is special. There's this incredible spiritual power here. The last thing you should do is sell it. Tell me you won't sell it!"

Befuddled, Lyndon stared at his brother. "I won't sell it," he said.

"Thank you," Woody said, and he shuffled up to Lyndon and hugged him. "I have something I need to confess to you, Lyndon."

A night, apparently, for confessions. "What?"

"Do you remember Henry Chang?"

"Henry?" Lyndon asked, still enwrapped in Woody's arms. "From high school?"

"I paid him to take the SATs for me."

"You did?" During high school, Woody had been obsessed with posting a perfect 1600 score on his SATs. He had taken preparatory classes, buried himself in workbooks, carried around vocabulary flash cards, and run through nightly practice exams, often asking Lyndon to quiz him. He'd always aced everything. He hadn't needed to cheat. He would have done absolutely fine without Henry Chang.

"It feels so good to be able to tell you that," Woody said. He drew back and grasped Lyndon tightly by the shoulders. "You are my brother," he said weepily. "We are brothers. I have to go to sleep now. I am so tired. Let's go, Bob."

They watched Woody, followed by Bob, amble toward the house.

"Dude," JuJu said, "I think your brother is *stoned*."

．　　　．　　　．

LYNDON AND JUJU were not, by habit or association, UCLA fans, but they knew about the UCLA-USC rivalry. They knew that before the annual football game at the end of the season, students went to each other's campuses on search-and-deface missions. They poured soap and dye into fountains and pools, left obscenity-laden tributes, released herds of farm animals, hijacked delivery trucks and substituted school newspapers with parodies, and stole and vandalized emblems, most notably the bronze statue of Tommy Trojan on USC's campus, on which some UCLA Bruins had once famously dumped five hundred pounds of manure from a helicopter.

A few months ago, when a facsimile of the statue had been erected in the middle of the circular driveway to The Centurion Group's new hotel, Lyndon and JuJu took up UCLA's cause. Every once in a while, they dressed Tommy up in bras, lingerie, makeup, eye patches, jockstraps, various coats of paint, always in Bruin blue and gold. Before Kitchell hired twenty-four-hour security to guard the statue, they kidnapped it one night, took it into Lyndon's workshop, then returned it safe and sound after a couple of days, save for Tommy's arm, which had been rewelded so his sword was stuck up his ass.

As the sod for some of the fairways of the new golf course was laid down, they did some nighttime gardening, spreading rock salt so in due time brown patches appeared, spelling out in huge letters: U$C Sucks. As the concrete for the new hotel's patio dried, they sprayed a polymer sealant onto the surface so after a rainstorm slick discolorations suddenly became visible, reading in huge letters: Fuck $C.

Tonight, they landed their kayaks on the beach below the fourteenth fairway of the golf course, removed their supplies from the storage compartments of the boats, loaded their knapsacks, and climbed the sandstone cliff, hunkering down in a bunker to wait. After the security guards had driven past on their scheduled patrol, Lyndon and JuJu snuck across the fairway to Kitchell's cavernous house, which, like all the McMansions on the golf course, was designed to resemble an Italian villa. The Centurion Group had built this home first as a model, landscaping and fully furnishing it, but soon deemed it too small for the demands of the current market—it was a mere five thousand square feet—and constructed another one next door that was eight thousand square feet.

JuJu had gone to a spy hobbyist shop in San Francisco and purchased a lockpick set in anticipation of breaking into the house, but it wasn't necessary. The back door was open, the alarm disengaged. Kitchell must have been in a hurry to leave for the home opener in L.A. They took their boots off on the deck outside and entered the kitchen, which was outfitted with the latest high-end appliances: gleaming Thermador oven, stainless-steel double-sided Sub-Zero, black granite center island.

"Looks just like my place," Lyndon said.

He opened the refrigerator, which was stocked with bottles of Gatorade, water, light beer, wheatgrass juice, cod liver oil, and liquid vitamins. On the counter, lined in neat rows, were tubs of whey and egg protein, creatine, glutamine, ground flaxseed, and various other fat burners and muscle builders.

"Where do you think he hides the steroids?" JuJu asked.

They worked quickly. In the master bathroom, they put cooking oil in Kitchell's shampoo and tamped a staple into his deodorant so mysteriously, for days, his hair would be lank and greasy and his armpits would itch and burn. They inserted blue fabric dye in his showerhead and baby powder into his hair dryer. They smeared Vaseline on his toilet seat and poured clear gelatin in his toilet bowl. They shorted his sheets and swapped out the legs on his bed with empty beer bottles. They superglued the handsets for all his phones to their cradles. In the study they rigged his stereo to blast a CD of UCLA's fight song, "Sons of Westwood," when the lights were turned on, and they superglued all the papers on his desk to the desktop. In the gym they superglued his barbell to the bench press. In the kitchen they put crushed-up laxatives in his protein mixes and sugar bowl, and smokeless tobacco in his ground coffee. In the laundry room they replaced his detergent with bubble bath and stuck a dead salmon that they'd found on the beach in his dryer. Throughout the house, they hid cute little stuffed bears of UCLA's mascots, Joe and Josie Bruin, everywhere—in cupboards, cabinets, cans, closets.

In the garage, they poured baby powder into the front window defroster and air vents of Kitchell's SUV and superglued the blower lever to high. They put yellow paint in the windshield wiper fluid reservoir and superglued the wiper knob to high. They put a CD of "Sons of Westwood" in the stereo and superglued the volume to high. They superglued a coach's metal whistle inside the tailpipe and covered the end with an unrolled extra-strength Trojan condom that contained a three-day-old egg yolk. Finally, they superglued his gas cap and swapped out his USC TROJAN license plate frames with ones that read HONK IF YOU'RE GAY TOO.

    ■   ■   ■

SOMEONE WAS IN THE ROOM with him—that was what roused Lyndon, not long after they had returned to the farm and he'd begun to doze off. Sluggishly, he turned over in his bed and saw Sheila looming over him, holding a knife in the air.

"Jesus!"

"It's just me," she said softly. It wasn't a knife. She was sitting on the edge of the bed, hooking her hair behind her ear.

"What are you doing here?"

"For a misanthrope, you have a lot of people staying in your house."

"There're only three," Lyndon said. "I think."

Sheila stretched her neck, tilting her head back and then rolling it. She exhaled heavily. "God, I am so tired," she said.

"Get into bed with me."

"I'm not going to have sex with you again."

"Come on," Lyndon said, pushing aside the sheets. "Lie down with me."

She stared out the window, thinking about it. "I'm keeping my clothes on," she said. She slipped off her shoes and lay down beside Lyndon, spooning against him, and he pulled the sheets over them and nestled into her body.

"You smell good," he said.

"You smell awful. What have you been doing? You stink of ocean."

"Shhh," he said. "Let's just lie here." He pulled her closer to him, and she entwined her fingers around his, and they lay quietly, getting warm and snug, their breaths calming into a mutual rhythm. "Isn't this nice?" he whispered. "This is nice." This was perfect, he thought. Why did people always insist that relationships had to change? Why did they always need to analyze them and discuss them and pick them apart? Why did everything have to be redefined and progress to another level? Why couldn't people just be together? Why couldn't it be simple, like this?

"Are you going to see her again?" Sheila asked.

It was never, ever, going to be simple. "I'm not planning to," Lyndon said.

"That's not a definitive answer."

"No, all right? I'm not going to see her again."

"Good."

"Did you come over tonight to see if I was alone?"

"Maybe."

"You're still in love with me."

"I am not."

"You are," Lyndon said.

"You know, you don't look anything like your brother," Sheila told him.

"Well, thank God for that," he said.

"And you say you have no vanity," she said. "Why is JuJu sleeping here?"

"He's sort of made himself at home."

"Because you lost his job for him?"

Naturally she had learned of the collapse at the Oar House. "I had nothing to do with that," he said. "That wasn't my fault at all."

"It's always the same song with you, isn't it? So to speak," Sheila said. "JuJu's girlfriend is a little old for him. Not a criticism, just an observation."

How far had she gone into everyone's bedroom? "I don't think either of them is looking at it long-term."

"You never know about these things. Maybe they'll surprise you. Maybe they'll stay together until they shrivel up and die."

"Somehow, that statement lacks a certain romance," Lyndon said. "Is Hana leaving making you feel old? Is that what's going on, all this drama?"

"It's about you and Steven," Sheila said.

"About making a choice between us?"

"Yes."

"Who's winning?" Lyndon asked.

"I don't know."

"Choose me," he said.

"You haven't been making a good case for yourself."

"So you've made apparent. I take it you haven't been putting holes in Steven's tires."

"I don't think he'd appreciate the joke."

"That's precisely why he should be disqualified. No fucking sense of humor, that man. Though the joke's getting a little stale now. And expensive. When did you get a hunting knife?"

"What?"

"The knife you used tonight."

She lifted her head off the pillow and turned to him. "What are you talking about?"

"What'd you slash my tires with, then?"

"I didn't do anything to your tires tonight."

"Okay," he said. If she wanted to play coy, if she wanted to pretend that her actions had not escalated from harmless vandalism to something approaching homicidal rage, so be it, that was fine with him. But then he had a thought. Could Steven have slashed his tires? He had been at the scene of the crime—the parking ticket. He had means, opportunity, and a shitload of motive. Then Lyndon had another thought. "You're not visiting Steven in the middle of the night like this, are you?" he asked Sheila.

"No."

"So I am winning."

"I wouldn't attach undue significance to this."

"Whatever you say," he told her, and tucked his chin into her collarbone. "As long as you don't go out with Ed Kitchell."

"That's really bothering you, isn't it?"

"You're not seriously considering it, are you?"

"There's more to him than you might think. He's a volunteer organizer for the Avon Walk for Breast Cancer. He has a sensitive side you'd never expect."

"You can't do it. You won't do it, will you?"

"I'm going to torture you a little longer and not answer."

"That's an answer."

"No, it's not."

"It's not like I need any more reason to hate the guy."

"So you've made apparent."

"You know he wears Brut cologne? Who wears Brut anymore?"

"How do you know he wears Brut?"

After they had gone from the bedrooms to the study, from the gym to the kitchen, from the laundry to the garage, Lyndon had looked around Kitchell's house and said to JuJu, "I feel like we're forgetting something."

In the master bathroom, they had emptied out half of Kitchell's spray bottle of Brut and filled it with cod liver oil.

CHAPTER 8

STONE UNCONSCIOUS. BLACK BLACK BLACKNESS. NOTHING. NO dreams or gauzy, half-remembered peeps during the night. A complete void. He slept like that until late in the morning, then awoke with a start. Someone was covering his mouth, not allowing him to breathe, shoving him underneath the water, trying to drown him. But, no, Woody's face was mashed square against the pillow, in a pool of drool from his open mouth, the saliva pink with blood from the scrape on his forehead. He had the most tremendous headache. Searing, pounding, unbelievable pain. He reeled out of bed, still in Lyndon's clothes. He gulped down water from a bottle he had kept on the dresser and began popping down aspirin and double doses of his meds and supplements. It had been a mistake, a terrible mistake, to miss a day.

He went to the bathroom and looked in the mirror. God, what a horror, blood caked on the side of his head, bags under his eyes, skin alternately sallow and ruddy, peppered with— what were those things? Pimples? Little red bumps in clusters. And dirt. Dirt everywhere. On his face, in his hair, in his ears, in his nostrils. He washed his face, put a bandage on the scrape, and blew his nose. Brown snot, like he'd been in a dust storm. Then, when he unzipped his jeans to take a leak, he met a hideous sight. There was something wrong with his penis. It was red and covered with a line of bumps, as if it had been caught in the zipper. Multiple times. And then Woody began to feel an itching, an unbearable, overwhelming itching, on his penis and, mystifyingly, on his ass, right in the crack between his cheeks, actually on his anus, on second thought it felt like it was up his anal canal, like he had been given a rectal exam during his blackout and a nest of mosquitoes had swarmed up there. No, forget mosquitoes. An army of red fire ants. What in the world?

He unbuckled his jeans, bent over, and took a gander. Everything was red, covered with those same bumps that were on his face, only there were more of them down there, and they were bigger. What *were* those things? Hives from an allergic reaction? The measles? Was it possible to get measles on your genitalia and ass? Good God, they itched.

He heard an engine rumbling toward the house. He looked out the window and saw Lyndon driving his tractor to the shed. Woody leaned out of the window and waved. "Hey, hey!" he yelled.

Lyndon turned off the engine. "What's up?"

"I need help!"

His brother mumbled something under his breath.

"What?" Woody asked, then deduced that Lyndon had said, "You're not kidding."

"I'll be up in a second," he told Woody.

He took his sweet time, stowing the tractor underneath the shed and unhooking the plow behind it before coming into the house. "What is it?" he asked when he reached the bathroom.

"I have some sort of rash," Woody said, holding up his jeans.

"Where? On your face? That doesn't look too serious."

"No," Woody said. "On my . . ." He glanced downward, and Lyndon did, too.

"There?" his brother said, smirking.

"Yes."

"Who have you been consorting with?"

"It's not an STD."

"Are you sure?"

"I'm sure."

"Okay."

"I think it might be the measles."

"If it were the measles, it'd be all over," Lyndon said. "It wouldn't be isolated on Pat and Mick."

"Could you . . . take a look for me?"

Lyndon winced. "You have got to be joking."

"Come on, we used to take baths together."

"Forty years ago."

"Just a peek."

Lyndon laughed. "No way, José."

Woody hopped up and down. "Holy fuck, it itches. What the hell is the matter with me?" He described the rash and bumps to Lyndon.

His brother nodded. "You have poison oak."

"Poison oak?"

"You said last night you took a shit in the woods. You used leaves for toilet paper."

"I did?" Woody had no memory of this. He barely remembered last night at all.

"The sap oil was still on your fingers when you touched your dick and face," Lyndon said. "Don't worry about it. It'll clear up by itself in two weeks."

"*Two weeks?* Isn't there something I can do? I can't live like this!"

Lyndon rummaged inside the cabinet underneath the sink. He pulled out a bar of brown soap and a pink bottle. "Take a shower with this—it's lye soap—in cold water, then put the calamine lotion on. The best thing you can do is keep it cool and dry. You have any antihistamines?"

"Of course."

"That might help. Try not to scratch. You'll get some blisters, and you don't want to get them infected. And take all those clothes to the washing machine and run them on hot-hot."

Woody read the label on the calamine lotion, then frowned at his brother. "You don't have to look so amused," he told him.

"It *is* pretty funny, you have to admit," Lyndon said. "Now I have to find Bob. You might have gotten some sap on him."

The shower, calamine lotion, and antihistamines did help. Not much, but a little. He still felt nauseous and hungover, however, and he needed coffee. Good coffee.

Outside, it was bright and sunny, but blustery—very windy, in fact. Ling Ling and JuJu were in the greenhouse, doing their training exercises or whatnot, and Lyndon was in front of the barn, hosing down Bob, who was less than pleased with the bath, arching his back under the stream of water.

"I'm going into town," Woody said.

"We'll catch up with you there," Lyndon said. "We're all going to the chili and chowder fest later on. Starts at noon. Maybe we can have lunch together."

Lunch? Woody thought. His brother was softening toward him.

He heard a piercing trill overhead, the song of a bird, *gurrga-lee, chu-laak, deeek*. He glanced up.

"That's a—" Lyndon began.

"Red-winged blackbird," Woody said.

"How'd you know that?" Lyndon asked.

"I'm not a complete city yokel," he said.

As Woody approached his Rover, he noticed, in addition to the damage on his bumper, grill, and headlight from hitting the tree on Friday, that the Buckingham Blue Metallic paint on the passenger's side was scratched. At first he thought he might have brushed against some branches as he had squeezed down that narrow road to the marsh preserve, but as he peered closer, he came to a different conclusion. Someone had deliberately keyed his car, raking a sharp implement several times across the paint, from stem to stern. He had been vandalized.

"Son of a bitch," he said. Unbelievable. But when had it happened? He'd come straight to the farm from the marsh yesterday evening. Had someone defaced the Rover the day before, when he had been in town? Maybe with all the mud and dust on it, he hadn't noticed. Or had it occurred while he'd been parked in the marsh? Those kids from the ice-cream store on horseback, they might have decided to get their revenge, payback for being chased off the beach by Trudy and her pellet gun.

"I meant to ask," Lyndon said, "what happened to your headlight? Get into an accident?"

"This is a hazardous town," Woody said. "Call me later on my cell."

The Rover stuttered when he started it, and it made a swishing sound as he drove to town—squirming, trying to keep his butt raised from the seat—and it coughed when he finally found a parking spot and shut off the engine. There was no way he'd make it back to L.A. without breaking down. He would have to buy a new car somewhere nearby, maybe in Santa Cruz.

They had closed off Main Street, and though the festival wasn't due to begin for another hour, there were quite a few people milling around already. Woody picked up a copy of the Sunday *Los Angeles Times* inside Cuchi's Country Store and got into an interminable line at the checkout. After a few minutes, he summarily cut to the front, ignoring grumbles and raised eyebrows, flicked off a twenty-dollar bill—the smallest he had—from his money clip and laid it in front of the cashier, and walked out. He went across the street to the Java Hut, saw a man vacating an outside table, and scooted across the patio into the chair.

An elderly woman said to him in a pique, "We were waiting for a table."

"I was, too," he said, and opened the Calendar section of the paper.

With so many customers, it took a while—too long—to get served. Woody was a bit irritable by the time the waitress got to him and wiped down his table, but she was chatty with him, giggly, and she was sort of cute, in a wholesome, freckly, small-town way, and he cheered up as he realized that she was flirting with him. And why shouldn't she? He was wearing a Roberto Cavalli shirt, Helmut Lang jeans, and Prada driving moccasins. Odds on, he was the most stylish, cosmopolitan man within a fifty-mile radius.

He asked her for a double espresso, a walnut and raspberry scone, two large orange juices, and a large glass of water.

"Thirsty this morning?" she said, smiling at Woody.

"Just a bit," he said, smiling back at her.

She tarried, standing in front of him. "You're not contagious, are you?" she asked.

"What?" For a happy second, he thought she might be making an extraordinarily brazen proposition, offering to consort with him, barring an STD, but then he understood she was referring to the spots of calamine lotion dotting his face. "Oh," he said. "No, I'm not."

"Just checking," she said, and gamboled away. He returned to his paper, his ass beginning to itch again.

WRACK AND RUIN | *251*

He was deep into an article on the Toronto Film Festival when a caravan of three cars, with stacks of windsurfing boards strapped to their roofs, idled up the side street, double-parking next to Cuchi's. A pile of young men noisily disembarked, stretching and joking, shoving one another. They went into the store and, after ten minutes or so, came out again, arms full of snacks and sandwiches and drinks. As Woody watched them absently, one of the men—Asian, ponytailed—caught his eye. It couldn't be, but he looked just like the director Dalton Lee.

"Yo, Dalt," one of the windsurfers said as they were getting back in their cars, and tossed a bag of potato chips to him.

Woody stood up. "Dalton?" he yelled across the street.

Dalton Lee turned, located who had spoken, and blanched. He jumped into the car, and Woody could see him motioning to the driver to go, go.

"Oh, no, you don't," Woody said aloud, and ran to his Rover, which he had had to park two blocks away. He headed in the general direction in which the caravan had taken off and was momentarily afraid he would lose them, but with the boards on their roof racks, the cars were hard to miss. He spotted them turning south onto Highway 1. As he sped after them, he said, "Call Roland," activating the Rover's hands-free phone.

"Yallow," Roland said.

"The little chickenshit didn't leave!"

"Who?" Roland asked.

"Dalton Lee! He never left Sausalito. There was no emergency. He was lying! I just saw him. He's going windsurfing!" Dalton Lee, according to reports, was an avid windsurfer, quite a good one. When *There Once Was a City* had won the Audience Award at Sundance, he'd been profiled on several entertainment news shows, segments showing him sailing off Crissy Field into San Francisco Bay.

"Maybe he got back early," Roland said sleepily.

"That's bullshit. Whose side are you on, anyway?"

"No one's," Roland said. "I mean yours. Ours."

"He thinks he can weasel out of our deal? Well, not so fast, pretty boy." Over the phone, Woody could hear Roland yawn. "Late night last night, as usual?" he asked.

"Not too late. Just tired," Roland said. "Hey, that PI's been trying to reach you. Did you get his message?"

Woody hadn't checked his voice mail. Roland told him the only additional information Christopher Cross had unearthed was that Kyle Thorneberry had gone to see a psychiatrist and gotten a prescription for antidepressants, though he'd never filled it. He was, like many New Yorkers that fall, dealing with the aftereffects of 9/11. He'd been at the Goldman Sachs headquarters that morning, three blocks south of the World Trade Center. There had been no scandal. There had been no problems with his career or his marriage or his family. He hadn't been in any money trouble, and there had been no drugs or gambling or terminal diseases. He wasn't having an affair, and he wasn't being blackmailed or extorted. Kyle Thorneberry—who'd treated Woody like the brother he always wished he had, who indeed appeared to have had everything—had shot himself in the right temple for no discernible reason.

The absence of a reason was far more disturbing and depressing to Woody than if there had been one. If Kyle had had everything that Woody ever wanted, if he'd possessed the life, the dream, *vita pulchra est*, and he still hadn't been happy, then what hope was there for someone like Woody? What was the point? How would he ever stop his monkey mind from torturing itself with regrets and loathing and envy?

He heard the brief announcement of a siren.

"What's that?" Roland asked.

In the rearview mirror, a sheriff's cruiser was tailgating him, its lights flashing. "I'll call you back," Woody said.

He pulled over to the side of the highway and, after putting the transmission in park, gazed straight ahead, hands at ten and two o'clock on the wheel, and watched Dalton Lee's windsurfing caravan drive away from him.

"License and registration."

It was one of the cops who'd responded to the ceiling collapse at the Oar House on Friday night—Lemke, the name tag on his uniform said. Perhaps Woody could finagle his way out of this. "Remember me?" he said to Lemke. "Woody Song, Lyndon's brother? Listen, I know I was going a little fast, but I'm trying to catch up to a group of cars. It's sort of an emergency. I'm a film producer, you see. Maybe you've seen something of mine. *Lethal Enforcer*? *Lying in Wait*?" Naturally, as was born out by audience demographics, cops were huge fans of his action remakes.

Lemke, impassive as a telephone pole, didn't respond.

Woody tried another tack. "That woman I was with Friday night, that was Yi Ling Ling. You might have heard of her— the queen of Hong Kong cinema? *Black Night Lady*? *Undercover Dragon Heart*?" Audience demographics also showed that a significant percentage of rice chasers—white men with a fetish for Asian women—were cops.

Nothing. Not a word. Lemke seemed to be staring at the spots of the calamine lotion on Woody's face. He tugged out a pair of blue vinyl gloves from his pants pocket and put them on his hands, took Woody's license and registration, and walked back to his cruiser. All day he sat in there, and then came back and silently gave Woody a ticket.

"Fuck," Woody said as he rolled up his window. And now he had no idea where Dalton Lee was. He could be anywhere.

Getting back on the highway, the engine rasping, he tried Dalton's cell phone, but of course the twerp wouldn't pick up. "Call Roland," Woody said.

"Yallow."

"I need you to do something."

"What happened, get busted?"

"Speeding ticket."

"Ouch."

"I need you to do some research for me."

"I'm not in the office today."

"You have a computer at home, don't you?"

"I'm, uh, not at home."

"Where are you?"

"I'm, uh, at a friend's."

Woody sighed. He didn't care to know what sort of friend Roland was consorting with. "Does your friend have a computer?"

"I don't know. Let me see. Okay, yeah."

"Look on the Internet for me and find out where people windsurf between here and Santa Cruz."

As he waited for Roland, Woody felt his ass tickle and prickle. He put the car on cruise control, clumsily dabbed some calamine lotion on a cotton ball, and unzipped his pants. As he lifted his hips and bent his hand between his legs with the cotton ball, he drifted out of his lane and the car beside him honked, the woman driver looking at him in horror and disgust.

"Yeah, that's right, lady, I'm jacking off in my car, I can't help myself, you're so fucking hot, you're turning me on so much, you stupid bitch," he said.

"What?" Roland said. "And I thought I knew you."

"Find anything yet?"

There were three wave-sailing sites on the coast favored by Bay Area windsurfers when the swell and wind came up:

Wads, Scotts, and Davs—or Waddell Creek, Scotts Creek, and Davenport Landing. The first, Wads, was about twenty miles south of Rosarita Bay—Roland didn't give him anything more specific than that, no address or landmark, Woody's GPS navigation system useless to him. But after driving half an hour, as the road curved down a hill toward the ocean, Woody located it easily enough by the collection of cars parked along the highway, all with roof racks. He couldn't tell, however, if Dalton Lee's car was among them. He had been in a late-model blue Nissan, and the other two cars in his caravan had been generic Japanese models as well—a silver sedan and a black SUV. Practically all the parked cars were nondescript, monochromatic Japanese makes.

It was blowing like crazy on the beach. On the water were dozens of windsurfers, zipping every which way. Woody had thought he knew what windsurfing was. He'd spent a week on vacation in Playa del Carmen trying to learn the sport. But he was entirely unfamiliar with this type of windsurfing. There were no wide longboards, no uphauling sails from a standing position, no putt-putting along at a leisurely pace. These guys were *moving*, gaining breakneck speed as they skimmed out to sea on tiny shortboards, hitting the chop and launching straight up into the air, some of them looping in somersaults. They barreled offshore and then jibed back in, timed the swells, and then took off down the face of breaking waves, carving bottom turns and snapping their boards off the lip.

From the beach, he could hardly distinguish any of the wetsuited windsurfers from one another. He thought he recognized Dalton Lee several times, but it always turned out to be someone else. How many Asian windsurfers in their early thirties with ponytails could there be? Apparently quite a few. He watched a guy wipe out on a wave, his rig flipping and twisting after him. Woody was going to have to attach a special insurance rider to Dalton's contract, forbidding him from windsurfing while they were on this project.

More than Ling Ling, Dalton Lee was integral to the financing of Woody's movie. As low-budget as *There Once Was a City* had been, it'd only taken half a reel to appreciate that Dalton Lee was brilliant, a savant, a budding genius auteur. But he was Woody's genius. He was his employee. He had signed a development deal, a contract. Woody *owned* him. He couldn't permit Dalton to lie to him and ditch him. He needed to put Dalton Lee in his place.

He wasn't at Waddell Creek, and, after Woody wasted an additional forty-five minutes searching for him at Scotts Creek, it appeared he wasn't at that beach, either. That left Davenport Landing, and Woody twice passed the road to the cove (because some joker had removed the sign) before he saw a pickup with its bed heaped with boards turning onto it. Woody followed the truck down the road and, after parking his Rover, walked down to the sandy beach, which was flanked by promontories to the north and south. Windsurfers were launching into the channel in front of the beach, then coming back to ride the reef breaks in front of the steep outcrops. The lower reef seemed to be the one generating the best waves today, almost everyone sailing over there, and Woody trekked through the sand and climbed the shelf of rocks underneath the limestone cliff. The rocks were slick and covered with sharp mussel shells, and when a wave crashed onto shore and sprayed over the shelf, Woody slipped and—goddammit to hell—fell onto one knee, cutting open his jeans.

He backed away from the water's edge and looked out at the waves, shading his eyes. He couldn't tell who was who from this distance. Among a handful of spectators underneath the cliff, a woman was videotaping the windsurfers, and he asked her if he could look through her camera for a minute. He zoomed in and out, and at last saw Dalton Lee catching a wave in. He carved out some S-turns and then jibed, after which he stalled a second, waiting for a gust.

"Hey, hey, Dalton!" Woody yelled, waving his arms. "Dalton!"

He couldn't hear him, and even if he could, Woody knew he would have pretended not to. The wind came in, and Dalton pumped his sail and hooked in and disappeared, speeding out to the horizon.

Another set of waves rolled in, and a windsurfer charged down the first of them, cut back up its face, floated above the crest, landed hard, and tripped off his board. Everything— board, rig, and sailor—tumbled inside the big wave, a washing machine, and then was flushed out in the whitewater, the gear crashing against the rocky shore and breaking into pieces. It appeared the sailor would be next. He was drifting perilously close to the rocks, unable to swim out with the current and tide. "Man," one of the spectators beneath the cliff said, "he is going to eat it." But then a man on a jet ski—a rescue sled attached to its rear—roared up to him, swooped him up, and motored him to safety.

It was no ordinary jet ski—not, as expected, a lifeguard or Coast Guard vessel. The jet ski was tricked out like a hot rod or low-rider, painted in jade green with a metallic flake finish, adorned with THUNDERDOME and MFP in flowing mother-of-pearl script, and decorated with airbrushed illustrations of kangaroos and crocodiles, flames on the sides, and an elaborate, exquisitely detailed depiction of a woman, naked, spread-eagled, on the rescue sled.

Woody hobbled to the beach, where the jet ski had slid ashore. The rescued windsurfer and some of his pals were walking back in Woody's direction to fetch his gear from the rocks, and the jet ski driver was securing the ropes that connected his rescue sled.

"How much to rent your jet ski?" Woody asked. He knew how to operate a jet ski. Years ago he had rented one for an hour in Manzanita.

The man stood up. He wore mirrored sunglasses, a green canvas hat with a chin strap, the brim pinned up on both sides of his head, and a farmer john wetsuit, his jacket and life vest unzipped to accommodate an immense beer belly. "What do you think this is, bush week?" he said in a heavy Australian accent.

"It's an emergency. I have to talk to one of the windsurfers. I need to get him to come in."

"Not for sale, mate. No one drives this ski but me. Now rack off."

Woody took out his money clip and began flicking off bills. "You drive, then. I'll sit in back. I'll pay you five hundred dollars."

The man looked at the bills. "Well, g'day, cobber, reckon that's the go, onya," he said.

"What?"

"What's your name?"

"Woody."

"Everybody calls me Mad Max," the man said, crushing Woody's hand (why couldn't people shake hands normally around here?) and revealing a horsey, brown-teethed grin framed within his scraggly fu manchu. He had curly brown hair spilling out from underneath his hat, and was grossly hairy in general, curlicues matting his chest and the backs of his hands.

"Mad Max. As in the movie?" Woody asked.

"One and the same. You gotta wettie?"

"What?" This was ridiculous. He could hardly follow a thing the Aussie was saying.

"Wetsuit. You gonna get wet out there. Water's fifty-two degree."

"That doesn't matter to me."

"Will if you fall off. That cut's not going to help, neither."

Woody glimpsed down at the rip in his jeans. He hadn't realized that his knee was cut. It was bleeding rather freely.

"Noah will *love* you," Mad Max said.

"What?"

"Noah. Big Mac. The holy mother of shit-your-nicky-na-nas scary motherfuckers, mate! Great white shark! They don't call this the Red Triangle for nothing. Three attacks in the last five years. Woman at Wads got her arm gnawed to a stump, surfer up at Rummy Creek had his foot bit clean off, bloke here got ripped to shreds, don't think they found anything below the nips. Once saw Whitey myself half mile out, thought there were two of them, his fins were so far apart. Big big big! They had a dead humpback beach herself up the coast couple weeks ago, heard some scientists took her out for a feeding frenzy and got Noahs from hundreds of miles away to congregate in the area. So don't fall off, mate, or with that cut you'll be yum-yum din-dins!" He laughed. He had hanks of nose hair that seemed to meld into his mustache. "Just kidding, mate. Don't listen to me, I'm just an old drongo. But I'm an ace waterman, anyone here will tell you."

He opened the front storage compartment of the jet ski and pulled out a life jacket for Woody—"Personally, I'm opposed to these, for political and religious reasons," he said, "but it's the fucking law in California"—and also handed him a pair of foul-weather bib pants, made of slick orange PVC. "These will keep you a little dry."

Woody stepped into the pants, which were several sizes too large for him, and tightened the suspenders as far as he could, but he was still swimming in them.

"Nice dacks," Mad Max said. "Ready?"

There was nothing to hold on to, no hand grips or railing. Mad Max told him to put his arms around his waist, but, given his girth, that was impossible, so Woody feebly grasped the straps on the sides of Mad Max's open life vest as they roared off to sea. Just past the shore break, it became apparent to Woody that this might not have been the best of ideas. First they smacked into the chop, which came from every direction, completely unsystematic, churning, roiling, foaming, heaving mounds and peaks, making Woody seasick, the wind howling, the water freezing and spraying up and splashing all over them, and then there were huge swells, inexplicably breaking in the middle of the ocean. Mad Max would drive over the top of a pitching wave, and the bottom would drop out behind it, the jet ski free-falling and slamming down into the trough. He'd have to gun the throttle to get them going again over the next swell, and the jet ski would whine and tip back, nearly vertical, and they'd be staring straight up to the sky. To counter the weight, Mad Max would stand and lean forward, and Woody, now absolutely terrified, would have to rise off the seat with him, hanging on to the Aussie for dear life.

"Coo-eee!" Mad Max yelled. "Coo-eeeeee!"

"What are you doing?" Woody screamed. "You're crazy!"

"I'm calling out to the goddess Wuriupranili!" Mad Max said. "Coo-eee!"

He banked the jet ski around toward shore, and windsurfers began crisscrossing their path, one of them catching air off a swell and floating downwind *over their heads*, taking one hand off the boom and casually waving his fingers at them.

"Jesus!" Woody said, ducking.

"You're hilarious, you prick," Mad Max shouted at the wind-surfer, laughing.

"There!" Woody said, pointing. "There he is!"

Dalton Lee was coming toward them, and Mad Max immediately spun the jet ski upon a parallel course, angling just a few feet away from him as they raced side by side at over thirty miles an hour.

"Yo, Dalt!" Woody said. "Yoo-hoo!"

Dalton gawped at Woody—the last person he had expected to see out here. Without warning, he laid down his sail and swept out a wide, screaming-fast jibe and sped away in the opposite direction.

Woody slapped the back of Mad Max's life vest. "Don't lose him!"

"He don't seem all that happy to see ya, mate," Mad Max said, but obligingly turned the jet ski around and revved after Dalton.

Back and forth they chased him, following him to the reef break and out to sea again, but they couldn't get him to slow down or even acknowledge them.

"Cut in front of him," Woody told Mad Max.

"What?"

"Make him fall."

"I'm not going to do that," Mad Max said.

"I'm *paying* you."

"Don't go acting the yobbo. Somebody could get hurt."

"I'll give you another hundred."

"You're being a bloody nuisance."

"Two hundred. Here he is again!"

Dalton was whizzing toward them, going so fast, his board was almost continuously airborne, skimming over the whitecaps.

"Do it!" Woody said.

"Rack off!" Mad Max said.

Woody stood and reached around Mad Max and pushed his hand over the Aussie's on the throttle and shoved the handlebar, making them lurch in front of Dalton.

"Cark it!" Mad Max said, swatting at Woody's arm, and at the last second he veered the other way, causing Woody to lose his balance and cartwheel off the jet ski into the frigid water right in front of Dalton, the nose of whose board was plowing directly toward Woody's head.

Dalton bailed, dropping his sail, instigating a spectacular crash, his board flying up and then ramming to a dead stop. "What the fuck are you doing!" he yelled when he surfaced, treading water.

"Pick me up! Pick me up!" Woody shrieked to Mad Max, swiveling around in a panic, searching for fins.

"Get stuffed," Mad Max told him. "You can swim in. I've had enough of you." He cruised back toward the beach a quarter mile away, the spread-eagled invitation of the woman on his rescue sled slowly withdrawing.

"Help me!" Woody, bobbing in his life jacket, said to Dalton.

"What the hell are you doing here?" Dalton asked, paddling to his gear.

Thrashing his arms, Woody could feel his bib pants filling with water, pulling him down. "Help me! Do something! I'm not going to make it. I'm bleeding. There are *sharks* out here!"

He could see Dalton deliberating, thinking of leaving him to fend for himself, but he said, reluctantly, "Grab the strap on the back of the board," and hoisted his sail into the air, letting it lift him out of the water and onto the board, after which he towed Woody to shore, trolling him like bait, the trip an agonizing eternity, Woody expecting, at any time, to be eviscerated and devoured from below.

       ■   ■   ■

THEY WENT TO A RESTAURANT to let Woody warm up. He was shivering, certain he had hypothermia. Dalton had lent him a hoodie and a T-shirt, and he'd talked a couple of friends on the beach into donating a baseball cap, some ratty cargo pants, and a grubby pair of sheepskin uggs. A ridiculous outfit for a grown man. While Dalton unrigged his equipment, Woody had sat in his Rover with the heat blasting. His key remote no longer worked. Neither did his cell phone or BlackBerry, everything waterlogged and fried.

The restaurant, the closest to Davenport Landing on Highway 1, was a hole-in-the-wall called the Cuckoo's Nest, with neon beer signs, rickety wooden booths, and tacky checkered oilcloths. There were Harleys and Ducatis parked outside. It was, evidently, a shrine of sorts, a tribute-themed establishment, for on the walls were dozens of movie posters and framed eight-by-tens dedicated to a single icon: Jack Nicholson.

Dalton looked around admiringly. "This is fantastic," he said. "I've never been in here. I always passed by and assumed it was a biker joint."

"Know what you want yet?" a waitress asked. She was wearing tinted Ray•Bans.

"Soup," Woody told her.

"We've got tomato bisque and chowder."

"Chowder. And coffee. And one 'As Good as It Gets' burger, medium rare, blue cheese. And an order of onion rings. And potato salad." Diet be damned.

"You still serving breakfast?" Dalton asked, smiling at the waitress. She was young, blond, pretty, in a wholesome, freckly, small-town way.

"All day, hon."

"A western omelet, but tomatoes on the side instead of home fries."

"Gotcha," the waitress said. "Coffee?"

"That's not a problem?" Dalton said. "Substitutions?"

The waitress glanced at him, then, catching on, tapped her pencil against her notepad, stuck it behind her ear, and placed a hand on her hip. "No substitutions."

"I can't have tomatoes?"

"Only what's on the menu," the waitress said.

"Okay, then whole wheat toast."

"No toast."

"No toast? You make sandwiches here, don't you?"

"Sure."

"Then a western omelet, coffee, and a chicken salad sandwich."

"Gotcha."

"But hold the mayo, hold the lettuce and tomato."

"All right."

"And hold the chicken."

"Hold the chicken?"

"Between your knees!" Dalton said, and he and the waitress laughed. "I bet that gets pretty old," he told the waitress apologetically.

"Never," she said, picking up the menus.

"What was that about?" Woody asked Dalton.

"Don't you remember the scene in *Five Easy Pieces*, the scene in the diner?" Dalton asked. "Come on! You've got to remember that."

Woody pulled out his asthma inhaler and sucked in a dose, unimpressed. Jack Nicholson's box-office numbers stank these days.

"Are you all right?" Dalton asked.

Woody nodded, though his face was covered with calamine lotion, he had a bandaged cut on his forehead and now on his knee, he was cold to the bone, and his ass itched excruciatingly; though in the course of less than forty-eight hours he had almost drowned, sunk in quicksand, and gotten hit by a truck, killed by a Samoan drug dealer, crushed in a building collapse, and eaten by a coyote and maybe a lurking great white shark. "There was no family emergency, was there?" he said.

"The truth?" Dalton asked.

"Yes."

"Son, you can't handle the truth," Dalton told him with a Nicholsonian snarl. "Sorry, couldn't resist."

The waitress came back with their coffee. "So you're a fan?" she asked Dalton.

"Totally. I'm a director."

"Really?"

"You ever see a little film called *There Once Was a City*?"

"You made that?" the girl asked. "I loved that movie. I saw it in Santa Cruz at the Asian American Showcase."

"You go to school there?"

"Community college."

"What are you studying?"

"Multicultural media."

"We should talk," Dalton said.

"Maybe we should," she said.

Dalton watched her walk away, raised his eyebrows at Woody, then tore a sugar packet and poured it in his mug.

"You didn't have to go out of town, did you?" Woody asked.

"No," he said, stirring. "I didn't."

"What's going on?"

"The truth is, I've sort of had some reservations about this project."

"It's Yi Ling Ling , isn't it? You don't want her. Well, that's fine. Between you and me, I don't really, either," Woody said, although he'd admired Ling Ling's recent demonstrations of discipline and had begun to think she'd be just fine in the role. "We can change that. We can cast someone else—someone younger."

"No, it's not her, not entirely."

"What, then?"

Dalton shrugged. "You know the types of scripts I've been getting since Sundance?" he asked. "Asian gang stories, Asian immigrant stories, Asian racism and war and internment and adoption stories, Asian kung-fu/sex-tourist/bootlegging/drug-smuggling/slave-trafficking/human-rights-abuse stories. It's been so depressing, seeing these things, one after another. I even got a treatment from a studio for a remake of Charlie Chan. You believe that?"

Brilliant, Woody thought. Why hadn't he come up with that himself? "That's why our movie's going to be fresh and hip," he said. "It's cross-genre, cross-ethnic, cross-market."

"It'll still be just another martial-arts movie, you know. It's just going to perpetuate all those tired, old stereotypes about Asians. Especially women."

"What do you want to do, reduce the female lead? Flip it around and make it more a male vehicle? We can do that, I suppose. Maybe that'd even work better. Maybe we could get Andy Lau or Takeshi Kaneshiro." They would, however, have to alter the love-interest angle of the story. Demographic studies indicated that audiences might accept Asian women with white men, but not the other way around.

"You're not getting what I'm saying," Dalton said. "I mean, why is it we can only do fresh-off-the-boat, three-generations-of-immigrants, interracial-relationship, cultural-misunderstanding movies? Why are we stuck with comfort women, picture brides, geishas, and greengrocers, with exploring our roots and searching for our birth parents and examining what it means to be Asian American? I mean, come on, why does it always have to be about race and identity? I'm sick to death of race and identity. You understand what I'm saying?"

"Uh-huh," Woody said. Dalton Lee had gone activist on him, he'd become a bleeding-heart, Asian Nation, Yellow Power crusader while being bankrolled with Woody's $100,000 pay-or-play guarantee.

"So if we don't do those kinds of stories, we've sold out?" Dalton said. "We've gone white-bread? Who came up with that? Who planted that shit? Here's a radical thought for you: maybe the white hegemony did. They like us over in this corner, you see. They like it when we segregate ourselves. They want us to endlessly mull over our cultural heritage and wrestle with discrimination and assimilation. They want us to keep thinking of ourselves as victims, just whine whine whine. I mean, for fuck sake, aren't you bored with that shit? Doesn't that shit just bore the hell out of you? It does me."

This tirade went on—sometimes making sense, sometimes not, every argument contradicting a previous one. Of late people had a tendency, it seemed, of making long, impassioned speeches to Woody. He didn't know why. Their lunches came. He squirted antibacterial lotion on his hands and cleaned his utensils with a napkin. The chowder was lumpy and too salty, his burger overcooked and dry, appallingly served in a red plastic basket.

"I mean, why is it," Dalton said, chewing on his omelet, "that when Ang Lee does Jane Austen or gay cowboys, it's showing his range as a director, but if I were to do it, it'd be race betrayal? Because I'm from Menlo Park and he's from Taiwan? Look, I'm not naïve. Nothing happens in this country without the involutions of race. But if we let it dictate what we can and cannot do and start limiting ourselves as artists, then we're no longer free. We're oppressed. We're slaves."

Woody nodded, bored, not even bothering to disparage Ang Lee's gay cowboy movie, which was scheduled to open in December and was sure to bomb. Woody knew he was being played. Dalton was engaging in this grand disquisition not because he believed anything he was saying, but because he wanted something. Evangelists of all stripes—political, religious—were always motivated by a hidden agenda. Dalton was positioning himself for a negotiation. So Woody finished his gooey potato salad, wiped his mouth, and came right out and asked, "What is it that you want?"

"What do I want?" Dalton said. He raised his arms and gestured to the posters on the walls of the restaurant. "Look around you. *The Passenger. One Flew Over the Cuckoo's Nest. Five Easy Pieces. Chinatown. Carnal Knowledge. The King of Marvin Gardens. The Last Detail.* Fuck, that was a good movie. They all were. I want to make movies like that—great movies. That's what I want. Simple as that."

"We could make this movie great," Woody said. "*You* could make it great."

"Oh, come on, let's not kid ourselves," Dalton said. "It's a shame. The original screenplay had a lot of potential. I really thought I could do a sort of dystopian, post-apocalyptic, neo-noir send-up of martial arts movies."

"That's precisely what I envisioned," Woody said.

"But with a lot of dark humor, something playfully absurd, almost a kind of metaphysical Feydeanesque farce, a burlesque mixed in with a little magic realism."

"Exactly!" Woody said. It sounded so much better, the way Dalton was describing it.

"With coincidence as a motif," he said, "so we'd have all these crisscrossing destinies, these intertwined story lines, all the characters searching for ascendancy from their daily lives."

"Yes!" Woody said. What a fantastic pitch. He had to memorize this. This movie *could* be good. It could be something to be proud of—a moneymaker and a critical darling, a cult classic. It could rack up a bunch of awards at film festivals and be Woody's calling card to much bigger projects. People would be clamoring to work with him. Studios would bid to sign him up to a long-term, multiple-film production deal.

"But there's no way I'll ever be able to make that movie," Dalton said.

"No?"

"No."

"Why not?" Woody asked.

"Because of you."

Woody felt the blood in his face drain. "Me?"

"You," Dalton said. "You've let these investors and distributors and God knows who else water down the script to the point where it's now unrecognizable. You let them put Yi Ling Ling— she's not even B-list, she's, like, never-listed—in the lead, and you stripped the production budget to the barest possible bones. You've ensured that this thing will never have a chance. There's not a shot in hell it could ever be any good. You sucked the life out of it. You killed it."

"All of those things can be changed," Woody said. "This is

what the business is all about—it's push-pull, give-and-take. Everything's negotiable, nothing's irrevocable. It's an equation with an attainable solution. We can still make this work."

"No, I don't think we can," Dalton said.

"Why do you say that?"

"Look me in the eyes, Woody. Look me in the eyes and tell me, honestly, that this movie won't be a stinker. Tell me you don't know that already."

Woody looked Dalton in the eyes and, despite not quite believing it, not really, not if he truly had to be honest about it, said, "This movie won't be a stinker."

Dalton smiled wryly. "Then you're not as smart as I thought."

"You want more money, don't you?" Woody said.

"That's not it."

"More control."

"That's not it, either."

What else was there? Woody thought. "Just tell me," he said. "Tell me what you want."

Dalton swallowed the last of his coffee. "I want out."

Woody slid his plastic basket away. He'd eaten too much, his belly straining against his belt. He wondered if the YMCA in town would be open today. "I know you're new to all of this," Woody said to Dalton calmly. "You're—how should we put it?—you're a bit idealistic about the transactional nature of the movie business. What you don't know yet is that we all start out with the best of intentions, we really do, but we have to accept that compromises will be made. The truth is, no one gets exactly what they want. No one. With the constraints given, we do the best we can, we hope to deliver a decent product and make a decent return on our investment. Once in a while it all comes together and you hit it out of the park, but most of the time it doesn't. You end up making something that's respectable but not high art, just a modest entertainment. That's nothing to be ashamed of. You do it, and you move on. You see, Dalton, you can't get out. Contractually you're bound to this project. If you try to renege, we'll sue you. We'll make it very expensive and nasty for you, and it'll be protracted, and we'll file injunctions so you won't be able to work on anything else in the meantime, and your reputation will end up in shit. You don't want that. I don't want that. No one wants that. So let's just do the best we can. We'll work together and do the best we can. What do you say to that?"

"I changed agents," Dalton said.

"Yeah?"

"I'm with CCC now."

A little shudder traveled down Woody's intestines, the mere mention of CCC making him pucker. CCC was the most powerful agency in Hollywood, the most feared collection of sharks among a sea of sharks, evil, ruthless ball-crushers, the holy mothers of shit-your-nicky-na-nas scary motherfuckers.

"They're the ones who told me to delay our meeting. They're talking to their attorneys. They think losing Vivienne Cheung and all the other changes makes my contract null and void."

His movie was dead. It was as good as dead. "They have something else they want you to do, don't they?" Woody said. "Something from a major studio."

"No," Dalton said. "I found something on my own. I ran across a book. Have you ever read any Richard Yates?"

Yates. He dimly recalled reading Yates for AP English in high school. "Sure," he said. " 'The Second Coming,' the spiral gyre."

"You're thinking of William Butler Yeats, the poet. Richard Yates was a novelist, a contemporary of Styron and Vonnegut. Brilliant, pitiless, heartbreaking stuff, unremittingly bleak. His first novel, *Revolutionary Road*, was a National Book Award finalist, but then he faded out of the picture, even though he continued to write, and write well. Eight more books. Eight and a half. When he died in 1992, he was pretty much out of print. A really tragic figure, an alcoholic. He smoked four packs a day and had emphysema. He died alone, living in a crappy little apartment in Alabama hooked up to a portable oxygen tank with tubes in his nose. They found the unfinished manuscript of his last novel in his refrigerator. It was based on his experience working as a speechwriter for Bobby Kennedy. I got to read it. I bought the rights to it."

"*That's* what you want to do?" Woody asked.

"Yes."

Bleak, tragic, and pitiless were not adjectives you wanted attached to any film. He was insane. Woody couldn't believe CCC was even letting him consider this.

The waitress dropped off the check, looking at Dalton meaningfully. He turned it over and smiled. The girl had written her name and phone number on the check. "I think she wants to 'interview' me," Dalton said to Woody.

What a sleazebag, Woody thought. What a hypocrite. He was perfectly happy to be Asian American if it was advantageous for him, if it might get him laid. He was just like Lyndon— everything had always just fallen in his lap, a golden boy, gifted, lucky, blessed—and Woody hated him for it.

"I already started the screenplay," Dalton said, "and a couple of people have expressed interest."

"What people?"

He mentioned three A-list stars, all Academy Award nominees, all CCC clients who would never deign to give Woody the time of day, much less a meeting.

"I'm sorry," Dalton said. "It's nothing personal. It's just, you know—"

And here he crossed the line. He could have let it go at that and been done with it, but he had to take it one more step and humiliate Woody, put him in his place.

"It's just," he said to Woody with a veneer of vindictive glee, "the way the business works."

．　　　．　　　．

IT WAS A PIECE OF SHIT. Dalton was right. His movie would be a piece of shit. But it was all Woody had, and he had too much riding on it to abandon it now. He had ignored the first rule when entering any negotiation: always retain the option to walk away. He couldn't walk away. It was possible he might lose his production company. He might lose his house, his car. He might end up peddling bootleg DVDs on the street again. He might have to take the Glock 17 from his nightstand drawer and stick it in his right ear and pull the trigger, just as Kyle had done.

What was he going to do? Unquestionably, his investors, once they heard the news of Dalton's defection, would quickly drop out, one after another, the first of which would be his German distributor, for whom he had done nothing to persuade Lyndon to sell his farm—did he, in fact, tell him last night *not* to sell it?—in service to the conglomerate SBK. How could he let himself get in this position, Woodrow Wilson Song, power broker extraordinaire, *éminence grise* of Machiavellian persuasion? He was on the verge of failure and destitution, while Lyndon, his idiot slacker brother, was thumbing his nose at fifteen million dollars. It infuriated Woody. That sort of money bought independence. It bought security. It bought immunity from the perils and vagaries and injustices of fate and luck.

He went back to the farm, which was deserted, everyone presumably at the chili and chowder festival, and he took a long hot shower. He reapplied the calamine lotion and swallowed two more antihistamines. He replaced his bandages and changed into another set of clothes, throwing the hoodie, cargo pants, and uggs in the trash. Grabbing his PDA and Bluetooth headset, he went outside and wandered around the yard in search of a better signal. The PDA was an older model, its phone capabilities rather weak.

"Hello?"

"Dan, it's Woody."

"Oh," his therapist said, disappointment bleaching his voice. "Woody, it's Sunday. Can't this wait until our regular time?"

"I don't know what I'm doing here, Dan. It's all falling apart. I don't know what I'm doing."

"Okay, slow down, slow down," Dan said. "Take a deep breath. Can you do that for me?"

"Yeah," Woody said, and he breathed in, breathed out.

"One more," Dan said. "Feel the tension dissipate."

He breathed in, breathed out, and the tension did dissipate a little, although the scalene muscles in his neck remained cramped and stiff.

"All right, then," Dan said. "Where are you? Are you at your brother's?"

"Yeah," Woody said.

"How's that going?"

"Okay, I guess. There are moments we don't hate each other."

"Well, that's good. Don't you think that's good?"

"Though I hate the *idea* of him, still. He's not going to sell his farm, which means my financing is in jeopardy, which means I might be homeless soon."

"Woody," Dan told him, "particalize what you've just said. This is exactly what I mean. You always look at things in extremes. Is it really that bad? If your movie fails, will you really become homeless? What's really the worst that can happen?"

"What did you say?" Woody asked. He couldn't hear Dan well. Besides the spotty connection, a bunch of white-crowned sparrows and scrub jays were making a racket in the trees, raucous and shrill, *shreep-shreep, quay-quay-quay, jree-reee, check-check-check.* Fucking birds. He picked up a rock and chucked it into the closest tree.

"What's the worst that can happen?" Dan repeated, louder.

"I'll have to kill myself."

"Come, now."

"I've never told you this, Dan," Woody said. "I have a gun."

Dan waited a second before responding. "Right now?" he asked quietly.

"What?"

"You have a gun right now, Woody? You have one with you, at this very moment?"

"No. It's at home, in L.A."

"Oh," Dan said. "Well, that's a relief."

"It's all falling apart, Dan. I'm hanging by a thread. I don't know what to do."

"Let me put on my headset, then you can tell me what's happening."

He told Dan everything, about Kyle and Trudy and Lyndon, about Dalton Lee and Ling Ling, about Ed Kitchell and the German financier and the SBK conglomerate, babbling in rapid non sequiturs as he paced in front of Lyndon's house, hands gesticulating wildly in the air to no one. It did seem like no one at times, talking to Dan. Woody often wondered if he was really listening. On the other end of the line, he could be doing anything—his bills, flipping through a magazine, watching TV on mute while reading the captions—and Woody always felt compelled to stop now and then and ask, "Are you there?"

Today, he wasn't mindful of needing any conversational

assurance, preoccupied with the crisis at hand, blathering heed-lessly, until he heard something very distinctly over the phone, a trickling of water, a soft, continuous, languid stream that was viscerally familiar.

"Dan," he said, "what are you doing? Are you taking a *piss*?"

"Of *course* not," Dan said, but Woody caught the tincture of embarrassment in the denial. He surmised that Dan, trying to be clandestine, had sat on the toilet seat and aimed for the side of the bowl.

"I forgot what I was saying," Woody said to test him.

"Never mind," Dan said. "Look, this is not your life, Woody."

"What?" What sort of ridiculous statement was that? This was not his life?

"This is not your *life*," Dan said again. "This does not *own* you. This is not who you *are*."

Woody thought of all the hours he had spent with Dan, all the money he had paid him. Had a single thing he ever said made a difference? Had anything ever struck Woody as truly profound, or had all of it been merely trite, touchy-feely, clichéd psychobabble—empty bromides and insipid, quasi-Eastern dic-tums, *Let it go, This is not your life*—straight out of some self-help book you could get off the shelf? Any shelf. Dan was the sole person in L.A. Woody could really confide in, and the sad, incontrovertible fact was, Dan only talked to him because every minute he spent with him was billable. "I have to go," Woody told him.

It was late in the afternoon, the sun low in the sky. He drove to town. He had missed most of the festival, many of the ven-dors already breaking down their booths, though there were still plenty of stragglers left on Main Street, parents holding hands with children who had their faces painted, carrying balloons.

Wandering past the art exhibits, he noticed a man and a

woman behind the booths in an alleyway between buildings. It was the boy and girl from the ice-cream store, the ones who'd been on horseback on the beach. She was standing with her back against the wall, one knee bent, foot flat on the brick. He was leaning against her, both arms raised overhead, hands on the wall, pinning her there with his hips, and they were staring at each other, giggling, the girl's head twisted slightly to the side, as if she were affronted with what he was suggesting, but the way she held her mouth open and askew—something about it looked so wanton—gave it all away. She would, eventually, comply.

"Woody! Woody!"

Trudy Nguyen jumped on Woody, wrapping her arms around his neck and hugging him. He had promised to visit her and Margot at the Bidwell Marsh Preserve again today, but it had slipped his mind entirely.

"I'm so glad you're here," she said. "I was afraid I wouldn't see you before we left."

"Where are you going?" Woody asked.

"What happened to your face?" she said.

"Nothing. You're leaving? What about AY:BO and WY:GO and their chicks?"

"They're gone. The chicks didn't make it."

The news, surprisingly, distressed Woody. "What happened?"

"They were taken by ravens. It was awful. I saw them coming, and there was nothing we could do. By the time we got down there, it was too late. But you know, I'm okay with it. I can accept it. It's part of the natural cycle of things, not something caused by people, so we did our job. Now we're going to another project, in Hawaii."

"When?"

"Tomorrow. We're going to try to lure the Laysan albatross

into nesting on Kaohikaipu Island, off Oahu, instead of on the airstrips."

She led Woody down the street and around the corner, where Margot was standing before—of all things—an elephant named Esther. Next month during the pumpkin festival, a local farm would be offering rides on Esther and another Asian elephant named Louise, and Esther was here today, corralled in a sandy vacant lot, for advance promotion, an exploitation that didn't sit well with the girls. Margot and Trudy had been harassing the elephant's keeper, Roger.

"We know all about your training methods, the way you abuse them," Margot said. "Blowtorches, bullhooks, electric prods. It's cruel and unusual punishment. We've seen the videos."

Roger, a stocky man in his thirties with a mullet haircut, rolled his eyes. "What are you guys?" he asked. "CEASE? PETA? Why don't you take your clothes off, then? Isn't that what you do at protests? Why don't you get naked and have a lie-down? I wouldn't mind seeing that. I might even join you."

"What's with the chain?" Trudy asked. A chain was wrapped around the elephant's back leg and anchored to a pole. "You could use a rope half as thick as this," she said, pointing to the bulky rope strung across the front of the lot, cordoning them from the elephant.

A little boy towed his mother toward the elephant, and Roger said to the child, "Hey, want to feed her?" He handed the boy some hay, which he eagerly held out in front of Esther, who scooped it up with her trunk and curled it into her mouth.

"You know, a kid got tuberculosis feeding an elephant not too long ago," Margot said, and the mother, alarmed, herded the boy away.

Roger, clutching a promotional flier that he had failed to

pass on to the woman, said, "Nice going, girlie. Now, really, kindly get the fuck out of here."

"Been tested yourself lately?" Margot asked. "Who knows what diseases you're carrying. You look none too savory."

"What time are you leaving tomorrow?" Woody asked Trudy.

"The flight's at one-thirty."

"Where are you going to sleep tonight?"

"A guy, a musician who was playing earlier, he said he'd take us to SFO. We're just going to spend the night in the terminal."

The thought of Trudy leaving further depressed Woody, puncturing him with loneliness. "Come here a minute," he told her. "I need to talk to you." When they were a few steps away, he said, "Don't go to Hawaii."

"Why not?"

"Come to L.A. with me."

"Why?" Trudy said, perplexed. "What would I do in L.A.?"

"Anything you want," he said. "Just be with me. It's as simple as that. I won't ask for anything more. We can figure it out later."

"You're not making sense, Woody. What are you talking about?"

"It feels right. It feels like we should be together. I don't want to lose you, Trudy. I want you to be with me. I'm asking you, please be with me." This moment—the present moment—seemed vitally important to Woody, the most critical of his life. He didn't want to be alone. He wanted to feel love, to swoon and weep and giggle, to be completely absorbed, to look at someone with the all-consuming passion and yearning that possessed those kids from the ice-cream store. He wanted to feel consoled in someone's arms, to be crazed when apart from them, to be thinking about the person all the time, first thing in the morning and last thing at night, to be besotted, enraptured. He wanted, just once, just once in his life, for someone to feel that way about him. And, for once, he was willing to quit trying to orchestrate everyone's behavior, disregard prudence and ignore appearances, lay himself bare, and ask a fellow human being for clemency. "Please, Trudy. Be with me," he said.

"Oh, Woody," she said pityingly. "I can't. I can't be with you. I'm with Margot. We're together. Didn't you know that?"

He blinked back shame. Of course he knew that. Now that she said it, he realized he had known it all along. How could he not? Could anything have been more obvious? Trudy was a lesbian. She and Margot were lesbians. He was overcome with humiliation. What had he been thinking? He was not in love with Trudy, yet he had practically proposed to her. He had made a colossal fool of himself. What was he doing in this stupid, godforsaken town? "I'll be right back," he said.

"Woody, don't go," she said.

He intended to get his clothes from the farm and, if his ailing Rover allowed, drive straight home to L.A., but then he saw Ed Kitchell, wearing a USC sweatshirt, walking down Main Street.

"Hey, chief," Kitchell said, "did you catch the game on TV?"

"What game?"

"Last night! The home opener!"

"No, I missed it," Woody said.

"Oh, man, it was a great game. Unbelievable. I just got back an hour ago." He seemed dazed, not quite awake, sporting a goofy grin. He was unshaven, his blond hair unkempt. "I want to ask you about something—something I just heard," Kitchell said. "Is it possible your brother is growing marijuana on his farm?"

Woody wavered only a few seconds before he said, "I found plants in two places near his Brussels sprouts, in the southeast and southwest corners. They must be in pockets of trees all over the farm. Just follow the irrigation pipes. But most of it is inside his barn, an entire crop."

Kitchell's face lit up, very alert now. "I'll be damned," he said. "That explains a lot. And resolves even more."

Woody felt suddenly sick. He couldn't lie to himself that he was betraying Lyndon in the hopes of saving his movie. At this point, he knew that anything he did for The Centurion Group would not make a bit of difference. He was doing this, he had to admit, out of spite.

"Don't make any moves until tomorrow afternoon," he said to Kitchell, for he spotted Ling Ling and JuJu approaching on the street and realized he had forgotten about her—he needed to get her on a plane back to Hong Kong tomorrow—and then it occurred to him that he could give Trudy and Margot a ride to the airport, too. He could have them spend the night at the farm, steal a little more time with Trudy.

Ling Ling was carrying a painting. "Look what I bought!" she said, flipping around the oil seascape. "Isn't it gorgeous?"

She was in such a good mood. Woody decided against telling her just yet that she would be returning home forthwith, her movie career dead.

"What did Kitchell want?" JuJu asked him.

"Who?"

"Ed Kitchell. You were just talking to him. Was he harassing you?"

"He was asking if there's anything to see down the street. Why would he be harassing me?"

"Lyndey sort of has a history with him. Did he seem agitated?"

"No, not particularly. Why?"

JuJu chuckled to himself. "Guess he hasn't been home yet," he said. "He's in for a few surprises."

"Where is Lyndon?" Woody said.

"Around here somewhere," JuJu said.

They were walking back toward the end of the block, slowed by Ling Ling, who insisted on stopping at every remaining booth to examine their wares, when they heard a loud pop, like a gun firing, followed by a horrendous scraping sound. Around the corner, they witnessed Esther the elephant ramming her head against a dumpster, sliding it across the pavement, trying to get free, trumpeting an awful keen. The dumpster was tied to one end of the bulky rope that had been used as a cordon, the other end around a telephone pole, and as Esther pushed against the dumpster—her trainer, Roger, waving and scream-ing at her—the rope was being swung around, pinning Margot and Trudy against a parked van.

Woody, JuJu, and Ling Ling were so flummoxed by the sight, they did nothing for half a second. Then JuJu and Ling Ling—dropping her precious painting to the ground—sprinted toward the girls, and Woody found himself beside them, trying to tug on the rope and extricate Trudy and Margot, who were groan-ing in pain, their arms trapped awkwardly as they were being cleaved at the waist, lifted off the ground, abject terror in their eyes, like animals about to be slaughtered.

"Pull!" Ling Ling said, bracing her foot against the van.

"My knife," Margot moaned.

Woody saw the butt of Margot's bowie knife poking out from beneath her shirt, the sheath inside her pants, and he yanked it out and hooked the blade against the rope, sawing back on it as hard as he could, and abruptly the rope snapped apart, every-one flying to the ground, Woody spinning and landing with the knife still in his hand, plunging it directly into JuJu's left foot.

Woody, staring at the blade embedded in JuJu's boot, began shrieking hysterically.

"It's okay, it's okay!" JuJu said. "It's a prosthetic!"

"What?"

JuJu lifted his pants leg, revealing the black metal shank of a prosthetic foot. "No worries, dude!" he said.

They turned and watched the elephant, which had broken loose and was now lumbering down Main Street, crashing apart everything in its way.

CHAPTER 9

THE FIRST ANNUAL ROSARITA BAY CHILI AND CHOWDER FESTIVAL was a miniature version of the town's larger, more established pumpkin festival, the usual five blocks of Main Street closed off to traffic for the usual arts and crafts booths, live music, children's games, and other activities, with one notable exception, the chili and chowder cookoff itself, which caused some organizational problems. An inspector from the San Vicente County Health Department was on-site to ensure that the guidelines for food treatment, per its environmental health standards, were being strictly enforced. This meant the only ingredients that could be prepared in advance for the cookoff were "nonperishables": canned or bottled clams and clam juice, tomatoes and tomato sauce, peppers and pepper sauce, broth, beans, and spices. All perishable items had to be prepared and cooked at the festival, especially the meats, which could not be cut or ground or otherwise treated in any way prior to the official preparation and cooking period—guidelines that the contestants, even though they had received them weeks ago, had not quite taken seriously. Thus, the chili and the chowder were not ready to be distributed, as planned, at noon, in time for the attendees to sample and purchase for lunch, but had to be, amid a chorus of complaints and finger-pointing, postponed until at least two o'clock.

Sheila Lemke, as the mayor, was thick in the middle of the fracas, and Lyndon watched her running to and fro with her megaphone, walkie-talkie, and clipboard, trying to mollify entrants, merchants, and members of the chamber of commerce, the city council, and the planning commission, and he knew, regardless of whatever stress and frustration and idiocy Sheila might claim were marring the proceedings, that she was in her element.

She had left his house at dawn, after waking him with a blow job—a rather unexpected act of philanthropy. "Don't put any undue significance in this," she had whispered to him. She had noticed his morning wood, she said, and had just felt like it. But he did put undue significance in it. Things were, he told himself, looking decidedly up. He was getting to her. There was, more than ever, hope for them.

His plants were faring better as well. Irrigating them with sprinklers had helped, and after applying rock dust on them with a spreader in the morning, he was reasonably confident he had staved off the infestation of aphids. His Brussels sprouts were looking robust and healthy. He was likely to have a good harvest after all.

All of this, on top of the amusement he derived from his brother's poison oak, put him in a rare good mood, one that could not be broken despite his sore knee and black eye and cracked molar and the gash on his forehead, despite being informed by the service station that he would need four new tires for his pickup.

It was a beautiful day, windy yet relatively warm. There was a pretty decent turnout for the chili and chowder festival, several thousand people—not anywhere near the quarter million who usually poured into town over the two days of the October pumpkin festival, certainly, but not bad for a newly manufactured occasion—and Lyndon ran into townsfolk he hadn't seen in quite a while. He talked to Hank Low Kwon, a former public defender for San Vicente County who was now a real estate attorney (Lyndon's attorney), his wife, Molly Beddle, and their toddler, Wilder. He exchanged hellos with Ariel Belieu, the reference librarian, Beryl Pappalardo, the bookstore/café owner, and Gene Becklund, who'd quit the sheriff's office recently to run the Moonside Trading Post with his wife, with whom he'd reconciled after a long separation. He chatted briefly with the chairmaker Dean Kaneshiro, who was the only true artist in Rosarita Bay, his wife, the poet Caroline Yip, and their two kids, Anna and Doc. He waved to B. J. Daniel, the photographer for the *Rosarita Bay Horizon,* Missy Stiegel, a waitress from the Java Hut, Will and Karen Somers, the proprietors of the trattoria La Bettola, and Katie Mitchell, who managed Cuchi's Country Store. He nodded to Janet McElroy, a half-black, half-Korean psychotherapist (Sheila's psychotherapist), her oncologist husband, Eugene Kim, and their four children. He shot the breeze with Evelyn Yung, a math teacher at Longfellow Elementary, her adopted Amerasian son, Brian, and his brother, Patrick, a Navy fighter pilot who was visiting from Coronado. It surprised Lyndon, how many locals he actually knew, and the realization comforted him. He was a part of this town, and, for better or for worse, it was a part of him. Not a single person, God bless them, mentioned The Centurion Group's bid to buy out his farm.

With the chili and chowder postponed, he suggested to Ling Ling and JuJu that they eat lunch at Rae's Diner. From the pay phone in the restaurant, Lyndon tried to call Woody on his cell phone, but his brother didn't pick up, so he left him a message, telling him where they were.

Ling Ling ordered a brunch of blueberry flapjacks, sausage, and hash browns, JuJu asked for a Reuben, and Lyndon got a bacon cheeseburger. There was no better burger in town than Rae's.

As they waited for their food, JuJu fidgeted, his right knee a sewing machine. Finally he blurted out to Lyndon that he had an announcement of sorts. "It doesn't look like I'll be here for the harvest this year, bro," he said.

"Where are you going to be?"

JuJu and Ling Ling glanced at each other affectionately. "Hong Kong," he said. "Then Vietnam for a couple of months."

"A couple of *months*?"

"At least. Maybe more. So, uh, I might not be going with you to Baja in January, either, Lyndey."

"What are you going to do in Vietnam?" Lyndon asked, miffed.

"Help Ling Ling set up a new prosthetic center in Ho Chi Minh City."

Not comprehending, Lyndon turned to Ling Ling. "You're setting up a prosthetic center?"

"There're over a hundred thousand amputees in Vietnam," Ling Ling said. "Most of them were maimed during the Vietnam War, but there are still anywhere between three hundred fifty and eight hundred thousand tons of UXO, unexploded ordnance, spread out through the country. Since 1975, almost forty thousand people have been killed and an additional seventy thousand injured. There's a desperate need for orthopedic surgical care and clinical outreach there."

A nice fundraising speech, but Lyndon still couldn't wrap his head around the first part. "No, I mean, *you're* setting up a prosthetic center? *You're* in charge of it?"

"Well, I wouldn't say in charge," Ling Ling said, "but I'm the regional VIP volunteer director for the International Red Cross Millennium Movement on Land Mines."

That Ling Ling—this heretofore self-centered, self-aggrandizing boozehound of a kung-fu actress—had an entirely different life as a humanitarian, one of substance and significance, floored Lyndon.

"She's arranged for me to train there," JuJu said. "Learn how to fit people with prostheses and assist with their rehabilitation."

"How'd you get involved in this?" Lyndon asked Ling Ling.

She blushed. "Well, if you must know, it was because of Princess Di."

"Princess Diana?"

"Yes. I loved her. She inspired me to volunteer. I saw her visiting Angola and Bosnia. You know, you must have seen the videos, with her helmet and flak jacket. But once I started working with these NGOs, once I saw the pain caused by all these UXOs, the victims, it's so often children, any associations—or should I say, shamefully, aspirations—for glamour faded rather quickly."

"What about Woody's movie? Aren't you supposed to start filming in San Francisco in November?"

She unfurled her fingers in a resigned wave. "Oh, that's possible, but I doubt very much it will happen. Realistically, I know that this movie probably won't get made—there are so many things that can disrupt these deals, it's very arbitrary at times, this business, the financing can disappear with a single person's whimsy—and even if it does get made, realistically, as much as I would like it not to be the case, I have to prepare myself that I probably won't be in it. If you haven't been able to guess, my career has been on the decline for quite some time now."

"You'd be so fabulous in this role," JuJu told her.

She kissed him on the cheek. "You're sweet to say so."

"You see what I was talking about, Lyndey? The coincidences?" JuJu said. "I mean, what are the chances that the queen of Hong Kong cinema would be marooned on your farm for the weekend, and I'd get to meet her, and she'd be the regional VIP director for the International Red Cross Millennial Movement Against Land Mines and I'd end up going to Southeast Asia with her? What kind of Vedic rabbit hole of temporally acausal connections have we tumbled through? I mean, holy mother of Carl Gustav Jung, throw down the *I Ching*, man, this is heavy, the serendipity of this, the Deschampsian plum-pudding wheel of karma that's spun me off in this direction. Once Ling Ling mentioned it, it made total sense, everything that's happened, the Oar House being destroyed, losing my foot to Big Mac at Rummy Creek. All those years looking for satori in Uluwatu and the Maldives and Lagundri Bay, I had a *quest*. Everything was so simple and pure, just searching out those secret, mysto spots for the perfect wave. And then it was gone, and I've just been floundering. I was *lost*, dude. I'd lost the one thing I'd loved most in the world. But now it feels like it's all come full circle, this yin yang of alchemic interconnection and fate, lives and souls bound together." He looked at Ling Ling. "I'm going to help people who are going through what I went through. This is, like, what I was meant to do, you know? Be part of something larger than myself. No pun intended. You understand what I'm talking about, Lyndey?"

Lyndon did understand, but the idea of JuJu—his buddy, his compadre, really his only friend—leaving, perhaps forever, saddened him immensely. "When are you taking off?"

"Next week. Yeah, I know—soon. Listen, Tank and Skunk will help you with the harvest. I talked to them already."

"Thanks a lot," Lyndon said.

"Come on, don't be that way. They'll be good workers. Be happy for me, man."

"I am," Lyndon said. He genuinely was, but he also felt something else, a shade of another emotion, which weirdly approximated envy.

They ate their lunch, and then returned to the festival, first to the kids' stage, where there were jugglers and a puppet show. At the Bank of America parking lot was the main stage, a cover band called the Skyline Waybacks playing the Eagles, America, the Stones and Beatles, Christopher Cross, Stevie Ray Vaughan, and, inevitably, the Beach Boys. And all along Main Street were rows and rows of white canvas booths that housed a panoply of arts and crafts, remarkable only for their collective mediocrity: glass-beaded trees, tapestries and quilts, aromatherapy soaps and soy candles, doggie apparel, cigar-box purses, Zapotec rugs and Oaxacan wood carvings, Japanese *shakuhachi* flutes, feng shui wind chimes, and all manner of jewelry, ceramics, sculpture, photography, and bad paintings, several of which, to Lyndon's dismay, captivated Ling Ling, particularly the endless iterations of moonlit waves crashing onto rocks. "I want something to remind me of your beautiful farm!" she said.

They each bought a five-dollar tasting kit, which consisted of a plastic spoon, a stack of small paper cups, and ten tickets, and got in line to sample the chili and chowder. At the table for Gregorio's Fishtrap, they were surprised to find Mark Beezle, a.k.a. Beelzebub, and Mandy, the erstwhile waitress whose myriad cases of litigation were presumably pending, serving the restaurant's clam chowder entry, and even more surprised to discern that the two former employees of the Oar House were an item.

Mark put his arm around Mandy and greasily nuzzled her, cheek to cheek. "I've been in love with her from the minute I laid eyes on her!" he told Lyndon. "But I couldn't do anything!

Not while she was working for me! It would have been sexual harassment!"

Wonder of wonders, Lyndon thought, even the wretched and the woebegone found love.

Alas, Gregorio's Fishtrap did not win the competition. Controversially the R. B. Feed & Hardware Store, instead of one of the food establishments, took home both the Best New England and Best Manhattan Chowder prizes (one hundred dollars each). Da Bones won Best Traditional Chili, and the Coastside Institute of Shiatsu snagged Best Nontraditional/Vegan Chili. Lyndon perked up, expecting Laura Díaz-McClatchey to pick up the award, but someone else, a tall blonde in a white gossamer dress, stepped forward to accept the check.

Because of the delay in the chili and chowder cookoff, after the prizes had been announced, a much larger crowd than expected migrated to the Bank of America parking lot, where the Skyline Waybacks were wrapping up their set with a spirited rendition of Loggins and Messina's "Vahevala." When the band vacated the stage, Tommy Fulcher, owner of Tommy's Tunes, stepped to the microphone and went into a long-winded speech, acknowledging and thanking the festival's organizers and sponsors, most notably The Centurion Group. Then he introduced the next act, crowing, "Now give it up for the winner of Java Hut's open-mike competition, Rosarita Bay's own Hana Frost!"

Hesitantly, Hana stumbled up onto the stage, clearly dazzled by the number of people before her. She had on a god-awful getup: a mod red trench coat over a distressed brown T-shirt, denim miniskirt, white pantyhose, and green tennis shoes. She was sporting a pair of Windsor glasses with purple lenses, black lipstick, and she'd done something inopportune to her hair, teasing it into wild, kinky whorls that made her look emphatically asylum-bound. The sight of her generated a few gasps and laughs. "Test, one-two-three, test," she said unnecessarily into the mike, her voice weak and craggy. Then she began nervously tuning her guitar, an excruciatingly long process that became all the more tedious since, with the adjustment of each peg, the bulky dreadnought sounded more and more discordant. Her hands were visibly shaking.

This is going to be a disaster, Lyndon thought. While they waited, he glanced around the crowd, which was murmuring and giggling. Chief among the twitterers were Hana's would-be paramour, André Meeker, and his ice-cream hussy, Jen de Leuw. They stood with their arms wrapped around each other, their bodies squeezed together in such a lascivious, hormonally intoxicated lock, Lyndon knew Hana would never have a chance of prying them apart, no chance at all. A few yards beyond them was Sheila, but strangely she wasn't paying the least bit of attention to Hana. She was glaring off to the side, and Lyndon followed her gaze to discover the object of her ire. Her first ex-husband, Hana's father, Chris Frost, was in attendance with his new, very young trophy wife.

At last, Hana got her guitar in tune, and she started strumming, and strumming. Her head down, she repeated the intro to the song five times, in danger of being stuck interminably in the same cascade of notes, but finally she busted out into the first verse with a robust, bluesy contralto. It was a luscious, rich voice, rootsy and growly, sort of country and western, though the song distinctly fell into the indie folk-pop category, and the most startling aspect of it was how big and deep and powerful the voice was—a completely unexpected projection from an uncertain high school girl. She barreled ahead now, pitching perfectly up another register into a haunting falsetto. In the next song, she rumbled out like a gospel howler, and in the next she performed a little vocal trick in the chorus, half yodel and half warble, able to quaver at will.

Her songs were well structured, complex, with good melodic lines, the chord progressions catchy and inventive. Her only failing, as Hana herself had intuited, was in her lyrics. She was trying to convey songs of wistful introspection, blue-collar, lonely-girl ballads, but they weren't at all convincing, utterly derivative, with obvious shades of Patsy Cline and Jeff Buckley and Patty Griffin. Worse was their sentimentality. She crooned about loss and longing and heartache, but the rhymes were sappy and unimaginative, hand and understand, forever and never, tears and fears, and the images were mawkish and cli-chéd, sitting alone, a prisoner in her own room, the moon and the rain outside, lovers going down the lonely highway, away, away, goodbye, goodbye.

Still, it was a beguiling performance, and the audience gave Hana her due, clapping and whistling. Breathless, flushed, and elated, Hana basked in the applause for a few seconds, and then ran off the stage, not to Sheila but to her father, burying her head in his chest.

"Not bad, eh?" JuJu said to Lyndon.

"Yeah, not bad," Lyndon said.

"I want to go back and get that painting of the water and cliffs," Ling Ling said.

"Which one?" Lyndon and JuJu said at the same time, there had been so many.

Ling Ling and JuJu went off to locate the painting, leaving Lyndon behind in the parking lot. He was joking around with Todd Kemel, an artichoke farmer. They both sold primarily to Veritable Vegetables in San Francisco, a women's collective that was the biggest organic-produce wholesaler on the West Coast.

VV was run mostly by lesbians, and Lyndon liked to play little pranks on them. He was telling Todd about what he was planning for this year's harvest—insert some fuzzy pink handcuffs in among his Brussels sprouts—when he looked across the parking lot at Hana and Sheila, who were arguing, daughter doing most of the yelling, mother staring at her murderously. Without warning, Sheila reached up and slapped Hana on the face.

Lyndon ran over to the other side of the lot. By then Hana had already fled and Sheila was walking back to the main festivities. "Oh, Sheila, what are you doing?" Lyndon said, grabbing her by the arm.

"Don't touch me," she said, twisting out of his grip. "Don't you dare say a word to me. You have no right. You are not part of this family."

But he was. He felt, for better or worse, that he was.

Sheila stalked away from him, and Lyndon turned in the other direction to look for Hana. She was probably already in her car, heading home. Lyndon hiked down Main Street toward the service station near Highway 71, where his pickup was supposed to have been repaired, but as he crossed the creek bridge near the end of town, he saw Hana below, near the water. He stutter-stepped down the steep embankment and sat next to her on a boulder.

"Hey," he said.

"Hey."

"You all right?"

"My father offered to pay for Berklee," she said. "I didn't think he'd even come today."

"Your mom know you invited him?"

"Where is it written I have to tell her everything?" She flung a rock at the creek, and it skipped twice on the surface and then plopped into the water.

"She's just trying to protect you, you know," Lyndon said.

"She's jealous. Jealous of my talent. She's jealous I have a purpose—something she's never had."

"I think it's more complicated than that."

"She has no *soul.*"

"Hana, you didn't tell her that, did you?"

She stood up and threw another rock.

He joined her at the edge of the creek, picked up a stone, and flicked it sidearm, making it skip on the water's surface. "Got three," he said.

"More like two and a half," she said. "That last one shouldn't count, it was so anemic." They traded turns for a while. Hana flung a low-trajectory beaut—six long skips. She brushed the dirt off her hands and asked, "What did you think today? Honestly. Do I have what it takes?"

"You were good," Lyndon said. "But honestly, I can't say whether you have what it would take."

"You didn't think I was very good, then."

"That's not it. It's just I don't know the music business."

"You can give me your uneducated opinion."

"You really want to know what I think?" Lyndon asked.

"Yes."

"Okay. I imagine it's a lot like the art business—ruthless, arbitrary, agonizingly unfair. With any of the arts, talent isn't always the deciding factor. Even if you have a shitload of it, you could still go unrecognized. It doesn't happen for everyone. But let's say you do make it, let's say you manage to hit it big, you have to sustain it somehow, or you'll just be a one-hit wonder, a flash in the pan, and you'll grow old playing that one minor, inconsequential hit over and over, hanging on to a faded dream, looking for relevance, pathetically chasing lost glory. You could end up begging for gigs at coffeehouses and chili and chowder festivals in little pough towns. On the other hand, let's say you become a star. There will be people out there whose sole mission in life will be to tear you down. Not just your music, but your personal life, your appearance, everything you say and do. Nothing will ever be good enough. You'll have this enormous burden to keep topping yourself, keep coming up with something new, different, but not too different. You could become a parody of yourself. You could end up doubting your own worth and feel like a total fraud. You could end up hating yourself, asking every day why you ever became an artist. It could be a terrible life. You could regret not becoming a doctor, doing something more tangible to contribute, something not as subjective, not so dependent on other people's judgment and the whims of public opinion and taste."

Hana stared at him with grim consternation. "Jesus, forget I asked."

"It won't necessarily get you laid, either."

She flicked a stone. "I don't care about that anymore. I'm over him," she said.

"Oh, yeah?"

"You were right. He's a complete wanker and dipshit moron. Jen de Leuw can have him."

"What made you change your mind all of a sudden?"

"He has some really bizarre theories. He's kind of a weirdo punk, if you ask me."

"Young love can be so fickle."

"Does age make a difference in that respect?"

"You have a point there."

He climbed up the embankment and walked back to town. Hana would be all right. She might not make it as a singer-songwriter, but whatever happened, whatever she decided to do, she would be able to cope.

The festival was winding down, the scaffolding for the cooking tents being dismantled, workmen carrying the framing to a truck. Lyndon crossed to the sidewalk to maneuver around them, and the world went black. Someone—it must have been two, maybe three goliaths—placed a hood over his head and clamped a hand over his mouth and dragged him away from the street as he tried to yell and writhe and escape. He was, it appeared, for a reason he could not begin to imagine, being kidnapped.

He was lifted off his feet and thrown to a hard metal floor. The hood was lifted off, and sitting across from Lyndon was Sunny Padaca, smiling at him in the back of a van.

"Howzit, brah?" he said.

"Sunny!"

Two of his *vato* crew stood outside the van. "Shut it," Sunny said, and they slid the door closed, leaving them alone.

"Aren't you supposed to be in jail?" Lyndon asked.

"Well, you know, it's funny how, with a couple of good lawyers, these things can turn out, yeah? Seems there were a couple of technicalities that weren't identified in the original indictment. Turns out it was all just a misunderstanding, a big misunderstanding, solly solly, velly solly, you know?"

"I thought courts weren't open on weekends."

"Helps to have connections, brah. And I got connections everywhere."

Lyndon shifted on the corrugated floor. "Good for you," he said.

"Yeah, good for me," Sunny said. "Not so good for you, bruddah."

Lyndon felt something internal quiver. "What do you mean?"

"What I mean? What I mean? Oh, I think you know exactly what I mean, Linda. No secrets here, right? No little birdies have to tell us nothing, do they?"

"I don't know what you're talking about."

Sunny sighed. "You and the pogo stick, you got ten Christmas trees from South Africa saying aloha, Nelson Mandela, on your farm."

Adiós, motherfucker, Lyndon thought. "Look, Sunny, they're purely for personal consumption."

"Ten trees? That's a lot of pakalolo. You and peg-leg must have some kind of habit."

"It was totally an experiment. I didn't think they'd all make it. We were just fucking around."

"Just fucking around, yeah? I'd think you'd have more confidence in your abilities, Linda, seeing how you're the local Brussels sprouts king."

"I'm a pretty bad farmer, actually. I barely make a living from it."

"So you decided you need to supplement your income," Sunny said.

"Absolutely not. We never, in a million years, ever thought about selling the stuff."

"No?"

"We'd never be that stupid."

"That's right, because, you know, this isn't a business for barneys. Nasty things happen to barneys. There's frightful, major, serious consequences for barneys. A lot more serious than a little vandalism here and there. More painful than Mac attacks, know what I'm saying? The Messiah would come to visit with righteous indignation. But as I assess the situation, I get the sense that nothing so dramatic would even be necessary, yeah? I get the sense, with your financial situation, one little phone call to old Five-O would be enough to take you down, permanent-like, you know. What's your feeling on that?"

"Listen, I'll go home right now and chop down the plants. I'll burn them."

"You'd do that for me, just to put my poor Nanakuli pea brain to rest?"

"Without hesitation."

Sunny removed a pack of gum from his back pocket and folded a stick into his mouth. "That might be kind of a shame, though, huh?" he said, chewing contemplatively. "Because I hear it's some good shit. Is that right? Is it good shit?"

"We haven't sampled it yet."

"But it's ready to harvest?"

"Pretty much."

"And they're looking tasty? Ripe and mongo and Buddha-licious?"

"Yeah."

"They're totally organic?"

"Of course."

Nodding, Sunny folded his fingers together across his stomach. "Okay, then, here's what I think we should do. It happens I got a little supply-chain problem at the moment. So you could do me a favor, you could help me out. You could give me the plants. What do you think of that? Isn't that a good idea?"

"All ten plants?"

"All ten."

"For free?" Lyndon asked.

"Linda, Linda . . ."

Knowing he was pressing his luck, Lyndon said, "Couldn't we, you know, negotiate a little, uh, transaction of some sort?"

Sunny laughed. "Like I said, man, you got *cojones*, brah."

"At a substantial complimentary discount, of course."

"A discount, yeah? How about this, then? Tell me if you

think this would be fair. What say we make it completely complimentary?"

"Completely?"

"Am I being too generous? Let me know if I am. I'd hate for anyone to think I'm being ripped off. I don't want to come off as a chump."

"Sunny," Lyndon said, "what about letting me keep a *tiny* little supply for myself?"

"I'd be happy to sell you dime bags whenever you want."

"You're going to make me pay for my own pot?"

"It's a hell of a world, isn't it, for the enterprising opportunist? Your brother and his kung-fu mama still staying with you? When they leaving?"

"Tomorrow morning, I think."

"Let's say I swing by one-ish, then. You'll have 'em ready for me, brah? Gift-wrapped would be nice."

Lyndon had little choice. "Yeah, okay," he said.

As Lyndon was about to exit the van, Sunny said, "Yo, Linda, it's not like me to mess with family, but let me throw you a bone. Don't trust your brother."

"Why?"

"I just saw him talking to that developer, Kitchell."

"So?"

"They looked kind of cozy, if you ask me."

Lyndon didn't know what to make of the information. What could Woody be conspiring with Kitchell about? What was he up to?

He jumped out, Sunny's crew slammed the door shut, and they peeled off. Breathless, Lyndon slumped down, leaning against a dumpster for balance. The truth was, with the aphids threatening his crop, he had actually been *thinking* about selling the pot—just a small amount to tide him over. Who knew what kind of trouble that would have led to? Plenty, he was sure, if what had happened over the last few days was any indication. He was glad not to have the temptation anymore. He wanted this long weekend to be over. Whatever Woody was scheming to do was immaterial. He'd be gone in less than twenty-four hours, and Lyndon could have his life back. Everything could return to normal, be quiet, uneventful.

He walked through an alleyway and emerged onto Main Street again. He saw Sheila talking to a vendor at her booth. The woman specialized in bronzes of "canine heroes," the statuettes dedicated to honoring K-9 police dogs across the country. As Lyndon neared the booth, a pop cracked the air, and then there was a tremendous ruckus, a piercing, grating, screeching noise, followed by an inhuman sonorous moan, like the song of a humpback whale, yet a hundred times more portentous— bloodcurdling and terribly lonely. Everyone, including Lyndon, turned toward the sound. In the distance, the white canvas tops of the arts and crafts booths were billowing up strangely, as if from updrafts of wind or from the rippling groundswells of an earthquake, one after another, a steady, rolling oscillation that appeared eerily familiar to Lyndon, evoking images of lanterns, anchors, oars. The growing din was familiar as well. Crunching, crashing implosions, imminent death by building collapse. Only it wasn't a building, and it wasn't an earthquake. It was an elephant stampeding toward them, head down, hell-bent on destruction, razing everything in its path.

Lyndon ran at Sheila and tackled her, shoving her out of the way from the rampaging elephant, and in the process bowled into a row of canine heroes, knocking his head against a bronze of Snowball, a five-year-old Belgian Shepherd in Harrisburg, Pennsylvania, who, as a plaque on the base of the statuette explained, had saved his partner, Sergeant Michael Torres, from further injury and very possibly death by attacking a suspect who had shot the officer, neutralizing him until backup arrived.

"This is all your fault!" Sheila screamed at Lyndon, standing over him amid the wreckage. "You caused this! You've ruined everything!"

As absurd as the accusation was, Lyndon had the distinct feeling, as he began to slip into unconsciousness, that—given the orbit of this weekend's catastrophes—she was probably right.

．　　　．　　　．

HE AWOKE IN ST. CATHERINE HOSPITAL in Moss Beach, and this time—third possible concussion in three days—they insisted on taking him in an ambulance over the hill to San Vicente Memorial for a CT scan. He also needed an MRI for his left shoulder, which he had apparently dislocated crashing into the bronze canines, but which a doctor had graciously popped back in the socket while Lyndon was still out.

This all took hours, of course, and when he was finally released, with a pounding headache and an arm sling to immobilize his shoulder, he had to pay for a fifty-dollar cab ride back to his farm. More than from anything physical, he was wounded that Sheila had not accompanied him to check on his welfare. No one else had been hurt during the rampage other than Lyndon. The elephant, after tearing down the final arts and crafts booth, had trotted to a stop on Main Street, docile enough to allow capture, leaving the town undamaged, *nada* defiled except unsold bad art (although the insurance claims for it would probably be astronomical). Sheila, if she really cared, should have come to the hospital. Lyndon could have called someone else to pick him up, he supposed, but he didn't feel like waiting. He just wanted to get home and have a peaceful night to himself—a beer, a bowl, a shower, dinner, sleep.

As the taxi rolled up to the house, he saw a fire. Someone had started a bonfire near the edge of the bluff, and Lyndon could make out silhouettes of people dancing around the blaze.

There was JuJu, Woody, and Ling Ling, and two young women who looked rather nappy, grooving to Santana's "Black Magic Woman," which was blasting out of a boom box, the women undulating their arms and bodies—bellies, pelvises, hips swaying. As the song reached the trippy instrumental crescendo, electric guitar going into high sustain and reverb, cymbals and congas and timbales voodooing out, everyone began twirling and flailing and hopping up and down, and at the song's conclusion, they raised their arms into the air and hooted and howled. "Oye Como Va" began playing next on the boom box, and the dancing resumed.

Woody jogged over to Lyndon as he got out of the cab. "Where have you been?" he asked. "We were getting worried." He stank of booze.

"Having a little party?"

"I wouldn't call it a party. What happened to your arm?"

"Who're the gypsy girls?"

"Friends of mine, Trudy and Margot. They were kind of stranded, so I invited them to stay the night. You don't mind, do you?"

"Why would I mind?"

"Come on, it's only for one night. I'm driving everyone to the airport tomorrow."

"Early, right?" Lyndon asked. He wanted the place cleared out before Sunny arrived. "You have that meeting with the director?"

"Well, that's kind of off now," Woody said.

"What happened?"

Woody shrugged. "You know, shit happens. It just wasn't

meant to be. But I'm okay with it. I can accept it. Things will work out."

This sort of equanimity seemed very unlike his brother. "What time are you leaving, then?"

"I don't know. Eleven? Twelve? What, can't get rid of me fast enough?" Woody joked.

"You don't think your visit's been a *little* disruptive? Fuck, look at me!" Lyndon said, gesturing at the totality of the injuries to his head, his shoulder, his knee, his eye, his tooth.

"Hey, man, chill out," Woody said.

"Chill out?" Lyndon said. "Did you just tell me to chill out? Are you out of your mind? Are you stoned?"

Woody stiffened. "No," he said too quickly.

Lyndon noticed his brother was concealing something behind his back. "What have you got there? A joint?"

"No," Woody said again.

"Yeah, sure, raid my stash anytime you want," Lyndon said. "Gimme." Woody handed him the joint, and Lyndon took two deep tokes from it, a couple of seeds popping.

Woody motioned for the joint's return, pinched it between thumb and forefinger, and dragged. "You know, I saved a life today," he said dreamily. "*Two* lives."

"It involved an elephant, didn't it?" Lyndon said.

"How'd you know?"

He plucked the roach from Woody's fingers. "Lucky guess."

While the elephant's trainer, Roger, had been distracted, arguing with Trudy and Margot, someone had snipped the chain off Esther's leg and then lit a firecracker, which had spooked the elephant into charging forward into the rope and the dumpster. On the back wall of the lot, "PLF"—the calling card for the Planet Liberation Front, the extremist organization—had been spraypainted in blood red. In the aftermath, the police—Steven Lemke chief among them—had threatened to arrest the girls for felony vandalism, inciting a riot, reckless endangerment, and malicious destruction of property, but, ironically, Roger, the trainer, had come to their defense, saying they couldn't have been responsible, at least not directly.

Lyndon looked over at the group around the bonfire, dancing now to "Soul Sacrifice," and said to his brother, "You are just a magnet for disaster."

"You are such a hard man, Lyndon," Woody said. "Why are you so fucking cold? What is wrong with you? Everything's always been so easy for you. You've never had to work for anything. You had it all, and you threw it all away. It was your choice to walk. *You* did it. You have no basis to be bitter."

"How's that different from what you did?"

Woody tilted his head back and groaned. "God, it was all so long ago. It was a lifetime ago. I made a mistake. I've said I'm sorry a thousand times over. Can't you forgive me? Mom and Dad did. Why not you? You had all that money. Why didn't you help me? You could have bailed me out, but you let me sit in jail. I'm your flesh and blood." He reached behind his back and pulled out a bowie knife from his waistband.

"Jesus, where'd you get that thing?" Lyndon asked.

"Flesh and blood, Lyndon," Woody said, holding the knife in front of him.

"All right, all right, calm down." Lyndon stared at the knife. Had Woody been the one who'd slashed the tires on his pickup truck? But why? Did his hatred of him run that deep? Was he going to stab the knife into him now?

"You know how many times I've wanted to kill myself?" Woody asked.

"Hey, come on."

Woody tipped the point of the knife toward his chest. "I have nothing," he cried. "Nothing."

"It's okay," Lyndon said. "Everything's going to be okay. Let's talk about it. We can talk about it. Why don't you pass that thing over to me?"

Woody looked down at the knife. Vacantly, he flicked the edge of the blade over his left palm, slicing his skin.

"Fuck," Lyndon said. He grabbed the knife from his brother. "Woody, what'd you do that for? We need to wrap that up. Keep your arm raised."

As they walked toward the house, a light suddenly blinded them. A spotlight was being trained on them from the sky, and Lyndon heard the whomp-whomp of a helicopter, then the thumping of drums and the earsplitting blaring of horns. Lyndon recognized that ominous heralding of trumpets. It was a recording of one of USC's fight songs, "Tribute to Troy," played by the Trojans' marching band.

Kitchell!

As Lyndon and Woody shielded their faces from the dust and dirt swirling with the shear of the helicopter's rotors, something dropped down to the ground, something hard and pink and shaped like a jagged rock. Several more pieces fell to earth, bouncing in a line toward Lyndon's panel truck. Kitchell was towing a large orange cylinder beneath his helicopter—it looked like a firefighting bucket—and once he was in position over Lyndon's welding truck, he released the contents of the bucket, letting loose a veritable cascade of what Lyndon could now see were pieces of blubber, frozen whale blubber, raining down on his truck, hammering and denting and piling up on the hood and roof.

Had Kitchell been saving the blubber from the humpback

carcass in a freezer for expressly this purpose? In anticipation of needing to retaliate if Lyndon and JuJu went a little too far with their pranks, as Kitchell most certainly must have felt tonight, assailed by the booby traps in his house? Lyndon, however begrudgingly, had to hand it to the guy, he had some chutzpah, maybe even, it could be said, some *cojones*.

"I'll give you this round, Kitchell," Lyndon screamed up at the helicopter. "You're still a fuckwad, but I'll give you this one."

· · ·

EARLY MONDAY MORNING, Lyndon walked his fields, turning on valves to the drip tape. He had an irrigation controller on the wall of his shed that was capable of automatically opening the valves on a programmed schedule. There were even fancier units that could factor in climate and water-usage data, even some with their own weather stations and meters that measured "soil tension." The sales rep had told him they were as easy to operate as a VCR, all he had to do, practically, was plug in his zip code, but Lyndon couldn't be bothered, and he no longer installed zone wires with his submains or electric solenoids on his valves. He preferred checking the plants and the ground himself, then deciding how much and how long each block needed to be watered. He only used his controller to regulate the pressure and flow rate and as a relay to start the pump near his irrigation pond.

He waded between rows, occasionally stooping down to inspect an emitter on the tape, his movements hampered by his knee brace and arm sling, and when he bent down, he caught the waft of a funny smell, something rancid—not putrefied whale blubber, something else, sharper, more astringent, like gasoline. The night before, after tending to Woody's hand, he had gotten everyone, including his two new female guests, to help him transport the blubber in wheelbarrows to his own freezers. He didn't want it to melt and stink up the farm, and he thought the blubber could be put to future service. He and Kitchell might trade it back and forth in perpetuity.

He heard an engine whining and revving over the berm. Woody spun around the corner of the tractor path in his Range Rover and slid to a stop. He rolled down his window and waved at Lyndon, saying in a panicked voice, "Something's wrong with Bob."

"What's wrong with him?"

"I don't know. He's sick!"

They drove back to the house, in front of which Bob was panting and staggering around in a wobbly circle. Lyndon hopped out of the SUV and squatted down beside his dog, stroking his throat. "Hey, hey, big guy, are you sick?"

Bob coughed and hacked as if choking. He was twitching, and his heart was beating rapidly.

"You swallow something?" There were so many things around the farm—ordinary, innocuous household items—that dogs could ingest by mistake, bringing them harm: detergent, alcohol, disinfectants, even coffee and chocolate, which contained theobromine, toxic to canines. Or maybe Bob had gotten ahold of a piece of blubber they'd missed. "Get me that bottle of hydrogen peroxide from the bathroom," he told Woody. "And a turkey baster, from the kitchen, the drawer with the knives and spatulas."

He led Bob to the side of the barn and flushed out his mouth with the hose. Woody returned with the hydrogen peroxide, and Lyndon mixed it with water and squirted it down Bob's throat with the baster. Bob gagged and squirmed, but Lyndon held him and massaged his belly to blend the peroxide with the contents of his stomach.

"Is he going to be all right?" Woody asked. Bob began dry-heaving. "What'd you do to him? Do you know what you're doing?"

"We need to make him throw up," Lyndon said. He kept shaking Bob's belly, and finally he vomited. "Hang on to his collar," he told his brother, and he knelt down in the dirt and sniffed the vomit. It smelled chemical, and he realized it was the same smell he had whiffed out in the field.

"Shit," he said quietly. He ran-hopped-skipped down to his irrigation pond, scooped up some water in his cupped hand, and tasted it. He spat it out and hurried back to his shed.

"What's going on?" Woody asked, holding Bob.

Lyndon shut off his pump, knowing it was already too late. "Turpentine," he said. "Someone dumped paint thinner into my irrigation pond."

"By accident?"

"Not an accident."

"Are your sprouts going to be okay?"

"My plants are dead. All of them. The entire crop." Just the tiniest bit of solvent was enough to kill them. And not only was this season's entire harvest lost, but he wouldn't be able to plant in those spots for years, the turpentine having leached into the soil. Worse was the pond. He'd have to empty it, dredge it, hope it hadn't gotten into the water table, and still he wouldn't be able to use it again—ever. He'd have to dig a new pond, and that would require money and time to get a new off-stream impoundment approved, money and time he didn't have. His farm was as good as finished.

"Why would anyone do that to you?" Woody asked.

"You tell me. You tell me, Woody."

"What are you implying?"

"What have you been up to, Woody?"

"*Nothing.* I can't believe—"

"I hear you've been palling around with Ed Kitchell," Lyndon said.

"Come on, you can't seriously mean it. I wouldn't do this," Woody said, stroking Bob. "Not this."

"Then what? Exactly what would you do, Woody, to get what you want? You'd pretty much be willing to do anything, wouldn't you? You'd hire someone to take the SATs for you. You'd embezzle your own parents' money and wipe them out. What else would you do?"

A car drove up to them, Laura Díaz-McClatchey's car. She opened the door and stepped out, and Lyndon saw that she had someone with her, a man around fifty who was well dressed and well fed—quite portly, actually.

"Well, Day-Glo my ass," the man said to Lyndon. "Look at you, you little fucker. How is it you haven't gotten fat like the rest of us?"

Lyndon stared at him. His thinning hair was long and swept back, and he had a silk kerchief in the breast pocket of his sports jacket. "Alvin?" he said. It couldn't be. He'd heard somewhere that Alvin had closed his gallery long ago, shortly after contracting HIV.

"Come here," Alvin said, and he hugged Lyndon warmly.

"I thought you were . . ."

"Dead? Ah, happily the rumors of my demise were extravagantly premature. No doubt wishful thinking by my competitors, most of whom I've happily outlived. Antiretroviral therapy is a miraculous thing. You're looking well, my old friend."

"You are, too," Lyndon said. "But what are you doing out here?"

"I called him," Laura said.

"Imagine my surprise," Alvin said. "A Brussels sprouts farmer! What an improbable twist! I love it!"

"We want to put together a retrospective," Laura said.

"A what?"

"I've already been in touch with the Hammer Museum," she said. "They were *wild* for the idea. After L.A., we're thinking of touring the show nationally."

"I've been putting feelers out to MoMA," Alvin said. "Wouldn't that be nice symmetry?"

"I don't understand what you two are talking about," Lyndon said. "What would be the point? Why would anyone be interested? Didn't you say I'm just a footnote?"

"The new work," Laura said. "The new work is what would make the show significant. We'd round up your old work and exhibit it with the new pieces."

"*What* new pieces?" Lyndon asked.

"She said you've been working all this time!" Alvin said. "You've always been one secretive bastard, Lyndon."

"I can attest to that," Woody said.

Alvin and Laura regarded him quizzically.

"My brother," Lyndon said.

"You see?" Alvin said. "I didn't even know you had a brother!"

"There is no new work," Lyndon said.

"What?"

"You've made a long trip for nothing."

"Stop," Laura said. "Stop pretending. I know what you've been doing in your barn."

"Can we see?" Alvin asked. "Will you show us what you've been doing?"

"This is ridiculous. You want to see my barn? All right, I'll let you see my barn."

He led Laura and Alvin inside his workshop to the barn doors and fished in his pocket for the key to the chrome padlock, but just as he was about to unlock it, he heard a helicopter approaching from the ocean. "Oh, fuck me," he said, not believing the nerve of Kitchell, coming on another bombing run so soon. "Stay here."

Outside, Woody told him, "I think we should take Bob to a vet. He's still looking pretty shaky."

"In a minute," Lyndon said.

He didn't have enough time to load the spud cannon. Instead, he grabbed his Viper M1 paint gun from the shed. Standing in the yard, he tossed off his arm sling, braced the rifle's buttstock against his shoulder, and waited for The Centurion Group's chopper to draw into a hover.

Yet the helicopter that appeared over the bluff wasn't cardinal-red with gold trim. It was black, and its side door was open, a man hanging out from a harness, his boots anchored on the skid, machine gun in his hands.

"What the hell?" Lyndon said.

A dozen SUVs swarmed the house then, men in black with helmets and body armor jumping out and aiming their weapons at Lyndon.

"Drop the gun, Lyndon!" Steven Lemke said.

"Steven? What the fuck is this?" Lyndon asked.

"Drop it!" Steven said, pointing his shotgun squarely at Lyndon's chest.

"Don't shoot!" Woody shouted, hands raised in the air. "It's a fake!"

"Is this your idea of a joke?" Lyndon said. "This is not funny, Steven."

Steven fired the shotgun, and Lyndon flew back, the impact yanking him off his feet and landing him several yards rearward, flat on his ass.

A horde of men flipped him onto his stomach and hand-cuffed his wrists behind his back. He moaned in pain. He couldn't breathe, his sternum burned. Out of the corner of his eye, he saw JuJu, Ling Ling, and the two girls coming out of the house and being promptly manhandled and shackled, the vests on the SWAT teams stenciled with "FBI," "DEA," "ATF." Had Steven enlisted every existing federal agency for this raid?

"It's a paint gun," an FBI agent said derisively, and fired a poodle-pink blob into the dirt.

"Get him up," Steven said.

Lyndon was hoisted upright, his shoulder searing. "You shot me," he gasped. "I can't believe you shot me."

"Relax," Steven said. "It was a beanbag."

Perplexed, Lyndon looked at his chest—no gaping hole, no gushing blood—and at the red object on the grass. He'd been hit with a beanbag projectile from a riot gun.

Lyndon and Woody were hustled behind Steven into the workshop, where Alvin and Laura, wide-eyed with terror, were being detained on their knees, hands behind their heads, in front of the barn doors.

"Open it," Steven said.

Lyndon was confused. Who had snitched on him? Sunny? Kitchell? Someone Tank and Skunk B. had blabbed to? More pertinently, he could understand why the authorities might take an interest in the ten Durban Poison plants in his fields, but why the barn?

A DEA agent chopped off the padlock with a bolt cutter and slid open the doors, revealing an orchard, a jungle, really, so dense with thickets and roots, it seemed as if the entire door-way was blocked by a solid arbor wall. These plants, these trees, however, were wholly made of metal—bent rods and wires, hammered sheets and plates, all welded together and twisting intricately into thousands of branches.

"Lemke, what the fuck is this?" the FBI agent said, punching a bank of electrical switches on, streaks of light illuminating the interior of the rusty hollow structure.

There was a small opening on the far side of the doorway, just big enough to slip through in a crouch, and they squeezed past it into the barn, stepping into a cramped rain forest of gnarled alloys and steel, wending their way between ory shoots of grass and undergrowth and iron trunks sprouting up from ground, vaguely in the form of bamboo and palm trees, willows, redwoods, and Monterey cypress, that covered nearly every foot of available space, vines, limbs, and tendrils extending upward to the roof, wrapping around the rafters, and spreading over the walls like mercuric ivy or kelp, like invasive weeds that had been steroidally fertilized, an elaborate latticework of climbing shrubs, tangles, and flanges, the canopy of leaves above populated by copper and aluminum birds of paradise, hawks, bats, butterflies, and cockatoos, and down below, perched on mesh resembling moss, were burnished lotus blossoms, orchids, and wild mushrooms, and dotting other parts of the floor were interweaved strips of bent wire, *écorchés* of geckos and snails and snakes, turtles and frogs and fish.

They stood staring in wonder at the sandblasted, oxidized, patinaed grove, which shimmered in luminous shades of red, orange, black, blue, and green.

"It's like we're inside a giant banyan tree," Laura said.

"Yes, exactly," Alvin said. "You know, there's a Buddhist sanctuary in Guangzhou called the Temple of the Six Banyan Trees, so-named by the poet and calligrapher Su Dongpo, during, by coincidence, the Song Dynasty! New parents go there to receive blessings for their children. Lyndon, I adopted a Chinese baby. I'm a father! I can see it now, this is a logical extension of your last show, 'Certain Epistemological Issues of Bestial Perversion,' an offshoot of Borges's Chinese encyclopedia. We could call it, oh, let me think, how about 'Subpatriarchial Abstracts in Botanical Objectivism,' something like that?"

But slowly what dawned on him, what dawned on each of them as they peered at the vast, strange metallurgic anarchy around them, was that, like a banyan tree, everything inside the building—the thick, crisscrossing tubes of lignified roots, the intertwined branches and long aerial vines, the bursting mayhem of flora and fauna—was fused together. It was a single, massive, linked sculpture that would be impossible to separate from the barn, that could never be dismantled or moved or installed in any gallery or museum. And, while the individual parts were lovely and exquisite, with their workmanship and detail, the whole made no sense—no sense at all. It had no shape, no definition, no pattern or apparent meaning. It was impressive, but, as Lyndon had long known, it was not art. It was a product of seventeen years of getting stoned nightly and holing himself in the barn and welding and sculpting to the accompaniment of jam bands on his boom box, first on the ground, then on ladders, then scaffolds, then with a seat harness and climbing ropes and Jumars; a product of working without design or scheme or foreseeable end, letting himself go with whatever impulse that arose, unchecked by any aesthetic restrictions or commercial concerns; a product of an imagination allowed to run amok; a product, everyone inside the barn gradually came to conclude, of artistic madness.

They had drug-sniffing dogs comb the entire property, and the helicopter buzzed every inch of the fields. They found nothing.

"No plants?" Steven asked. He had believed Lyndon was the leader of a local cell of the PLF, of which everyone on the farm was a member, and that they were planning to fund their eco-terrorist activities by growing and dealing pot.

"Oh, there are plants, all right," the FBI agent said. "There are plants galore. But no marijuana plants."

"How can that be?" Steven said.

Lyndon asked himself the same thing, but wasn't about to voice dissent.

"What about this?" Steven pleaded, pointing to Lyndon's stash—baggie, bong, joints, hemostat—that had been discovered in his workshop. "We can at least arrest him for this."

"Less than an ounce," the agent said. "Misdemeanor possession, hundred-dollar fine. You want to arrest him for it, go ahead. But if I were you, I'd be worrying more about what this is going to cost your career."

The SWAT teams drove away in their SUVs after uncuffing everyone except Lyndon, leaving Steven with the ignominy of having to release him personally. Alvin and Laura departed in her car with dispatch.

"Who tipped you off?" Steven asked.

"You took the words right out of my mouth," Lyndon said. He rubbed his wrists and then unbuttoned his shirt, examining the softball-sized bruise on his chest. "Fucking-A, look what you did, you maniac."

"Why can't you just stay away from Sheila?" Steven said. "You're never going to be the right person for her. You know that. I know that. She knows that. Why can't you just go away? Sell your farm. Move."

"I like it here." He eased the arm sling back around his aching shoulder.

"Don't you see?" Steven said plangently. "I love her. I love her so much more than you ever will." He unstrapped his body armor, his T-shirt soaked through with sweat. "I'd be there for them. I could give her and the baby my whole being, every fiber. They'll need someone who's responsible, dependable, not a habitual punk like you."

"What are you talking about?" Lyndon said. "What baby?"

"I don't get why Hana's always liked you more than me. I was her stepfather. I was good to her. Whereas you—you're a fuckup, Lyndon. Look at you—too stupid to accept ten million dollars for this shithole junk heap."

"What baby?"

Steven puffed disdainfully through his nostrils. "She didn't tell you. She didn't tell me, either."

"Hana's pregnant?" Lyndon asked, confounded.

"Not Hana, you dopehead. Sheila. A nurse at St. Catherine's let it slip. She assumed it was mine and congratulated me. It says something, doesn't it, that she's kept my name all these years? That's got to mean something."

Everything made sense to Lyndon now, Sheila's behavior over the past few days, the dramatics and hysteria. "It's my baby," Lyndon said.

"Maybe," Steven said. "Or maybe it's mine. She wouldn't say. It doesn't matter. She's gone to a clinic in the city to have it terminated."

"When?"

"I don't know, sometime this morning."

"Which clinic?"

Steven shook his head. "Nothing in this life is fair. You do everything you're supposed to do, and it turns to shit, anyway. I'm a good guy. I deserve better than this. Isn't there supposed to be such a thing as karma? Why are people like you anointed and not me? Yeah, I knew all about you. You think I didn't do a background check on you from day one?"

"Which clinic, Steven?" Lyndon asked, grabbing him by the shirt.

"I don't know."

He let go of him and ran to Woody. "I need to borrow your car," he said. His pickup was still at the service station, and his panel truck, thanks to Kitchell, had been flattened and would no longer start.

His brother was sitting on the ground with Bob. "I think he's getting worse," he told Lyndon, who squatted down and rubbed Bob's back. He was lying on his side, lethargic, and, ever so slightly, he seemed to be convulsing.

"Wrap him in a blanket and get JuJu to drive you to the vet," Lyndon said to Woody. "I need your keys. And your cell phone."

"It's not running very well these days," Woody said, hesitating.

Unbelievable. His brother was worried Lyndon might damage his precious SUV. "I won't leave a scratch on it, all right?"

He got into the Range Rover and turned up Highway 1, heading north to San Francisco. Awkwardly he hooked Woody's Bluetooth headset around his ear, jabbed at the PDA, and dialed Sheila's house, where Hana answered. "Do you know where your mother's gone?" he asked her.

"She said she had a meeting," she told him.

"Find her—what's it called?—that big calendar thing."

"Her Filofax?" After a minute, Hana came back to the phone and said, "She has an eleven o'clock at the Baycare Clinic. What's this about? Is she all right? Is she sick?"

"Did she write down an address?"

It was on Fillmore, near Geary. If he was lucky, he could

make it there in forty-five minutes. But just past the town of Montara, he hit a standstill. He had taken Highway 1, thinking since it was a holiday that the coastal route would be faster this morning than going over the hill on Highway 71, but he hadn't counted on another Caltrans blockage at Devil's Slide. The narrow, winding road on the steep bluff had been impeded or closed dozens of times over the years due to mudslides and rockslides, boulders the size of minivans sometimes crashing down from the hills and splintering the asphalt. The geology here was unstable, water in the soil, and the road had been slipping inexorably toward the ocean.

The hillside on the southbound side of the highway had evidently given way again and cracked the road surface, causing a mile-long backup with single-lane traffic control, which gave Lyndon time, sitting in virtual gridlock, to ponder what he would say to Sheila if and when he got to her. The thought of it—Sheila pregnant with his child—was almost unfathomable. A baby at his and Sheila's age? His entire life would have to change, his schedule, his preoccupations, his routines subordinate to the caprices of an infant. And what would this mean with Sheila? He would have to marry her, move in with her. She would probably force him, at last, to sell his farm. He didn't know if he was willing to do or compromise on any of those things. It was an enormous adjustment to ask of him at this stage. He had fashioned a life he was comfortable with—one that was solitary, selfish—and he didn't know if he was capable of relinquishing it.

The Range Rover, true to his brother's anxiety, was idling roughly, misfiring once in a while. Blue smoke was coming out of the exhaust, most likely oil leaking into a cylinder, fouling up the sparks, and the temperature gauge on the dashboard was rising, the engine beginning to overheat. As Lyndon squinted at the smoke in the rearview mirror, he noticed something sweeping past the front of the windshield. A paper airplane. A Volvo station wagon was creeping forward on his left flank, merging, as were all the cars, onto the northbound side of the road. The driver was a woman with a shaved head, dressed in an orange and red Buddhist nun's robe, and in the back seat was a little girl with brown hair, mumbling angrily to herself as she scribbled in a notebook. She tore out a page, hastily folded it into an airplane, and chucked it out the window.

The Fourth Noble Truth was that the end of suffering could be attained through the pursuit of morality, meditation, and wisdom, as described by the Eightfold Path: right view, right intention, right speech, right action, right livelihood, right effort, right mindfulness, right concentration.

The little girl sensed Lyndon staring at her. She looked at him and stuck her tongue out. She contorted her lips and gritted her teeth. She squashed her nose up against the back windowpane to confer him with pig's nostrils. She pulled her eyes slanty and wagged her head, silently chanting, "Ching chong, ching chong, Chinaman."

Lyndon spun the steering wheel to the right—right intention, right action—and accelerated, straddling the bank of the hill with the wheels, the SUV tilting and on the verge of rolling over as he sped past the stalled cars, ignoring the Caltrans workers who were waving at him, knocking down traffic barrels and crashing through barricades, pieces of wood whirling up and fissuring the windshield. The glove compartment popped open, revealing a USC baseball cap.

To get beyond the last part of the bottleneck, he had to squeeze through a narrow space between a concrete retaining wall and a backhoe, a space that didn't look like it would quite accommodate the full width of the Range Rover. He gunned it nonetheless, almost able to edge through intact, except he sheared off both sideview mirrors and crunched up the doors and snagged the rear bumper onto something, shredding the back quarter panels and leaving the bumper behind, tumbling end over end on the road.

With a high-pitched whine emanating from the differential, the oil and temperature gauges warning of imminent failure, Lyndon proceeded on, racing onto I-280, then taking 101 to the Civic Center exit and Mission Street, swinging onto Van Ness, and turning left on Geary. He parked the Rover in a bus zone, and as he shut off the ignition, the engine coughed and smoke began drifting out from beneath the hood.

"The Baycare Clinic, the Baycare Clinic!" he said, accosting passersby. One of them pointed across the intersection, and he hobbled in front of oncoming traffic to the other side of Fillmore, saw the sign for the clinic, and pressed the buzzer for entry. He told the receptionist he was there for Sheila Lemke, she had an appointment, then he went through the metal detector and hurried inside to the waiting room, where Sheila looked up at him, a clipboard on her lap.

"Great," she said, watching him sit next to her. "Just great."

"Why didn't you tell me?" he asked.

"There's nothing to discuss."

"Are you joking? Nothing to discuss?" Lyndon said. "You're having my child."

"I'm not having it," Sheila said. She was filling out a questionnaire, and she checked off a box.

"You're not going to let me have a say in this?" Lyndon asked.

"What, you're willing to jump into full-fledged domesticity all of a sudden?"

"I might be," he said. "I just might be."

"Don't kid yourself," she said. "So to speak." She placed the clipboard on the adjacent table and rubbed the heel of her hand against her forehead. "God, how did I let this happen? I'm forty-one years old. How could I have let things devolve like this? Was I intentionally trying to destroy my life?"

Lyndon glanced at the other people in the waiting room—a couple of college students, a woman in her thirties—not very crowded, it was Labor Day, after all. He was surprised the clinic was even open. "Let's go get a cup of coffee," he told Sheila, adjusting his arm sling. "Let's get out of here for a while."

"It's not your baby," she said.

Lyndon turned to her. "It's not?" he said. "It's Steven's?"

"I don't know."

"You don't know? What do you mean, you don't know?"

"I was still living with Steven when I came to your house in July. It could be his, it could be yours. I can't really say. Isn't that the stupidest thing you've ever heard? I suppose we could wait a few weeks for an amnio. Or we could all just wait until April and see what color pops out." She laughed mirthlessly.

Lyndon leaned back in his chair, at a loss as to what he should say now.

"You probably think this is all hormonal, the way I've been acting," Sheila told him. "The thing is, I don't know who I am. I have no idea. The only thing of any worth I've ever produced is Hana, and now she's leaving, and you know what? I resent her. My God, why did she have to become so fucking beautiful? I've seen the way men look at her. *You've* looked at her that way. Don't lie and say you haven't. And now this singing thing. She's so *young*. She has her whole life ahead of her—very likely an exciting life, an extraordinary life. Mine's pretty much over, and what do I have to show for it? Two ex-husbands, three failed businesses, and a lamebrained sometime lover. I always thought I would do extraordinary things. It's terrible to realize the moment is gone."

"That's ridiculous. You've accomplished more than that, and you have an entire lifetime ahead of you. There's still so much you could do."

"What have I accomplished?" she asked. "I hated being an attorney, absolutely detested it. I couldn't quit fast enough. I just took the money and ran. I retired at *thirty-one*. That's obscene when you think about it."

"You have your chocolate boutique," Lyndon told her.

"I've become a cliché," Sheila said. "I'm a postfeminist, over-privileged suburban matron, a middle-aged dilettante looking for fulfillment. A hysterical bitch with no purpose. I've done nothing with my life."

"You've done a lot of good as mayor."

"Now you're just patronizing me," she said. "You've disagreed with everything I've ever implemented."

"I like the new bike paths."

"Thanks."

"The beaches are cleaner."

"That they are," she said.

"You're still young, Sheila. You're not too old to have another child."

"What if it's Steven's child? The earliest you can do a DNA paternity test is the tenth week, but it's not a hundred percent until the second trimester, and then it'd be too late for an abortion. I wouldn't be able to go through with it then. If it turns out to be Steven's, what would you do? You'd walk—that's what you'd do. That's your particular specialty, Lyndon, your singular talent. You'd walk away, you'd retreat to your farm to do God knows what."

Lyndon read the titles of the pamphlets on the rack across

from him: prenatal care, STDs, birth control, adoption alternatives, breast health, cancer screening, sterilization services. "Would you go back to Steven?" he asked.

"No," she said. "Never."

A nurse called one of the college students—she could have been in high school, Hana's age—and took her down the hall. Lyndon and Sheila sat quietly in the waiting room for a few minutes, staring at the wall before them. A poster announced that you could register to vote at the clinic. Another had a photo of George Bush and Dick Cheney in a jocular pose, the caption underneath them reading, "Do you trust these men to make decisions about your reproductive rights?"

"People who've never had children think it's such a joy," Sheila said. "It's not. It's about exhaustion. It's about total collapse. Oh, there are those brief moments of unconditional love, innocence, but those moments get chipped away, bit by bit, and it becomes, 'I hate you. Get away from me. Where's my dinner?' You know what that's all about? It's about them looking at you as a parent, as an adult, and finding you wanting, finding you're not the person they'd hoped you'd be. It's the saddest thing in the world, to have someone look at you like that. It's devastating. It's like being abandoned. It's one series of departures after another. You love them and worry about them and do everything you can to shelter and provide for them, and then they leave you, feeling you're a disappointment."

"Hana loves you, Sheila," Lyndon said. "You know she does. And she'll be less than an hour away."

"Not if she goes to Berklee. Boston is three thousand miles away. I won't be a part of her life. I won't be able to do things for her, help her. Not that she lets me help her now. She won't confide squat to me anymore. For all I know, she's already come to a clinic like this."

"She's a virgin," Lyndon said.

"What?" Sheila asked. "How do you know that?"

"She told me."

"She tells *you* and not *me*? Great. That's just wonderful. That's just peachy-keen."

"Let's go home, Sheila. We don't have to decide this now. We can decide this later. Come home with me."

"What home, Lyndon?" she said. "What home? We don't have a home. We're fuck buddies. We've never lived together. We've never done all the things that couples have to do. We've never bought a house or a car together, we've never had to figure out careers, we've never had to deal with kids or schools or bills, we've never shopped or done chores, we've never gone to teacher conferences, vacations. What kind of relationship is that? We hardly know each other. Sometimes I feel I don't know you at all. I don't know the first thing about you—not really."

She began to cry, and he laid his hand over hers, but she swatted it away. "Fuck you," she said. "Oh, that's right, I already did that. Which is why I'm presently in this absurd predicament."

"Sheila—"

"Shut up," she said, and pulled out a tissue and blew her nose. "What a mess," she said. "What an ungodly, unbelievable mess."

"I'm a Brussels sprouts farmer and a welder and an ex-bartender," Lyndon told her. "I was a famous artist once. I made more money than I knew what to do with. I gave most of it to my parents. I gave them the money to keep my brother out of jail sixteen years ago, but I will never tell him that because I can't bring myself to forgive him. I smoke pot every night. I have a sculpture in my barn I can't stop working on. I occasionally engage in petty criminal activity and mischief. I am far, far from perfect, but I think I'm a loyal person, a person, given a chance, who can be counted on. I have my faults. I need to be alone a lot. I'm moody and sullen. I need to withdraw now and then, and sometimes I don't like to talk. I have problems with authority—any authority. In many ways, I admit, I'm immature. I'm someone who doesn't like to look inward much, and probably never will. I am afraid—afraid of so many things, most of all change. I'm not expressive or especially communicative. I'm a guy incapable of spewing out niceties, who will refuse to go to parties or barbecues and make chitchat with people I don't know or like. I'm not at all ambitious. I don't have any interest in making more of my life than I have. I prefer my obscurity, and I don't think there's anything wrong with that. I'm a man committed to a simple, quiet life. I am a man, against all sense and reason, who is pathetically, incurably in love with a woman. I am yours, Sheila. Yours and this baby's. If you will have me, I am yours."

CHAPTER 10

THEY HAD A LITTLE MISHAP EN ROUTE TO THE VET. JUJU WAS DRIVING them to the animal hospital in town in his beater car, Ling Ling in the passenger seat, Woody in the back holding Bob, who was nearly comatose, when the front right tire blew out. The car began shaking and yawing, they smelled burning rubber, there was a loud, rapid thumping against the chassis, then the shriek of metal grinding on asphalt. JuJu squeezed his hands around the steering wheel and tried to stay in control, but they fishtailed and skidded sideways and spun into a telephone pole, crushing the rear door and imploding the window, glass shards showering the back seat.

Woody picked up Bob and ran the rest of the way to the animal hospital, and as he leaped over the curb to the entrance of the clinic, he landed on a crack in the sidewalk, supinating his foot and badly twisting his ankle, which made him cartwheel head over heels onto the concrete. But as he tumbled, he kept Bob wrapped in his arms, protected, and somehow he rolled upright in a continuous motion and limped inside with the dog.

The veterinarian pumped Bob's stomach and performed blood tests for possible kidney and liver damage. She would keep him overnight at the clinic and administer him with IV fluids, but he would be just fine, she assured them.

Woody's injury was another matter. The X-rays at St. Catherine Hospital showed he had broken his fifth metatarsal, a minute but functionally essential bone. His foot was placed in a plastic boot, and he would have to be on crutches for six to eight weeks.

He sat in Lyndon's kitchen that night, his foot propped up on a pillow and chair, an ice pack folded over his throbbing ankle, as his brother cooked dinner for him. Trudy and Margot were long gone, as was Ling Ling, all three on flights across the Pacific. JuJu had taken them to the airport in Skunk's car and then had retired to his own apartment. The house was quiet, attended only by the sounds of the wind, cicadas, and ocean outside and the sizzle of the pans on the stove.

"Want a beer?" Lyndon asked.

"Yeah, sure," Woody said.

Lyndon opened the fridge and popped off the tops of two bottles, and he limped over to Woody to hand him one, his knee brace strapped to the outside of his jeans, left arm in the sling.

Woody winced as he reached for the bottle. He was certain he had busted a rib or two in the car crash, although the radiologist had stubbornly contradicted him. The ER doc had also been skeptical about Woody's self-diagnosis of whiplash, but he'd relented and given him a neck brace anyway, simply to get rid of him, no doubt, the son of bitch, good-for-nothing doctors.

He shook out a couple of Percocets (from his personal supply, way better than the useless anti-inflammatories he'd been prescribed) and swallowed them down with a swig of beer. He smoothed down the curling edges of the bandage—which matched the one on his brother's forehead—over his temple.

His face was covered with remnants of calamine lotion and tiny scabs, as if he'd been hit with birdshot, from the pieces of glass they'd picked out of his skin, and his left hand was bundled in gauze. "Jesus, we're a sorry-looking pair, aren't we?" he said to his brother. The first thing he would do when he returned to L.A. was see his dermatologist. And his allergist. And maybe a cosmetic surgeon. And set up a phone appointment with Dan. Then he planned to make the rounds with a pitch for a new project, spurred by the mention of studio interest in Charlie Chan. His brainchild was to do a feature remake of *The Green Hornet*. He could hold a worldwide search for the next Bruce Lee to play Kato—a competition, a reality TV series in multiple countries. The prospective payoffs were simply outrageous.

The bandage made Lyndon think of something that had happened when they were children, maybe in junior high. They were walking to the movies, passing a golf course, Lyndon on a low fieldstone wall that bordered a chain-link fence, Woody below him on the sidewalk. Just as Lyndon reached the corner of the wall and jumped off, Woody threw a rock, supposedly at the fence but hitting Lyndon in midair, striking him smack on the head, just above the ear. Lyndon crumpled to the ground and put his hand to the side of his head, his fingers coming away with blood. It was streaming down his neck, pooling in the hollow underneath his throat, staining his T-shirt. It enraged Lyndon, the blood, and he rose and tackled Woody, punching him and wrestling him to the ground. They returned home, smeared with blood and dirt and sweat. They refused to talk to one another for weeks. Their mother tried to convince Lyndon that it had been an accident, a complete fluke, jumping into the path of the rock, that it was a statistical impossibility for Woody to have actually been aiming for his head and been capable of hitting him, but Lyndon would not be swayed.

It might have been pure luck, the fact that Woody had found his mark, but Lyndon knew, he knew, that Woody had wanted to hit him, bring him down, it was his will, his nature, his deepest impulse, he had *meant* to do it, and nothing—not then, not now, all these years later—could ever convince Lyndon otherwise. Such was the power and persistence of fraternal enmity. Cain and Abel. He knew that Woody had been plotting something against him with Kitchell. He would not forget that. He would never trust his brother. Although a few things about him had surprised Lyndon during this visit.

"You know," he said, "you don't seem too upset about your car."

"Well," Woody said, "I'm pretty well insured. Besides, I'd been thinking of getting rid of it."

Lyndon had been able to talk Sheila into leaving the clinic, decision pending another day, but the Range Rover had not been where he had parked it. He assumed it had been towed and called San Francisco's DPT, but they couldn't check their logs without knowing the plate number. Lyndon had been unable to reach Woody, and it was only after his brother came back to the farm from the hospital that they determined the SUV had been stolen. Later on, they'd learn it was taken to a chop shop and swiftly dismantled, the parts shipped off to Colombia and other far-flung corners. Even in its mangled condition, the car had worth—its leather seats, touchscreen, sound system and DVD, its one intact Xenon-gas headlight. Lyndon would also figure out that Sunny Padaca had been the one who had filched his pot plants, sneaking onto the farm in the predawn hours before the raid, about which he had been somehow tipped, for a little nighttime gardening. The turpentine had not been intended for Lyndon. André Meeker and Jen de Leuw, the Udderly Licious lovers, were the self-appointed PLF terrorists, finally caught as they tried to torch Kitchell's house. They had been responsible for firebombing the trailer and discharging the elephant, among other infractions—addled by lust and hormones and cannabis into becoming Rosarita Bay's teenage Bonnie and Clyde. They had been transporting two fifty-five-gallon drums of paint thinner in the back of a borrowed flatbed truck, planning to dump them into The Centurion Group's water supply, but they hadn't secured the cargo very well, and the drums had fallen off the bed of the truck and rolled into the creek ditch that fed directly into Lyndon's pond.

"Let me ask you," Woody said, "that thing in your barn—what does it mean?"

"It's not supposed to mean anything. That's not the point."

"What is, then?"

"The process," Lyndon said. "Just doing the work."

"Don't you want something to come of it?"

"No. It's just about being in that state of mind—the state of invention, spontaneity. That's all I want. To be attuned to it. To be present in it—inside of it. That's the only thing that matters to me."

"I still don't get it," Woody said.

"I wouldn't expect you to—or anyone else."

"What are you going to do, Lyndon?" his brother asked. "Your Brussels sprouts are ruined."

"Not all of them," he said, pointing to the pot on the stove. Yesterday morning, before his crop had been tainted, he had happened to pick off a quarter of a bucket of Oliver—an early variety—from the bottom of a few plants.

"You're going to have to sell your farm," Woody said, wiping his flatware with a napkin.

"Yes, I am," Lyndon said. "But not to The Centurion Group.

There's a nonprofit trust that's been offering to buy my land and lease it back to me to farm. There would be a conservation easement so it could never be developed." It wasn't the best of arrangements—he would no longer own his farm or house out-right, and, as a tenant, he was vulnerable to unforeseen changes in the land trust's management. He could get kicked off at any time. That was why he had ignored them—their calls and let-ters—for as long as he could.

"What are they offering?"

"Enough. 1.2 million."

Woody was flabbergasted. It wasn't fair-market value, not anywhere near it, but it was a substantial chunk of change, enough—if properly invested—to carry Lyndon through to retirement. It would allow his brother, the stupid, intracta-ble relic, to stay exactly where he was. Maybe he couldn't hide from the world, but he could still manage to outwit it, eternally charmed, and Woody had to give him credit for that. "How long have you known about this?"

"I don't know," Lyndon said. "About a year, I guess."

"You really are a secretive bastard, aren't you?" he said, glad that his betrayal of Lyndon, snitching on him to Kitchell, had been a lapse without consequence. He would have regretted it as an unnecessary act of malice, perhaps cowardice. He was, he wanted to believe, a better person than that now. He had saved Trudy and Margot. He had saved Bob. Who knew what else he had the potential to do? A reservoir of goodness was there within him, somewhere.

"I've got chocolate ice cream—and a bowl of 420—for des-sert," Lyndon said, "if you're interested."

He took the lid off the rice cooker and scooped out two mounds for their plates. He forked the steaks from the pan and stirred the Brussels sprouts he'd been braising. He had browned slices of thick diced bacon, sautéed them with shallots, added chicken stock, thyme, parsley, as well as some sherry, salt and pepper, and a bay leaf, then the sprouts, brought everything to a boil, and simmered it, covered, for fifteen minutes. Now he served the sprouts with the steak and the rice to his brother—a simple meal, not much to it, just the basic elements, but filling.

AUTHOR'S NOTE

FOR THEIR EDITORIAL INSIGHTS AND SUPPORT, I WOULD LIKE TO THANK my editor, Alane Salierno Mason; my agent, Maria Massie; and my friends Jennifer Egan, Fred Leebron, Katherine Bell, Kathy Herold, Scott Buck, Katherine Palmer-Collins, and Rebecca Lee.

I'm particularly indebted to Don Murch of Gospel Flat Farm, who told me everything I needed to know about growing organic Brussels sprouts. Thanks as well to David Dewitt and Ilene Bezahler, formerly of Allandale Farm.

Laura Kina was instrumental in guiding me to a seminal text about Asian and Asian-American artists, *Why Asia?* by Alice Yang. Another source of substantial influence was *On Seeing Nature* by Steven J. Meyers, as were articles on Lee Bontecou by Calvin Tomkins in *The New Yorker* and Michael Duncan in *Art in America*. Jon Kabat-Zinn's *Mindfulness Meditation* and Steve Hagen's *Buddhism Plain and Simple* also deserve acknowledgment.

Thanks, too, to my copy editor, Dave Cole, and to Don Rifkin, Alexander Cuadros, and Winfrida Mbewe at W. W. Norton.